FINDING MY FIGHT

R. G. CORR

Cover design by Sofie Hartley, Hart & Bailey Design Co.

Editing by Claire Allmendinger, Bare Naked Words Editing.

Copyright 2018 R.G. Corr

ISBN-13: 9781720184676

All rights reserved. This book or any portion thereof may not be reproduced or used in any manner whatsoever without the express written permission of the publisher except for the use of brief quotations in a book review.

This book is a work of fiction. Names, characters, places, and incidents are either products of the author's imagination or are used fictitiously to give a sense of authenticity. Any resemblance to actual persons, living or dead, events, or locales is entirely coincidental.

Recommended reading age 18+

BOOKS BY R.G. CORR

THE HAYWATER SERIES

Autumn's Rise

Monday's Promise

STANDALONE

Finding My Fight

For A and L, with love

CHAPTER ONE

PRESENT DAY

*H*e can't be back. It's impossible.

My breaths come thick and fast as I run frantically down the road. Peering around the edge of my hood, I check over my shoulder. I can't see him. But just because I don't see him, doesn't mean he isn't there... biding his time.

Hopelessness shrouds me as reminders of him continue to attack my mind. Blake... he can't be here. He can't be back. It's impossible. The rushed pounding of my boots landing on the concrete causes my panic to surge. I want to cry out but what if he hears me?

Stumbling the last step to the house, I drop my keys and shopping bag to the ground below, the contents spilling over the path around my feet. A sob catches in my throat as I desperately pick up the key. I have to get inside, away from him. Raising my right hand, I try to steady the trembling with my left. When the key slides into the lock and the click sounds, I push on the door with all my weight, almost falling inside.

Leaving the shopping splayed outside, I spin around and slam the door closed. The echo reverberates around the small hallway, but I don't pause for a second. I twist the lock and jerk the chain across. Only then, as I lean back against the door, do I fight to take control of my breaths.

How can this be happening? How can he be here?

My head judders from side to side in a state of shock and disbelief. The first tear forms before more follow, falling to my cheek.

The freedom I've had a taste of is now at an end. He warned me it would always be us, no matter what. He won't let me go twice, and I know I won't be able to survive. Not again.

Hesitantly, I tread into the kitchen. The room appears uncharacteristically dark, but I don't put on a light. I don't want to be seen. My focus flitters from corner to corner, door to door, searching for anything that is out of place—but everything appears to be how I left it.

I move towards the window, standing back as far out of sight as I can. Gently, my fingers slide in between the blinds so I can peer outside.

Dark clouds make their way across the sky, droplets of rain are starting to fall again, and the trees sway with the impending storm that's been predicted. I scan over the few people that are walking down the path on the opposite side of the road.

When I don't see him, I look beyond, to the open fields.

"Where are you?" I say out loud. "You're dead. You're supposed to be dead!"

Withdrawing my fingers from the blinds, I move quickly to the cutlery drawer and take out a sharp knife.

"Dead!" I whisper in desperation. The fear encroaches as I think of the unimaginable and the possibility that somehow my husband is still alive.

I retreat until my back hits the wall. Like I did months ago when I knew he was near. When I knew it was time.

I tighten my grip on the cold metal of the knife knowing that this time, I have no choice but to be ready for him.

My mouth feels dry, and I lick my lips reliving what fear feels like. The hairs on the back of my neck now stand on end and my heart thumps louder, taking over the silence.

My legs slowly start to give way, and I slide down the wall as a broken sob rips from my chest.

I thought the nightmare had ended, but as I sit, gulping back my cries in an attempt to remain quiet, I fear it's only just beginning.

My husband is back, and there's only one reason he's here. For me.

When a voice calls out, my body jolts against the wall. The letterbox rattles as he calls my name through the opening.

My fingers tighten around the knife in my palm. He won't hurt me. Not again.

CHAPTER TWO

EIGHT MONTHS EARLIER
HEREFORD

I glance down to the faded and weathered-looking wood panels of the bench I'm sitting on. From a distance, you don't notice the beaten, worn appearance. It's only when you get closer you see the extent of the damage. The colour stain on the wood lifts in various places. One slat is cracked and brittle to the touch. It even feels damp underneath my legs due to the coldness of the day. It's damaged, but it's still here, providing what it promises. A respite.

Some would choose not to sit on this bench, instead preferring the modern shiny versions further down the road. Yet for me, this bench is a flicker of hope. Sitting here means I'm one step closer to talking to somebody. One step closer to proving that the situation I'm in is *not* normal or right.

My focus rests on the alley across the road where today I had hoped I would find the courage to walk. But uncertainty lingers in my heart and mind like a dead weight, holding me down.

To passers-by, you'd be forgiven for believing I possess courage. I appear well groomed and in control. How can I be anything else? Why would I want to admit that I'm ashamed of the person I've become? I'm so used to faking a smile that at one time, I wondered if it was fixed permanently on my face. Now I know it isn't. My smile no longer presents itself freely. It's displayed as an act. A performance.

My hands jitter in my lap, the only physical indication of the fear and uncertainty that racks my body. If I go in there, I admit I'm *that* person, that woman who allows herself to be beaten. Only allowing isn't really the right term. I don't give permission. I beg for him to stop. I plead like a helpless child. How can I still love him, when I hate what he does to me? With each word and every shock of pain, I fear the love I have for him is lessening and the hatred growing. But the loathing isn't solely for him, it's for me too.

Walking away from Blake requires a strength that I don't hold. Take now. I've been here for over half an hour, only occasionally daring to glance at the building I should be walking into. I sit, surrounded by high-rise buildings and impressive monuments, emphasising how small and insignificant I truly am. *So full of self-pity, Ginny.* I curl my lip up at the truth of my thoughts.

Company arrives on the other side of the bench, surprising me. On the four times I've been here, I've not seen one person even come near the bench. I don't look up to acknowledge whoever it is. Instead, I move even closer to the armrest on my right, increasing our distance and feeling that little bit safer with the wood by my side. I shift my attention to the brick built buildings in front of me. There are a number of offices, some shops, but it's down the wide alley where my focus lies. A trail of shops and offices lead to an alcove with the blue door that holds my attention. It's only just visible from where I'm sitting.

I clasp my hands together in my lap in a bid to cease the

shaking, but the movement causes my sleeve to ride up slightly, and the edging of the bruise on my wrist comes into view. Immediately, I tug on my jacket pulling the cuffs into my palm. My cheeks heat with shame, I dip my head and retreat further into the back of the bench, hoping for whoever it is sitting near me, not to have seen.

Out of the corner of my eye, I see the person move. I can tell by his hands and sleeve that it's a man. He has his mobile in his hand and touches the screen before lifting it towards his ear, out of my sight.

"Hey," he begins. "I don't suppose we can delay lunch by an hour?" His voice is soft, almost calming. I want to cling to the sound, but that would be foolish. Life isn't calm nor is it soft.

He goes quiet, presumably while the other person talks.

"There's something I need to do," he continues then stands. I can tell by the sound of his voice that he's walking behind me. "I've been putting it off for too long, and if I don't do it now…" He continues his conversation, but his words quieten as he walks away. But it's no longer the sound of his voice I focus on or the shameful way I feel in his company. It's what he said, the words linger in my head.

If I don't do it now… I raise my focus to the alleyway. If I don't do it now, will I ever do it? Will I ever work up the courage to speak to somebody?

My mind swings to last night, to how the new bruises got there in the first place. Bruises that are conveniently, or purposefully, out of plain sight. I close my eyes at the thought of reliving it. The familiar taste of blood tinges my taste buds. The image of my cowering pathetic body appears in my mind, sickening me.

Steadily, I force myself to stand. Reaching for support from the bench, I wince in a breath at the tenderness in my side. Then straighten myself up and make my way closer to the edge of the path. *It's twenty yards, Ginny. That's all.*

In an attempt at shielding myself from the cold that stems from my bones, I pull my coat tighter around me before compressing my hold further in a bid to push away some of the pain. Checking for oncoming traffic, I cross the road. Urging my feet forward, I walk by a few pedestrians but am unable to look up, until finally, I'm standing, facing the blue door.

I focus on the tiny flaws embedded in the wood, hoping it's a sign that they welcome the blemished person I've become.

My shaking hand rests on the handle, and I pause. How did this get to be me? This happens to other women, weak women, not to me. Yet here I am, standing rigid as stone and more petrified than I've felt in my life.

Mist surrounds me as my breaths leave my mouth quicker. I look back, take in the people passing by. I don't see *him*. I don't see anyone I recognise, but a shudder runs through my body all the same at what I'm finally daring to do.

As I push down on the handle, I hope more than anything I've ever hoped for, that someone behind that door is going to help me. That someone is going to help me believe that I'm worth saving.

∼

The first thing I notice is how quiet and calm it is. I'm not sure what I expected, but at a time when agitation stirs as though anticipating turbulent times ahead, calm is not what I was preparing myself for. I guess I expected to see tears, sadness, and fear.

A large empty space surrounds me, and I suddenly feel even more isolated and alone. A woman standing in the corner of the room catches my eye. I have the urge to run, but she keeps her eyes on me, lowers the phone from her ear and smiles a kind smile. She starts to move towards me but sidesteps and passes her phone to a companion who is sitting at a desk close by.

Quickly, I glance around the room and realise that the only person that is looking my way is the blonde woman who is now approaching me. It's as though they've all been trained not to stare and intimidate the pathetic woman that falls through their doors.

She comes to a stop in front of me, her lips lifting in an unthreatening smile. Something I haven't seen for a while. "Hi," she says.

I can only nod, suddenly unsure of what to say. My focus lowers to the floor. This was a mistake. I can't even bring myself to say the words.

"Come with me," the woman says. She walks on ahead, her pumps quietly pressing on the floor as she goes. I open and close my hands in an attempt to alleviate the clammy sensation that's settled in my palms, then follow like a lost lamb in the wilderness. My heart is thumping so heavily in my chest that I half expect her to turn and query the sound, but she doesn't.

She pushes through a door, then stands against it, propping it open, indicating for me to pass her. I do.

Immediately to my left, I notice two chairs, pale taupe in colour, a small table between them—a box of tissues and a shaded lamp in the same tone as the chairs, sitting upon it. Vertical blinds hang from a frosted glass window in front of me, ensuring privacy from the outside world. A few pictures grace the walls, but they're not enough of a distraction to divert me away from the reason I'm here. It's a room lacking in warmth yet somehow completely devoid of cold. It's a room with a purpose.

"Please, take a seat."

I lower myself to a chair and hear the door close softly before the woman sits down herself.

"My name is Katie."

I remain quiet, sitting and staring at my hands as they twist together nervously on my knee. I don't know where else to look because the confidence that finally pushed me to walk through that blue door has now deserted me.

"The first thing I want to tell you is how brave you are for walking in here today. I know how hard that was for you. Every woman that walks through that door has a story. It's their own story. The thing that makes you different to them? This time the story is about you. And you are who matters."

I matter? I dredge my focus up, and she nods her head as though silently reassuring me. I know she's waiting for me to say something, for me to tell her *my* story, but all I can do is avert my gaze.

I can't tell her my story! What was I thinking? My life is turbulent enough without me adding an extra element of danger to it. Blake would never forgive me for coming here.

"I shouldn't have come," I whisper.

"Why do you think that?"

"He wouldn't like it. He doesn't mean the things that he does. He always regrets it. But he can't seem to stop."

"Do you want to tell me what it is that he does?"

I don't offer an answer, and Katie doesn't question me further.

When I glance up, she's looking at the floor in what can only be described as sadness. *Why is she the one that's sad?* She's not the one sitting in the 'visitor' seat. She's the one who gets to hear the stories, not live them.

A woman like Katie wouldn't ever be told how worthless she is. With her fair colouring and delicately placed freckles on her nose, she's beautiful. No man would want to ruin her. I almost want to laugh in her face at how well she's managing to falsely empathise with me. She has no idea what kind of monster I married.

"I'm sorry." Her voice breaks, entering the silence, and I find myself continuing to stare at her. Slowly, she brings her eyes up to mine, and I see that she means it. She isn't apologising for anything that she has done, but she's expressing regret for the reason I am here. There's something in her eyes that tells me she understands. That she believes me.

I turn away as pain takes me by surprise, crushing my chest. Knowing instantly that this woman believes me, makes my situation so much more real.

"I feel so ashamed," I whisper. My fingers gravitate to my wedding band, and I gently twirl it around. "It never used to be like this," I admit, my focus remaining low. "*We* never used to be like this."

It wasn't like this in the beginning. Everyone loved him. Marci, my best friend, looked at him like he was golden chocolate encased in a diamond wrapper. She feigned disappointment when his attention seemed to lie solely on me. Claiming he was the *perfect* man, and I was the luckiest woman on this earth. Marci was happy for me, genuinely happy. She saw how he made me feel. How he *used* to make me feel. How he *used* to treat me. I slam my eyes closed to stop the tears from forming.

"You think you've changed?"

"I've had to. I try and do everything right, to do all I can to avoid disappointing him, but I still fail." Katie opens her mouth to speak, but I hold up my hand to request her silence. "I know it's not all my fault. You don't have to say it, but I don't know what to do. There was a time when I believed myself to be brave—"

"You're here now. That takes a lot of guts."

"Does it?" I look up, sceptical. "It's an act of stupidity. It's a risk I shouldn't have taken."

"We're here to help you—"

"But you can't stop it, can you?" I accuse unnecessarily. It's not Katie's responsibility to stop the abuse. Stopping it would take a miracle, and I know for certain that this pretty blonde woman in front of me is unable to provide the miracle I need.

"No, I can't. But I can tell you things that right now you need to hear." A sarcastic laugh bursts from my lips but Katie ignores it, choosing to continue. "This isn't your fault. Nor are you stupid for coming here—"

"If it isn't my fault? Whose is it? What made him this way?"

"I can't tell you why he is the way he is. There can be many factors, traits, and changes in behaviour. It's an endless list and not a definitive one. There can be warning signs, but you are not the cause of them."

I feel myself frown, not really listening to her. "Did something happen in his past?" I question like she should know the answer. "His parents are both dead." Or at least that's what he told me. "He doesn't have any siblings. When we first met, he told me his past was unremarkable." I mumble to myself trying to find a reason.

She swallows, seeming to hesitate. "What you need to know is you should be safe, you should *feel* safe in your relationship and loved—"

"Enough," I call out downhearted. "I don't need to know what my human rights are." I suddenly realise what it is I need from this woman seated in front of me. "I need to know if you think I should leave him. If you consider me foolish for putting up with this?" The answer to my questions determines whether I will be walking back out of the door in exactly ten seconds. I need to know that she understands. That this isn't something I've asked for. But I also want to know if she believes I'm crazy for still living with Blake.

"They're very difficult questions for me to answer." She leans back in her chair, watching me. "I know very little about what's going on. My main priority is to keep you safe," her focus never leaves me, "...And alive. And no, I don't think you're crazy. Not one bit." Her face softens. "Sometimes it's hard to see a way out, but we are here to help you. *I*," she states she word strongly, "believe you, and I want to help you."

I nod my head as my defensive exterior takes a battering and tears start to fill my eyes. She believes me, there's no questioning of whether I'm telling the truth. No belittling of my worries like Blake does. She isn't telling me to walk out and leave him right now. My shoulders start to shake as my vision blurs. Katie hands me a tissue.

A simple agreement, that's all it took and somehow, for now, that's all I need.

I lift my arm to dab at my eyes, but the movement causes my breath to hitch with the pain.

"Do you need help? A doctor?"

"No." I'm quick to respond. I blink hard, needing to see her face. When I look into her eyes, panic reverberates through my body. "And no police!" I warn, jumping up. Immediately, I cry out as pain slices through me. Katie gets to her feet just as fast. I stoop over and draw in some breaths, trying to adjust to the pain.

The resting of her palm on my back momentarily causes me to remember what caring feels like, but I don't allow it for long. My hand clutches my side as I force myself to stand up straighter. "I'm fine," I say on a breath.

"I'd like to help you."

I shake my head, realising how unwise I've been. I came seeking advice and have given away too much already. If Blake knew what I was doing—the punishment doesn't bear thinking about.

"I have to go. This... it's not where I should be."

Katie looks at me with sad eyes, and I feel disappointment flood through me. I walked through that blue door expecting someone to help me. But how can they? What can they do? I won't go to the police because even if they believed me, Blake would be free within hours, and I know exactly what he would do. He would find me like he did before. Then I would pay.

"I'm sorry to have wasted your time," I say with regret.

"You haven't wasted any of my time. Please come back, even if it's for five minutes. Or I can meet you, anywhere. Ring this number and ask for—"

"Katie. I remember."

She hands me a card. "It would be best to memorise the number then destroy the card." I take in what it is she's saying, she's warning me that Blake *cannot* find the card. "Can I ask your name?"

"Ginny," I answer distractedly. I stare at the card in disbelief at the situation I'm finding myself in.

"Ginny, do you have children?" Her words break through my thoughts.

"What? Oh! No." I should at least be grateful for that, Katie nods like she read my thoughts.

"Then one last thing..."

I pause in the doorway, silently allowing her to continue.

"Work through your home, room to room, look at areas within those rooms that are your safest place to fall. Avoid places such as the bathroom where there is no way out. If you sense he's angry, avoid the kitchen."

"The kitchen?"

"There are more items in there than any other room that can be thrown or used as a weapon," she explains, and I nod in understanding. "Do you have another room with an outside door? Think of escape routes. Do you have a friend or neighbour that you can trust? You could speak with them. If they were ever to hear shouting, they could call help for you."

I look away, wishing I had an answer. The one true friend I have, I've not seen in months. The distance Blake's career move created has had more than one impact on my life. Marci and I have now resorted to weekly phone calls, and then we can barely make out what the other is saying due to the poor signal at home. Which secretly, I'm grateful for. How can I even begin to explain any of this to Marci? I'm not sure she'd believe me anyway, not when it's about Blake.

As for neighbours, nobody would be able to hear me. Our house is too isolated. Is that why he chose where we live? I'm aware I'm frowning as Katie looks at me.

"Sorry, um not really, not nearby. I'm sorry. I have to go." I open the door and leave the room.

"Remember our number," I hear Katie call after me.

I walk through the building as fast as I'm able, not once looking up until my feet hit the path outside. Then I swerve right, joining the other pedestrians on the main street and set walking, my pace a little more laboured than theirs.

Staring blankly ahead, I think of what happened only a minute ago. I told somebody, and she didn't throw it back in my face, claiming I was too sensitive or being ridiculous. She didn't laugh. She believed me instantly, without question.

The small sense of relief is suddenly whipped out from under me when something unnerves me. The sense that I'm being watched causes me to come to a standstill. I turn around and for some reason, I look first towards the bench, but it's empty. So I scan the flurry of the crowd but don't see a soul looking my way.

Brakes creaking cause me to jump. People passing by look at me strangely before uttering words of annoyance. I feel my cheeks flush with embarrassment. Dipping my chin low, I move towards the bus. With my head bowed, I get on board and scan my ticket.

"Morning," The driver addresses me. I mutter a greeting in return before making my way towards the most deserted side of the bus.

As I lower myself to the seat, a little girl sitting a few rows in front of me with her mum draws my attention. She's wearing a tiara and waving a wand around, the low-level winter sunlight bouncing off her tight blonde curls. When she turns around, she's giggling, I imagine at something her mum said. A set of dimples press in her cheeks. The sight should make me smile in return, but all it does is highlight what I can never have. I twist away from the sight, my hair covering the side of my face, no longer wanting to look at part of life I won't allow myself to have.

It's hard not to think of anything but where I've just been. Katie wasn't shocked or surprised. There was no threat of a call to the police. I'm guessing because she knows if she had, I'd have been out of that door immediately. But it's what she didn't say that holds me with the most dread. She never said it would end.

Instead, she talked of finding areas of safety in the home, of asking for help when I will need it the most.

I fiddle with the ticket in my hands, and my mind starts working. Pushing my hand down the back of the seat, I wedge the ticket in place, technically littering but needing to cover my tracks. Then I pull the contact card Katie gave me from my bag and run my fingers along the number, repeatedly saying it in my head before looking away and testing my memory.

Once confident that I remember the number, I tuck the card down the seat with the ticket, then focus on the dirt-stained windows as we travel past buildings and people. Above all, I avoid the laughs and fond mutterings between the mother and daughter. Because there is no magic wand, nor will there be an easy escape, if escape is even a possibility at all.

CHAPTER THREE

After a restless night's sleep, I find it difficult to think of anything but my journey out yesterday. Even with my hands submerged in the heat of the dishwater, the rest of me continues to feel the chill. As winter approaches and the weather turns colder, I'm uncertain if the cold is due to the house being unable to hold any heat or if it stems from fear and unease.

"Ginny?" Blake calls my name on his way out of the door. I pull my hands from the sink, look to the hallway and give him my attention. He glances at the bruises he created on my skin days before, some more visible now my hands are out of the dishwater. "I'll be home on time tonight, okay?"

"Yes, Blake." I smile weakly.

"And about Saturday, you like the dress, don't you?"

"I love the dress." I nod my head in confirmation, knowing my words alone will not be able to convince him. I *like* the dress but would have preferred to choose one myself—one that was a little less conspicuous. Social gatherings have never really been my thing. I used to prefer being in the company of close friends, smaller groups, but I don't really have a choice on Saturday. The firm Blake works for holds an annual gathering to celebrate everyone's effort and success. Evidently, Blake has more than proved his commitment to the company since we moved here. It's therefore a requirement that we both attend.

"Well, they're all looking forward to meeting you." He takes his coat off the stand and tosses it over his arm. "I'll see you tonight."

When he closes the door behind him, I turn back towards the window and lift my arm to wave him goodbye.

The sound of the tyres crunching on the gravel of the lane slowly dissipates as his distance grows. I wait until the car has been out of sight for at least five minutes before I finally feel able to breathe more freely, but as I look around the room, at the tall walls and high ceiling, I know I'm far from being free.

My focus settles on my tan leather bag that hangs from the chair at the table, or more precisely, where my phone is. I need to ring Marci. It's been two weeks, and for once I feel strong enough to face any questions she may have and able to lie for the sake of my safety. Or is it for the sake of Blake's reputation? The reasons merge into one and have become too clouded for me to even make sense of.

I drag the heavy chair out from under the table and sit down, scrolling through the very short list of contacts, Marci's name appears, and my finger hovers over it. I close my eyes and smile as I think of her strolling around work, instructions to staff rolling from her tongue. She'll be telling Justine for the tenth time how to arrange the clothing on the rails.

Then I imagine what she would do if she saw me. She would stop immediately, her wide smile would appear, and she'd drag me into her arms. I'd rest my head on her shoulders and take in the familiar scent of sunflowers. I used to tell her how overpowering the perfume was, that she wore too much. But I'd give anything to be back home and smell the intensity of sunflowers again.

However, the risk is too great, or the shame too powerful, again the reasons combine but result in the same outcome.

Drawing in some deep breaths, I open my eyes and press dial.

I try a number of times, before getting up and walking around the room until I finally get a signal. But as soon as she picks up, her voice breaks. Deciding higher ground may prove more successful, I rush up the vast mahogany staircase and head straight for the only spare room where I've managed to get a signal.

A rare beam of winter sun gleams through the window. I perch myself on the window sill, right in the middle of the glow, thankful it found its way through the trees. With two bars lit up on my phone, I quickly dial as the sun starts to warm my face.

"Ginny? For Christ's sake! Ginny?" That's all it takes. One exasperated comment from Marci and a laugh breaks free.

"Hey," I respond before I wipe away the tear that's taken me by surprise rolling down my cheek.

"Oh my God. About time, Ginny! I was beginning to think you'd forgotten about me!"

"H—"

"You haven't, have you?" Her interruption and incessant need to talk are a welcome sound in the stillness of the home.

"How could I forget about you? Marci, you know how awful the signal is here."

"Tell me about it! I was gobsmacked when I finally got through a couple of days ago, but then Blake said you were out. You know you could always step away from the beautiful mansion you apparently live in to get a better signal, or hell you could ring me while you're having lunch. That is what you do now you have all this spare time, right?" Her words continue, but the only thing I centre on is, she rang two days ago?

Two days ago was Sunday. I wasn't out. If Blake was at home, then that's where I would have been. "When exactly did you ring?"

"What? Oh, two days ago like I said. Sunday. Blake said you were loving it and it was about time I came up to see how stunning your new home was myself. If he weren't so blasted important at work, I'd have made it up before now, but you two are always so busy! We were trying to organise it for a weekend I have off, but then the signal disappeared on us again. He sounded happy, Gin. This move, it was the right thing, wasn't it, for both of you." There is confirmation in her voice, believing Blake's own take on the move.

"Yes," I say quickly, trying to sound genuine. Marci and Blake got on well from the very beginning. She admires him—like most do. Not long after we moved here to Hereford, Blake and I went back home to visit everyone. It was before the abuse really took hold. I had a rare moment of being alone with Marci, and I remember mentioning how Blake liked me to be at home. She laughed and said something about it being good that I knew my place. It was a flippant comment, one that I know she wouldn't really mean if she knew what being at home meant, but it was enough of a comment to quieten me at the time. Yet somehow, the silence continues.

It's not something a person would ever want to freely admit to, suffering from abuse. But it's not even that which creates my silence. I know I haven't seen the worst of him yet. He scares me more than I believed a man could ever scare a woman.

With my fingers, I draw swirls on the small beads of condensation on the lower half of the window.

"So, tell me how you are? I'm bloody missing you like mad."

My hand stills and a lump rises in my throat. Briefly, I close my eyes hoping to seek some strength even if only temporary.

"Ginny?"

"I'm here. I miss you too."

"Is everything alright, Ginny? I mean truly?" My lips part. I could tell her but deliberating over what to do only makes it harder to admit. "I can't believe we've gone from seeing each other every day to this. If I didn't know any better, I'd swear Blake was purposely torturing us by dragging you away!" She chuckles. "I'm going to tell him so when I actually get to see him!"

"No!" I'm quick to respond. Luckily the recovery is just as fast. "This isn't torture, Marci." The words feel like poison in my mouth, and I want to spit them to the ground and come clean, but fear renders me unable to do so. Instead, I hold back and talk to my friend as though life is perfect. Yet with each lie that is told, each bruise that is created, my self-loathing is fuelled some more.

"I can imagine exactly the kind of torture you must be experiencing." My heart clutches at my chest. "A husband who's at the top of his company, working as hard as he does. I bet he can't wait to get home to you at night, you lucky sod." I try and laugh as though I'm smiling when her words only fill me with sadness. "Although a house that's in the middle of a forest, miles from another human being? Does the wind howl in the trees at night and the shadows from the branches creep across your bedroom?"

I look out over the area of land in front of me. There are a number of trees, clustered along the lane that leads up to our house. Branches appear spindly, their bright green leaves now darkened and shed to the ground due to the time of year.

"I'm kind of desperate to come and see your pad, but at the same time a little bit scared."

My breath hitches. "Why would you be scared?"

"You're kidding, right? Have you forgotten about my phobia of scary movies? Although I'm sure it's nothing like that. I can imagine how perfect Blake's made it for you."

"Marci," I dread the words that are about to leave my mouth because asking them alone, causes my chest to ache. "Have you been to see her?" The line goes quiet. "Marci?"

"I went last week. I put some fresh flowers on her grave."

I close my eyes and draw my knee up to my chest resting my forehead to it. "Thank you." It's been three years since my mum passed away, and I still miss her as much today. The pain doesn't seem to ease any.

I hear her sigh on the other end of the phone. "Did you not want to come and see her?"

Of course I do, I want to yell. I used to go all the time. It was always my mum and me—until the day it wasn't. "I'll come soon."

Marci isn't aware but Blake drove me down a couple of weeks ago so I could go to my mum's grave, but we didn't have time to drop in on Marci or her family as Blake had to get back for work. If my car ever comes back from being repaired, there's a possibility I could drive myself down there, but it's only a possibility. For some reason, my car has been in the garage for months now. Blake claims there are numerous things wrong with it, but I hadn't noticed anything.

"Speak to Blake, try and convince him to take a day off work. You can both come down, and in two weeks, I have the weekend off, so I can come and see you. Mum and Dad are desperate to see you, Ginny. So is Liam."

I haven't seen Marci's parents nor her brother Liam for far too long, and I miss them all.

"How is everyone, Marci?"

"Missing you, Gin."

"I miss them too. I'll speak with Blake." I try and add a sense of promise to my tone but recognise that it's only been falsely placed there. It isn't likely that either of those plans will come off. Swiftly, I swipe at the tears that roll down my cheeks.

Needing to change the course of the conversation, I draw in a deep breath. "Marci, how's work?" I don't just ask for a distraction but also out of interest. Marci loves her job. She works in retail, a sexy boudoir type shop, and she gets to meet all kinds of clientele. She used to spend night after night regaling Liam and me with tales of customers.

"Oh my god, Justine! Put it down. That is *not* how you use it. I'll be with you in a moment, sir." I feel my cheeks bunch as a smile lights up my face. "Shit, Ginny!" she says under her breath. "You wouldn't believe what she was just doing. This guy's eyes are popping out of his head! I'm going to have to go," she adds apologetically.

"Okay." I'm desperate to know what Justine was doing, but I guess I don't get to hear those stories anymore. Chats are limited due to the time of day I always call her.

"Holy crap! Does she know anything?" she adds with further exasperation.

"Maybe it's because you know too much," I say.

"You can never know too much, Ginny." She laughs. I look around the room, and for once I have to disagree with my friend. Sometimes you're better off not knowing anything at all.

"Let me know what Blake says."

"I will." I lie because Blake's choice of words won't be anything I'd repeat to Marci.

∽

My hands start to vibrate on the worktop as the water in the kettle begins to boil, pulling me from my thoughts. The remainder of the afternoon seems to have passed in a blur, and any minute now he'll be home. I've made certain that everything is as he likes it. The air is tinged with the smell of lasagne cooking in the oven. A newly baked lemon drizzle cake sits perfectly in the middle of the table.

Surfaces sparkle and remain clear of clutter. All that's left to happen is my husband to arrive home, and then uncertainty can ensue.

I pour the steaming water onto my coffee, then pick up the spoon and watch as the brown flecks mix with the milk. My vision elevates, and I take in the encroaching night sky through the window. Clouds conceal what little sunlight is left, yet the heavy branches on the trees are still indicating a calmness. I know it won't last, the wind will arrive, and the few leaves that remain will be left with no option but to batter against each other. Eventually, one will break free and fall to the ground below.

I remove the spoon from the cup and drop it to the sink with a clank. Wrapping my hands around the cup, I move to the table as the heat makes an effort to warm me.

While I sit waiting, there isn't a sound.

Silence never used to bother me, but now it comes in many different forms. The past two days' peace is the aftermath—it's about picking up the pieces. When remorse follows my husband around, and his hands are no longer the cause of pain but the method by which he soothes me.

By far, the worst form of silence is right before detonation. I'm learning the signs but seem unable to avoid the actual explosion. The path is always directly in front of me and no matter which way I turn, I'm unable to avoid it.

Even though today is a day I'm expecting calm, the sound of his car on the gravel still causes me to stiffen in apprehension. Resting my elbows on the table, I swallow and look at the door, awaiting his arrival.

As he enters the house, I briefly see his face before he disappears further into the hallway. His keys jangle as he tosses them to the bowl, their usual place of rest. Then I hear the shuffling of fabric as he removes his coat and hangs it up. They are all sounds I'm used to, none of them out of the ordinary. Briefly, I close my eyes and breathe a sigh of relief.

When he steps through the doorway, he does a double take at me sitting at the table. I would normally be making dinner or carrying out household chores.

"Ginny." He acknowledges my presence and briefly glances to my cup in front of me. "Is everything okay?" He glances around the room clearly confused by the change in routine.

"Yes. Dinner's nearly ready," I say by way of explanation. "I'll make you a drink." I wince unintentionally as I twist when standing, surprised that my side is still tender from a few days ago. The pain eases, and I continue forward.

Then as though it suddenly clicks into place, he moves towards me and the second the kettle is in my grasp, he takes it from me.

"Go and sit down." I do as I'm told and take my seat. When I bring my eyes up, he's already looking my way. I expect to see regret, but all I see is a blank stare.

His vision flicks briefly to my side where he knows it's hurting, but he doesn't pass comment. "I forgot to mention, your car should be back tomorrow morning. First thing," he remarks casually.

"Oh, thank you," I say surprised, I wasn't sure my car would ever be returned. I'm pretty sure Blake likes the idea of me being housebound. The few trips I've made into the city he's been unaware of because I know it's something he wouldn't like.

"So what have you been up to today?" he asks, taking his usual cup from the cupboard.

"Not a lot," I reply. "A little gardening, clearing up some leaves. I've made a lemon drizzle cake," I remark. It was always Marci's favourite, and she'd rarely let anyone share it. Blake frowns as I quickly wipe the small smile from my face.

"What's so funny?"

"I was thinking of Marci, that's all. Lemon drizzle is her favourite."

He passes a look of distaste at the cake. "Marci." He states her name without emotion. "Have you done anything else today other than gardening and baking? You haven't spoken to anyone?" His tone is icy causing my posture to freeze. My lips part as I seek breath like I wish for an escape.

"I, err, did speak to Marci." My voice is so pitiful that I shake my head. He continues making his drink, not stilling for a second. Somehow he knew I'd spoken with Marci and he was testing me.

"And how was she?" His words are brittle, yet he turns around and smiles. Blake used to think and speak of Marci only ever in complimentary ways but not anymore. I'm not sure what or even when it changed.

"She's fine." I force myself to return his smile.

"Did she tell you I spoke with her on Sunday?"

"Yes, she did."

"I guess I forgot that too." His stare starts to harden. "But I presume that's why you brought it up, to prove my thoughtlessness."

I didn't mention Marci's name for any other reason than she came into my thoughts. It was unrelated to missing her call on Sunday. But as I look to him now, I recognise he doesn't believe me. I feel my breathing start to accelerate.

"I-I didn't mean anything," I mumble. "She didn't have any urgent reason to get in touch with me or anything. I was letting you know we spoke." My babbling only flusters me more.

"Why would it be urgent? A phone call to tell you of her latest conquest would barely be classed as urgent," he gripes. I'm mindful not to pass comment. There was a time when I would defend Marci, but not anymore. I only do it quietly in my head. He continues to look at me. "I didn't *mean* to forget, Ginny, if that's what that look is about." His tone puts me on alert, and I try to portray a neutral expression. "You know I have a lot going on. Acting like your secretary is the last thing I need."

"I know you do, Blake." I lower my focus in shame. Why did I even say anything? But wait... I didn't. He brought it up, didn't he? I stare at the cup on the table in front of me as my heart continues to hammer in my chest.

This is unlike before. After the pain usually comes regret, but it's not even been forty-eight hours. My hands start to turn clammy. I release them from the cup, and I'm lost at what to do.

The moment I hear his feet on the tiled floor, I know I backed down seconds too late.

He arrives fast. I don't have chance to get out of the chair. His right hand clasps my jaw, and he yanks me to standing. The pain shoots through my jaw, and I whimper before I shudder at the pathetic sound. His fingers dig into my skin and with the sound of my pitiful cry reverberating around me, I force myself to look directly into his eyes, my self-loathing coming at him with full force. The blame, the torture, and the shame are all there, fighting its way through.

My self-hatred spurs my words. "You know what this is?" I begin through my forcibly pressed jaw.

"Tell me what it is," he taunts seeming to enjoy my new-found confidence.

"Abuse!" I manage to spit the word out. He appears unaffected by my accusation as he laughs out loud but then his mouth seals shut and his nostrils flare.

"Who's filled your mind with that bullshit?" he fumes through clenched teeth, as his face edges closer to mine. "Marci? You fucking told her what you make me do? Have you, Ginny? Because this isn't all on me. You know how to work me so I have no option but to do this!" He juts his head in the direction of my jaw.

"I didn't tell her," I cry out in panic, his eyes focus on mine and he curls his lip up at the weakness he sees before him. Releasing his grip, he shoves me hard against the table. A jolt of pain spreads through my back. Then he spins on his heel and paces across the kitchen, dragging his fingers through his hair.

"I didn't tell her," I repeat, wanting above all, to protect Marci. I stretch my hands out behind me and tread steadily until I reach the far wall.

As his pacing continues, hopelessness combines with fear. He pauses and stares at the cake, then seizes it in his hand, hurling it across the kitchen. "Your baking is fucking shit! Marci probably kept it to herself to avoid you facing embarrassment while everyone gagged at the taste!" A whimper leaves my lips. This is never going to be over.

I try and say the right thing, but it always ends up being wrong. I tried leaving once before but he found me. He says he will always find me. So I choose to stay, aiming to limit the abuse by adhering to what he wants, but my methods are somehow failing me, and it's only getting worse. Yet remaining here with him means I'm slowly losing Marci and the only family I have.

Realisation dawns and an ache spreads throughout my chest. I crumble to the ground, my knees landing on the unforgiving hard floor.

Marci. No longer watching him, I stare blankly into the air around me, recognising what I've been scared to admit all along. I thought I would lose them all, but the reality is, I'm already losing them. I'm choosing to stay here. This is down to me, yet, I can't see any other way out. Gradually, I tilt my chin, and my focus settles on him.

"It doesn't really matter… any of it," I whisper.

He stills and turns his head in my direction. "What?"

I look away from him because the words aren't only for his benefit, they're for mine too. "The pain is something I'm getting used to. I'm used to cleaning my wounds and wiping the tears from my face. I'm used to seeing you regret the pain you cause, and each time I'm becoming more ready to accept the blame."

His shoes click across the floor as his feet enter my vision. They come to a stop, but I don't expect his hesitancy to last long.

When I bring my eyes up to meet his, he's standing above me, appearing more powerful and in control than ever. I know the position will please him. I also know he's going to hurt me, no matter what else is said or done tonight.

I inhale deeply, in preparation, but for once I'm going to make this pain count.

"Each time you raise your hand, it's one step closer to losing me. I don't know how it will happen, Blake, but it won't always be like this. Steadily but surely you're making me believe that I don't matter."

"What are you talking about?" A scowl crosses his brow, and his intolerance is evident.

"If I don't matter then I won't care what happens to me."

I feel the weight of his stare but refuse to look away. Not this time because I'm not sure I have anything left to lose. The rise and fall of his shoulders become more exaggerated as his breathing becomes heavy. Movement of his fingers as they curl into fists causes me to lower my gaze. They're level with my head. I look at his neatly trimmed fingernails and wait. I know this time it's going to hurt, but running serves no purpose. It will only hurt more.

I open my mouth wide in shock as he turns and storms out of the room. Keys scrape along the bowl right before the door is slammed closed. Revs from his car's engine spring to life before the wheels spin on the ground as he veers away from the house.

I stay motionless before my chest starts to heave with breaths that spurt from my mouth. Dragging myself up, I stumble my way to the sink in front of the window. The drive is empty. He's actually gone.

My hands are trembling uncontrollably, and I shake my head in disbelief at my small show of defiance. Could this be it? Could he have shown some comprehension of what it is he's been doing to us? To me?

My hands can't stop shaking though, and, once again, a dreaded silence fills our home. I raise my hands in front of me and wonder why I can't control the tremors that run through my fingers. I move one hand to my jaw and skim my fingers along the tender skin. It's rare he marks my face but tonight his clasp was hard, and it's still tender to the touch. But was that it? That's all I get tonight?

I glance outside at the darkness of the night. Skimming past the trees, I wonder where he's gone. If I've angered him or made him realise what consequences are in play.

"What's happening?" I cry out in desperation.

The strength of the moonlight on the trees starts to build. I take a second glance before looking up at the moon, but I see only cloud cover. I look back to the lane. Petrified.

The light isn't from the moon.

Blake's car reappears at a speed that causes me to step back from the window. Even in the dimmed light, I see the gravel and dust spit out from behind the wheels. He slams his foot on the brakes, the red taillights illuminating the drive like the igniting of a fire.

The car door is pushed open with such force that it swings back on itself until Blake rights it. Then as he comes into view, he straightens himself up, displaying his full height. With a threatening glare, he looks to the window and directly at me.

My lips part, fear renders me immobile and unable to look away. He backs up a step and gently closes the door, his glare unmoving.

An evil sneer kicks up the corner of his lip, and I know this time it's different. This isn't an act of anger residing from stress or frustration. It's not even a threat. It's a promise. An intentional assurance of pain.

My heart races, feeling like it's going to explode in my chest. I force my feet to move and start to run across the kitchen, but my feet slip from under me. On my knees, I reach for the table top and grab my mobile. I shake it in desperation at the lack of signal, and I cry out, powerless.

My attention switches to the door that leads into the hallway as I hear him enter the house, opening with ease the only barrier that was between us. *Why didn't I lock it?* Like he heard my thoughts, the lock clicks, shutting us both inside.

"Darling, guess what?" he calls out, sauntering into the kitchen, pushing the keys deep into his trouser pocket. I stumble to my feet, my hands jittering behind me to find the safety of the far wall. "I'm home," he says with a smile that causes a strange yelping noise to break from my throat. "You look scared, Ginny." He tilts his head in what I can only call glee. "After that little speech, I didn't think I could scare you."

Suddenly, I remember what Katie said about avoiding the kitchen. My eyes dart to the drawer containing the knives. He notices and briefly glances in the same place. "Are you looking for you... or for me? Because I don't need a knife, sweetheart. Although I have to say it's rather considerate of you."

Pushing off from the wall, I run from the room as fast as my trembling legs are able, but he's as fast off the mark. Only his legs are longer and more stable than mine, anger and evil driving him forward. I head for the stairs but as my foot reaches the third step his hand makes contact with my ankle. He pulls my legs from under me. I try to reach out to cushion my fall, but I'm too slow, my head lands with a shuddering bang on the edge of the step.

Dazed, I'm unprepared for the remaining two steps, my head

colliding with them as he drags me down. Cries leave my mouth as I writhe around helplessly trying to free my foot, but his grip is unyielding.

My sickening screams fill the air as he hauls me to the living room at the back of the house. It's dark. I can barely make out the furniture. He stops but maintains his hold on me then shoves my knee into my abdomen as he leans above me, his breath landing on my face.

"You have some fight in you tonight, oh wife of mine." Instinctively, my free leg kicks out in an attempt to push him from me. I can barely see where I'm aiming, but I hit something.

He drops his hold, and I see his form step away, so I scuttle backwards further into the dark. He alters his position and steps into the only ray of light that's shining into the room. His eyes aren't visible, but the smirk on his lips is clearly evident.

"Ginny, that isn't a kick, darling." I witness his leg draw back before he launches his foot directly into my already bruised side. I yelp like a defenceless animal. Winded, I struggle for breath. "That... is a kick." I curl into a ball, wanting the ground to swallow me up. "Now get up." I peer up at him through my hair and realise he's serious. "I said, get the fuck up!" Again he kicks me, equally as hard. "Now!"

Clutching onto my side, I stagger to my feet. He brings himself closer and grabs onto my upper arm, yanking me back, pushing us both into obscurity until I slam against the wall.

My head quivers from side to side, anticipating the unexpected. I scream as he gathers a fistful of my hair and tugs it hard to the side, exposing my neck. I sense his face come close and feel the warm breath on my ear.

"So I no longer scare you because you don't care," he states, sounding intrigued. "Yet we both know Marci and her family care about you, don't we?" I freeze, not moving a muscle. "How is Jim's heart these days by the way? I asked after him when I spoke with Marci. It doesn't sound too good to me." All breath leaves me as the darkest fear settles in the pit of my stomach. "I hear stress can cause serious problems with people like Jim. His heart won't last out forever.

No. He can't. He wouldn't. "No." I sob.

"Please..." My voice trails off helplessly. "Just stop," I beg.

He pushes my head from his grip, releasing me. "I'll take that and accept it as fear, Ginny." I hear the sound of his feet on the carpet, retreating. "You *are* scared. Sometimes it's so much easier to admit you were wrong in the first place."

I fall to the ground, and my hands cover my face as I quietly weep, and wonder how this will ever end.

CHAPTER FOUR

My hand is tucked underneath his arm as we step into the grand lobby of the most exclusive hotel in the city. My heels click along the white marble floor, and I sense people watching, but I keep my eyes low to avoid the attention.

Nearly a week has passed, the bruises have almost faded, but my fear has only grown. Each beating is getting progressively worse, his apologies becoming weaker, and threats more severe. The strength to run from him is diminishing. Being the person that spends a lifetime running, and permanently looking over her shoulder is steadily becoming second place to being the wife that stays with him, hoping that predicting his moves will reduce the episodes of abuse. Survival, but on the run, versus survival with pain. It's an impossible choice.

"Did I tell you how beautiful you look?" I glance up at him and smile. It's no wonder he sees it as beauty. I'm wearing the dress and shoes he chose. My dark hair falls in glossy waves down my back, the style precisely as he suggested. My makeup is subtle yet provides the shell to my much-needed flawless mask.

"Thank you." I find the words that should come easily.

The elevator arrives, and he guides me inside. Mirrors cover each wall. So I stand and face the doors. Only when they close, again I'm faced with my own reflection and my husband by my side. I drop my focus, not wanting to see the image that stares back at me because that woman, that man, they are strangers, and the image is far from any version of beauty.

"Ginny?" he says my name, and instinctively I turn to face him. His stare hangs on me a little too long. "You know how important tonight is? Everyone at work respects me, Ginny. You can't mess this up for me."

My vision sinks at the reminder of the last work event I went to. It was before we moved—before everything. I'd been nervous, so ended up drinking way more than was necessary. I made a fool of myself, ending up on the floor of the restroom by the end of the night, clutching the toilet like some inexperienced teenager after their first heavy taste of alcohol. Blake had been unforgivingly disappointed in me.

"I won't, Blake. That won't ever happen again," I state with honesty.

His chin lifts and his eyes maintain their steady scrutiny. "Don't look so nervous. You look beautiful. Perfect." Blake makes an offer of reassurance believing that my inability to look at my reflection stems from nerves when instead, it's from the residual feeling of shame.

He brings his hand to rest on my lower back, and I have to force myself not to recoil from his touch. Instead, I twist and offer my practised smile up at him.

The elevator finally stops. When the doors open, he reaches for my hand ensuring a show of our unity. He guides me out and into the vast room.

Glass windows from floor-to-ceiling extend all around,

providing a panoramic view of the city skyline. The bar sits in the middle of the room but, minimalistic in nature, with soft lighting, it doesn't detract from the true beauty of the top floor of the hotel —the city around us.

I'm still standing in admiration when I hear laughter to my side. I turn, my focus immediately landing on Blake, and I remember where I am, and unfortunately, who I am. Dutifully, I walk straight to his side where his arm finds its way around my waist.

"It's beautiful, isn't it?" he confirms. It looks like Blake has his own mask fixed in place tonight. "Let me introduce you to some annoyingly handsome and wealthy people," he adds with a humour that I haven't witnessed in many months.

"Ginny, this is James, my right-hand man." A man in his fifties with a pinstripe suit as smart as Blake's steps forward and leans in, placing a kiss on my cheek.

"It's lovely to finally meet you, Ginny, although, Blake's description of you doesn't do you justice, my dear. How on earth did he convince you to marry him?" Thankfully, he crosses his focus to Blake as my cheeks grow warm, feeling uncomfortable with his comment and praise. "You bribe her?" he asks laughing.

"I'm lucky, that's for sure," Blake replies as he takes two champagne flutes from a passing waitress and hands me one.

"Thank you," I say.

I must have stared at the bubbles rising in the glass a second too long because James laughs. "It's the good stuff," he reassures as though that is the cause of my hesitation. Blake looks down at me, so I take a quick sip.

"Ginny, this is my wife," James looks behind him. "Kirsty!" he calls. A lady briefly turns before passing her excuses to the group she was talking to. All I can focus on are her legs. Very long immaculately prepared legs. Realising how rude I'm being, I quickly glance at her face. "Kirsty, this is Ginny, Blake's wife."

"Oh wow!" she says. "Finally, we get to meet you. We keep telling him to bring you to one of these functions." *One of these functions?* This is the first one I've heard about. There have been occasions Blake has been home very late, but he'd told me he was at the office.

"Nice to meet you." I smile, feeling Blake's eyes on me.

"Come on, Ginny." She hooks her arm in mine. "Your husband may be a man at the top, but you get to spend every night with him. Right now, there are far more important people that you need to meet," she adds, laughing fondly at Blake before she tugs at my arm, giving me no choice but to follow. I glance back at Blake, wondering if I should have put up some kind of refusal, but with a look of approval brimming from his eyes, he nods his head discreetly, then turns his attention back to James.

"So, how long have you two been married? I have to tell you there are going to be a lot of unhappy faces around here now you've turned up."

"What?" I ask panicked.

"Oh, don't worry." She leads me to the bar and indicates for me to sit on a bar stool as she climbs onto one herself.

"Why will there be unhappy faces?" I query. I don't need to look around the room to know eyes are already boring into my back.

"Your husband, he's, how shall I put it? Desirable to a number of the admin staff, even some of the partners. So trust me, I know how you're feeling right now. It was the same when James arrived. New meat you see and they had hoped your husband was the kind that was readily available. Just try not to look so intimidated. You're the boss's wife. Own it, girl, like your husband does!"

Kirsty's eyes settle on Blake as he starts to work his way around the room. Mine follow. Blake knows how to act at social gatherings. It's one of the things that initially drew me to him. His confidence and aura pull people in his direction like metal to a magnet. His body glides, people rush towards him, but he always remains steady and controlled. His hands reach out to colleagues, somehow showing how valuable he believes them to be. I remember the feeling myself.

I've always chosen to hide in the shadows, the limelight was more Marci's preference. So when Blake saw me and refused to take no for an answer, it gave me a confidence boost like never before.

As I take in their faces, it's obvious everyone looks on at him with the admiration and envy I once did.

I'd love to sink into the depths of oblivion, if only for one moment, to forget everything that's happened and instead, go back to those first few months.

"You don't like champagne?" Kirsty asks drawing my attention away from Blake.

I place my glass on the bar. "I'm just a little nervous."

"Which is why I can tell champagne isn't your drink. Nerves would have meant that champagne flute would have been emptied by now, but you've barely had a sip." She pauses and narrows her eyes up at me in contemplation. "So what do you like to drink, Ginny Daniels?" she asks seemingly interested.

I used to drink lager or white wine, but it's been a while since I've had a drink at all. I take a quick look around the room and see mostly spirits or wine in glasses. I'd take either of those, but my nerves are creating a thirst. "A white wine maybe?"

"But that's not what you want, is it? Don't worry about what everyone else in here is drinking! I'm glad I've found a kindred spirit." Kirsty calls over the barman. "Two bottles of lager, please. No glass, just as they come. That's right, isn't it?" I bite my lip and wish I'd drunk the champagne. Blake thinks it's uncouth to see a woman drinking from a bottle.

"Thank you." I smile, but worry instantly fills me, wondering what Blake will think. We wait a moment until the barman has left us with our drinks. "Should I go and meet people?" I ask, despising the shyness that appears to have taken hold. I don't want to meet anybody else, but I sense Blake would prefer it.

"They'll come up and introduce themselves. Mark my words. You never answered my question? How long have you been married?"

"Seven months," I reply barely able to believe it myself.

I expect further questions, but another woman comes to stand beside us, her attention lying solely on me.

"Evening, Josie."

I glance briefly to Kirsty as she acknowledges the woman and simultaneously rolls her eyes.

"You must be Ginny," Josie remarks, snubbing Kirsty. "I'm Josie, Blake's personal assistant." She smiles coyly over at Blake and twirls some of her auburn hair between her fingers. *Seriously?*

I draw on a smile and offer out my hand. "Nice to meet you, Josie. Blake talks a lot about you." I lie. Blake hasn't mentioned her name at all, and I wonder why. But then Blake hasn't spoken to me about anybody from work. Other than James. I assumed it was taking time for him to settle, but clearly, I was wrong.

"You look beautiful, Ginny. Do you like the dress?" Josie questions.

"Thank you and, erm, yes, I love the dress," I reply a little puzzled by her question. I run my hands down the silky material questioning if there's something else I should have noticed about the dress.

"I had a selection brought to the office. I knew by the picture he has of you on his desk that this was the right one for you."

Oh. That's why. She wants to point out that *she* chose the dress, not Blake.

I see Kirsty's eyebrows lift. "You actually chose his wife's dress? Did you not think she could choose it herself, Josie?" Kirsty questions. Josie ignores Kirsty as though the comment was never even passed.

"*You* understand, don't you, Ginny? It's part of my job?" She directs to me, her question sounding almost belittling. I want to tell her that I can choose my own goddamn clothes. But of course, I don't.

"Well, you have beautiful taste," I say finally.

"Thank you. Well, I wanted to come and say hi. I must get back. Hopefully, we'll catch up again later."

"Hopefully," I respond. As Josie walks towards Blake, I'm aware that Kirsty is watching me. "So, she wants to screw my husband?" I say twisting back to face her and taking a drink from the lager.

She bursts out laughing. "Like I said, you've caused quite a stir. No one expected you to be as beautiful as you are either. Yes, he has your photo, but there are only a few members of staff that will have seen it. Not everyone is important enough to make it into Blake Daniels' office."

"I'm not beautiful," I utter. I'm far from beautiful. The

makeup and preened hair may help, but inside I'm angry, I'm bitter, I'm hurting, and I'm sad, but most of all I'm lost.

"You're joking? You're the envy of every single woman in this room right now and even some of those that are taken!" Tears sting my eyes, and I can't help but turn away. "Ginny, I'm sorry. What... what did I say?"

"Nothing. I'm fine. You're being very kind, and I haven't had a drink in a while. One is clearly my limit before my emotions get the better of me." I smile fondly at her. "I could do with the ladies room." I scan the area around me but see only glass windows and the lift.

"There are some stairs beside the lift. It's just down there."

"Thank you." As I get down from the stool, Kirsty grabs my hand.

"I'll be here, okay?" She looks at me, and I can tell she knows there's more to my story. I need to do better than this. I won't be coming back to the bar. I'll be heading toward Blake. Bizarrely, it seems like the safest place. Kirsty looks like she has the ability to read people with barely a word being exchanged. At least I won't suddenly break out in tears by Blake's side. Instead, his presence will ensure my façade is more firmly in place.

I notice Blake across the room. He's deep in conversation, with Josie by his side. Perhaps I should feel jealous or perhaps pleased, but I don't. I feel indifferent.

As I walk down the short flight of stairs, I release a breath and know for all of five minutes I will be able to let Ginny Daniels go.

Once I enter the ladies room, I head straight for a cubicle. I don't need the toilet. I need some space alone. Twisting the lock, I pull on the toilet seat cover and sit down.

Laughter erupts as I hear the door open. "So what do you think?" a voice asks.

"Well, she's clearly not the boring, frumpy housewife everyone believed her to be. I can't understand why Blake hasn't brought her before."

"Sam, maybe?"

"No! Do you actually think that's true?"

"I can't imagine Blake has much to worry about with Sam. I mean yeah, Sam's good looking, athletic, but Blake, well he's—"

"Don't you think she looked a little sad?" The woman interrupts her friend. I wish they'd backtrack. I'm not sure I'm prepared to know what others really think about me.

"Who?"

"Blake's wife." My chin dips to my chest. *Please... just stop.*

"No! Are you crazy? Why would a woman like her be sad?"

"She clearly adores him. She barely takes her eyes from him."

Because rocking a boat that's already on dangerous shores is never a wise thing to do. If only it were due to adoration.

"If you ask me, she's the silent boring type and wants nothing more than to go back home with a hot water bottle. Blake's strained I tell you, as though he's checking if she's okay. She doesn't even work apparently." Her words become less clear as though she's applying lipstick. "I bet he treats her like a princess."

My heart slumps at how quickly people are willing to judge. If Blake treats me like a princess, I'd much rather live like a pauper.

Knowing I've heard enough, I flush the toilet which causes their voices to resort to a whisper. Then, pulling back on the door, I walk directly to the sink beside them to wash my hands. I feel the weight of their stares on me. When I look up into the mirror, one of the girls is ruffling her hair. The other turns round to face me.

"I'm sorry. We didn't know you were in here." She at least manages to look regretful.

"It's okay," I say in response. "But whether you like me or not, I know my husband wouldn't appreciate you talking about us that way," I say in warning.

"You're right. We're so sorry," she answers in an apologetic tone.

I could explain that I used to work for an accountancy firm before we moved here. It was the first and only job I applied for because I barely managed to scrape through college. At the time I was nursing my dying mother, so obtaining a career wasn't exactly a priority for me. They think my husband treats me like a princess? I'm sure I could find evidence on my skin that would prove otherwise. I could ask who Sam is, but I don't because it doesn't really matter and as they've highlighted, gossip is rife, and the last thing I need is for Blake to hear of my ramblings in the toilet. So I place my hands calmly under the drier before making my way out of the bathroom, fighting to blink away the glistening of tears in my eyes.

Only, as I do, I crash straight into something hard and solid. When I glance up, I realise I have my hands on a man's chest. Immediately, I recoil, muttering my apologies.

"Hey, it's no problem," the man says. I glance at his face, and he's frowning at me.

"Excuse me." I try to walk around him, but he sidesteps in front of me.

"You're Blake's... girlfriend, right?"

"Wife actually," I say back with a polite smile.

He holds out his hand. "Well, it's nice to meet you." Reluctantly, I shake his hand. "I work with your husband, along with the rest of them up there. He's certainly making an impression at the firm." *Another Blake supporter.*

"Apparently so," I say. But my response is curt, and I regret it the second I open my mouth.

The man looks at me as though he's waiting for me to continue but those two words were already too many.

The door to the ladies room opens, and the girls who had been talking about me walk out. "Sam." The blonde pushes out her chest and nods as she passes us.

"Courtney," he acknowledges. *Sam? That's who they were talking about.*

Heels tap on the steps, and I don't have to watch to know taut, firm backsides will be sashaying their way up the stairs. I get the distinct impression from what the girls said, that I shouldn't be talking to Sam. I'm certain Blake wouldn't like it.

"Excuse me. I should be getting back," I offer my excuse.

"Probably a good idea. It was nice meeting you, Ginny."

The second the room comes into view, I search for Blake, knowing I've been gone way too long. The second I find him, his eyes are already on me. He's been watching and waiting. The panic starts to rise as I walk towards him. But then he holds out his hand.

"It's time to dance," he states, and I know it's not an invitation. It's an order.

But the moment our fingers touch, his focus moves behind me, and he follows something or someone with interest. I start to look in the same direction.

"Do *not* look at him," Blake asserts under his breath, but not before I see it is Sam where Blake's attention lies. Blake's back stiffens beside me. I turn back but feel the hatred stream from Blake in Sam's direction. I feel like I should defend Sam as all he did was say hello, but I'm learning when to keep my mouth firmly closed and now is one of those moments.

"Oh, what a great idea, Blake." Kirsty arrives with a smile, and I feel guilty for leaving her stranded at the bar. "Come on, James, let's get those two left feet of yours on the dance floor." She leans in and whispers in my ear. "Time to prove who he belongs to," she adds with a wink and nods in the direction of the dance floor before walking away holding on to James' arm.

Blake turns slightly, sheltering me from his colleague's sight. "Don't ever speak to him again." His emotionless smile rises then he lifts my hand, cradling it between his.

I look at Blake in surprise as he draws me towards the dance floor. We're actually going to dance? Dancing used to be something I loved but haven't done it in a long time. It was a regular Friday night tradition for Marci and I until I learnt of my mum's ill health, then the dancing stopped.

I walk a step behind him, but we remain linked by our hands. People stare our way, and for one night, I want to not fail. I want to believe what everyone else does as they look at Blake and me. So the fire that started burning in Blake's eyes when he saw Sam needs to be diminished. It can't flourish because pain will only follow.

Blake spins me around to face him, ready to dance. For tonight, I need to see the man that I married. I want him to see the woman he fell in love with. Only then, do I actually stand a chance of getting through this night unharmed.

∼

He doesn't speak one word to me in the lift. Instead of the warmth I'd hoped for after we danced, I experience a chill that runs down my spine and a sense of dread that sinks to the pit of my stomach as we both sit in the limo.

I feel myself pale as the engine comes to life and we start to move. I don't look out of the window to see the lights of the city. They can pass by in a haze. Instead, I keep my eyes forward on the headrest of the driver in front of me. I concentrate on the dark grey leather, trying to discover flaws, anything to take my mind off what is happening. But it's impossible. The strain and tension are evident. It was stupid of me to believe I could try and make a difference, but I thought if he could see what it used to be like, perhaps he'd grasp how awful things have become.

"You know where you're going." Blake addresses the driver, his words dangerously precise. It's a warning that the driver *should* know where he's going and for him not to question.

"Yes, sir."

The bright city lights outside start to fade as we drive into the countryside.

The slight waft of whiskey drifts towards me, and I grip onto my clutch bag a little tighter. Blake's tolerance levels are at ground zero, and I know it's down to me. I shouldn't have said hello to Sam. I don't know what I was thinking.

I can't even hear him breathe. I dip my head slightly, and hair falls over the side of my face as I peer out of the corner of my eyes. His hands are clasped together in his lap. There's no shaking, no movement, nothing. Only an icy stillness.

Time passes slowly, but I know we're getting closer to home. I pluck up the courage and glance across at him. His unsmiling eyes are there, staring right back at me, appearing darker than I've ever seen. I'm paralysed by his unmoving focus. The discontent he holds me in, growing and festering beneath my returning look. When I can cope with the singe of his stare no more, I look away and maintain a downward glance.

Dread and fear weaken me as the car is steered onto the lane and steadily takes us to our home. The second the car stops, Blake gets out, but I'm rooted to the seat, not sure my legs will be able to hold me up.

A second later, the chauffeur opens my door. I glance up nervously before forcing my foot to lift and step out of the car.

I'm unable to speak and offer my thanks. When I peer up through my lashes, the kitchen light turns on. Blake steps in front of the kitchen window and closes the blinds without even looking up. I jump at the sound of the car retreating back down the lane. I look into the woodland and wish I had the guts to run, to hide, but I know he'd find me, and even hidden, I would hear him call my name and know that he was getting closer. Then the punishment would be far worse than what it is about to be. I return my focus to the house and make my way inside.

His back faces me, his stance tense and solid. Whiskey lines the glass as he pours himself a generous measure.

"What did he say to you?" My heart rate spikes at his tone.

"Who?"

He swiftly turns around and glares at me. "SAM!" he yells.

"He d-didn't say anything."

"You lying bitch. You went to the toilet, and he followed you. What did he say?"

"Blake—"

"You thought that fucking dance would distract me? He's the company fuck! Do you know what that means, Ginny?" I walked into the house expecting to face his anger, but the look of disgust and hatred that seeps from his eyes tells me I've walked straight onto a battlefield. Only Blake is the one with ammunition and fire, and I'm open to all forms of assault.

Before I know what's happening, the glass is hurled into the air. I curl my shoulders and bury my head in my hands expecting the glass to hit me but at the sound of it shattering, I peer through my fingers and see the shards of glass scattered on the floor around us.

"Fuck! Why do you have to be so stupid? He fucks as many people as he can," he spits out in revulsion. "He doesn't give a shit if they're married, engaged, or in a relationship. He takes what he wants! And you!" A vein protrudes in his reddened face. "I bet you fucking smiled that sickening bitch smile of yours and thought you'd make me the latest laughing stock!"

With wide eyes, I feel the tears start to form. Hastily, I try and blink them away, knowing weakness can aggravate him further. "Please, Blake. I would never do that to you. Ever." Even though the words leave my lips, I recognise that no words of explanation can calm him down. "I love you." The words come out as a sob, but he doesn't hear me.

I retreat slowly until I feel the wall at my back.

Then I watch helplessly as his chest rises and falls with the weight of his breaths.

"No!" I start to scream as he storms towards me. His hands grab on to the scarf around my neck. I feel the material drag against my skin as he yanks me closer to him.

"I thought I had everything when I met you. Yet, with that one stupid move, you could have ruined it all."

"Nothing happened, Blake," I beg apologetically.

The skin on my neck starts to burn. I clutch at the material in an attempt to loosen it, but he catches me off guard, yanking me, and I fall to the ground. I don't manage to free my hands in time and cry out as my shoulder collides with the unforgiving slate floor. The impact of the fall somehow causes my scarf to loosen. Scuffling on the floor, I manage to slide the red material over my head then scramble up and make a run for the door.

But the dress is pulled tight against my abdomen as his grip once again lands on me. Feeble sobs keep breaking free from my mouth. When I'm hauled back against him, the delicate material of the dress rips apart at the seams.

"Blake," I hear my voice over and over again but know my pleas are futile. He yanks again at my dress, and with nothing left to hold it up, it falls from my front leaving only my bra in place. His arms clamp around me, preventing me from going anywhere. He tightens his hold, making it impossible for me to move a muscle. It's hard to expand my chest to draw in a breath. I start to panic, trying to shove him off.

"You're struggling," he comments calmly before easing the pressure slightly. "Look at yourself."

With frantic breaths, I do as I'm told and look down at my body to see the torn dress hanging around my waist. I feel the burning around my throat where the scarf caused friction.

His hot breaths land on my skin. "How can a husband love a wife that looks like this? You're a mess."

Shame and confusion shroud me. I didn't mean to do anything to hurt him, but I know by his tone, that's what I've done.

"I'm sorry." I start to weep then spurt out a moan as he tugs at my waist, demonstrating his powerful hold. "Do it," I beg. "Please... hit me until I black out, so I no longer have to feel this."

In one swift move, he takes hold of my hair, spins me around like a ragdoll and pins me up against the wall. Then he releases his hand, and for a second I get a brief respite. But all he is doing is altering his path of pain.

His hand wraps around my throat. I gasp, fighting for air.

"You hate yourself that much?"

My arms flail helplessly against him. He's too strong. I feel the tears sting my eyes as I recognise that this could be it. So I drop my arms helplessly to my side and wait... wait for it all to end.

"You *are* the one doing this. I love you with my whole heart. It's yours forever." His eyes blacken in front of me. "But your heart isn't mine, and that stings, Ginny. It fucking hurts like a jagged knife tearing its way through my soul."

My eyes close and each breath becomes harder to obtain.

When my legs are no longer able to hold me, he lets go, and I crumble to the floor. I gulp at the air before desperately looking around for him. He's pacing around the room, dragging his hands through his hair. I shift up against the wall and drag my legs towards my chest, wrapping my arms around them. I want to apologise again, to tell him that I love him, but I'm scared of what he'll do if I talk.

He mumbles away to himself, words I can't make out. I don't know what to do anymore. So I sit, petrified, and watch him march back and forth.

"You keep goading me. You keep pushing me until this happens." In the next breath, he stills and looks down at me.

Whether by an act of stupidity or sanity, I speak, "Then finish it."

It's like time stands still. His body remains unmoving, as rigid as a statue. His dark brown eyes take on a colour of their own, and I witness nothing but sinister and evil. Then his lips kick up into a menacing grin.

"You pathetic bitch. One minute you're pleading for your life, the next you wish for me to end it." He laughs, a sickening taunt of a laugh before his glare intensifies. "Those big brown eyes of yours reel men in. But they only see what's on the outside. If they saw what I see, Ginny, you'd be sitting on the floor in the exact same position you find yourself in now. There's a difference between people like you and me, darling wife. You sit and wait, hoping that one day things will change, that someone will give you an easy out. Whereas I take and get exactly what I want. You're weak. Worthless. You're only here because I agreed to take you in so Marci's family could get back to how they were supposed to be... just the four of them." A sob catches in my throat. It wasn't like that. Or was it? Was I a burden on them too?

Taking me by surprise, he grabs at my arm, yanking me up. I stumble, feeling disorientated. Then he presses my head to his chest. For one brief second, I remember a time when this was all I wished for. This was the only place I ever wanted to be. He still smells the same. His muscular build is familiar. Yet it's all so different.

His hands come to rest on the sides of my heavy head then he starts to squeeze. I feel it on my cheekbones as the pressure increases until it feels like he's crushing my jaw together. My arms are up, fighting to push him away, to stop the pain and break the skin to skin contact. The flesh on the inside of my mouth pushes into my teeth, and I taste the familiar metallic presence of blood. I can't see clearly for my tears.

"Do you think anyone will be able to save you now?" He lets me go, but the pain remains. "I'm the only one that can save you, Ginny."

"I don't want to be saved." I blurt out as blood drips from my mouth. "I want to die."

"Make it known, that even in death we will be together. I will find a way to get to you. Whether it's your breath that ceases to exist or mine, we won't be apart for long. Trust me. It will be you and me for eternity."

I feel like I'm stumbling with my eyes barely open, I can't find anyone to reach out to because there's nobody there, only Blake in the background, laughing, taunting. This is how it's going to be. No one will save me, and I'm too much of a coward to walk away. He's right. I'm worthless.

"I hate you," I sputter, "But I hate myself more."

His strong hand reaches out and grabs at a chunk of my hair. I whimper at the immediate stinging in my scalp. Cries dribble from my mouth, sounds of desperation and pain. One of my hands tries to ease some of the pressure on my scalp while the other covers my face, attempting to provide a shield. But when I see something moving fast towards me, I know there's no escaping the expanse of pain that's coming. His fist pummels into the side of my face, battering against my upper cheekbone. The harsh contact causes a ringing in my ears, and the coppery taste of blood from my mouth builds as my cheek once again knocks into my teeth. I'm unable to even duck my head due to his grip on me. Again, his knuckles make contact, and the pain spreads. His hold releases, my body fails me, and I plummet to the floor. Even though I'm here, it's as though my mind becomes distant from my body.

I hear the zip on his trousers. What's left of my dress is ripped from my body. My underwear scrapes down my thigh, exposing my naked skin. Pressure is applied on my calves as he kicks my legs out. I have no strength nor will left to fight the pain that is inevitably going to be mine.

His heavy breaths resound in my ear before he talks. "No one will rescue you. Nor will anyone else have you because you're mine, and I'm going to make sure you'll *only* ever be mine."

Blake is slowly killing me, and right now it feels like the only way out. The light starts to fade and the little energy I had remaining, leaves me. As the pain invades, darkness surrounds, and I hope never to wake until this all ends and if that means only in death, then so be it.

CHAPTER FIVE

*I*t hurts to swallow. My throat feels dry and sore, and as I swipe my tongue across my lips, clumps, of what I can only assume is dried blood, lay stuck in place. I swallow again, then force my eyes open when I remember what happened.

I try to look around, to search the room but I can't see clearly. Everything is obscured and blurry.

I don't hear movement. I don't hear anything.

There's silence. No longer a good or bad kind. Existence is poor, with or without sound.

I'm where I remember falling on the kitchen floor. Light fights its way between the gaps in the blinds, meaning another morning is casting its vicious presence.

I look down at my body. The only piece of clothing left intact is my bra. My torn panties and dress lay beside me on the floor.

Each small movement I make causes an ache somewhere in my body, but I pull myself along, eventually getting on all fours before crawling to the stairs. Reaching for the railing, I grab onto it and haul myself up. Pain immediately assaults my head. I grip at my temples to try and ease it, but the sensation of nausea arrives. I clamber up the stairs, my chest heaving with the movement before I collapse to my knees at the toilet.

The sounds of my retching echoes around the room, increasing the pain in my head which only makes me feel sicker. I beg for silence, but it refuses to come.

When I have nothing left to give, I slump against the cold floor and curl up tight. Tears track down my nose before dropping to the smooth tiles. I'm not sure how long I lay there for, nor do I care. My skin is icy to the touch, but I don't feel cold inside. I only feel pain from head to toe and a sorrowful ache in my chest.

I struggle to my feet and lean over the sink with my focus pointing down, preparing myself for the bruises that will be covering my face. Slowly, I bring my eyes up to meet in the mirror. I inhale sharply at the sight in front of me.

My upper lip is swollen, dried blood is congealed around my mouth. I'm unsure if the skin is split or if the blood is from the inside. I try to open my mouth to look at the damage, but it's too painful. My left eye is puffy and bloodshot, and the beginnings of a bruise are already appearing on my socket and cheekbone. Even if you exclude the new cuts and bruises, I'm unrecognisable.

Then I still. Palpitations give way to panic. *What if he's still here? Hiding... waiting for me.*

I move to the window but don't see the outline of his car through the frosted glass. So I open it. His car is gone, but mine is there. Waiting. A sign of what I have to do.

I push all of the doubts aside and think only of getting away from here.

Moving steadily, I head to our bedroom and begin taking clothes from the drawer before I start getting dressed, breathing heavily through the pain.

Gently I go down the stairs, two feet per step, refusing to look back, I only focus on the direction I have to go. Taking my bag from the coat stand, I put on my jacket, then lift up the collar to hide as much of my face as I can.

I leave the splatters of blood on the walls, the ripped underwear and dress on the floor. He can see those as a dirty reminder of the person he has become.

Blake is no longer the man I married. He's a monster.

∼

I ease my grip on the steering wheel, flex the ache from my fingers and glance further down the road to Marci's house. Panic starts to rise. I'm not even sure that she's home. As I twist to undo my seatbelt, I catch sight of my face in the rear view mirror. Specks of dried blood are still fixed to my skin, and my eye is even more swollen than it was this morning. I probably shouldn't have driven.

Scanning the car, I search for a cloth or something to wipe my face with but there's nothing, and just the twisting action causes me to hold my breath with the pain.

With a heavy sigh, I pull the key from the ignition and step out of the car. Every muscle and bone throbbing with each move I make.

Keeping my focus low, wanting to remain unseen, I walk closer to her house. The tarmac beneath me provides a smooth surface for me to pass. Even the small wrought iron gate has been left open.

When I enter her yard, I pause and look around. New potted shrubs are placed either side of her door, the sill of the windows have been newly painted, a job she always used to despise. The addition of a bistro-style set of chairs and a small table are tucked neatly in the corner, where the sun always falls in the summer months. We'd talked together about the idea so we could sit and watch life pass by with a bottle of beer in our hands. Only, Marci had actually done it. The disgrace overwhelms me. The changes to her front garden highlighting how long it is I've been away.

I find myself staring at the familiar white door. Only now I'm here, I'm unsure what to do. What if everything inside has changed too? What if Marci can't even bring herself to look at me?

My finger lifts to press the doorbell, but I'm unable to move that last inch.

I look back to my car, an overwhelming sense of doubt swamping me.

The hinges of the door squeak as it's pulled open and suddenly I'm facing her. My best friend.

At first, she appears confused as though she doesn't recognise this beaten woman standing on her doorstep but then the shock registers in her face. Her focus travels from my eye to my lips as embarrassment and shame cast their spell.

"Ginny? Oh my God!" She grabs my arm to pull me towards her. Without thinking I draw in a breath with the pain. She instantly lets go and steps back. "Okay... it's okay." Her hands go up in the air as she looks me over from head to toe.

So I walk past her, not wanting to see the looks of pity and disappointment that will follow the current expression of shock.

Marci remains standing behind me, and all I want to do is pause this moment, so I don't have to provide any kind of explanation, so nothing for her changes.

But she steps in front of me. Her face a picture of shock and concern. "What happened? Have you been in an accident? Have you been to hospital?" Her panicked words fall from her mouth in a rush. "Oh my God, look at you!" She raises her arms and moves towards me, but I step back fearing if she embraces me, I may fall to pieces in her hold.

Her brow furrows in confusion. "What? What's going on?" The distress is evident in her voice, but I'm not sure what I can say that will ease it. "Is it only your face?" She looks me up and down. "I don't mean *only* your face. You've lost weight. You look different... everywhere." She glances out of the window before returning her focus to me. "Ginny. Goddamn talk to me!"

I open my mouth but nothing comes out, and she frowns, recognising that my lack of speech is just as concerning as the injuries I have on display. "I'm putting my arm around you, Ginny, so don't back away this time." She does as she says and this time I let her. "You need to sit down."

She leads me to one of the two stools at the breakfast bar and slowly, I ease myself on.

Where do I begin? I close my eyes wondering why I came here if I can't even bring myself to tell her. The sound of running water causes me to look up. She carries the glass over to me and puts it down.

"I can get you something stronger? I don't know what I'm dealing with here, Gin. You have to help me out a bit. You're in pain, there's blood and bruising but why do you look so damn scared? What's happened?"

Her lips click as they open, a slight draw in of breath follows. Then she exhales. She was going to say something but changed her mind. I've learnt to become in tune to small sounds, learning to read moments of quiet and recognise what each movement, every form of breath inhale and exhale could possibly mean. To be familiar with the cues of hatred and aggression is a talent I can't afford to give up.

"Ginny, for Christ sake, you're scaring me. Listen, I know you hate hospitals, but I really think you should go."

"No!" My voice cracks but I remain firm. "No hospital." This is all too much. I want to tell my friend how beautiful she is. How the image of her face has been the light in an increasing world of dark. But it's like I daren't speak.

"Well, where's Blake? Maybe he can convince you?" Again she looks out of the window as though expecting him to be outside parking the car or something.

"He's not here." My voice is raspy and dry.

"But why not?" Her voice is shaking, and tears start to form in her eyes. "Why won't you let me hold you? Does it hurt too much?"

I only look back at her, without being able to utter the words of explanation, I just look. The colour begins to drain from her face. They say it happens in moments of realisation or fear, but I've never actually witnessed it before. Her focus dips to my lips then moves to my bruising. She can't stop looking at my injuries. A line gathers between her brows.

I shake my head slowly, wanting to protect her from hearing the truth for a minute longer, but she barely gets a second.

"No," she whispers. "He did this? Blake?" I don't confirm it nor do I deny it. She turns away, walks around the small room and stares to the floor trying to process what has happened. "I don't understand. Did you have an argument?"

Did we have an argument? The comment stings because, like me, she believes there has to be a reason why I deserve this.

"Yes... no... it's difficult to explain."

Finally, she comes to sit beside me. "He did this?" I know it's hard to believe, so I have to allow her questions of doubt. This time I nod my head. "But why? Why would he do this?"

I hang my head in disgrace, unable to explain the reason.

"Marci... I don't know." I understand she has questions, but I'm struggling to hold myself up. I'm hurting, I'm scared, my emotions are all over the place, and I've never hated myself more. "Give me five minutes," I plead. Marci's disappointment has cemented my own self-loathing to the depths of my soul.

"Give you five minutes? Are you for real? I haven't seen you since April. You've done everything to avoid me coming to visit. Is this why?" She screws up her face and looks me up and down. She storms to the other side of the room before she turns on me. "I'm going to fucking kill him. Where is he?"

Fear starts to invade my soul as I understand the result of my actions. I'd left without thinking... without giving a single thought to the consequences. I had to get out, that's all I could think of. Now, the nightmare I've been living suddenly drops me straight into the pit of hell.

"No," I whisper.

"No?" she almost screeches in response.

I shouldn't have come. Looking over my shoulder, I glance at the door. He's going to follow me. I thought once I was here, it would be okay, but all his promises echo in my head. It won't ever be okay, and I've pushed my friend directly into my world of torture. Even if Blake never lifts a finger to her, seeing his control over me will crucify her. What have I done?

My focus lands back on my best friend and my eyes start to water. "I have to go... I can't be here." I stand up. "I can't believe I've been so stupid." I turn towards the door, but she sidesteps blocking my path.

"You're not going anywhere. You may be scared of him, but I'm bloody not. We're going to call the police."

"You can't," I say in defeat.

"I can't? Why? Because they won't believe you?" She pulls on my elbow, and I yelp out like an injured dog, but she marches me to into the lounge regardless and stands me in front of the mirror. "Did I hurt you then?" she fires at me. "I'm guessing you already have bruises because I didn't grab you hard, Ginny!" She looks from me to the mirror. "Look! Look at what he's done."

I don't look at my reflection. I already know what I will see. Instead, I divert my focus and stare into Marci's eyes. I know my friend, and I recognise why she's reacting in the way she is, but any minute, I also know she's going to be full of regret. Another reason I shouldn't have come.

Slowly, she starts to recognise who I've become. A cry breaks free, and her hand jolts to her mouth in an attempt to stop any more sobs being released.

"Oh God, Ginny." She turns me back so I'm no longer facing the mirror. Her eyes search mine. "I'm sorry. I-I didn't mean... when I asked if you'd had an argument... Shit! You know this isn't your fault, don't you?" Her face creases up in sorrow as she looks at my arm. "You're hurting. You're in pain." Her lips start to quiver as this time her approach is slower. Her arms carefully wrap around my shoulders, and she clasps onto me. Her whole body starts to shake as her heart breaks for the friend she used to know, the woman who I now feel detached from. Tears slowly trickle down my cheeks, but there is no deep sob waiting within, no snap of my emotions. My tears are for Marci because as much as she thinks she can help me, she can't.

I know what is coming.

This is it. This is my life. Blake's right, I won't be able to escape him. I can't move back to my old life and expect to be the person I once was. I'm different now. Life is different, and even if it all ended today, the memories would remain. I would carry the burden of his love and his hatred for the rest of my life. Blake is slowly ensuring he owns me whether I survive him or not.

Marci draws back and tucks a piece of my hair behind my ear, but even that small touch of affection hurts due to the soreness of my scalp where he yanked at my hair.

My hair.

Katie talked of irons and vases, but my hair is becoming a regular crutch of pain. I break free and set towards the kitchen knowing what I need to do. Marci trails closely behind. I go straight to the knife block on the side and pull out the pair of kitchen scissors.

"Whoa! Ginny!" Her mouth opens wide. "What the hell?" She stares at me as though I'm about to do something stupid. I let out a hysterical laugh because the stupidity is already deep-rooted and well settled in my soul. Stupid? I'm the living breathing definition of it.

I lift the scissors and start hacking at my hair, the sound of the metal slicing against the strands filling the silence. Marci's eyes almost bug out of her head, looking at me like I'm going crazy.

"What are you doing? Ginny!" She charges towards me, but I hold the scissors in front of me stopping her in her tracks.

"I need to cut my hair, and I need to do it now." I fire at her. She nods her head, backing up a step, and once again I lift the scissors, cutting the hair until there's virtually nothing left to pull.

When I'm done, Marci glances to the floor at my shredded brown locks. It doesn't even look like my hair. My hair used to have a shine, and a warm, rich colour. The hair on the floor can only be described as mousey brown, appearing dry and brittle.

"Why did you do that?" she asks aghast before looking back up.

"To stop some of the pain."

"What?" She narrows her eyes, not understanding.

"He sometimes... he can pull my hair." The explanation sounds pathetic when said out loud, and my confidence wanes. I stare at my hair. He will hate what I've done. Another impulsive decision leading to a foolish mistake. What the hell is wrong with me?

"Sometimes? How long has this been going on for?" She stares at me, expecting an answer. "You've left him now, Ginny," she states adamantly. "He can't hurt you."

I'm so confused. Last night I saw no way out of this. Then, when I saw my car, I wanted to run, to leave, to flee. Now I'm here, I know I can't stay. I'm scared of him. Terrified of what he's capable of, which should force me to stop here with Marci, but then I'll be running forever, and Blake won't just be controlling my life, he'll be ruining Marci's too because I know she'd do all she can to protect me. But this isn't her battle.

I pause because she has no idea what I've done by coming here nor what I'm about to do.

"It will be okay, Marci." She stares at me, and frowns, uncertain of the meaning behind my words.

The harrowing thing is, I know it won't be alright. The second he comes here, I have to get him out of this house. Hurting me is bad enough, but I'm not going to put my friend at risk. To keep her safe and to limit the punishment he will inflict on me, I have to return with him. Which, in turn, will mean turning my back on Marci. I will be choosing my husband to prevent any pain being inflicted on her. I have no doubt of my actions. This is my mess, and I can't allow her to witness this again.

"I'm sorry, but I have to call the police. You can't let him do this to you."

Is that what I'm doing? *Letting* him do this to me? How can I explain to her that I don't give my permission? She scoops her phone from the side.

"Please... don't," I plea.

"Why, Ginny? Give me one reason why I shouldn't."

She doesn't understand. Why would she? Marci is one of the strongest and most independent women I know. This would never happen to her. But then there was a time when I thought the same of me.

"Please, I'm begging you. Don't call them."

"You can't still love him after this!" She looks at me with a lack of understanding. "Is it because you're scared of what he may do?"

"Yes," I say, the reply sounding simple when it's as confusing and complicated as can be. "And no." He used to regret it, to loathe his outbursts but something's changed.

"But it's the police, Gin. They'll stop him." I pity her naivety, yet wish I owned it myself. They may stop him temporarily, but he would find me.

I should have figured a way out of this without involving Marci, yet by coming here, that's all I've done. I've made a huge mistake. "If it makes you feel better, then ring. But I won't confirm anything you say." It's all I can say as I walk from the room.

Lowering myself down to the sofa, I remain still and quiet. I used to curl back on these cushions with my feet tucked beneath me, I don't own that right anymore. Marci is never going to forgive me after today. Never. By coming home, I've forced the hand of choice. Except, I don't really have a choice. Coming home was the worst mistake I could ever have made, and he'll be here soon, I have no doubt.

"I haven't called them yet, but it doesn't mean I'm not going to," she says as she enters the room before flopping down beside me. I'm not sure whether to believe her because I'm certain I heard her talking to somebody on the phone.

"*I* could have helped. The second he lifted his finger to you. I should have been told."

I don't deny or confirm it. She's right. I should have told her, but I'm not sure it would have made a difference. If she'd have told me to walk away, I'm not certain I'd have done it. It started with a few cruel words, a slight touch of control over what I did. Before I realised what was happening, I was spending all of my time trying to keep him happy. When he first hurt me, he felt so bad that I actually felt sorry for him.

"If we call the police, they'll put him away for a long time, Ginny. He won't bother you again." Her promises fade into insignificance as she continues telling me how everything is going to be okay.

I take the words, allowing a friend to grieve for a friend she no longer recognises. But I can't do any of the things she's suggesting. I could tell the police, but Blake wouldn't go away for years. Even if, and it's unlikely, that a restraining order was put in place, Blake would steer his way around it. Inevitably the punishment would be more severe and brutal and possibly widespread, involving those that matter. Marci, Liam, even her parents, Jim and Claire. The mere thought of them makes me see how much I have to lose.

Before I came here, I believed I wanted to die. Yet here I

am, admittedly, I wish I hadn't come, but I did. I came to Marci. I don't want to die. I don't want to lose them. I want to leave him.

"Why are you not even saying anything?" Marci is losing her patience with me, and I can't say I blame her. She jumps to her feet and walks from the room. I hate what I'm doing to her. The regrets keep coming.

I'm not sure how long I sit there for, but I know Marci's been in the other room for some time. I stand up and walk into the kitchen. She has her back to me, and her shoulders are quivering beneath the emotion as she stifles back sobs.

"Thank you, Marci, for trying to help me, but I'm okay." I force the words and nausea takes over.

"No, Ginny, you're not." The shaking of her shoulders eases somewhat as she twists to look at me. "You always thought you could hide your feelings, but not with me, Ginny, never. You're terrified. I've never seen you look like this. Your words don't convince me otherwise. Do you know what scares *me* most of all? Although you've come here, where you knew you'd get help, it's like you don't *want* the help."

I try to respond, but I can't. I thought by coming here I was fighting, but now I see that all I've done is make it worse.

Loud knocking deafens my ears. I look in panic at Marci as my heart pounds.

"It's Liam. Seeing as though you don't want the police involved, I asked him to come, in case… in case Blake turns up." *Liam.* I close my eyes as Marci goes to open the door. I haven't seen him in months. I look at the ground, nowhere near ready to see him.

Footsteps make themselves known then they pause. "Fuck! Ginny?" Briefly, I close my eyes before raising my focus. He tracks to my swollen and bruised eye and split lip before his eyes widen at the sight of my hair.

"It looks worse than it is," I respond.

"No, it doesn't. It'll always be worse than it looks," Marci interjects.

Liam takes a few, deliberately slow steps towards me. Almost like he's trying to tiptoe, scared I'm going to run. My eyes grow wide, and he stops a few feet away. His vision crosses to Marci for confirmation. "*He* did this?" he asks her, not me, and I look away as the shame envelops me. *He* may have created the bruises, but I believe more than ever that I didn't try hard enough to stop him. "I think some of this needs looking at, Ginny. What does the rest of her look like?" Again, he directs the question at Marci like I'm not really here.

"I don't know. I haven't—"

"The rest of me is fine." The lie comes easy.

"It's not fine!" Marci fires back.

"Your hair? He cut it?" he questions, and I can see the confusion on his face.

"She cut it," Marci interjects, gesturing to my hair scattered on the floor. "Because that's one of his *favourite* ways of causing her pain."

Liam stares hard at Marci like she's the one who hurt me but all she's doing is speaking the truth.

"What's wrong with you?" Liam continues to glare at Marci as her defiance starts to build. "This is the first place she thought of coming. It's probably the only place she could have come, and you make it sound as though it's her fault. Shit, Marci, this is Ginny!"

"Liam, please don't—" I try to defend her, none of this is Marci's fault. She's reacting the way she is because of how helpless she feels, how helpless I'm *making* her feel because deep down, she knows what I'm going to do.

"I get it, Ginny. She's hurting, so she's lashing out. I'm male, but not stupid. Christ, I've grown up with you both. You always had my back, then I started covering yours, and that's not about to change. But she needs to stop with the shit comments that are making her sound like a shit friend. Because she's not shit, and she'll regret what she's saying." He looks back at me, taking in the sight of me once again. Then he shakes his head. "But I'm going to fucking kill him."

"No!" I squeal. "You can't. Please, Liam." I approach him quickly. "You can't do anything. You have to stay out of this." The begging comes easily.

His brows dip until almost meeting in the middle. "What? You're defending him?" He juts his head side to side. "Ginny, I can't stand back and let him do this to you. I can't." His jaw clicks, and it's suddenly impossible to stop the tears from coming.

Before I even have chance to move, he takes a step towards me. He's too close, leaving me with no room to back away. My breathing picks up as a strange sense of claustrophobia starts to kick in. But as his strong arms slide around my shoulders, Marci approaches from the side, and she too covers me in her embrace.

I nod, finally giving in to their offering of comfort. As their hands encase me, I've never felt so loved, yet I can't let it continue. It's a false sense of security.

I hear the desperation in his voice. "Don't be scared, Gin. We've got you." My eyes glisten as the boy who's been like a brother to me is acting more of a man than my husband ever has. He's five years younger than me and Marci, still a teenager. Although he's taller and stronger than us both, I can't allow him to fight for me. Their hold eases, but Liam keeps his arm over my shoulder, guiding me back into the living room.

He leads me to the sofa then crouches down in front of me as Marci stands at his side. "You have to stay with us. Okay?" He widens his eyes waiting for me to respond. "Ginny, I have your back. We have your back. He won't ever touch you again, I promise." When did Liam get so grown up? My eyes water at the man he's become and what he's willing to do for me.

"I wish you could understand, but you can't. You can't touch him, Liam. I mean it. I don't want him having the satisfaction of seeing you being carted off by the police. I shouldn't have come in the first place, and for that, I'm truly sorry." Then I glance up at Marci with tears in my eyes. "I'm so sorry for putting you in this position. I know you both think I'm crazy. Perhaps I am, but I'm not having any more bloodshed over me... or him. I'm going to sort this, I promise. But I'll be doing it my way." Alone.

CHAPTER SIX

*A*n exaggerated knocking on the door, the sound I've been expecting, alerts us to his arrival. Liam's up on his feet in a second. I'm not far behind him. The tension elevates in the air as my heart rate kicks up in response.

"Please, don't," I beg, glancing helplessly from one to the other, but I know my plea is wasted.

"Stay in here. It might not be him," Marci orders but I know it will be.

I want to argue with them, to ask them to stand back and let me answer the door, but I know they won't allow it because they're trying to protect me.

All I've had is half an hour with them. That's it. It's not long enough.

They both head to the doorway but come to a stop. Liam's hand stretches out blocking Marci's path.

"I'll get it, Marci," Liam's tone is assertive, one, which Marci will not appreciate from her younger brother.

"It's my house, Liam. I want to see if he has the guts to face me!" I glance in panic between the two, not wanting either of them to face him. I don't know what to say to change what's happening. As I look at Liam, it's clear he's not going to back down.

"Marci. Let me do this. Please." With hesitation, she finally steps aside.

"Well, I'm coming with you," she adds. The simple display of protection causes an ache in my chest because this is the last day I will allow such an act. "Stay here," Marci instructs, before adding, "Please," in hindsight.

My shoulders slump as my sight plummets to the ground.

The door closes behind them, providing a provisional and feeble barricade between myself and Blake.

I hold myself still, my poise stiff, anticipating his arrival. Even with my bruised and battered exterior, I'm portraying a woman who is holding it all together. Yet, my hands are clasped tightly to hide the endless shaking. My stomach is in knots, and I have to keep swallowing down the bile that is rising in my throat.

Raised voices seep through the gaps in the door. After a scuffle, I know Blake's now pushed his way into the house. It's only a matter of minutes before he'll be in here. Every part of me wants to run and hide, but I know it would be a wasted attempt, and I'm not sure how many more I'll be able to survive.

As the raised voices continue, I choose to savour my final moments here. Turning away from the sounds, my eyes seek the familiarity of the room. The drift of sunflowers touches the air, and my sight settles on the lamp in the corner. We chose it together, well, I advised against buying it, the price was ridiculously high, but Marci was adamant she wanted that particular lamp. We walked out of the shop, Marci's purse a lot lighter and out of nowhere, a kid on a bike whizzed past us. Marci jumped out of the way, and the box with the lamp crashed to the floor. She ran after that kid until she couldn't run anymore. When she came back her mascara had made tracks down her cheeks, she was barefoot, her heeled boots hanging from her palms and a trail of mud ran from her knee down to her ankle. I'd never laughed so hard in my life. But Marci being Marci, picked up the box with the shattered lamp, took it inside and demanded a replacement. She got it, of course.

My focus moves to the log burner. The glass doors are open. A box of matches with one stray match placed beside it sits on the hearth. In the grate, clumps of screwed up newspaper lie beneath some sticks, and a large log rests on top. Marci must have been about to light it when I turned up.

I stand and walk stiffly to the fire. Carefully kneeling down in front it, I light a match. The orange flame bounds to life before it quickly lessens. Calmly it tracks its way along the thin stick of wood. When it's almost on my finger, I put the flame to the newspaper and let go. The fire starts to take hold, so I close the doors and open up the vents before drawing myself back up to stand.

I blink slowly, with dread, as the shouting turns more hushed, yet strained, so I concentrate on what is staring right in my face. In the centre of the mantelpiece is a picture of Marci and me. It was taken four years ago, Marci and I had clubbed together to buy her dad a camera for his birthday. It was the first picture he'd taken, and he must have been watching us as he managed to capture the moment Marci and I sealed our promise with our pinky fingers. We stood, facing each other, fingers clipped together with grins of innocence shining back at one another.

'We will always stand by each other. No matter what choices we make,' I remember saying.

'Even when they're soooo wrong,' Marci had teased at the time because she'd been dumped by a loser called Mike that same day.

'Even when they're wrong,' I confirmed.

'Your wish is my wish.' We said it together.

"Your wish is my wish," I repeat the words quietly, not quite believing what my wish for today is.

I scoop the frame into my hand and turn round in time to see my husband fall through the door. I guess he must have thought it was bolted closed. He quickly rights himself and finds me, but Liam tries to yank him back by the collar of his coat. Blake stops struggling, instead, focusing on me.

"Ginny?" He narrows his eyes and, unlike Liam, he stares at my hair first. Of course he does because he's seen the marks on me before. But my hair? That's something he won't be happy with.

Anger starts to flare in his eyes. I sink my focus beneath his glare.

"It's time to go home." I was half expecting an apology, but that would be an admission of guilt. I bring the photo to my chest and hold it in place with both hands.

"The hell it is!" Marci cries out. "She doesn't *want* to go with you Blake."

He tries to come a step closer, but Liam's grip is unrelenting. "I'm not letting go, you piece of shit!" An amused smile flickers on Blake's lips, and I know it's time for me to step in and end it before things spiral further out of control.

"You have to come home, baby. I can't live there without you." He may believe the lies that spill from his mouth, but I don't. Not anymore. I know what will happen when I leave with him, the punishment will come eventually. But at least the punishment will only be mine. I will not involve Marci and Liam again.

"The police are on their way, Blake, so you may as well stop your pathetic begging." My eyes flicker in panic. She told me she didn't call them. Oh my God, we have to leave now. Blake will go crazy if he thinks I had anything to do with calling the police.

Blake manages to shrug himself free from Liam and in an instant he's at my side, but Liam and Marci are just as quick, only they falter when they witness him resting his arm tenderly around my waist. Marci looks at the touch, confused. She doesn't understand what that touch means, but I do. I'm still his, and I'll be leaving with him. Today. But I already knew that anyway.

"Has she actually told you that I did this, Marci?" he questions her. "Did she actually say those exact words?" I glance up desperately and look at Marci. She catches my eye, and a slight frown burrows its way between her brows. Steadily I turn the photograph around, and her focus drops to the image of us together. She pauses then looks back at me. All I can do is hope she recognises my silent plea for help.

"I'm not sure," she mutters, and I release a breath.

"You know what? You don't get an explanation. If you were any kind of decent friend, you would have visited before now." My heart misses a beat at his brutal accusation. He'll make sure everyone takes their own share of the blame, but what Marci hasn't learnt yet, is disagreeing will not change the seed of doubt he has already planted in her mind.

"What?" Marci cries. "I have rung you both, numerous times. Neither of you has even told me where you live. I've wanted nothing more than—"

"Sad excuses, Marci. All you're bothered about is making sure you have someone to fuck on a night time." Blake twists his head and glares at Liam, deliberately trying to irk him. "Your sister still the town tramp?"

"You fucking bastard!" Liam leaps forward, but I step between them just in time. Liam rights himself managing to avoid falling into me before he shifts backwards and drags his hands through his hair. "You're kidding me, Ginny? Why would you defend *that?*" He curls his lip up.

"I told you what I wanted, and this isn't it," I say my voice barely above a whisper. I sense Blake closing in on me from behind, and when I feel his breath skimming over my neck and shoulder, I know what I need to do. "No more fighting."

"Ginny?" Blake says my name in the fondest of ways. When I feel his hands softly rest on my shoulders, I wish for his touch to always be this gentle. But I no longer have the privilege of such a wish. He guides me around until I'm facing him. He smiles, but the threat in his eyes is unmistakable. The warning that there is no choice here. He loves me, and he will never let me go.

Marci and Liam step either side of Blake, leaving me to stand and face all three. The accusations, the condemnation continues spurring from Liam and Marci's mouths while Blake's focus remains on me. Holding me still. Instructing me on what I'm to do.

I step away from Blake, move around Liam and Marci, and walk out of the room. They all stop talking. I know there will be varying looks of concern, but there will also be one of triumph. I pause my steps halfway through the kitchen, and Blake meets my side like I knew he would. I will not make the same mistake again. I know what walking out of Marci's house means. She will see I am picking Blake over her when the truth is I'm choosing Marci over myself.

For a second, I ignore the man that owns and ruins me both at the same time, and I look at Marci. Biting back my tears, I smile at my heartbroken friend.

She nods her head in encouragement, fighting to give me the strength she so badly wants me to own. "Come back." Her hand lifts and she brings herself closer. "This isn't the life you should be living. Stay here. Let us protect you." As I keep my eyes fixed on hers, I shake my head slowly from side to side. She grasps what I'm silently saying. "No, Ginny." Her voice is thick with emotion. "You can't do this."

The pain in my side, the throbbing in my head, the stinging on my lips, it now feels insignificant to the crucifying shards of pain that are cutting through my chest. I came here, and through all of the darkness, I saw the light. I came home. But I have to turn my back on it, and I will never forgive Blake for forcing my hand. Marci will believe I've chosen him over her, but that's something I would never do. I did it once, and it was the biggest mistake of my life and the cause of my lifelong regret.

Blake's hand lifts and comes into my vision. I stare at the hand that can create such pain. He thinks I'm beaten. He actually believes I'm choosing him. I move closer to him, and his arm snakes around my waist. Whether to give me support or to show ownership it doesn't matter.

As we make our way out of the house, Marci scrambles past us and blocks Blake's path. "I'm going to find out where you live, and when I do, I'm coming for her. I don't understand this hold you have on her, but it's only temporary, mark my words." She looks at me as I stand mutely by his side. "She doesn't have any fight in her, but do you know what? I've got enough for the both of us." Blake's grip clenches tight around my waist, and I inwardly flinch through the pain.

I take a hand from the frame and reach out to Marci, demanding her attention.

"There isn't a fight to be had, Marci. You will stay out of this. We will get the help that we need and make this work." I pause as I struggle to maintain my composure. On an exhale I pass the cherished image to my friend. "This is my wish." I bite my jaw together, fighting against the tears that desperately want to be released.

I can only see the tops of her lids as she looks at the photo, the younger, carefree version of ourselves staring back. When she looks back at me, her eyes are brimming with tears, and it crushes me that I can't allow myself to join her in our grief.

This is it. This is our final goodbye. I'm not sure that Marci is aware, but I certainly am. I cannot come here again. It will be the first place he'll come to look for me.

As I stand and study my best friend, I want to tell her that this isn't over. That coming here has made me realise what I need to do, the only thing I can do. Marci believes the fight has left me, but it's only just begun.

Blake wants to treat me as though I shouldn't exist? Then perhaps it's time for me to become a ghost.

I look up at Blake and smile, then nod, providing the permission he doesn't need. As I walk away, and the heart-wrenching sounds of Marci's cries fall from her mouth, I keep going.

We pass my car first. "You won't be needing that," he informs me, and I accept it. Because with each move I make towards Blake's car, with each instruction he provides, and the sound of my best friend sobbing onto her brother's shoulders, I'm overcome with hatred. It continues to build and for the first time, I welcome it because, with the hatred, a newfound determination bubbles away in my gut.

Blake may believe it's time to go home, but it's going to be for the very last time.

We've been in the car for at least half an hour. His hands have remained in the ten to two position on the steering wheel, knuckles whitened by strain, no doubt from the anger that's churning away inside of him.

"Your hair's a fucking mess. That really was a mistake, Ginny," he sneers, finally speaking.

I take the insult because I imagine it does look a mess, but I don't see it as a mistake.

"Marci." The word is spat from his mouth. He's not bringing her name up for any other reason than to state the error I've made.

"It won't happen again," I say truthfully because it won't. That was our final goodbye.

His hand lifts, and I close my eyes expecting to feel a force I know I'm due. He can beat me black and blue, which no doubt he will. As long as I keep it together. I no longer want to die. I want to beat him, and I have every intention of ending this.

No matter how strong I suddenly believe myself of being, I still flinch and jolt open my eyes when I feel something drop in my lap. A bunch of flowers lies pathetically on my knee. Flowers. He thinks flowers are going to make all of this better?

"I went out to get these this morning, then when I came home..." His voice fades, and the flowers are ripped from my knee as he hauls them into the back of the car. "I can't believe you have done such a thing to me, Ginny." Out of the corner of my eye, I see him shake his head. I don't need to look at him to know his jaw will be set in a rigid line. I've humiliated him which in turn will fuel his anger. "You are my WIFE!" he shouts.

All I do is sit and take his words. Arguing will not change his mind. Disagreeing will only result in pain. I keep my eyes forward and concentrate on the little droplets of rain as they start to fall on the window. The wipers take a swing at them, casting them aside easily, and I think how lucky they are to have such an easy escape.

"The police!" His tone causes a chill to my spine. "She fucking called the police!" My fingers wind around each other, and I push down on my lap as the muscles in my legs jerk in trepidation.

"She didn't," I whisper.

"WHAT?" he shouts in return.

"I-I told her not to."

"Well, that's the only thing you've done fucking right today, isn't it?"

The sound of his silence ensues. Every muscle in my body tenses in wait. But no matter how much I'm expecting it, the pain always manages to take me by surprise.

A jab to my temple knocks me sideways. My skull bashes against the seat belt hook and an intense shooting pain radiates through my head.

"Did you fucking hear me?"

"I heard you," I mumble, trying to right myself from the stabs of pain. "P-Please... she thought she was helping. It won't happen again. I won't give her the choice."

"What?" he snipes, peering at me sideways.

"I won't be going back, Blake. I made a mistake." My mind churns on the words like they're poison, but I have to force them from my mouth. "I was hurting, so I went to her. I was scared, Blake." He glances across, but I don't reciprocate in case he sees through my lies. "I love you," I say quietly.

"Then it shouldn't be too much to ask for your loyalty, should it?" He steers onto the motorway, his driving becoming less erratic. "You didn't tell her where we lived?"

"No." Why would I?

There's a pause as he keeps his eye on the road, and I think that for a minute, maybe he's concentrating on the traffic giving me a minute of reprieve.

"Finally, you're making sense."

I went to her for help, showed her a fragment of the pain I've been going through then walked away, tossing her help back in her face like it was worthless.

"So you won't be going back?"

"No, I won't."

The car slows, and he twists to look at me, for a second I think I see remorse but the look disappears just as quickly. Which is a shame because this battered and bruised wife is ready for him to suffer.

CHAPTER SEVEN

*G*lancing down at my feet as one foot steps in front of the other, I peer beside me at Blake's shiny tan brogues. His heels click as they land on the pavement, my own shoes somehow maintaining a silence. My willingness to fall in place irks me, so I purposefully falter a step, no longer walking in time, needing to be out of synchrony with my husband.

It's been seven days since I came home. It's silly to say 'came home'. Not only was I gone for a matter of hours, but the term 'home' is no longer deemed appropriate.

"We're nearly there." His words aren't said by way of reassurance but to warn me. There is no need though. I'm aware when to put on an act, to conform to requirements. I've learnt the hard way what happens if I don't.

Running to Marci last week had been a big mistake. The way everything unfolded remains as chaotic in my mind as it was then. *I should have known better. I* should not have run without thinking it through. Now Marci and Liam have seen it all, and I'll never be able to take that back. I'm ashamed and embarrassed that I went for help but instead, walked away with the man that hurts me.

"Let's hope a miracle can happen, dear wife of mine and they can sort out your hair." He looks down at me, and I manage to feign regret when it's probably the wisest decision I've made in months.

That aside, I can't abide my reflection. When we returned home, and Blake shoved my head into the mirror to show me what a mess I'd made, the retching started once again. Blake believed the nausea was from the sight of my hair. I think he almost felt sorry for me. But it was insignificant to the marks of abuse he'd scarred me with. My face was even more of a mess. I was barely recognisable. And I let Marci and Liam see me like that.

That afternoon I made myself a promise. I will escape Blake, as of yet, I'm unsure how, but I will be leaving him. No one else is aware, not Marci, Liam, or Blake. But in my mind, the battle has begun.

Blake stops walking, and I look up to see we've arrived. It's only now Blake extends his hand to mine. He pushes the door and guides me inside. With a soft, almost tender look he nods towards one of the chairs in the waiting area. The loyal, loving husband has come out of the stern, unforgiving man's shell. Perhaps I should be grateful for the reprieve, but it's difficult when I'm starting to despise both versions.

"Why don't you sit down, darling?"

I smile and nod my head, doing as advised and take a seat. It only takes a moment before an attractive well-styled woman in her thirties makes her entrance.

"Blake! Darcy said you were coming today. The appointment is for your wife though, isn't it?"

"Yes, Jo, it is." Blake then looks over his shoulder at me and only then does Jo actually notice that I am here.

"Oh fabulous. How lovely to finally meet you." She smiles briefly before her focus passes over my face and lands on my self-inflicted messy crop. Her smile soon dips.

Blake lowers his voice, and I turn away in embarrassment, wondering what lies he's now filling Jo with. Whatever it is, when I look back, Jo is on her way over with a saddened smile gracing her pink lips.

"I'm ready if you are," she says coming to a stop in front of me. I stand up matching her own height. She glances at me surprised, as though she expected me to be much smaller. "Come this way." I follow on behind.

In a line along one side of the room are five chairs, positioned opposite mirrors. Three of them already have customers in. I don't look to see if anyone glances our way, I already know the kind of effect Blake will have on a salon filled with women, jealousy will no longer come though.

Jo continues walking until we reach the sink area. "That will be our chair over there." She points to an empty seat opposite. "But first we need to shampoo." She holds out a black apron for me to put on. "And don't worry, we don't have anyone else booked in, so Blake can sit right there beside you," she adds quietly like she's trying to reassure me, and I wonder what story Blake has told her to indicate I *need* him beside me to make me feel better.

Sure enough, Blake takes the chair at the end, ensuring I will be on my best behaviour. But he needn't worry. Right now I have no intention of doing anything different. My time for that will come.

Once I've put on the apron, I sit down and rest my head back as she gets to work on my hair.

"Your hair is a beautiful colour," she remarks. "Blake said next time you may want it changed? I'm not sure I would."

"Oh!" I never said I wanted to change my hair colour. "Erm, thank you."

My brief answer is the last we say until she finishes washing my hair. Jo blots a towel over my head, absorbing any excess before wrapping it over my shoulders.

"Let's see what we can do, shall we?" Once again, I get up, this time making my way to the seat beside Blake. "So you fancied a change, is that right?"

Although the question is aimed at me, it's Blake that's quick to reply. "Her hair was long before, wasn't it, Gin? I thought it looked beautiful actually, but Ginny had other ideas. Apparently, it was frizzy and out of condition," he says with a roll of his eyes. "You know what you women are like, never quite happy with the good looks you were graced with." Although there was possibly a compliment hidden in his remark somewhere, I know it was only meant as criticism.

"It was time for a change," I reply for myself.

"Well, it suits you." Her hands grip my shoulders in reassurance. "I sure wish I had your bone structure. We'll make this a proper pixie cut, all it needs is a tidy up. You'll walk out of here like a new woman," she adds with an unknowing smile.

The haircut won't make me feel like a new woman, but it's a step in the right direction. I've made Blake think I didn't want to come here today. That all I wanted to do was stay inside our house and live with the shame I'd created by running. Once I admitted blame, we've been managing to live under a temporary and false sense of calm.

I feel Blake's eyes boring into my side, but I don't look at him.

For once, I actually want to smile freely because he doesn't have a clue what the future may hold.

Neither do I, not truly. But for the first time, I possess hope.

Seeing the reaction my pain sparked in Marci and Liam has strengthened my determination. I *want* to leave, and I will do, but I'll be doing it properly. With the help of Katie.

CHAPTER EIGHT

I walk with purpose, knowing exactly where I'm heading this time. The familiar bench comes into view across the road, and I'm saddened to see it's empty. I imagine if someone were to re-varnish the wood, giving it a brand new appearance, people would soon sit down. Sometimes there is a beauty to imperfections, but often there is a sadness to the reason behind them.

The wind whips around my neck, so I tug up my collar and pull down my woolly hat. Scarves and long hair are no longer a barrier to weather, but I'd rather go cold than be dressed in a weapon. I come to the side street where my journey ends and remind myself of why it is that I'm here.

They say there's a cycle to abuse. That women like me move through each stage at the hands of their abuser. The tension builds before leading to violence. Then, for a while, you may get a reprieve before it starts all over again. Some manage to alter the path and run but never quite live freely. Others break free, but that's the last thing they ever manage to achieve. A number leave, return, then leave again, finding it impossible to break the cycle.

I have to break the cycle.

Living with the fear and pain that is part of my everyday life can no longer be classified as living. I could end it all. It could go away indefinitely. I think of the medication we keep in the kitchen cupboard or the sharp knives in the drawer. Everything could be over, but that would leave people I care about to face guilt that rightfully should not be theirs.

There is only one answer. I need to learn how to survive.

Stopping, I face the blue door. The wind is unable to reach me now, but I still hold my coat tight around me, feeling cold and nervous at the same time. I lift my hand, wrapping it around the faded gold metal of the handle, its tarnished appearance somehow providing me with reassurance that damage does not mean the end. With a twist of my wrist, the door opens.

I take a deep breath and step inside. The lady at the desk has her attention on the computer in front of her. It only takes a second before she looks up and smiles. Then she slowly stands from her desk. I guess they've all been advised never to make any sudden movements. My eyes sink to the floor below because unlike last time, I now know I belong here.

Sensing somebody to my left, I glance in that direction and recognise her immediately. Katie. The woman I met last time. She doesn't appear surprised to see me here, and she too gives me a brief smile.

"Would you like to come with me?" I dip my head in confirmation before walking behind her.

I'm guided into a room, positioned opposite from the last time I was here. There's a different picture on the wall, but the furniture is the same, the colour of the walls a little darker maybe.

"The other room is in use," she says feeling the need to explain.

"This room is fine." The room doesn't matter. I wait for Katie to talk but recognise she's doing the same.

Unlike before, I sit down without prompting. Katie follows suit.

"Things have changed," I finally speak before elevating my eyes to hers. "I-I... I belong here. I know that now." Katie briefly closes her eyes like she's in mourning. I take off my hat. The movement must have caught her attention as she looks back up, her focus landing on my pixie cut before flitting to the remaining bruise on my face I thought I'd concealed well enough not to be seen. Obviously, I was wrong, or maybe her eye is more 'trained' at seeing such marks on the skin.

"I went short," I say by way of explanation. "You advised me to find safer places in the home where he couldn't reach things to harm me with." I ruffle my fingers through my hair and tug gently on a gathering of short strands in my fingers. "He likes... liked to use my hair."

"It suits you... you look beautiful."

My eyebrows flick up, and I want to laugh at her misguided belief. Someone who made her friends suffer like I did is not beautiful. I went and showed them what a mess my life was and then walked away, not giving them any other option but to grieve.

Putting a halt to my tumbling thoughts, I straighten my back, take in a deep breath and force the confidence to appear. If I'm expecting Katie to help me, then she has to know that I'm no longer burying my head.

"These bruises may be fading, but I know more will come."

"The bruises I see usually aren't the worst. I'm aware they are a speck of ice in an ocean filled with icebergs. It's beneath the surface that usually holds the worst of it, but you know that, don't you?" She sits back in her seat, places her notepad and pen to the table beside her.

"I do," I confirm. Katie is right, at first I downplayed his behaviour, made excuses, believed that maybe I was somehow the reason. Grabbing my arm and causing a bruise hurt, but it wasn't *that* bad. However that was only the beginning, quickly the pain became worse.

Katie watches me and waits.

"He pushes me," I begin and Katie nods by way of encouragement. "Grabs, punches, it can get quite bad." I pause. "He's dragged me down the stairs, holding onto me by only my hair. He's raped me when I've been too beaten to stop it."

Surprisingly Katie doesn't react how I expected. Her eyes aren't laden with pity—her chest didn't sink in anguish. She's witnessing a person weakened by months of physical and emotional abuse, and I've reached the point where I have to give in entirely or learn to fight. Katie knows which route I've chosen. I can tell. She knows this time I'm not running from the room.

"I'm so sorry for you, Ginny." Her tone is so kind and caring that I wish I could talk to her all day. She somehow provides me with a sense of peace when everything I'm telling her belongs in the realms of hell.

"He controls me. He controls everything. I don't have a penny to my name. I had a car but, well, I don't have it now." To my knowledge, it's still parked on Marci's street. I haven't dared to bring the subject up with Blake. I widen my eyes and stare at Katie. "But I'm also aware I brought some of this on myself. I used to work. It was only in the office for an accountancy firm, but I loved the job. When we moved here, Blake suggested I give up work. He didn't force me. It was merely an idea." Although at the time, I had known it was what he preferred. "With Blake's salary, I no longer needed to work, and at the time, I was happy to stay at home making sure everything was perfect for him. It made him happy, so you see, *I* chose to stay at home."

"So you think because you chose to stay at home, you invited the abuse?"

"No. But because I stay at home, I rely on him for everything. He pays for the house, the car, every bill we have. He buys the clothes I wear, I don't contribute a penny."

"And if you go out? With friends? Socially? What does he think then?"

"He doesn't like it," I say quietly. "So I don't try, but again that was my wrongdoing. I should have been stronger."

"Men who control and coerce can make you feel excluded from any form of socialising. Whether it be work or seeing friends. You don't want to cause any friction between the two of you, so you end up living to how he wishes. It's manipulation, and it can be purposeful." She allows a silence to pass between us as I try and find belief in what she's saying, but it's so hard when I always thought, and possibly still do, that some of my own decisions haven't helped our situation. "Ginny... You're talking in the past tense." Katie points out.

"I know."

"Why?"

"I left. It was the second time I'd tried to leave. Last time I barely made it more than a few miles before he got to me. This time I actually made it to my friend's house. I drove for over two hours. I arrived beaten, bloody." I hang my head, disgusted at what I allowed Marci to see. "I was a mess." My words are spoken with bitterness. "The worst I'd ever been... and she saw it." My chest starts to shake as sobs begin to form. "I'm sorry," I mumble, and I gulp away my emotions.

"Don't apologise, Ginny," Katie's voice trembles. "Never apologise for this. Ever!" A box of tissues come into my distorted vision, I take one and rub at my eyes. When I can see more clearly, I once again look to Katie and notice a scrunched up tissue in her own hand. I've upset her.

"I'm sorry." Again, I mutter my apologies. The softness of Katie's palm gently comes to rest on top of my hand. Then her fingers slowly clasp. "I let her see that... me like that... but then he came like I should have known he would, and I left her behind. She believes I chose him over her." I grind my teeth and swallow. "But that's the last time."

I sit up straighter, and Katie's hand falls from mine.

"I'm talking in the past tense because I want to leave. I have to leave. When he's with me, I breathe quietly, consider every word I say, ponder over every move I make. When he's not with me—when he's at work, breaths are a little freer, but they're still laced with dread, uncertain of what's to come. That dread will not go away, but I have to take him out of the equation. This time, when I leave, it's going to be for good. I will not be going back home. I failed Marci, and I won't do it again."

"I can help you."

I smile weakly at her because she knows that's why I came. "I want to be invisible to him, to endure his world no longer. I have to go somewhere he'll never find me."

"That also means—"

"That Marci can never find me either," I confirm with regret.

She leans forward in her chair and bows her head. "Why?" As though afraid of the answer.

"Because I have nothing left to lose. Each day I live in fear. I used to hope that it would stop, that he would change. But I keep falling. What happens if one day I don't get back up? I used to think I deserved to stay down on the ground. I didn't care if I never got back up."

"And now."

"I need to fight." For Marci, for Liam, but also for me.

Peering up through her lashes she utters. "You know this isn't going to be easy."

"None of this has been easy," I say, the desolation overwhelming.

I exhale and for the first time truly look at Katie. She's wearing a yellow-gold band on her wedding finger. Her style of dress is casual, yet somehow she makes it appear smart with the accessories she chooses. I glance sadly at her scarf and hope she never gets to experience what I have.

"Why do you do this? Sit here and listen to the same horror story. More often than not, women like me choose to return to the man that's hurting her. That's got to be difficult to understand."

"It's complicated. Ginny." She draws in some breaths. "Somebody told me..." She shakes her head. "What I mean is, you remind me of somebody I once knew."

"Knew? Did she die?" There's no panic in my question, only a desire to know the truth.

"No." She smiles. "She didn't."

"She was younger than you, a teenager, she didn't even know places like this existed." Katie waves her hand around the room. "Her upbringing was less than ideal. There was lots of shouting and other stuff... from her mum's latest boyfriend. She didn't really have anyone, so the only person she could rely on was herself. She thought she was strong, but I think maybe she was lucky. She met a boy, he was a young man in the making. He saw past the withdrawn teenager, looked through the bullies that tended to walk behind her, taunting the girl about her appearance. But he also saw something beyond the pain. He saved her, Ginny. Him and his brother." Her eyes narrow as she looks at me in consideration. "She didn't save herself... so really, I'm not sure where the comparison is." She appears confused but then her brown eyes focus on mine, and I see an understanding I've not witnessed before. "Survivors, we come in all forms, Ginny." She goes quiet. Her long dark lashes splay out on her skin as she closes her eyes, and I recognise a familiar sadness.

I nod my head silently in acknowledgement because I think deep down I already knew, I just didn't want to see it before.

"I want you to understand, Ginny, that my mum, she's different to you. She went from one abusive relationship to the next. Her idea of a stable relationship is a boyfriend that doesn't beat her as much as the last. The majority of the beatings were hers, only occasionally did they become mine. But do you know, the thing that I remember most about my childhood? I can't remember seeing my mum smile. I have no idea what her smile looks like, even now. My mother may still be alive, Ginny..."

"But it's not a life you want her to live," I finish for her. "Yet, you choose to still live and breathe the abuse through other's stories."

"It's not the same, trust me. Back then I had friends that helped me. They're still with me. In fact, I married my saviour, Ginny."

"You married him?"

She nods her head and tears glisten in her eyes. "I did, and I'm thankful every single day."

"Why are you telling me all of this? Is all of what you said true?"

"You think I'd tell you a story like that to make you believe that it can happen? That people can escape it?

I shrug. "Possibly, yes."

"What do you want to believe, Ginny?"

"I hope that girl, the one who was hurting and lonely, I want to believe it's the woman I'm staring at now."

"Then believe it." She sits back and studies me. "You know we all fall, Ginny. It's an inevitability of life. Some falls may be more painful or further than others, but when you've fallen, know that the climb becomes the making of you. If you're lucky, you get to climb with somebody special holding your hand."

"I don't... I can't think about that."

"I understand, but remember it because one day, I'm hoping you will."

"So what do I do now?"

"*We* start to make plans."

CHAPTER NINE

I'm lying on my side with my back to him while he sleeps. The early morning sun is starting to creep through the gap in the curtain. The time for me to get up is drawing closer which only heightens my nerves. I breathe in and out slowly in an attempt to reduce the panic that has been steadily building. I force myself to feign sleep until the alarm sounds. I can't risk any change in routine, can't arouse suspicion because Blake would notice. The day has to continue the same as the days that have passed before them.

When this day is going to be the day that changes everything.

The alarm finally goes off. I jump out of bed as I always do, giving Blake an extra five minutes sleep. I put on my robe and slippers then tread quietly downstairs. As I walk through the house, I scan each room. They were bleak and empty when we first arrived, but over the months, I've made each room into a home, trying to brighten the décor, hoping in return it would brighten our lives.

Now all I see is a home that's become a prison, and all I seek is escape.

I click on the coffee machine then go to collect the newspaper from the hall. As I place it on the table, the pages shake in my grasp. I grip the chair closest to me and take in some deep breaths fighting to regulate my behaviour. *He can't notice. Everything has to be normal.*

Rubbing at my brow, I swallow and set back to carrying out my normal morning tasks in the habitual way we've both become accustomed to. Only today is different, and the complexity of it is overwhelming.

I close my eyes. *Calm breaths, Ginny.* The breaths halt as I sense company. I shoot round in a panic and let out a shriek as he's standing right in front of me, watching my movements.

"You scared me, Blake."

He doesn't reply. Instead, he continues to stare as I step away from him and finish the coffee. He'd normally be sitting at the table now, but I know he's still standing only a yard from me.

Finally, my chest sinks in relief as I hear his steps on the tiles. The chair grates along the floor, and he sits down. The rustling of the newspaper has never been such a relief to my ears.

"I'm sorry I got in so late last night. There was a deal I needed to close, and it involved a fair bit of research."

"I understand." He got home at half past eleven. I'd been lying in bed awake praying that he wouldn't come home at all.

"Did you sleep well, Ginny?" He never asks if I sleep well.

"Yes, thank you. Did you?" I didn't sleep. The entire night was spent running through the plans I'd made with Katie.

"I did." I nod my head and smile before resuming my normal duties and prepare his breakfast.

"Do you have any plans for today?"

"The usual. I thought I'd go out in the garden this morning for a couple of hours and try and tidy up some of the leaves. What about you?" I take the jug of coffee and make my way towards him.

"It's Thursday, Ginny. I'll be in the team meeting all morning, but I'm sure you know that already." I go to fill his cup, but he grabs my hand harshly. Luckily the coffee doesn't spill. "We're becoming creatures of habit don't you think?"

"I guess we are," I agree and force a smile trying to make him believe it's a good thing. I look at the grip he has on my hand, and he slowly releases it. I pour his coffee before moving away and filling up my own cup.

I watch the toaster, waiting for the bread to pop up. When it does, I spread the butter thinly, just as he likes it, before taking it over to him. He's sitting back in his chair, his palms gripping the newspaper again. Only he's not really looking at the text.

"I think we should book a weekend away," he announces. I stop and stare at him in astonishment. "No need to look so surprised. I think we both deserve a break. It might help," he says seemingly with regret. I feel the small tug in my heart, but I force the sensation away. There are no more regrets to be had. I cannot be that person anymore.

Sliding his plate onto his placemat, I walk around the table and sit down opposite him. "I think a break sounds perfect." My answer pleases him and a brief sense of relief washes over me.

"Are you not hungry?" I ask noticing he hasn't yet picked up his toast.

"I have an early appointment before the meeting, so I need to get going if I'm going to catch her."

I simply nod as he narrows his eyes at me.

"You have nothing to be jealous of, Ginny." Jealous? The emotion hadn't even entered my thoughts. "There will only ever be you in my life."

"I'm glad." I blink and drive the corners of my lips into a smile.

Pushing back from his chair, he gets up and approaches.

Resting his hand on the back of my seat he bends down. I meet his gaze.

"I'll book it today. Okay?"

"Okay."

His lips land softly on mine causing the seed of doubt to once again appear. *This is what he does.* I remind myself of the see-saw of emotions Blake manages to create but recall the moments of pain that always follow.

I watch him as he retreats to the porch and collects his briefcase. With a lasting look, he walks out of the door. I sit frozen to the chair not daring to move until I hear the sound of his car leaving the driveway.

When I do, I finally release the breaths I've been holding. "*You are doing this!* He's being nice because that's what he does. Right after he's beaten you," I say out loud by way of convincing myself further.

I remain seated for another ten minutes or so. Blake leaving early has thrown me. His meeting doesn't start for another hour and a half, which means he could come back and surprise me at any point. So even with him not here, my routine has to continue for a while longer.

I look around the kitchen. This is what it's come to. My life, my belongings, Marci, all to be left behind. Not even for a fresh start because I won't ever stop running. I'm leaving to survive with the hope that one day, when it's safe, I can make contact with Marci again.

By way of habit, I take the pots to the sink, looking out of the window as I go, ensuring his car has gone. As I start to wash the first cup, I stand and stare at it, wondering what I'm doing. I don't need to wash the dishes, but I resign myself to doing them anyway.

When the dishes are clean, dried, and put away, I walk into the lounge and sit staring at a blank television screen. Over an hour has to pass before I can walk out of the house.

Time passes slowly, allowing doubt to enter my thoughts frequently. But I keep drawing in deep breaths and force myself to see the image of myself after the last attack. I think of Marci and Liam and how desperate I am for them to know that I'm fighting back. That I'd rather live my life on the run than stay here another night.

When the hour has passed, I make my way to the doorway and take one last look outside. There is nobody there.

I dash upstairs, two steps at a time. When I reach the landing, I look back down at the stairs that lead to the grand hallway. I make myself remember the times he dragged me down the stairs, the moments he slammed my head into the wall or when he clasped his hands around my throat. I swiftly turn, a slight charge of defiance running through me.

With a list of what I need to take memorised in my head, I enter my bedroom and work methodically, but hurriedly, until my bag is finally full. Leaving it propped up against the wall, I sit down at my dressing table, taking out the notepad and pen from the drawer.

The words are implanted in my memory, so I start writing straight away. I tell him looking for me at home will be a thankless journey. That contacting Marci would be a wasted task. Nobody knows where I am going. Not one person. Finally, I tell him that his actions have caused me to despise him so much that if one day he does find me, it will be the last time he will set sights on me because I would rather end my life than spend the rest of it with him.

I fold over the piece of paper, scribing his name on the front and do nothing but stare at it. My departing gift.

But I know the main reason for my delay. There's one last thing to do, and it's what is destroying me the most. Slowly I stand, then make my way to the far bedroom, the only room guaranteed to give me a phone signal. As I enter the room, melancholy rules me. It's time to sever all strings in my life—only some strings should never be forced to break.

I approach the window and dial his number.

Liam answers on the second ring.

"Ginny? What is it? What's he done?" Liam's voice is rushed and filled with panic believing that I'm reaching out to him for another reason. My heart instantly aches.

"I'm okay, I don't have long to talk, but it's important that you listen."

"Ginny, where are you?" he questions dubiously.

Raising my hand, I press it against the window, spreading my fingers wide, somehow trying to connect myself to him. To her.

"Liam, I'm leaving. Now."

I hear rustling over the phone and then the jangle of keys. "I'm on my way, where are you?"

My eyes close briefly as I will the courage to rise. "I'm not coming home."

"Shit, Ginny! No, you have to come to us. What the hell has he done this time?" he growls.

I raise my voice defiantly, wanting him to take notice. "Please, hear me out. This is the hardest thing I've ever had to do. This is the only way. There is nothing you can say or do to convince me otherwise. I'm leaving, and I won't be coming back. I need—"

"I can protect you, Ginny, I promise. Don't do this." The desperation in his tone tugs at my sore and bruised heart.

Pushing my forehead to the window, I look up to the sky, seeking strength to come from somewhere. "I need you to protect Marci. Blake will come looking for me, and Marci will be the first place he'll look. You have to be with her."

"Of course I will, but, Ginny—"

"No!" I stop him from saying anything further that may change my mind because it can't happen. "Please, Liam. This is how it has to be."

"Damn it! This is it, isn't it? Fuck!" He lets out a heavy sigh. "Where are you going?"

"I can't answer that. I won't answer that but know that I'll be safe." This is the last time I run. But at least with Katie's help, I hold some hope that I might be able to break free. If... if he finds me this time, then there will be no point in running anymore. The only conclusion would be for it all to end. Everything.

"Ginny, you have to tell me, please..." He goes silent. All I can hear are his steady breaths as realisation sinks in. I want to stay on the line for eternity clinging onto the only good part of my life, but I know I can't. I need to go.

"Goodbye, Liam."

"You're not going to ring Marci are you?"

"I can't." I squeeze my eyes shut, trying to fight back the tears. "I can't say goodbye to her. Liam, tell her I'm fighting back in the only way I can. I know she won't understand, but believe it or not that's a good thing." I sniff and search for a tissue in my pocket but resort to my sleeve. "I'm sorry... he'll come there, Liam. You have to be ready. Call the police. Do what you feel is right, but don't try and look for me."

He starts to say something, but I interrupt. "Take care of each other. I love all of you."

I end the call, then immediately double over, wrapping my

arms around my middle as great sobs heave from my chest. My entire body feels weighted down with loathing and uncertainty because of what I'm doing. I'm leaving and losing the few people I care about, and I'm scared. Even though I'm finally finding my fight, it's never hurt so much.

The sound of a car coming up the lane has me jolting upright. I rush to the edge of the window, swipe at my eyes and peer out from behind the curtain. My heart hammers in my chest and the curtain starts to shake with my desperate grasp. Then I remember my bag and the note. *Oh my God! This could be it. All of it over.*

I dart from the room, making a leap towards my bedroom. Quickly gathering up my bag and the note, I shove them to the back of the wardrobe. Rushing towards the stairs, I make my way down as fast as my legs will take me. If he knows I'm upstairs, he'll want to know why. Excuses for everything I'm doing differently this morning start charging around in my head. As I slide onto the tiled kitchen floor, I take in the view from the kitchen window in front of me. My phone drops from my hand, crashing to the floor.

Two police officers step out of a car. They take the hats from their heads, glance at each other before looking solemnly towards the door. Why are they looking at my door like that? Are they expecting to see something sad when they walk through it? They don't know me. How would they know?

As they get closer, I recognise one of the officers is male, the other female. Her hair is pinned in a low bun at the back of her head. She straightens her uniform, and they both set towards my door.

The knock causes me to jump even though I knew it was coming. My legs start to feel weak, and the dread I've come accustomed to takes over my body. My footsteps land unnoticeably on the floor like it's not really me making them.

Again they knock, the sound much louder now I'm standing right behind the door. Reaching out I tug on the dense hardwood and the police officers come into my vision.

"Mrs Daniels?" The policeman asks.

"Yes," I reply.

"Can we come in?"

I move back a step, allowing them to pass. I raise my arm indicating for them to go into the kitchen then tag behind. As I reach the closest chair, I drop down, not sure my legs can continue holding me up. *Why are they here?* I can't even begin to come up with an explanation. Perhaps my car's been vandalised or stolen?

The sound of the chairs scraping across the floor as the officers sit down causes me to meet their focus.

"Is your husband, Blake Daniels?" Why are they asking me that?

"Yes," I repeat. The only word I'm able to say.

The female officer moves her chair a little closer in my direction, and I frown. She then takes the lead in the conversation.

"I'm very sorry to have to tell you this, but your husband has been involved in a car accident." She glances towards her partner before returning her sombre look to me. "We're afraid your husband died at the scene, Mrs Daniels."

I freeze, don't move a muscle, not even to blink. I just sit and stare at them. *Dead? That's impossible.*

"Mrs Daniels?"

"How do you know it was him?"

"It was his car, Mrs Daniels. He was carrying personal

belongings with his identifiable information on. A formal identification will be needed, but we're certain it's your husband. We're extremely sorry for your loss."

"Blake's dead," I say the words out loud as though that will somehow convince me.

"We're so sorry. Do you have anybody we can call?"

Gone. After everything.

I see the policewoman's mouth move as she says something to me, but I don't hear her. She stands and steps towards the kettle.

No more words. No more pain. No need to run. It's all over?

"Mrs Daniels? Mrs Daniels?"

My attention drags to the man sitting opposite me saying my name.

"Is there someone we can call? A family member?" I stare at him blankly. "A friend?"

Marci. They could ring Marci. My chin starts to quiver, and my vision blurs remembering last time I saw her. "No. We don't know many people."

He looks to the policewoman.

"No," I say again. "There isn't anybody. But the people he works with, they should know. He should be in a meeting now." I glance at the clock.

"Mrs Daniels, is there anybody we can call *for you*."

"No. Thank you." I push back from the chair. "Excuse me. I need a moment," I mutter then walk out of the room. I pause at the photo taken on the day of our wedding, positioned neatly in a silver frame. I scoop it into my hands and make my way up the stairs.

I tread calmly when inside everything is in turmoil. When I enter the bedroom, I stare at the bed covers that Blake pulled tightly after he got up this morning.

"I don't believe them," I vocalise as though he's here in the room with me. "You wouldn't allow this." My fingers curl reminding me of the photograph I have in my hand. "You said I'd never be free," I utter the words to the only version of his face I can see.

Tears start to fall. I don't know if they're due to sadness, loss, confusion, disbelief, or relief. "You changed everything!" I call out as I throw the picture frame across the room. It hits the opposing wall and the glass shatters, scattering across the bed. "How do you get to leave so easily?"

"Mrs Daniels?" The voice of the police lady comes from behind me, and I drop to my knees. Her arm wraps around my waist as she joins me on the floor. Soothing words fall from her mouth, but they are a waste of her breath. No words will take away what I'm feeling.

It can't be this easy. It can't.

I'd found my fight. I wanted to fight. To show that I could do this.

He's dead… Blake's dead.

Even in death, he said he'd be with me, and it's only now I truly know what he meant. Everything he did will be with me forever.

Silence surrounds me. A silence I'm not used to. Because for the first time in a long time, I have no idea what's coming.

CHAPTER TEN

I jolt up in bed, my heart thumping in my chest as breaths seep in and out of my lips. Moonlight breaks through a gap in the curtain, casting shadows around the room that fill me with fear. My focus searches in panic before I gulp in a breath.

"You're not here," I whisper trying to take control of my breathing. *They're shadows. Only shadows.* Warm tears cascade down my cheeks, and I press my hands over my eyes in an attempt to stop them. "You're not here," I repeat wishing that somehow the truth could offer some form of comfort but it doesn't. Blake may be gone, but his presence has never felt so strong.

My body slumps forward with the realisation of what today is. The day I bury my husband, and the last day I'll ever set sight on this house.

Reaching to the floor, I pick up my phone to check the time. It's 4.40 a.m. Which means I have just over three hours before Marci arrives.

Although I'm desperate to see her, I'm not sure what to expect when she arrives. Even if she does forgive me, I'll find it difficult to accept because I don't believe I deserve it.

I think back to last night when I finally called her. She'd been quiet, perhaps it was shock or anger. Maybe there was a part of her that felt sad hearing of Blake's death?

Either way, her reaction was justified. I walked away from her when *I'd* been the one who went to her for help. *I* was the one who shut her out, and I choose this life with him when Marci had given me an opportunity to escape.

I've read that people feel numb going through an experience such as this. I wish I felt numb. Instead, I'm confused. I feel sadness and regret for a man that shouldn't deserve another second of my time thinking about him. I can't help but mourn him. But then, my thoughts become tinged with relief that he's gone. Frequently, I go back and forth, through every emotion imaginable, but I still don't know which one it is I should be feeling.

I miss his presence. Yet, I loathed it when he was here. I loved him, but I also despised him.

I shake my head as exhaustion starts to roll over me. The effects of the past few days, weeks, even months, taking its toll. Rolling to my knees, I get up on all fours before standing up fully. With a backward glance at the mattress, the only furniture left in the house, I make my way to the bathroom to shower. When I enter the room, I come to a stop when faced with my navy 'A' line dress that hangs on the back of the door. A few months ago it would have fit me perfectly. Only now as I look down at my body, I'm aware the material will cascade over me like drapes. My curves, it seems, have disappeared without me even noticing.

Turning on the shower, I step into the warm spray and continue to mourn a man who left me with scars that I expect never to heal, and nightmares that I fear will never end.

There are still two and a half hours before Marci is due to arrive. There is nothing else for me to do in the house, no television to watch or even a radio to listen to. I managed to make contact with a local furniture project that was only too happy to take the furniture off my hands along with various belongings, which had only served as reminders of the abuse. The dressing table... where I landed after a backhand across the cheek. The oak chest... I reach up and touch the scar on my temple. The mirror. I almost retch at the memory of him pinning my face against my reflection so he could show me just how ugly a person I was after I'd hacked at my hair. I look at the spot on the wall where the mirror used to be and turn away in disgust at the image that is still ingrained in my mind.

Treading into the kitchen, I head to the sink and pour myself some water into a cup. My attention swerves to the door as I check that the key remains in the lock and the chain is still in place. Then I move to the edge of the room to where the table and chairs used to be.

The silence surrounds me like it has done for many months. Now, the silence gives me nothing but time to consider an abundance of what-ifs.

When I last saw Katie, she spoke of how brave I was, of how I would have to fight for my survival. She warned me that *if* he did find me, I would have to be stronger than I've ever been before. She believed I could be that person, but now I'll never know. I may have packed my case, but I never actually got to walk out of my marriage and this house. Blake made certain it came to an end on his terms.

"What's wrong with me?" I say out loud with a shake of my head. How can I say such a thing? Blake didn't die on purpose! I'm wiping my hands over my face as bright lights flash over the kitchen units, catching my attention. Immediately, I'm on alert. I see Marci's familiar car travel up the lane towards the house. She's early, something I was unprepared for. She must have set off in the early hours.

I make a feeble attempt to straighten my dress, hoping that somehow she won't see her pathetically broken friend beneath the fabric. My feet land on the tiles, creating an echo from the deserted room as I walk to the door and unlock it. With a deep inhale, I pull it open.

She's already out of the car, her focus on me. I'm not sure what I expected, but I wasn't prepared for anger. Not today.

My brows draw together as the friend I thought I'd lost stalks towards me, her blonde hair fighting to keep up with the fast pace. The friend, who after one phone call, dropped everything she was doing to come to me. The friend, who right now, is very clearly pissed at me.

She comes to an abrupt stop in front of me, and I take a step back. I'm grateful she doesn't acknowledge my uncertainty.

"You're early," I mutter.

She raises an eyebrow and cocks her head to the side. "No. I'm far too late," she retorts.

I dip my head and mumble an apology. Marci has every right to be mad at me.

"Ginny, don't tell me you're sorry. Shout at me or something. Tell me I should have helped. *I* know I damn well should have so what's stopping you from telling me the same thing?" Her voice elevates, and instinctively I take another step back like the coward that I am. With disappointment shrouding my every cell, I lift my focus.

Her mouth is open wide, and she's staring back at me, but I'm as stunned as she is. I don't want to back away from Marci.

"Jesus, Gin." In a second she's there, her arms ready to wrap me in their fold. But as tears fill her eyes, she hesitates, and I know no matter how much I try to hide it, she recognises the look of fear that still resides in my eyes. Slowly her arms circle me. Initially, I can't help but stiffen at her touch, but as the seconds pass, her hold becomes familiar, the smell of sunflowers wafts under my nose, and I close my eyes, trying to blink the tears away. She's here. Really here.

"I'm sorry." That's all I can say, the words repeatedly roll from my tongue.

"Why are *you* sorry? I *let* you leave, Ginny," Marci murmurs. "I should have done more—" she whispers in my ear.

Disheartened, I shake my head. "You did what I asked," I respond quietly. I won't allow her to take an ounce of the blame, but I know today she won't listen to my reasoning. So I don't push the matter.

I'm barely holding myself up right now and when she eventually let's go, I know that's what she's seeing. Tears sting my eyes, and a silent plea leaves me, wishing for her not to push me. She steps back, runs her fingers over her temples before she looks out of the door and scans the surrounding scenery.

Half turning towards me, she says, "This is some freaky place you're living in," she remarks with her eyes wide as she looks back to the surrounding trees. "I mean seriously, Ginny? You've been living here? Who owned this place before you? Freddie goddamn Krueger?"

I laugh hard then. My laughter turning hysterical as Marci stands in a stunned state watching me.

"I can't help it," I fire back as though by some kind of explanation. She continues to stare wide-eyed, which only makes me laugh harder. "I know it's not funny," I exclaim as the laughter starts to diminish and shame fills me. My mouth sets in a straight line as I wonder how I could laugh on such a day. "You're going to have to give me some time. I'm more than a little messed up right now."

"Lucky for you, I have plenty of time to spare." Her look briefly changes to sadness before she pushes it from her expression, and I know she's trying to be strong for me.

"Now, am I safe to hook my arm through yours, or are those twiggy arms of yours going to break?"

"You can hook." Beneath hooded eyes, she steps forward, closes the door behind her and her arm glides into mine as she always used to, only this time, sadly she felt she had to ask for permission.

As we walk into the kitchen, she looks around. "Should I have brought a chair?"

"I like the minimalist look," I reply smiling at her ability to cause a smile for the second time, even when in the depths of despair.

"Coffee?" I ask withdrawing from her grasp. Other than the mattress, my belongings consist of a kettle and supplies to make a few cups of coffee.

"Of course!" Again a smile touches my lips. Marci and coffee go together like milk and cookies. You can't have one without the other.

"So you went to the hairdressers?"

"What?" My fingers reach up and twiddle with the short hair at the back of my neck.

"Well, you're good at plenty of things Ginny but cutting hair isn't one of them. You had your hair made into an actual style," she points out.

"Yeah, I did." I don't expand on who I went to the hairdressers with. All that would do is highlight to Marci another element of Blake's control that he continually had, possibly still has over me.

"It suits you."

"It gets a little cold," I add, rubbing the back of my neck. "I'll probably grow it again." I smile coyly at her.

"So? You wear a scarf?"

My smile drops. The image of the bright red scarf he wrapped around my throat flashes through my mind. I reach to my neck reliving the tight and restricted sensation. There will be no scarf.

"Or not," she adds, registering the shock on my face. She glances at my neck before a look of understanding passes over her expression, closely followed by the obvious yet unwanted reaction of pity. "He—he used a scarf?"

I simply nod.

She closes her eyes and exhales heavily. "I'm sorry."

"No," I respond immediately. "The apologies end now. I mean it, Marci." I turn my back and set about making the coffee. It takes a minute before I sigh in relief at the sound of her footsteps as they cross the tiled floor while she explores the house.

"This is some big pad, Ginny. Although I guess it didn't really matter..." her voice trails off as she cuts herself short of what she was going to say. "Sorry."

As I stir the coffee, I glance over my shoulder at her. The novelty that I can turn my back without fearing what may come is new to me altogether. She stands in the doorway to the lounge, questions must be whirring around her head, but she keeps quiet.

Walking towards her, I hold out her cup. When she takes it from me, I walk deeper into the room, grateful for the warmth of the carpet beneath my feet instead of the cold, tiled floor.

"I'm not sure what to say," she begins. "I don't know whether to say I'm sorry that he's... dead or that I'm glad."

"Then don't say anything."

"But—"

"I'm not sure how *I'm* feeling right now, Marci. I can't believe he's actually gone. I wake thinking I hear him next to me. I still smell his aftershave. I expect him to walk through the door any minute. It feels like he's here—as though he's never left."

"But he has," she points out. "And he won't hurt you again." I wish her statement to be true, but even now he manages to cripple me. "You wake? Are you not sleeping well?" she questions with concern.

"Not really." I haven't slept that great for a while now. I catch her balling her fists up. She notices me watching so relaxes her palms. "Take a seat," I say with a small smile as I sit down on the carpeted floor. Marci joins me. We both rest our backs against the wall and sit staring straight ahead at the view of the huge expanse of the back garden.

"Shit!" she interrupts the silence. "More trees?"

"More trees," I confirm.

"I'm not sure I would have chosen this place, Ginny, I mean it's big, and yeah, pretty spectacular, but all that!" She tips her head towards the trees.

"I didn't choose it, remember?" Blake organised everything, and at the time I was happy to go along with his excitement.

"Ginny... I wish I'd done something." Her words are heavy with regret, and I despise myself for making her feel that way.

"You did do something." She twists her head to look at me. "When I came to you, it was a wakeup call. I knew what I had to do. I couldn't have you believe that I was willing to choose him over you. I know it may have looked like I did, but I can assure you, that was the last thing I wanted. The day of the accident," I glance down at the cup in my hand, "I was leaving him." I keep my focus low. "I'd packed a bag. I was minutes from walking out of the door."

"Liam told me." She admits quietly. "He made me promise not to make contact with you. He said it was safer, he said it's what you wanted. But why, Ginny? Why wouldn't you come home? I get that you were scared but—"

I twist back to face her and shake my head slowly from side to side. "I had to go somewhere he couldn't find me. I know this is all a lot to take in but coming to you would put you at risk, Marci, and I wasn't willing for that to happen. Not again. I made that mistake once before."

"That's why you left with him before?" She stares at me incredulously. I nod, but it's not the only reason. How can I begin to explain how much power he had over me? How my fear ruled over every thought I had? "Bullshit! The police would have arrested him. You had bruises, Ginny, evidence!"

"But it wouldn't have been over. No matter what you believe, he would have got to me again. The only answer was to go somewhere he could never find me."

"I can't believe you weren't going to say goodbye." She narrows her eyes at me. "We've known each other since forever, Ginny."

"I know, but it was safer that way, trust me." The fact that Katie shared my view cemented my belief that Marci was best kept out of it.

"No!" she responds through gritted teeth. "You would have been alone. You shouldn't have been forced to run."

"Sometimes that's the only option." I recognise as I look at her that I need to take a step back. It's going to take time for

Marci to understand the extent of the situation I was in. I had months and months to get used to it because that's how he did it. Gradually, over time, little by little he took away my independence and placed it solely on him.

In the beginning, I argued because then it was unacceptable. But then I started seeing that a punch was not as bad as a kick. Twisting my arm back was better than slamming my head against the wall. He conditioned me into believing some days weren't as bad as others when every day was like living in hell.

"Marci, can we please talk about this another time?"

"You want to act like nothing has happened?" Her eyebrows lift in shock. But her disbelief stirs something inside of me.

"No, Marci." My words are assertive, and I'm unsure where I found the strength. "I will never be able to act like nothing has happened because something did happen. Lots of things. Awful things. I relive it every minute, so if I choose to not talk about it, it's because it's crucifying me. I'm not ignoring what I've been through. I won't ever have that privilege. I don't want to talk about it, just for a while." Which is probably stupid of me really because I haven't had anyone close to talk to since Blake died. You'd think I'd be desperate to talk.

"Well, I'm allowed to hate him," she directs at me, and I smile sadly but don't try and sway her opinion. Her eyes finally leave me, and she leans forward trying to peer through the other door that leads towards the stairs. "Your furniture?"

"Gone," I confirm.

"So you have your kettle, coffee, and what else left here?"

"Not a lot."

"So you're leaving?" She looks at me anxiously. "I didn't see your car?"

"I don't have my car. Is it not still at your place?"

"No, Ginny." She studies me. "The next morning it was gone from the road. I thought you must have known?"

"No."

Blake may have robbed me of my freedom, but I took away Marci's right to help a friend in need. It's only today, looking into her eyes, that I see her own guilt that she harbours for feeling so helpless. I've never seen her look so powerless or so vulnerable, and I know immediately that moving back home is the right thing to do.

"I was hoping you'd give me a lift."

On tenterhooks, she leans towards me. "To?"

"I'm coming home, Marci. Right after I've buried the bastard," I say with a seriousness I feel in the presence of Marci. Not only did he take my independence, he forced me to push my best friend away and create her self-doubt. I have to learn how to fight again because with Marci's help, we're going to get our lives back.

"That sounds like an insult to me."

"I'm allowed."

With tears rolling down her cheeks and without hesitation she pulls me towards her. "You won't keep trying to block my comfort, Ginny. This will get better. We're going to find a way to get you back."

"I'm sorry, Marci—"

"It's not an apology I want, Ginny. I want you to trust me. In fact—" She looks around the room before standing up. Then she walks over to the doorway and stares into the kitchen. "Is there a room in this mansion that has a wooden floor?" she asks looking back at me.

"Yes, the dining room. Why?"

"Please tell me it's a big room."

"It is." I stand up and walk past her. I take the door that leads to the staircase then look back, checking she's following. She is but is currently staring up at the wide stairs and balcony that overlooks the other entranceway. I stand and wait for her to join me at the dining room door.

"Sorry," she apologises. "It's just so big!"

Swinging the door open, I push it back letting Marci walk through into the dining room.

"Why do you want to see this room anyway?"

"Not this room per se," she adds grinning at me. "It's the floor. I'm guessing you haven't skated in a while?"

"Skated?" I question.

"Skated, Ginny, like we used to."

Then I'm hit with recognition. When we were kids, Marci had a room in her house with a wooden floor. Frequently, we'd toss our shoes aside, ensuring we had the softest and smoothest pair of socks on, then pretend to skate in every direction possible across the room, dodging varying amounts of furniture.

"I don't know, Marci," I say uncertainly.

"Why? Surely you should have one good memory of the place." Before I know it, Marci bends down and takes off her shoes, throwing them to the hallway past my feet. Her focus settles on my own feet for a second, and I do the same.

"Tights," we both say in unison, and I actually release a giggle.

Then she's off. Marci runs across the length of the room before her feet slide across the final stretch. Then she turns. "Your turn." Although she's at the other end of the room, she holds out her hand. So I run. I run as fast as my feet will take me before I too, slide over the wooden floor and almost collide into Marci.

We spend the next few minutes running, sliding, twirling like we did when we were younger and for those brief minutes, I remember what it is like to smile.

"So how's Liam?" I ask through heavy breaths, wondering what he feels about all of this.

Her eyes widen and Marci skids to a halt. "Shit! Christ! I've done it this time. He's outside! I told him to wait until I'd had chance to speak to you.

"What?" I say loudly. Then we both make a quick dash into the kitchen, and sure enough, Liam is standing with his elbows resting on top of Marci's mini cooper staring our way. When he catches sight of us, he sets his feet moving. Without knocking, he opens the door and stops in the doorway facing us.

"You finished talking?" He glares at Marci.

"Yes... well, I'll never finish... there's always something to say," she replies daringly.

"And you! You're coming home this time, right?"

"Right," I reply straight-faced but somewhat out of breath from the past few minutes' activities.

"Then get a move on because we need to get to the church. Someone has an appointment with the devil, and I want to make sure the bastard gets there."

CHAPTER ELEVEN

THREE MONTHS LATER

Marci walks into the bar before me. She turns and smiles over her shoulder like she's checking I'm actually still with her. I smile back, trying to offer some reassurance. I'm working on convincing her that I'm okay, in the hope that it convinces me.

I try and follow in Marci's footsteps to avoid bumping into the heavy crowds gathered. Again, she looks back, then reaches her hand out towards me, so I take it. When we're almost at the counter, she stops, concern flooding her expression. It's been three months, and with each hour that has passed, Blake has somehow managed to be in my thoughts, or if not in mine, in the thoughts of my friends.

"Are you okay? It's not too busy?"

"It's fine, Marci," I comfort her. If I'm honest, my heart is racing, and the clamminess in my hands is at an all-time high, but I *should* be okay with this. So I suck it up in the hope that one day I actually believe what I keep telling everyone else.

After we've been standing in the same spot for a minute, I glance at Marci wondering why there is hesitation.

"It's open mic night," she states the obvious as she jerks her attention briefly to me, her eyes almost popping out of their sockets.

My heart accelerates for a whole other reason this time. I haven't heard Marci sing in forever. "So what are you going to do?"

"Oh, I don't know. Grab a drink, get plastered, and criticise the hell out of every person that has the guts to get up there," she adds with a sideward glance at the current vocalist.

"I meant what are *you* going to sing?"

She widens her eyes and shakes her head. Submerging herself within a cloud of mumbling, she makes a beeline for the bar. I immediately follow.

"Hey!" I call when I reach her side. I glance briefly at the shots that are placed on the wooden counter in front of us. Marci instantly downs the liquid and shudders at the taste.

"Your turn."

"Oh, I don't know."

She lifts the glass in front of my face. "Nah! Don't know doesn't exist tonight remember? Nor does I'm not sure, maybe, or any other word that carries the same meaning. It's only a yes, Ginny!"

I scowl, but only because I agreed to it in the first place. Marci came to mine earlier with the 'fantastic' if not delusional idea that I had to do as she suggested tonight. I agreed, and I suppose a shot or two isn't too much to ask.

"Fine," I mutter before linking the glass to my lips and swallowing the alcohol straight down. Immediately, my mouth waters, so I gulp again to stop the threat of the alcohol making a reappearance.

"Hey, Ginny. Good to see you." I look at the man behind the

voice and recognise Callum, the same barman who used to serve Marci and me, what now feels like centuries ago.

"Hey, Callum."

"So Faye brought the shots over." He twists his neck smiling at his companion behind the bar. "Classic case of the nerves coming back to haunt you, Marci?" He laughs.

"Piss off, Callum. Oh, but two beers before you go."

"Oh, charming." He then directs his focus to me. "We've not heard her sing in months. Thought she must have lost her good luck charm, but now you're back, maybe she can get reacquainted with the mic."

"You haven't been here in months?" I ask aghast.

"No, I've been here." She snarls her lip at Callum then dims her voice. "I haven't been up there." She nods her head to the stage.

Without her saying it, I know there will be a number of reasons. Nerves used to get the better of Marci, which is surprising considering her confident exterior, but I always managed to talk her through it, convince her to get up and show everyone what she was capable of. Then I left. Even though I've been back home three months, I've only just started to make it out at the weekends. I only hope that my absence isn't the cause of Marci not showing her talent to the world.

When I look back up, Marci's watching me. "Don't even think what you are right now," she orders.

"But it's down to me, isn't it?"

"No, Ginny." She hands me a Bud. Even taking a bottle of beer brings back memories I don't want to face. Everything I do bears some resemblance to the life I shared with Blake. *Christ! I have to stop with this self-pity!* Screw you, Blake! I elevate the bottle to my lips and drink it until I can't take anymore. When I lower it down, Marci's gawping at me.

"Whoa! Thirsty there?"

"Right. Well, you said don't know, not sure etc. They weren't an option tonight, right?"

"Right," she adds with hesitation.

"In that case. Stay here. Okay?" I don't give her a chance to reply. Instead, I head over to the booth.

The man behind the table looks up from his chair and meets my stare before he slowly takes me in. I straighten my shoulders and try not to look as uncomfortable as I'm feeling.

"I want to add someone's name," I blurt out.

"And what *is* your name, sweetheart?"

"It's not for me. It's my friend, Marci."

"Marci?" He sits upright.

"Yes," I reply a little impatiently.

"Marci Sanders?"

"Yeah."

"Hell, she can go next." Again his gaze hovers over my body. "I used to watch her from the crowd before they gave me this gig. And you're her friend?" He finally looks back at my face.

"Yes." I swiftly turn, his voice disappearing as I step further into the crowd. But as I do, a shiver takes over my body, and I stop moving. I scan the nearby crowd as the familiar sense that someone is watching me starts to take over. I've felt it repeatedly over the past few weeks, while I've been at work, or even walking down the streets.

I find it difficult to swallow as my mouth turns dry. The jumble of sounds within the bar blur as my focus continues to sweep the room. I check out each person and every corner, but nothing seems out of the ordinary or provides me with a justified reason for my unease.

When I catch sight of a set of eyes looking directly at me, my body stills. It's not a passing gaze, it's a stare. The hairs on the back of my neck and arms stand on end as I try to figure out if it's discomfort I'm feeling or something else. Whoever he is, he's rendered me powerless to move, but I have no idea why.

"Someone caught your eye?" I briefly take my eyes from the stranger to see Marci standing beside me looking in his direction. *When did I make it back to the bar?* Confused, I right myself and look back to the man. Only now I'm facing his back.

"Who was that?" I ask, my voice sounding shaky.

"A man that was checking you out, Ginny and, damn girl, he's hot!" Marci proclaims. But as I keep my focus trained on him, I swear his back tenses beneath my gaze

"No!" I'm quick to respond. "It's just... he was staring at me." I turn to the side, facing Marci, and obscuring him from my view.

"Because he was checking you out," she teases.

I may have been out of this game for a while, but I'm not stupid. He was not checking me out. There was no smile on his face, only a blank, unreadable look in his eyes.

Marci reaches out to me, and I flinch, not expecting it. I quickly look at her as her hand tightens around mine. "You're beautiful, Ginny, guys are going to look your way. It's unavoidable," she adds with a shrug. "I'm bummed because you're back to being my competition!"

I open my eyes wide. "It's only been months, Marci, I'm not ready. I mean, you thought that guy was checking me out, I felt like he was an axe murderer!"

She opens her mouth and eyes, equally as wide. "It's that bad?" she questions sadly.

"No." I exhale. "Of course it isn't. Anyway, you're up any minute." I add, deflecting her attention.

"What?" she gasps.

With perfect timing, Marci's name is called over the mic, breaking our conversation.

"Shit!" she utters.

"Go!" I order, grateful Marci's interrogation has been brought to an abrupt stop.

"But, I—"

"But nothing. It has to be a yes, remember? Please, Marci, I want to hear you sing. I want to see you up there, where you belong."

With a scowl and an immense amount of puffing out of breaths, she drags her heels and walks towards the stage. I watch as she steps up to the small area sectioned off for the performers. She looks around, searching for something. Crap! She doesn't have her guitar, but then someone comes to the rescue and hands her theirs.

Happiness creates a smile on my lips. This is Marci. This is all she's ever dreamed of. When we were kids, she'd sit and play on that guitar for hours in an evening while I was working my way through homework. Her parents would complain and tell her to get on with her studies, but she didn't need to. She excelled in them too without ever having to put the effort in.

When her eyes find mine in the crowd, she winks. Then pulls the guitar strap over her head before resting the instrument on her knee. I smile at the familiar vision. The vision I believed I'd only ever hold in my memory.

The second her fingers hook on the strings, shock fills my face. It's a song I recognise instantly. The first song she'd ever written, and it's about us. About how we will always be together, by each other's side. As she's about to sing the first word, she pauses and looks straight at me. Pride rages through me. Then, before my eyes, she disappears into her own world, and it's mesmerising to watch. Her voice starts out low and soft then when the raw emotion hits, the crowd stops and takes notice. I don't see anyone looking anywhere but at Marci and pride rages through me.

"Holy fuck!" someone comments to my right. I glance over and see the man who'd been looking at me a few minutes earlier. Only the words didn't come from him. They came from his friend beside him. "You hearing this, Nate?" he says apparently unaware that everyone is hearing it.

"Yeah, Ryan. I hear it," he answers. His voice is deep and raspy. But as my focus moves back and forth from Marci to the men on my right watching her, I realise Nate isn't watching her at all. His lids are lowered forcing his vision south, away from the staging area.

As I watch the scene before me, I choose to back step; standing behind the crowd somehow makes me feel safer. I start to relax when my back meets the wall. I can see Marci and know that nobody is watching me. I breathe out quietly, wanting to merge into the background but to keep the perfect view of my friend and all that are taken in by her voice.

When Marci sings the last word and plays the final note, a silence follows before the deafening sound of applause and whistling erupts. I join her in grinning and watch her bow and blow a kiss right in my direction.

Then, without wanting it, heads turn in my direction. My shoulders hunch forward, and all I want to do is disappear within the bricks behind me. Feeling those same eyes on me again, I can't help but glance up. Sure enough he... Nate is watching me. His friend says something to him, causing Nate to narrow his eyes in return. Then without warning, his friend makes his way towards me. Nate looks at the floor, then rubs his hand over the nape of his neck before he follows.

I search for Marci, hoping to god she's on her way over. Thankfully she is.

"Well?" she says with a lift of her brow when she reaches me.

"You're seriously doubting yourself now?" I shake my head, suddenly having to hold back tears. "I love that goddamn song, Marci!"

"That's why I sang it, Gin."

I take a step forward and wrap my arms around her shoulders, pulling her to me. I hear her voice hitch at the shock of the contact, and it only makes me squeeze harder. "Thank you," I whisper in her ear.

She draws back and looks deep into my eyes. "I'd do it ten times over to get this reaction." A repeated cough causes us to turn in the direction of the sound.

"Sorry to interrupt but... well... you kind of blew me away." The man who was taken with Marci's performance leans towards Marci and holds out his hand. "You were great! Um, I'm Ryan."

Marci's face lights up in delight, and it feels good to see her happy. She lifts her hand to his and provides him with a full on smile, loving the praise. "Marci," she replies before she nods in my direction. "And this is Ginny."

Ryan briefly glances my way in acknowledgement, and I force a smile.

"This is Nate." Ryan nods indicating the man standing slightly behind him. I keep my smile in place and pluck up the courage to look across at Nate.

"H-hello." I manage to stutter on my word of greeting and inwardly cringe at my pitiful response.

"Hey," he replies before looking down, then away. He tucks his hands into his pockets and flexes his muscles on his forearm as though it's a strain standing here. Although his body is facing me, he twists his neck and looks over the room. It's hard not to miss the tensing of his jaw.

Clearly, I'm not the person he wants to be standing with on a Saturday night. I get it. Of course I do. He's standing there because his friend is here, but it's hard not to take the knock when he can barely look at me for longer than a second. I glance around awkwardly, noticing Marci and Ryan deep in conversation. I don't want to break them up, but nor do I want to stand here facing a ticking jaw.

I notice a girl approach, the kind of girl that men like Nate will do more than say 'hey' to and turn away from. Her eyes are hooked on Nate. She's a few inches taller than me and steps in between us, obscuring my view. I exhale, instantly feeling relief.

Leaning towards Marci, I mutter, "I'm going to get a drink." Then I set off towards the bar, grateful for the easy escape, but loathing that I feel so out of place. I never used to. One hot, brooding guy and I'm wishing for invisibility, or maybe it's safety.

Shaking my head, I make my way straight to one of the pillars on the side of the bar and slink back against it. With one arm on the bar, I stand sideways on, ready to gain eye contact with the barman but take a moment to control my breathing.

"Hey!" I hear Marci call as she reaches me. "What was that about?" she asks. "What did he say?" She looks back confused.

"He didn't say anything, Marci." That's the point. I expect my voice to sound snarly, but instead, it comes out sad, which surprises me.

"Damn, Ginny, I wish you could see what I do when I look at you..." her voice trails off as a look of sorrow covers her face. "You're hot! Always have been. Fact. If anyone deserves some fun right now, it's you, and he looked—"

"Uninterested. Which is fine by the way."

"Uninterested wouldn't be my label. He couldn't take his eyes off you earlier. Perhaps he's nervous. You ever think of that?" I huff out a laugh. He most definitely was *not* nervous.

"So?" Ryan slides up to Marci. "That drink?" he interrupts.

She glances at me with a look of apology before responding. "Thanks, but not tonight. Some other time?"

"Oh, um, right!" He acts shocked at her turning him down. Marci picks up on it too as she rolls her eyes at me, fighting a grin. "You're sure you don't want a drink?" Ryan seriously isn't a guy that's used to being turned down.

"I'm sure," Marci replies, hooking her arm around mine. I look away accepting the blame.

"Well, I'll be over at the other end of the bar if you change your mind," he adds with disappointment in his tone.

"Why did you say no?" I ask once he's moved away.

"Are you kidding? I'm not dropping you for some random bloke I've never met before."

"Oh really? Since when?" I challenge light-heartedly.

"Since I lost you, Ginny."

The comment stuns and annoys me at the same time.

"No. I'm not going to be the excuse," I say through pressed lips. "You can't make me the excuse, Marci."

"Come on, let's go." She steps away from the bar, trying to pull me with her, but with a glance at our joined arms, something starts to stir within me. What happened didn't only happen to me. It happened to Marci too, and even now, the collateral damage continues. Although the sacrifice may seem small, it's still a sacrifice—only this was my mess. No burden should have been placed on Marci.

I stand up straight, ignore her gentle tug and lift my free hand, gaining the attention of the barman. When he approaches, I order us both a drink.

"Ginny—"

I throw her a determined stare. "We're staying."

"I—"

"We're staying." Again I interrupt.

"Okay," she replies with a nod of her head. I give my attention back to the barman as he hands me the drinks in exchange for the money. I pass Marci's drink over and take a step away from the bar. "And when you've had this drink. You're going over there to talk to him!"

"Ginny—"

I hold my hand up to silence her. "That's what you would have done before, so that's what you're going to do tonight."

"But—"

"No, Marci," I shout before deciding to lower my voice. "This has gone on long enough."

She smiles. "Okay, boss, but you have to start believing that hot guys *do* want to do more than stare at you." I shrug by way of appeasing her but know this particular hot guy may stare but most definitely does not want to do more than that. He's no doubt thinking what a jittering freak I am.

The room starts to quieten as the next singer is announced. "I'm off to the ladies room," I say to Marci. She nods then moves a few steps away to catch a better look at the artist. At first, I don't recognise the tune because it's with a slower tempo, but the second the voice comes over the speaker, I freeze, no longer able to move. A tightness spreads across my chest as the familiar song thrusts me back in time.

I see him and his frozen glare, the one that could cripple me within a second.

I'd been making a drink... *he* wanted a drink. I hadn't been aware that he was listening to the radio, to this song. The kettle started boiling and he could no longer hear the music.

A pathetic whimper leaves my mouth. I find myself leaning onto the bar, my spine weakening as I grip onto the edge as my knuckles turn white from the strength of my hold.

Licking my lips, I swallow, then move away. Stumbling, I collide into a couple, then mumble my apologies, still hearing the song that reminds me so much of him.

I want to retreat into silence... anywhere but here.

Bypassing the toilet, I push on the side exit door and keep moving, gulping at the fresh air, desperate to catch a breath. My whole body is shaking. I rush forward, seeking a place away from others.

When I reach a wall set back from the car park, I stop and dip my head, resting my forehead on the coolness of the bricks.

I have to do better than this. He's gone, but he's still managing to control my every turn. I hold back a scream because the only person that needs to hear it is no longer here. Imagining his laughter, the type of laugh he did the moment right before he'd lash out, causes me to cower even more. I close my eyes, trying to block out the memories but even then, he's still there, lurking like the unwanted devil.

He's won. No matter what I do, where I go, who I see, he will always be there. Always.

A lone tear lands on my cheek, and I quickly swipe it away despising myself for still being so affected by my past.

Slowly, I turn round so my back is against the wall, but I jolt when I see somebody standing in the shadows. A gradual movement brings him into the subtleness of the streetlight. Nate. I stare at him, confused, wondering why he's here. My hands splay to the wall behind me, my heart rate increases, and I know I'm back to fear again. Then he drops his chin to his chest as though he can't bear to look at me.

"Don't be scared." His words are spoken softly.

"What do you want?" I challenge defensively.

He holds his hands up like he's trying to reassure me. "I saw you come outside."

"So?" He could barely muster more than the word 'hello' five minutes ago.

"You looked..." His voice trails off and doesn't finish his sentence. But he doesn't need to because I know what I looked like. "I wanted to make sure you were okay."

"Well, I'm fine," I lie as he continues to look at me, and I know he recognises my untruth. With his hands still up, he takes a stride back, recognising that one wrong move could mean I'm liable to run or break.

"When a woman says they're fine, it usually means they aren't."

"I said I was fine. Which means I'm fine." I am not fine. I look at the ground in shame, broken, and with no idea what else to say. I shift my focus and see his feet still standing in the same position.

"I'm sorry... for being rude in there. Ryan has this habit of trying to hook me up, and sometimes it's not what I'm after..." His voice fades, and I glance back up at him.

"It's an understandable reaction." In more ways than one.

Then he frowns. "I didn't mean you aren't what I'm after." He scrapes his hand through his hair appearing flustered. "Nor did I mean you aren't. Shit, look, I'm sorry. I just came out here to check you were alright. And we've already established that you're fine. So you'll be okay?" His voice is soft, his concern sounding genuine, and I realise that perhaps I've misjudged him.

I nod my head, and he pushes his hands into the pockets of his jeans before he turns away, then hesitates. "I'm sorry," he says clearly with his back to me.

"I said it was fine," I answer, my lack of tolerance towards my behaviour annoying me even more.

He glances over his shoulder and looks me straight in the eye. "No, I'm sorry for whatever it is that must have happened to you."

Then he walks away leaving me to stare after him.

"Ginny?" I hear Marci approach from behind me. "What are you doing out here?" I blink hard as I turn around. "You said you were going to the toilet." Her focus moves behind me as she spies Nate before she raises an eyebrow at me. "So? Believe me now?"

"What?"

"Well, it doesn't take a genius to work out why you are both out here?" Her eyes almost pop out of her head. "Christ, did I scare him off?"

"No." I force a smile before looking back, but he's already out of sight. "You didn't." That would have been down to me. "Trust me, he's not interested." If some stranger can tell how messed up I am, I've got to do a better job at pulling myself together.

"At least he's not an axe murderer," she adds sensing my reduced mood. "Every cloud and all that!"

I smile, even let out a little laugh. "Come on. Let's go back inside," I say with the intention of only staying for one more drink. Tonight's been eventful enough.

CHAPTER TWELVE

NATE

*W*hen I get to my car and climb inside, I stare straight ahead. A couple walk by before getting into their own car. Others pass through, using it as a shortcut to more bars on the street beyond.

Shit! I hang my head on the steering wheel, confusion clouding my mind. *Why am I here? Why am I doing this?*

The answer lies with the woman who I can't get out of my head. Her eyes are beautiful, there's no denying it, but the pain that's embedded in every single fleck tears at my already goddamn shredded heart. In that one second, it's like an arrow shot straight to my chest, and it still feels like it's rotating around in there. But not only is she sad, she's angry.

It was like looking in a mirror.

What's surprised me the most, is the reaction she's created within me. I didn't just see her pain, I felt a need, a desire to take it all away but that's goddamn insane, isn't it?

Damn it! I slam my hand on the steering wheel, unable to get her haunted eyes out of my head.

I push the key into the ignition, and the engine roars to life.

I pull out of the car park and start to drive away but can't help check the rear view mirror. I know she won't be there because it's impossible to see that particular bar from here but I look nonetheless. Just in case.

With a sigh, I sink back into the seat, ready for the half hour journey it takes to get to my parents' house.

Olly's going to go mental when I tell him what I've done tonight. He already thinks I'm verging on the edge of insanity. I'm beginning to think he may be right.

"Shit!" I mutter out loud. *What the hell am I doing?*

I spend the rest of the journey trying to answer that exact question, but the answer refuses to be found.

When I get to the house, I cut the engine and look up. Other than the landing light being on, the house is in darkness, which means they're all in bed. I breathe a sigh of relief. They don't need to see me like this—my thoughts twisted, my head all fucked up. All they need is the strong version of me, not the side that's ready to crumble to the ground.

My head falls back on the headrest, and I can't help but think about how wrong this entire situation is. I wanted to meet her once. That was it. I've done that now. I've watched her, and finally tonight we spoke.

It's clear that she is changing. The change is gradual, but it's definitely there. So now, I should walk away. That had been the intention after all.

In the silence of the night, the sound of my phone ringing scares the crap out of me. Quickly I answer it, expecting for it to be heard from inside of the house, which is stupid because there are a hundred yards and a brick wall between us.

"Yeah," I answer the phone to Olly, expecting a barrage of questioning.

"Hey. Thought I'd give you a call, let you know that

everything at the gym was fine." At weekends, when I'm out of town, my friends Olly and Shannon, his wife, look after the gym for me. Well, all they need to do is be present. I make sure all the work is completed when I'm there during the week.

"Thanks, man," I reply then drum my fingers on the edge of the dash in wait.

"What you up to?"

"Nothing much." Which right now is the truth.

"So where are you?"

I exhale heavily. "I'm parked up outside my parents' house."

"Outside? You been out?"

"Yeah. Just got back." There's a silence, and I know what it means.

"You saw her again, didn't you?" When I don't answer, he continues talking. "Look, Nate, Shannon's worried about you, well, about this entire situation."

"Your wife is the one that's worried?" I know that isn't the case. If anything Shannon's the one that gets why I needed to do this in the first place. "Why don't you put her on the phone, and I'll reassure her."

"Well, she's, erm, already in bed."

"So, Shannon's the one that's worried, yet she's in bed, and you're the one making the call?" I drag my fingers through my hair roughly. "Look, Olly, I went out to see a mate and now I'm home. It doesn't need to be complicated." We both know it's as complicated as it gets. "We're back tomorrow night as normal. Okay?"

"Right," he says with a sigh.

"Oh and, Olly, thanks."

"For what?"

"The gym... this phone call... I get why you're doing it, but we're good."

"What do you think your brother would think?"

Pain shoots through my chest at the mention of him. I have no choice but to mumble goodbye and hang up. Face the fact that I'll never know what he thinks, ever again.

I get out of the car and make my way to the house, entering as quietly as possible so as not to wake anyone.

Gently, I tread up the stairs and come to a stop outside Sophia's room. I frown when I see the door shut. She doesn't like it closed—they should know that. So I turn the doorknob gently, and the glow from the lamp on the landing casts a beam of light into her room. I walk in and watch her, as soft, delicate breaths seep in and out of her mouth. A familiar ache sweeps across my chest causing me to stoop before lowering myself to the carpeted floor.

Her small childlike hand hangs over the edge of the bed. The nail polish I applied to her fingers only a few days ago has started to chip away, but she won't mind. As long as some colour remains. Reaching out, I gently take her hand in mine, careful not to disturb her. The fear that somehow I'm going to fuck this up starts to bubble away in my gut. That I'm not who she needs. I'm not who she signed up for. But knowing there's no way I could give her up either. She worked her way into my heart from the second I set eyes on her, and I know I'll do all I can to do right by her.

As my lids start to feel heavy, I recognise how tiring life has become. Sitting up on my knees, I place a kiss on her forehead before standing fully and making my way to my old bedroom. It's been redecorated since I lived here, the colours more neutral because my parents didn't expect that I'd be living with them every weekend. None of us did.

I sink down on the single bed, hearing it squeak under my weight. It's barely big enough for me, but it wouldn't matter if it were a super-king size. Sleep is usually restless no matter where I am. Changing the bed won't alter the likelihood of a nightmare waking one of us.

I pray like I do every night that Sophia's the one who gets the reprieve.

CHAPTER THIRTEEN

GINNY

I'm running late, which means Marci will be standing waiting for me. I step around two strangers who seem to have more time to spare than me.

Oh crap! I see her slightly ahead, in our usual meeting place, so quickly pick up my pace and approach with apologies ready to flow.

"I'm sorry—"

"Don't worry about it." She cuts me off sounding strangely pleased.

Glancing at her, I frown. "Don't worry about it? Who are you and what have you done with my normally-so-vocal friend?"

She stops walking, as do I. "The old you used to be late. So if you want to be late, Ginny, I couldn't be happier."

"Oh." I grow silent at the mention of my past, but I instantly push it to the back of my mind choosing to forget and move on. "Well, we should still get moving." I can't say Carrie will be overly pleased if I show into work late.

Then she smiles, but it's a different smile to the ones I've seen from Marci recently. It's free and honest. She proceeds to wrap her arm around my shoulder. "I reminded you of how you'd changed, how he'd changed you, and you didn't sink into that abyss that reminders of him usually create, Ginny. Instead of looking back into the past, you saw it as a chance to see today. Right now, this day… it's a goddamn good day."

"Come on, let's turn that mush switch off and get to work." We steer around the corner and make our way closer into town.

"So, Saturday night. You had fun right?" She queries.

I've not seen Marci since Saturday. She left me in peace, other than the odd text, so I had a quiet day yesterday.

"I think some of us may have had more fun than others," I say raising my eyebrows. I went home not long after my freak-out episode that Nate happened to witness. Marci, on the other hand, stayed out until the early hours with Ryan.

"Talking of fun. Have you heard from Nate?"

I'd stop walking, but as I'm in a rush to get to work, I pacify myself with a look of disapproval. "Why would I have heard from him? We spoke maybe two words." A slight miscalculation but not too far from the truth.

"Every time I looked in his direction, he was watching you. Apparently, he owns his own gym. Which would explain his huge presence." She lifts her arms trying to mimic big muscles but not coming anywhere close.

"You appear to know a lot about him. You suddenly changed your point of interest?"

"Damn, girl, no! Besides Nate was clearly interested in you."

"Marci." I sigh.

"When he's back in town, we should all meet up."

Her comment makes me stop in my tracks, and someone walks into the back of me.

"Oh God, sorry," I mumble apologising as they step around me, providing me with only a scowl.

"Watch where you're going in future!" Marci calls after them.

"That was my fault," I say, and she grins.

"Yes, because I was talking about Nate!" We set off walking again, me being more mindful this time not to disturb anyone's path.

I want to tell Marci that I'm not ready for anything like that when her hopeful expression shines back at me. *Today's a good day.* That's what she said. So I shun my original thought and go with what's actually causing some intrigue. "Back in town? He doesn't live here?"

"No, apparently he comes back to see family every weekend."

"Let's leave it as a maybe," I say to appease her. I shouldn't let myself think about him anyway. I'm certainly not a girl Nate would normally think of approaching. On Saturday night he saw a woman, loaded with fear, run. He saw me too clearly that night. I'm positive he won't be in a rush to be around me again.

"Anything planned for next Saturday night?"

I sigh heavily this time. "Really?" I query looking across at her. "Is this going to become a regular thing?"

"Yes, Ginny." She rolls her eyes. "Early nights and evenings watching television are for old people." Her eyes twinkle with excitement. "Come on. It's good for you. Admit it."

I smile, faintly knowing that as annoying as it is, Marci is probably right. Sitting indoors, alone, gives me time to ponder on the past when I'm trying desperately to move on from it.

Glancing at the window as we approach Coffeeroma the 'Open' sign is already on display. "Crap!" I utter. It's my job to open up, which means I'm definitely late. "I gotta go. I'll catch you later." I've only been working here four weeks. I'm not ready to be given the push yet when I'm just starting to find my feet.

"Later, Ginny and remember to tell Carrie this is a good

thing, you being late." I roll my eyes and push open the door. "I'm so sorry," I shout out my apologies as I near Carrie.

"Not a problem, just don't make a habit of it!"

"I won't."

Ben, the other waiter, taps his finger on his watch. "Tut, tut, tut! Little Miss Perfect isn't so perfect after all!"

"Thought I'd make you look good for a change," I say with a shrug of my shoulders. Hearing laughter, I turn to Carrie who's staring at us both with amusement. Confused, I look back at Ben who's also smiling.

"She's glad to know you are *actually* alive in there," Ben states. The comment stings, but I force a smile to my lips.

"Back to work, Ben," Carrie says, but it sounds more like a reprimand. She then retreats into the back.

I try not to dwell on what Ben thinks of me. Instead, I set about ensuring all of the machines are on and the tables set for the customers.

The morning passes in a bit of a blur. My mind not quite landing on the tasks set in front of me. I don't want people to see how I feel, yet Carrie and Ben have highlighted that I've been unable to hide it, and it's hard not to feel frustrated with myself.

The espresso machine finishes pouring the drink in front of me. So I add the cup to the tray with the rest of table four's drinks on and take them over. Once I've checked they have everything they ordered, I wipe a table clean and take the empty cups back to be washed.

I vaguely hear the jingle of the door as another customer walks through. Distractedly, I look over my shoulder but pause when I see who it is.

Nate. I can't help but stare at him as he approaches,

somewhat apprehensively while looking around the café. I stand still in wait, hoping he's forgotten who I am.

"You work here?" he asks once he reaches the counter. Clearly not forgotten.

The vulnerability I felt on Saturday night returns with full force, so I simply nod.

"Sorry, stupid question," he adds softly as he briefly looks to my uniform. "Erm, I came for a coffee."

"Do you want a take-out or a table?" I question. *Please say take out.* I plead silently.

"Um, a table I guess," he replies, and I try not to let my face show disappointment. Nate saw me at a time when I was showing how weak and damaged I am, and it makes me uncomfortable. Feeling vulnerable and exposed, I sidle past him, aiming to at least do my job in his company. Briefly, I glance over my shoulder to check he's following and he is. He gives me a brief smile, so I narrow my eyes before turning back around.

Once he reaches the table, he sits down.

"Here's the menu." I try to hand it over, but he leaves it hanging. "Or do you know what you'd like?"

"Ginny." I lower the menu at the mention of my name because I'm surprised he remembered it. "Saturday night. I'm sorry if I was out of order." I drop my focus, wishing he'd stop talking but he doesn't. "I spoke out of place."

"You didn't, and it's fine," I mumble wishing he'd forget that he ever saw me how he did. The hint of a smirk touches his lips, and I know it's because I said the word 'fine'. Since when did a man know what fine meant? "Is it a coffee?" I ask, hoping he answers easily.

I watch as his lips part with the drawing in of breath before he leans back in his seat. *Why is he taking so long to answer?*

"You about to get the third degree for talking to a customer?" He tilts his head to the side, his vision briefly crossing to the counter, so I look in that direction and catch Carrie and Ben staring in our direction. *Great! Exactly what I need when I'm actually making progress with them.* Instead of allowing them to see my more vulnerable side, I remember where I am, and while Ben and Carrie look on in intrigue, I force myself to act stronger than I did on Saturday.

"So the drink?"

He winces. "No small talk, hey? It's okay. I get it. Some strange man talks to you on Saturday. Well, when I say talk, I mean blatantly acts like an absolute idiot when you are introduced. I'm sorry about that. I could try and explain, but I'm mumbling enough as it is. So, yes, a coffee would be great. Black, no frills."

"No problem." Before I have chance to move away, he starts to talk again.

"Ginny." Again it feels strange to hear him say my name. "It's quiet." He lifts his hand and rubs the back of his neck. "I-I don't suppose you fancy a coffee?" I stare at him. Just stand and stare. Why would he ask *me* for a coffee and look so ill at ease doing it? He stops rubbing his neck and instead, clasps his hands together on the table, giving the impression that he's nervous, which in itself is ridiculous.

"Pardon?" I say, wondering now if I heard correctly.

"A coffee?" His eyebrows pull together, then he judders his head. "You can say no. I thought that maybe... Sorry, you're busy now, but perhaps some other time. Or not." What the hell? He *is* nervous. Why would he be on edge around someone like me?

I take a quick look around me, wondering if Marci's lurking in the background somewhere, having put him up to this, but all I notice are two girls, I'm guessing in their late teens, waiting for their take-out, openly gawping at Nate. When I glance back to Nate, he's still waiting for me to answer, not paying any attention to the girls who are vying for his attention.

"I'll go fetch your drink," I mutter. He reclines back in his seat on an exhale, and I walk away, trying to maintain an air of calm, which is damn hard when I feel like his eyes are on me the entire ten yards it takes to get back behind the counter. I raise my brows to Carrie and Ben who are openly staring at my approach. Ignoring them, I collect a cup and tray to make his drink, keeping my back to them and ignoring the sound of laughter that starts to come from the girls at the counter, Ben clearly managing to work his magic with them.

In a second, Carrie is at my side.

"Who the hell is that? I've not seen a tight arse like that for years! They change you know, the older you get. Start to sag and droop. What I wouldn't give to get my hands on that set of steely buns!"

"Nice!" I reply sarcastically as I pour out Nate's coffee from the filter machine.

"So who is he?" Carrie continues enthusiastically.

"His name is Nate."

"Nate," Ben puffs out as he goes to the coffee machine I'm not using. "Sounds like a bug."

"Oh!" Carrie teases. "Are we not checking your arse out today, Ben? Feeling a little left out." She nods her head and winks behind her to the young girls. "You get plenty of attention, stop sulking."

As I place Nate's hot cup on the tray, I stare at it, and a thought pops into my head. Carrie could do me a huge favour. I push the tray towards her. "Be my guest." I nod to the drink. She grins and without hesitation, takes the coffee over to Nate's table.

I turn away and breathe a sigh of relief, but the reprieve is only for a second. Once Ben has finished serving, he comes to stand in front of me.

"What's going on?" he asks looking at Nate and back to me.

"Nothing."

"What did you do? Give him your number, and he never called you back?"

"Do I look like a girl that gives people her number?" I ask truthfully.

"Did he give you his number?"

"Christ, Ben, no numbers were exchanged."

His eyes fix in Nate's direction. "Well, he's damn nervous about something. He asked you out yet?"

I stare at him astounded. "Will you stop?"

"Well, little Miss Lady of Mystery, it looks like he's not quite done with you." My head darts to the side, and I see Nate approach.

"Is there something else we can help you with?" Ben interjects when Nate comes to stand in front of me.

Nate's gaze slowly hovers over Ben. There's something in Nate's eyes that seems to warn Ben off, but Ben appears unaffected as he stands his ground. I see Nate's jaw harden and wonder what the silent look means that's passing between the two of them.

Then Carrie sails past me, nudging Ben from his fixed position. "Table one asked for their bill five minutes ago, Ben. I think Ginny has it covered here." Ben hesitates before grumbling under his breath as Carrie turns on her charm to Nate. "You got five minutes with her, sugar, so treat her nice, or I'll set Ben on you. Not that I'm sure you can't handle him." She adds as she twirls in front of me with a wink.

"Carrie—"

"Five minutes, Ginny." She raises her eyebrows and mouths the word 'go'.

Once again, we're left alone, and for some reason, the confident façade I'd managed only seconds earlier starts to dwindle under his watchful scrutiny.

He frowns. "I should have asked for the coffee to go." His eyes continue to hold me as he pulls out some money from his wallet and places it on the counter. "Thanks." His lips don't quite close, and I wait, believing he's not quite finished with what he wants to say.

But then with a smile that any normal girl would go nuts over, he turns and walks out of the café, leaving his coffee behind. *Normal girl.* My heart sinks because I know that's something I'll never be again.

I stare after him as he crosses over the road and walks a few yards further before getting into a white car. I've no idea what kind of car it is, all I know is his arms are now draped over the steering wheel, and he's facing forward.

"Surely you didn't send him on his way?" Carrie whispers in my ear.

"Excuse me?" I answer, crossing my arms over my chest.

"You must be crazy, girl, saying no to a man like that!"

I blurt out a laugh and face my boss. "What have I said no to?"

"He asked you out. That's what he came for."

"No, he came for a coffee."

"A coffee that he didn't even drink." She raises her eyebrows as she empties Nate's full cup of coffee down the sink. "Now I know my coffee, Ginny, and ours is the damn finest in this town. So he did not come in here for the coffee. That man came in here specifically to see you. I'm telling you, Ginny, your hot man radar needs a service. He came here for you." She shakes her head and grins. "And you sent him away. You know you've piqued his interest even more now?"

I look at the empty cup before glancing outside. He couldn't have come here for me. Why would he?

He's still sitting in the same position when a 'coffee to go' is slid under my nose. "Take him that."

"What?" I swing round to Carrie.

She nods to the cup. "He paid for a coffee. He should have a coffee. Go now before he drives away."

"But, Carrie…" She pushes her hands to her hips like she's squaring up to me.

"But, Carrie what? Girl, you need some fun in your life. I've seen those big beautiful, sad brown eyes of yours stay the same dull shade. That man put a little light in there, and you aren't even aware of it, are you?" She shakes her head. "I don't know what happened to you, Ginny, but whatever or whoever you're mourning, they can't take all of you. Now go and take him that coffee, it's an order."

Ben comes to stand in front of me, adding a passing scowl to Carrie, before focusing on me with an expression filled with pity. "I'll take it, Ginny." But I keep my hands on the coffee. Do I want to be the girl that forever feels like the weakest link or should I take a simple walk across the road and do my job. With the phrase 'in mourning' bouncing around in my head, I know what the answer is… *not to be in mourning!*

With my heart hammering in my chest. I step around Ben and head out of the door. When there's a lull in the traffic, I move closer, then he notices me and almost leaps out of the car.

"Ginny? What is it?" He starts to dig about in his pocket. "Did I not leave enough—"

He quietens when I hold up the coffee. "To go," I explain.

A car sounds his horn as it passes behind me. Nate quickly reacts, placing his hand gently on my elbow he guides me closer to the path, away from the main flow of traffic.

"You didn't have to do that."

"I kind of did. Carrie," I signal to the coffee shop, "my boss, asked me to."

"Oh," he replies sounding disappointed. Why did I say that? Because I'm goddamn dumb at this stuff! I look over my shoulder with a grimace at the café and see Ben averting his gaze as he wipes a table back and forth near the window.

"Well, thanks," he says, and I turn back to face him. "Maybe I'll see you around sometime."

"Maybe," I respond. Then I check the traffic, and even though there's time for me to cross, I hesitate, knowing Nate still hasn't got back in his car. Whether it's the need to prove to everyone, including myself, that I'm doing alright or whether for the first time I want to do something for myself, I peer over my shoulder. "About that coffee, it sounds good." Then I walk calmly over the road when what I really want to do is dance. Carrie's right. Blake cannot take all of me. There has to be some left. I just have to figure out how to find it. Right this second as I walk back into the shop, I've never felt as close.

CHAPTER FOURTEEN

NATE

I got back over an hour ago, and so far all I've done is sit and stare at the paperwork that's scattered out in front of me. I took on another member of staff at the gym a couple of months ago to free up more of the daylight hours for paperwork, leaving me with evenings and weekends free for Sophia. So far, it's been working well. Except for today, when my unplanned outing has left me with something or someone else on my mind and now a backlog of paperwork to sort through.

My phone vibrates on the desk with Ryan's name showing up on screen. Picking it up, I pin the phone between my shoulder and ear, freeing my hands to try and organise the papers into some kind of order.

"Hey, Ryan, what can I do for you?"

"I think my friend, you mean what can *I* do for you?"

With that, I lean back in my chair and for now, ignore the unorganised scattering of bills, intrigue taking over. "Go ahead."

"Next weekend, you're back right?" Ryan's aware I only visit at weekends. This morning was an exception, a craze-fuelled exception. "The girl from Saturday, Marci the singer, she wants to meet up, and she's going to bring her friend."

Immediately, I sit up and pay attention. "I mean, I'm up for a threesome, but I don't think she had that in mind. You're still single right, so?"

Christ! Straight away I want to say yes, but I'm not sure it's the right thing to do. I shouldn't have gone today, nor should I have asked her out for a coffee, but it's damn hard to stop saying such things when she's around.

"Well?" Did Ginny actually agree to go? Before I have a chance to ask, Ryan continues. "Oh, and before you think of saying no. If you can't make it, I'll be asking Shawn to come instead?" *Fuck!* Involuntarily, I let out a groan and drag my fingers through my hair before rubbing the back of my neck. I've only met Shawn a handful of times, but he's not the kind of man Ginny needs introducing to which is exactly why Ryan made the comment.

"Does she know about this, Ryan?"

"Who, the friend?"

"Yeah, her friend, Ginny."

"I guess so. It was Marci's idea."

"I'll come," I say with a sigh. *What the hell am I doing?*

I hear him chuckle on the other end of the phone. "Thought so. Although not quite sure what took you so long, you clearly have a thing for this girl! She had you all worked up on Saturday."

I'm not about to explain myself to him when this entire situation is fucking with my own head. The only thing I'm certain of is that Shawn is not going anywhere near Ginny.

"We're meeting at Valentino's at eight."

"So you already said yes?"

"Of course. Why the hell would I say no to a girl like Marci? Did you see the rack on that? And, man, those lips! Oh Christ, what I picture her and that silky blonde hair wrapping itself around—"

"I've got it, Ryan!" I butt in causing him to laugh out loud.

"See you next week. Oh, and get a taxi for a change. Fed up of seeing you on soft drinks all night."

We end the call, and my stomach starts to churn. What have I agreed to? It feels like I'm walking into something I shouldn't, but the idea of standing back and allowing someone else to take her out doesn't sit well with me. It's clear as day that she's too wounded to be exposed to the wolves that Ryan hangs around with.

I drop my head into my hands as a knock sounds at the door. Peering up, I see Olly step into the office.

"Come in," I say sarcastically, and once again I sit back in my chair. I've been waiting for a visit from him. I'm surprised it took this long.

"Death by paperwork, is it?"

"Something like that," I answer.

"You get back last night?"

"We did," I reply somewhat curtly because I know I'm in for a grilling. He closes the door behind him, rests back against the frosted glass panel, crossing his muscular arms in front of him, proving he's a damn good advertisement for the gym. He shakes his head and looks around the open space of the office like he's searching for the right thing to say.

"Nate—"

"Olly, I know what I'm doing."

"You do?" he questions, knowing full well I have no idea what I'm doing, but the admission at least sounded good.

I lift my hand and rub at my temple. *Why does this have to be so complicated?*

"Perhaps you should concentrate on this place and on Sophia."

"Don't you dare make out as though she's not my priority!" Sophia takes precedence over everyone, and everything else and his flippant remark pisses me off.

"That's not what I said." At least he has the decency to look apologetic.

I pull my lip in with my teeth and stare at Olly. Should I be listening to him and walking away? It doesn't feel right. This pain, the loss, it all had to have happened for a reason, and if I break all contact, I might never know what that reason was. Whatever this is, it doesn't feel finished. I'm not ready to walk away. I drag my fingers back and forth over my scalp wishing I could clear this haze that's been lurking around since our lives changed.

"You wanna go lift some weights?" I peer up at him. "And punch shit?" he adds with a grin.

"Yeah," I say breathing out heavily. "I do." The paperwork can wait until tomorrow. I have an hour before I need to pick Sophia up from school, which will give me enough time to work off some of this frustration. I get up from the chair and walk over to him. He opens the door and clasps my shoulder as I walk past.

"The mums still hoarding around you like flies to shit?" He laughs.

"You're seriously referring to me like a piece of shit right now?" I close the door behind Olly and lock up before we set walking to the main gym downstairs.

"Your brother would have loved to have seen that."

I don't pass comment because the fact that I am walking in his footsteps makes me feel nothing but guilt that I'm the lucky son of a bitch who gets to do it when he no longer can.

I swerve into a space a few hundred yards from the school gates. I see other kids already leaving, so I jump out of the car and jog to the playground. Goddamn traffic. I'll have to leave work ten minutes earlier from now on. When my eyes land on her, I see the relief on her face, and it almost tears me apart.

She runs straight over to me, and I tug on her blonde ponytail. My skills in the hair department are steadily improving although it's a little weathered looking now from the activities of her day. "Hey, kid. Good day?"

"Yep. Jack asked me to be his girlfriend today, but I said no," she says with a shrug. Her response surprises me because I know how much she talks about Jack.

"You said no?"

"Yep. I am ONLY nine years old, Nate."

"True, very true. You're also the best nine year old on this planet, Sophia and don't ever forget that! Come on." I put my hand gently on her shoulder and ease her around to head out of the school gates.

At the sound of a loud groan coming from Sophia, I turn to look in the direction she's staring and immediately recognise why. One of the kid's mum is fast approaching. Penny... Penny... I struggle to remember her surname. She's taken an interest in me, but it's not one that's reciprocated.

"Say no!" Sophia whispers.

"She hasn't asked anything yet," I mutter through tight lips.

Penny steps directly into my path, forcing me to stop dead. "Hi, Nate. How are you?" Her voice is too sing-song and irritates the hell out of me. She's practically blocking the path but acts unaware, or perhaps that's her purpose.

"I'm good, Penny, you?" I reply stepping aside, giving others room to pass.

Her lips spread into a smile, and I see a trace of red lipstick on her teeth. She reaches up and brings a section of her hair so it hangs over her shoulder. I used to dig girls with long hair, lately not so much. "I'm great, thanks. I was wondering if Sophie would like to come and play with Grace one night after school. It'll save you having to finish work early. It must be hard having to do all of this on your own." Her little spiel immediately pisses me off. And it's goddam Sophia!

"That's very kind, but I don't leave work early. My hours are suited to our life. Nor is it hard, hey kiddo?" I put my hand on Sophia's shoulder and tug her towards me, and her little face lights up. This kid will never be seen as an inconvenience. I'm going to make damn sure of it.

"Oh, of course. Well, if you let me know when is suitable. Here's my number. Call me *anytime* for *anything!*" She hands me a neatly folded piece of paper, and it falls open as I take it. In fancy, swirly writing is her name and mobile number.

Sophia pulls at my waist, indicating she's ready to go home. "Thanks, Penny." We walk out of the school gate. I point to where the car's parked, and we make our way over. My hand falls to my side, and Sophia finds it straight away, enveloping her small hand in my much larger one. Without hesitation, I smile, but then immediately feel guilty for the second time today that *I* get to be the one lucky enough to hold her hand.

"She's so fake," Sophia says.

"Who? Penny?" I cast her a sideways glance and love the way her button nose is screwed up in dislike. "Since when did you start labelling people?"

With wide eyes she looks back at me with a 'you're kidding'

expression. "She shouts at Grace, but then with you, she flicks her hair and smiles. It's what you call fake, Nate. She's started wearing lots more makeup and bright red lipstick. She never used to when mummy…" Her delicate voice quietens, and I know the rest of the sentence was 'took me to school.'

We stop as we reach the car. Squatting down I put myself at her level. The familiar ache lurches in my chest seeing the heartbroken little girl stare back at me. "Sophia, you're allowed to remember your mum and your dad. I want you to, and I want you to talk about them as often as you like. Remember, I loved them too. Your mum, she was one of a kind." The corners of her lips lift in an attempt to smile.

"You always say that." Her smile grows.

"Because she was. She helped a lot of people, Sophia, a lot, and I couldn't be prouder of her." I squeeze her small hand, and she squeezes it back before I open the car door for her to get in. Then I walk round to the driver's side.

When I get in, her hands are on her knees, and she's looking down.

"Sophia?"

She twists to look at me, her lids lifting to reveal her big brown eyes that remind me so much of her mother's. "I know you're not my dad, Nate, but you're doing a really good job."

Her comment throws me, and all I can do is stare at her until my eyes start to mist over. Then I bite my teeth together and quickly turn away fighting to hide my emotion. "Thanks, Sophia." I choke the words out before I proceed to blink repeatedly so I can see clearly for the journey home.

CHAPTER FIFTEEN

GINNY

I stand, staring at the kettle as it starts bubbling to life, wishing that Marci would hurry up. Moments of quiet often lead to unease and a flashback of memories. Although I'm in a very different house and normally experience a sensation of safety, something's unnerving me today, and I can't put my finger on what.

Briskly, I rub my hands down my trouser leg to try and wipe away the clammy sensation that's taken over, before I take two cups from the cupboard. When my phone belts out its ringtone, a cup slips from my grasp and lands with a crash onto the worktop.

"Shit!" I breathe out heavily, then answer the call while glancing at the cup, surprised to see it isn't broken.

"Hello," I say, but all I'm greeted with is silence. "Hello?" I say again before glancing back at the screen to see if whoever it is has hung up, but the line appears still open and the words 'unknown number' stare back at me. Slowly, I bring the handset back to my ear, but I still don't hear a sound. Not a breath. Not a movement.

The memorable, eerie sensation returns and the temperature around me seems to drop.

"Who is this?" I question with mounting fear. A chill sweeps over my exposed neck, but I don't move, only force my now rapid breaths to quieten.

Still, nobody answers. Closing my eyes, I try to picture what's happening with some sense of reality. *There is nobody on the phone, it's... I don't know... some kind of missed call. But more than anything it is NOT Blake.* I rub at my neck vigorously to rid myself of this fearful feeling before pressing the end call button and dropping the phone to the side.

I lick my lips, trying to even out my breathing, and grip onto the worktop when in the corner of my vision, movement catches my attention. Jerking my focus up, I see Marci walking up the garden path. I've never felt so relieved to see anyone.

Some days I believe I'm actually doing alright and moving on with my life, then something happens, usually something minute, and it thrusts me back into the darkness he created. I have to keep visualising what is happening with reality. Blake died. He may have left me with a fear that will last a lifetime, but he can't actually hurt me. Not anymore.

"Hey!" Marci calls as she enters the house. "Don't you love Saturdays?" I swing around and smile, eternally gratefully for the intrusion. "The lock isn't on today," she points out as she closes the door.

I nod, but the only reason the door isn't locked is because she told me she was coming at one. Checking the time, I see that it's exactly that.

I continue to smile in her direction. "So, we're loving Saturdays?"

"Damn right. We both have the day off!"

I get back to making our drinks. "And we're going out tonight," I add to which Marci provides a strange smile causing a flash of confusion. "It's still on, right?"

"Of course it is."

I add the sugar to her cup, then hand it over, before making our way into the small living room that I've desperately been trying to make feel like home. We both collapse down on opposite sofas.

All rooms had been painted prior to me moving in, so I all I had to do was add a little furniture and personal touches. Slowly, I'm getting there.

When Blake died, I got everything. Every single penny. I limit myself to the amount of money I withdraw from the bank, taking only what is needed. I've not been extravagant.

I bought two *anthracite* grey fabric sofas. I didn't care what kind of grey the chairs were, but the sales assistant was set on emphasising the colour in every other sentence. The television is new and luckily came with its own unit. Then I purchased a bed. The bedroom already had fitted wardrobes and cabinets. Other than that, I've added lamps, the odd candle or ornament. The main thing is it feels like mine and most of the time I feel safe here.

"The white mice are back, I see?" Marci remarks before tossing the opened pack of chocolate mice over at me, managing to spill a few in the process.

"Back?" I bend down and pick them up, putting them beside the packet.

"I haven't seen you eat them in a while." Her voice fades as she disappears into some far off memory. "You used to get them every Saturday."

"I did." It was a tradition of mum's when I was a child that I continued into adulthood. We didn't exactly have a lot of money back then, but every Saturday we'd walk to the corner shop, and I'd be allowed to fill a paper bag with white mice. Blake hated any form of white chocolate. I can't even remember when it came to the point I no longer bought them.

We both stare at the bag of chocolate now perched on the arm of the chair. For once, I permit myself to imagine Blake here, in this very room. A stony, unimpressed expression would be fixed in place. He'd be less than amused at my choice of decoration for starters. He never saw the use of candles or pretty photo frames. But he'd be staring at the white mice in disgust. I don't know why he hated them so much?

Ripping open the bag, I take out a sweet and eat it deliberately slowly, savouring the taste before chucking one over to Marci.

She smiles. "I'm glad they're back."

"Me too." I grin, and for a while, I relish in the knowledge that he *has* gone. That I'm now free to do what I want.

Turning on the television, I pass the remote to Marci as I'm not fussed what's on, and I want to see if I can try and turn the pile of wool sitting beside me into something worth admiring.

Leaning over the arm of the chair, I collect everything I need. Settling the wool to my side, I pick up the knitting needles. Realising its gone quiet, I look over to Marci. She's staring at me as though I've suddenly broken out into song, which for her wouldn't be unusual but for me, it's rare, like extremely rare.

"What?" I probe.

Her eyes widen as her focus drops to the needles in my fingers. "You're knitting?"

"It's a hobby, Marci." I need something that calms and distracts me, and I think this is going to work. "My mum taught me, remember?" I add, in the hope that the mention of my mum will cause her to back off. Although when I say my mum taught me, I was never any good. She used to be so patient, but nothing I made ever lasted. The wool would somehow become undone.

"I know that, Ginny, but you were like eight at the time... You're knitting!" she repeats. It looks like not even my mum can help me now.

"I'm knitting," I confirm with confidence as I imagine my mum looking on at the scene from above with a gentle laughter ringing out. Not only at seeing Marci so stumped, but also because I'm trying my fingers at knitting *again*.

"You're twenty-four."

I nod my head and turn my attention to the task in hand, occasionally glancing up to the television, trying to avoid Marci's horrified expression. Only ten minutes ago I felt on the verge of a kind of nervous breakdown, now I'm desperately holding back laughter. It's amazing what the company of a friend can do.

"Okay." Out of the corner of my eye, I catch her shaking her head like she's dealing with shock or something. "It's fine," she utters, and I'm not sure if she's reassuring herself or giving permission for me to knit. Either way, it doesn't make a difference. I'm knitting, and that's all there is to it. Especially now it's created this response from her.

"So tonight, where do you fancy?" I question.

"Valentino's?" she says with another look at my hands. "What is it that you're making anyway?"

I have absolutely no idea. A week ago, I looked out of the window at work and saw the craft shop across the road so decided to take a look during my break. That night, when I came home, I unpacked the bag, picked up the needles and started. I look at... whatever it is I'm knitting and consider what it looks like. "It's going to be a blanket," I announce.

"A blanket?" Marci glances to the window. "It's almost summer."

"So I'll have it ready in time for winter."

"It's a good job we're off out tonight," she mutters to herself.

"Oh, and why is that?" I reply enjoying the mocking.

"Because you're turning into an old lady! That's why! And these things," she holds up the chocolate I threw to her, "they smell like puke!"

I chuckle at her comment before grabbing a handful of mice and shoving them in my mouth by way of defiance.

Marci looks at me like I'm steadily going crazy. Maybe I am. But then her lips break into a smile, matching my own and it feels damn good.

∼

As we walk together, her arm looped through mine, I know she's looking at me. I want to tug at the hem of my dress to make sure it hasn't ridden up while I walk. I'm desperate to take off the heels and put my flats back on, but I can't do any of those things because I'm trying to move forward with my life and because I'm twenty-four, goddamn it!

"I still can't believe... you look beautiful," Marci says apparently amazed.

With a kink in my brows, I glance sideways on at her. "You can't believe I look okay? Thanks for the vote of confidence, Marci," I say sarcastically.

"Didn't say okay, Ginny. I said beautiful, and it didn't come out right. I don't mean the dress, which by the way looks hot on you. You just look different."

"I'm trying to do better, that's all." We continue walking, our steps in time with each other's as a quietness falls over us.

After Marci left this afternoon, I glanced at the needles in my hands and considered what Blake would think of me. At first, I saw him laugh, amused at my choice of a hobby, but then I saw his mouth transform into a smug sneer believing even in his death, he was winning. I wasn't out shopping or having a drink with friends. No, I was nestled in safely behind closed doors. Alone. Knitting.

So I wrapped the wool up, tucked it back into the bag and walked upstairs with nothing but defiance starting to build. I had three hours until I needed to be ready, but I was going to make damn sure that tonight, I would *be* ready. Blake would want me to remain alone. He would loathe the fact that I was back home with Marci, but he no longer got to rule me with his clenched stern fist because its buried six feet underground.

Once I'd showered, painted my nails and buffed every part of me I could, I dredged up the guts and stood in front of the mirror. I was stunned by what I saw. I looked normal... like me. The old me.

I've put on a little weight, so I no longer look like the ghostly figure I did months ago. No one would ever know what's happened to me. The past... it could all disappear if I let it.

Then Marci arrived, and well, I've been fidgety ever since.

"Ginny, I'm up for you trying to do better as long as it doesn't come as a sacrifice."

"What do you mean?" I ask confused.

We both slow as we come to end of the road. Once we've

checked the coast is clear we cross over then come to a complete stop outside Valentino's. Marci glimpses inside and gently closes her eyes before returning her attention to me. "It's been three months, and I can't tell you how much I've missed you." She looks at her feet, uncertainty seeming to own her. "The fact that I'm starting to see my old friend again is amazing." Again she looks indoors.

"Marci?"

She steps directly in front of me so I have no choice but to return her gaze. "I don't have any idea what you went through, Ginny. Not really. I saw the bruises, but just because they've faded, it doesn't mean to say the damage has too."

"That kind of talk doesn't help my new outlook does it? Come on, this was supposed to drag me out of my old lady shoes, but all you're making me want to do is get back into the house, pick up those needles and shove chocolate mice into my mouth. You want me back in my old lady shoes?" I say it light-heartedly, but I'll try anything to move us away from the seriousness of my past.

Marci starts to shift on her feet. "I thought I was doing you a favour but after... well, after I've thought about it. I'm not sure that I am." She bites the corner of her lips and frowns.

"What is it?"

Again her focus steers indoors. "Don't freak out, okay?"

I twist my head to the side and narrow my eyes at her. "Why am I about to freak out?" I move my own attention to the inside of the restaurant but don't see any cause for Marci's strange behaviour.

"Just listen. Ryan wanted to take me out tonight. I explained I'd already made plans with you."

"Are you about to ditch me, Marci?" Because there's not a chance I'm going to sit and eat here alone.

"No, and it's not a big deal, I promise you. This isn't me

setting you up. This is me wanting to be with you." She hesitates. "We decided that Ryan could bring Nate along. As friends," she adds quickly.

"What?" I can tell my immediate reaction is one of shock by Marci's face. "You've set me up on a double date? With Nate?"

He'd mentioned a coffee, with a lot of hesitation, but it was a coffee, not a bloody date! I stare through the glass windows into the restaurant and search for them. I spy Nate straight away. He's looking directly at me.

I'm not ready for this. I hadn't prepared *for this!* It was supposed to be her and me.

"I could goddamn kill you right now," I seethe through my teeth then immediately regret my words. "I didn't mean that."

"I know, Ginny." She twists me round to face her. "This really isn't a big deal, if you don't make it into one. I'm the one that's put doubt in your mind. You were doing brilliantly before I went and opened my big mouth." I glance back at Nate who is now standing glaring at Ryan saying something that looks anything but polite. I'm guessing he didn't know about this either.

From somewhere off in the distance, I hear Blake's laughter, proving to me that he was right all along. That I would never be able to make it without him by my side.

Perhaps this is my chance to show that I can make it. That talking and dwelling on the past is something I am ready to move on from. When I face forward and witness Nate still on his feet, looking my way, I refuse to be the beaten, broken girl he saw last weekend.

"You owe me, Marci." I try to grab what dignity I have left, plaster an unaffected expression on my face and walk inside. Marci informs the waiter we're here, but I don't hang back like the shrinking wallflower everyone, including myself, believes me to be. I walk directly towards the table.

Nate's eyes don't leave mine, and it's difficult to gauge what he's thinking. I try not to look away in unease but know I blink a few times.

"Hi," he says when I reach the table. Marci slides out from beside me and moves towards Ryan. "Judging by your face, this wasn't what you had planned for tonight?"

"Not exactly," I reply. "But it's cool," I add in hindsight.

"I wouldn't have come if I'd have known." I'm taken aback by his comment. "Not that I didn't want to come. It's just—I thought you knew. I thought she'd have told you." Nate briefly crosses his focus to Marci, but it's not one of friendliness—more of annoyance.

Ryan laughs, and Nate glares back at him.

"What?" Ryan proclaims. "You two are acting way too serious. Have you never been out on a date before?" He directs at Nate in jest, then as though he realises the question should be aimed at me, his attention swerves my way.

"Ignore him," Nate remarks glaring at Ryan, forcing him to turn away and give his undivided attention to Marci. Feeling Nate staring at me, I raise my eyes to his.

"I'm sorry." I stop myself from fiddling nervously with my bag. "I wasn't prepared, that's all."

Slowly he shakes his head. "Prepared or not. You look beautiful," he says, his attention not moving from me.

Beautiful? He called me beautiful? "Thank you," I whisper.

As Marci takes her seat next to Ryan, Nate's jaw tenses slightly. "Did you want to stay? I can take you home or call you a taxi?"

"No," I respond, wanting the fuss I've created to disappear. I glance at Marci, who I know has done this with only the best intentions, and know that if I want people to start treating me with even the slightest touch of normality, I have to start acting normal too. So, as Marci passes nervous glances my way, I smile back. "I'd like to stay, but I need the ladies room first," I say almost apologetically.

"I'll come too," Marci adds sounding like she's about to be chastised.

Nate remains standing, appearing uncertain about what to do.

"The linguine always used to be good." I nod towards the menu on the table.

He nods and gives a hint of a smile. That's when I see it.

He's not looking at me with pity, or even like I'm a freak, at least not today. His smile, his gentle nod—he's offering support. He looks at me like he understands, and for the first time in a long time, I walk with my back straight, believing that maybe, just maybe I can get through this.

CHAPTER SIXTEEN

NATE

The moment they're out of earshot I make it known how out of order this is.

"You're a fucking idiot."

"Excuse me?" He doesn't have a clue. "How about, 'you're welcome'. You couldn't keep your eyes off her last week." I freeze at his words. Did anyone else notice? More importantly, did Ginny notice? "What is it about her anyway? I mean she's pretty but a little socially awkward."

"Shut the fuck up, Ryan."

"Whoa! What's going on man?" He leans forward in his seat lowering his voice. "Why does she have you so worked up?"

I sigh, frustrated. "Did you not see her when she walked in? She was totally unaware of this entire thing. She didn't have a clue I was going to be here!"

"What's the deal? Women are always falling at your feet, and you walk past them like they don't exist. Yet this one is provoking this kind of response in you. Why?" He narrows his eyes and annoyingly starts tapping his fingers against the table.

I turn to see where they are, not surprised when I see them on their way back. "Leave it. I've had a bad day." With a lasting scowl, I sit back down at the round table, again choosing the seat next to Ryan. At least this way she'll be sitting between Marci and me.

I briefly look at Ginny, to check she is okay with being here. She smiles. It knocks me for six. Not because her smile is *that* amazing, but because it isn't. It's a practised smile. She's putting on a brave face. Whatever her reason was for staying, it's not to suit her. My focus flicks to her friend before the truth sinks in. This is what she had to do before and she's still doing it.

This is down to *him*. I feel the tension radiate from my jaw as the familiar sense of hatred starts to build. Most likely she had to conform and adjust to whatever scenario *he* threw her way. Tonight, she's going along with it for Marci's sake, but as I look at Marci, I wonder why she'd push her friend into a situation she clearly doesn't feel comfortable in.

I glance back to the menu, the words a blur in front of me as I try to figure it all out. When the waiter comes to take our order, I'm nowhere near ready, so I opt for the crab linguine like Ginny.

"And to drink?" he questions. I notice Ginny glimpse at Marci.

"Ooh, shall we have a white or red?" Marci exclaims pulling her lip between in her teeth. "What do you think, Gin?"

"The pinot sounds good," she says.

"Yeah, but look at the merlot! That's our fave!"

Ginny eases back. "The merlot will be perfect." *What?* Marci orders the red wine, and I wonder if it's always been this way for Ginny. If the decisions have always been made by others or perhaps I'm reading too much into it.

Conversation flows fairly easily after that. Ryan and Marci talk nonstop, and although we cover safe ground, I can tell Ginny relaxes in my company. On occasions though, Ginny's reaction to something or someone has me distracted. A number of times, she's looked over at a couple seated at the other end of the restaurant. Marci's noticed too, but for whatever reason hasn't said anything, but it hasn't gone unnoticed that Marci's reached her hand over to Ginny's to give it a squeeze. All I know for certain is when Ginny looks their way, her fingers tighten around her cutlery, and a strained expression flashes across her face like it is doing now.

"Excuse me for one minute," Ginny says as she places her fork on the table and stands up.

As though predicting Ginny's move, Marci is up in a second. "Ginny, leave it!" Instinctively, I get up too, wondering what's going on.

Ginny halts her step, looks back at me and opens her mouth, but nothing comes out. I expect she's wondering the same thing I am. Why have I jumped up to her defence? What is it that keeps me wanting to be in her company, checking she's alright?

Because I like her.

Her eyebrows dip before she directs her words to Marci. "I'm okay. I just want to go and say hi."

"Well, I'll come too then."

Ryan and I look back and forth between the two women, Ryan clueless as to what's going on, and I'm not far behind him. All I know is I want to be walking beside Ginny to whatever situation she's heading towards.

"No, you won't!" Ginny responds almost challenging her friend. Marci sits down with a sigh but swings around making sure she can see what her friend is doing as Ginny walks away.

"What am I missing here?" Ryan asks.

"She used to work with her before—"

"Work with who? And before what?" Again Ryan asks, and

for once I'm grateful for his frankness as it provides me with a chance to learn more about Ginny.

"Before she moved away," Marci answers, her voice unusually quiet. She looks back to Ginny and doesn't appear able to concentrate on anything else. "I thought she was ready for this." She flits her focus to me briefly. "I wanted her to have some fun," she says, and it sounds like an apology.

I search to where Ginny's heading and see the exit beyond. "I'm going for a smoke."

"Since when?" Ryan calls after me, but I ignore him and walk around the array of tables, my focus not leaving Ginny. She stops and stands in front of a couple. They look up and notice her presence, the woman appearing surprised. I push through the glass door taking me to the designated smoker's area. Turning around, I back up against the wall, ensuring I can see her, needing to see if she's okay.

She's standing straight, her face in what she believes to be a flawless mask. As she talks, her hands hang by her side. I can't see the couple she's gone to face, but I don't want to—it's her I'm interested in.

To everyone else, she's portraying an image of grace and politeness. But I can see how tight her shoulders are. How much courage it's taken for her to even approach them. The look in her eyes tells me she's doing everything she can to get through this moment.

It only takes her two minutes to say what she wants to. For a moment I think she's going back to our table, but she makes a detour and heads in my direction. She steps outside, and although I'm standing in the shadows, she approaches.

Absently, she looks to my hands.

"I don't actually smoke," I admit.

"Neither do I, but sure as hell wish I did." She inhales and rests back on the cold brick wall beside me. "So why did you come outside if you don't smoke?"

I consider my answer and decide to go with the truth. "I wanted to check you were okay."

"So that's twice. What are you, some kind of saint?" Her focus stays forward, giving me the opportunity to look at her. Her hands are shaking, but when I look closer, it's her entire body that's trembling.

"I wish I were, but no, Ginny, I guess it's because I can tell that you aren't alright." She's trying her hardest to put on some kind of act, and I wonder who it is that she's trying to convince.

The glow from the patio heater illuminates her sadness. Her eyes brim with tears, but I'm unable to turn away from the tortured look on her face.

"That night, you said you were sorry for what's happened to me."

"I shouldn't have said anything." My vision lowers in regret. She believes she's shown me weakness.

"But you did. What did you mean? Is it that obvious that I'm screwed up?"

I sigh, loathing the branding she's tarring herself with. "I see how you look at people." I see how she surveys a room the second she enters it. How she backs up against a wall so there are no surprises coming from behind her. I've seen it before. "I don't pledge to know what you've been through, but I know you've been through something. Usually, with pain, comes sacrifice."

"Sacrifice." She ponders on the word. "Why did you come tonight?"

Christ, what do I tell this girl that will stop her from running away? "There's something about you that has me unable to look anywhere else," I admit, but at the same time, wonder why I allowed those particular words to leave my thoughts and become known to her.

"Did you come to the coffee shop to see me?"

Christ! "No," I lie. "But I'm glad I did."

When I see her body twist slightly, I glance back up to find her staring at me. She's confused by my response, and I hate the bastard she used to be married to for a whole new reason. She doesn't trust what I say because she doesn't believe anyone would think it.

"I-I feel like I should know you." She frowns, and I still at her admission. So I try and respond in a way that a normal man would respond to a woman in this situation. He'd be trying to bring that smile back to her face.

"Feel like you know me or that you should get to know me?" I grin and as she glances to my mouth, a shy smile briefly touches her own.

"What's your name? I mean I know its Nate but the rest of it."

I prepare to explain more than just my name. "Dawson. It's Nate Dawson." I look at her for any sign of recognition, but she doesn't show any and I wonder how that's possible. Even though I know her surname, I ask anyway. "And you're Ginny?"

"Ginny Daniels." She seems to struggle with her name. "I think you should step away from me, Nate." Her words are sincere, but there's a tease to her tone. "I might not be the best person for you to know."

"You don't possess a great deal of self-belief do you?" I tease, gently nudging her with my shoulder.

"It's that obvious," she says with a gentle laugh, and it's one of the best sounds I've heard.

I push off from the wall. "What if I said I want to get to know you, Ginny?"

"Then I would have to warn you that not all of it is good." Her brown eyes widen and the tinge of sadness I see there, grows.

"You're not scaring me, Ginny. I know life is rarely perfect, if ever."

She drops her gaze and transfers it back inside the restaurant to the couple she's just spoken to. I stare in their direction too. Whatever she said has unsettled their evening. The couple appear strained in their speech.

"Marci said they were old friends," I state, wondering if she wants to talk to someone about what just happened.

"Not really friends. A former work colleague and her husband." Again I hear a heavy breath leave her. "Marci will wonder what the hell I'm doing out here." She laughs, trying to bring lightness to the mood. "Sometimes, burying your head is no longer good enough," she begins. I want to look at her as she speaks but sense a single movement could halt her words. "I had to face the inevitable conversation that comes from someone you used to know before everything came crashing down."

My breaths stop, and I stand frozen to the spot. We both continue facing forward, overlooking the restaurant.

"You said you wanted to get to know me? I moved away with my husband, left my job. Lynne over there," she nods in the direction of the woman she was talking to, "happily stepped into my position. Right after she'd made an attempt at breaking up my marriage by trying to fuck my husband." She steps away from the wall and turns to face me. "I told her I wished she'd tried harder. It would have saved me from an awful lot of pain." Then she looks at me like she's challenging me. "Like I said, you should walk away. I'm damaged goods, Nate."

As I return her focus, I wish she could see what I do when I look at her. I don't know her full story, but I know enough, I want to take her in my arms and tell her that from now on, everything will be different, but she'd think I was crazy. We barely know each other. I just happen to know more than she's aware.

"You're still not scaring me, Ginny."

"Well, it scares me," she admits before walking back into the restaurant, leaving me staring after her before finally I bend over and draw in some deep breaths.

She talked about her marriage with regret. Ginny Daniels. I didn't need confirmation of her name, but she gave it anyway. Hearing her name caused an ache to well in the centre of my chest. The images of what he could possibly have done to her start appearing in my mind. My fist starts to curl for a man I never met, but who right now, I would gladly kill if it wasn't for the fact that he was already dead.

Yet the question that still burns in my mind is, did she know everything about him? The more I get to know Ginny, I don't believe she truly knew her husband because if she had, I think she would know who I am.

CHAPTER SEVENTEEN

GINNY

The bell rings above the door, and I glance up to see Marci walking through.

"You almost done, Gin?"

I finish stacking the last of the clean teapots on the shelf as Carrie replies. "She's all yours, Marci. Any exciting plans for tonight or is it a steady walk home?"

"A steady walk home," I answer at the same time I hear Marci say something about a bar. "What?" I say needing her to repeat herself.

She pulls out a chair and plonks herself down on it. "I've had a shitty day! I'm permanently correcting mistakes that Justine makes, but I don't want to get rid of her, she's so damn nice!" she wails before dropping her head to the table in front of her. "So I need wine," her muffled voice comes from beneath her long blonde hair.

I glance over at Carrie, and she lifts her shoulders. "Only have coffee here, looks like that steady walk home is on hold."

Marci raises her head and peers through her hair at me. "What do I do?"

I understand why Marci's in such a predicament. She likes

Justine who's genuinely a nice person who tries her hardest to please, yet all she manages to do is create problems for Marci to solve. But there isn't a chance I can make this kind of decision for her. So instead of agreeing with Marci, I opt for the easier option. "Let's go and get wine!"

She jumps up from the seat. "Yay!"

I turn, grab my coat and bag, leave my apron behind the counter and set off towards my friend. "Night, Carrie."

"See you in the morning. Don't forget you're opening up."

We walk out, and Marci steers me directly to the left. "You're a lifesaver! Just some days..."

Marci starts to talk endlessly about Justine and what a failure the day has been, then tells me to top it off, Justine's been dumped by her boyfriend.

"Oh," I say in sympathy.

"Oh?" She looks at me aghast. "No! Not oh! I can't get rid of her now, can I? I'd be a total bitch!"

Marci slows her pace as we reach the wine bar. Holding the door open, we both step inside.

"Finally!" A familiar voice calls out. I turn and see Liam and his girlfriend, Megan grinning over at us.

Marci steps in front of me. "I text them before I got to you," she responds sheepishly. "But it's okay, right?"

"Of course it is," I reassure her. A drink with Liam and Megan is probably what I need myself right now. Over the weekend my thoughts have regularly swayed back to Nate. Saturday was a good night. No scrap that, it was a great night even after I nearly ruined it. Nate had this ability to put me at ease. I didn't feel judged, or ridiculed and even when the discussion became intense—somehow he made me smile. Yet there's no escaping that I messed it up in typical Ginny style.

Liam stands up as we approach, and I halt my breath knowing what's coming. He gathers us both in his arms, squishing us together. I close my eyes, silently reassuring myself that it's okay, it's only Liam and that I'll be free any second.

Marci immediately calls out, "Jesus, Liam!" She bats him on the back giving him no choice but to let go. Marci looks nervously over at me, but I smile to reassure her.

"It's been like two weeks!" Liam retorts. Then with a thrust out of his chest, he glances down. "So? Do you think the weights are working?"

Marci rolls her eyes and lets out a groan as we both sit down.

"Of course they're working! Just don't bore them with gym talk like you do me!" Megan comments before lifting her hand to us both. "Hey! Wine anyone?"

"Ooh me, definitely!" Marci takes a glass from the table. "You are a star!"

Megan pours us both a glass and tops her own up, somehow managing to empty the bottle, and I wonder how long they've been here. I pick up my glass and take a drink. The red liquid trickles down my throat, and it starts to warm me instantly.

"Liam—" Megan remarks holding up the wine bottle.

"On my way." He jumps up from the chair taking the empty wine bottle and his lager glass with him.

Marci shakes her head and laughs. "I still can't believe how henpecked he is."

"It works both ways, Marci. Liam doesn't do badly, trust me." She licks her lips, jiggles her brows, and smiles.

"Oh god," I utter as both Marci and I reach for our wine glasses and take a huge gulp, hoping that Megan doesn't share any more details.

"I'm serious! You should see what I do with—"

"Please! I'm begging you to stop!" Marci intercepts, her voice loud, overtaking anything Megan may be trying to say. "Sisters," she points her finger between me and her, "do not need to know that kind of shit!"

With a giggle, Megan rests back in her seat while Marci and I try and compose ourselves back to some kind of normality.

"So? Not that I'm complaining about wine on a Monday, in fact, I think we should do it every Monday, but what's got you so stressed?"

Liam arrives back at the table and fills our glasses back up.

"Justine!"

Liam moans. "Christ, Marci. You do this all the time. Leave her where she is. She's happy isn't she?"

The bottle is put down on the table as Liam takes his seat again.

"Yes, but—"

"And you are perfectly capable of running that place with your eyes closed. So let the girl stay."

"Huh! Have you met this Justine, Ginny?" I swing round at Megan somehow involving me in this.

"Erm, yes."

"What's she like?"

"She's nice."

"Nice?" Megan leans back in her chair and crosses her arms over her chest. "Nice as in 'hot' nice, or nice as in 'kind' nice?"

"Ooh, my woman is jealous of Justine!" Liam pipes up, and Megan's bottom lip pouts.

"I'm not jealous. I want to know why you don't agree with your sister giving her the boot, that's all."

Liam lifts from his chair and shuffles it closer to Megan before reaching out and resting his arm across her shoulders.

"Because, my love, I don't want to dwell on whether Marci will fire Justine or not because I've had this conversation with her too many times, and the outcome will always be the same. Justine will stay. Besides, I'm more interested in what happened this weekend."

Oh crap! My heart sinks with the realisation that one of us is going to get the third degree. Under the table, I cross my fingers hoping it isn't me.

"Marci says you went out on a date, Ginny?" *Crap! Dumb fingers.*

"It wasn't really a date," I say scowling at Marci. How could it be a date when I didn't even know it was happening?

Her brows lift as she moves the wine glass from her lips. "I would say it was a date, Ginny, and I'm pretty sure that's what he would have called it." Would he? The chance that Nate saw Saturday as a date causes a little fluttering feeling to dance in my stomach.

"What I need to know is, should I be having words with him?" Liam's voice turns serious, and I hate that I'm somebody he feels the need to protect. It used to be Marci and me looking after him when we were younger. But then as Liam grew up he was the one that became protective over us. Liam was the brother I never had, and knowing he was around made me feel safe and kind of special —but then everything changed the day I came back and allowed Liam to see what Blake had done to me. I took away his ability to protect me, which is why now, I understand moments like these, when he's trying his hardest, but when I wish he didn't have to.

"No, you should not, Liam!" Marci intervenes, and I'm grateful.

But Liam isn't ready to give up. Part of me loves him for it, but the other part wishes he'd drop it. "Do you think you're ready for this? Hey!" he calls as he clutches his side where Marci's just punched him.

"Of course she's ready for this." Am I? A couple of weeks ago I'd have said no but since meeting Nate and spending time with him... I don't know, maybe it's possible? There's something different about him. It would be foolish to say I feel like I can trust him but I do.

He screws his eyes up, and I can tell he has more questions. "So what's he like?" He aims his question at me, but it's Marci that answers. He shakes his head in what I think is annoyance at his sister.

"He's bloody good looking. Oh and Megan you should see his body—"

"You've seen his body?" Liam's voice elevates, and he looks between Marci and me. I shake my head no.

"He owns a gym, and you can tell, that's what I mean. Jeez, chill out. Liam, seriously do you think I'd let anything happen to her?" Marci's eyes land on me. "I saw him, throughout the night watching you. He was looking out for you, Ginny. There's something about Nate that makes me think you can trust him."

All focus is on me as an uncomfortable silence comes over the table. It seems ridiculous to agree out loud with her when I barely know him. And the realisation that I've been wrong before will forever cling to my thoughts.

Megan stands up. "Well, I'll leave you to your sibling squabbling, I need the ladies room." I'm not sure how much Liam has told her, but I always hoped he'd keep most of my past private or at least the little that he knew.

Marci at least waits until Megan is out of sight. "It's been months since he's been gone and it was months before that when she stopped loving him, right, Gin?"

"Right," I answer although I'm not sure if I'm being totally honest. It's hard to pinpoint when I stopped loving Blake. The control kind of took over, and I can't be certain when one ended, and the other began.

"So are you seeing him again?" Liam questions, still sounding unsure.

I lift my shoulders in uncertainty. "I don't know." But I hope so.

"Well..." Marci's voice trails off, and we both look her way. "It's Ryan's birthday this weekend, and we've both been invited to his place for... well, drinks and food I guess. It's a bit of a party, so I'm assuming Nate will be there."

My heart rate spikes, creating another unusual sensation in me. I glance at the wine and wonder if my nervous excitement has anything to do with the two glasses of wine I've consumed. They were two *large* glasses. Deep down, I know it's not from the wine.

After I'd warned Nate off, he came back into the restaurant a few minutes behind me. I was subdued for a while, but somehow Nate changed that. The night became fun. He made me laugh, and it felt good.

"Nate, that's his name?"

Marci ignores him and empties the second bottle of wine into our glasses. Since when did wine glasses get so big? Taking the opportunity to escape, I jump up. "I'll get the next."

I walk away, and the sound of their voices fade. I understand Liam's hesitation, I truly do. But knowing I may see him again at the weekend gives me something to look forward to. Surely that can't be a bad thing?

"Another bottle?" The barman asks as he nears.

"Yes, please."

He walks away, and I'm thankful he doesn't feel the need for small talk.

I see Megan exit the restroom. She notices me and makes her way over. "You okay?" she questions as she comes to stand beside me.

"Yeah." I smile. "Thanks."

"You know, I'm not sure of the details of your marriage. I know your husband died and that things weren't great before that. I can tell by how Liam talks about you and how he's always checking if you're okay, that there's more to it."

"He checks on me? What do you mean?"

She glances to Liam guiltily. "He doesn't do it so much now, Ginny. In fact, barely at all. He likes to know you're safe. He feels he let you down."

"He didn't let me down," I reply sadly. This is so damn hard. I appreciate they worry about me, both Liam and Marci, in fact, I love them even more because of it. But it wasn't down to them to protect me. I can't keep feeling like someone's watching over me all the time, keeping me safe. It has to stop. I need to be free.

She nods gently. "If ever you want to tell them to butt out, I'll be there with you for back up."

A steady smile spreads across my mouth, and Megan grins back.

The barman places the bottle on the bar, and I hand over the cash.

"Come on," I say scooping up the bottle. "This wine won't drink itself." And right now, I'm craving another glass.

"Oh and Ginny, you have to make a cake for Saturday," Marci states as we arrive back at the table. "Pretty please, with cherries on top. Well, not with cherries on top, you know I can't stand cherries but, oh my God! With lemon! Lemon drizzle!"

"What?" I have to make a cake? I haven't made a cake since *he* threw it aside.

"I'm not sure you should have much more," Liam intervenes. "My sister's drunk. Did you not have lunch today?"

"Oh, be quiet, my little big brother—"

"Little big brother?" Liam mocks, lifting his hand and rubbing his chin. "How is that possible?"

"Oh, shut up, you know perfectly well. You're my younger brother but bigger than me! Anyway, what was I going to say?" She glances at me like I should know.

"I have no idea, Marci!"

She slumps back in her chair but almost missing the backrest, she wobbles to the side. Liam reaches out to stop her from falling, and we all burst out in laughter.

"Great! Just what I need, three drunk women."

"Most men would love to have three drunk women in their company."

"Not when one of them is his sister and another as good as a sister," Liam retorts.

Megan extends her arm, touching the back of Liam's neck. "Looks like you have to settle for me then, pumpkin."

"And I am not drunk." Marci does a double take at Liam. "Pumpkin? Did I hear you being called a pumpkin?" Marci exclaims before she blurts out in laughter again. I can't help but join in. To think that Liam, the boy who only ever climbed trees and got into fights with anyone that crossed his path, was now sitting here being called pumpkin. I never thought I'd see the day. But as I stare at them both, it's obvious they're happy, and I'm happy for them.

"You're doing well, Gin," Marci says under her breath.

I peer sideways on at her. "I am?"

"You are. You've got this."

I've got this? Do I have this? I don't want Liam or Marci to forever be standing in my corner, on the ready to attack. I want to move forward. I keep telling myself that's what I'm doing even when I don't actually believe that I am. Maybe it's time to step out of the corner and prove, not only to my friends but also to me, that I'm making life work.

"Marci? Do you happen to have Nate's number?"

"No, but I know someone who does." She grins.

With that, I lean back in my chair, ignore the concerned look that's written all over Liam's face and instead, get ready to text Nate.

I can do this, so I'm going to.

CHAPTER EIGHTEEN

NATE

"*D*amn!"

"Oh no," Sophia's little voice filters in from the other room. "What's happened?"

"Nothing! It's all good." *It's all good?* I stare at the burger in the pan in front of me. Rookie mistake, I clearly shouldn't have turned it yet, now the lump of meat that only a second ago resembled an actual burger looks like a crumbled pile of minced meat. Acknowledging the pile of mush will be mine, I decide to wait a little longer before turning Sophia's burger.

My phone vibrates in my pocket, but when I pull it out to see what the message reads, I pause mid-step.

Unknown: Hey, it's Ginny. I hope you don't mind, but I got your number from Ryan

I stare at the screen in disbelief. *Ginny's text me?* The phone vibrates again.

Unknown: Well, Marci got it from Ryan. I don't have Ryan's number

The fact she feels the need to explain how she obtained my number gets to me. The three bubbles appear on screen telling me she's typing out another text, so I wait, but then the bubbles disappear, and I know she's changed her mind.

My fingers hover over the keypad, wanting to reply but not knowing what the hell to say. I save her number and finally type out a reply.

Me: You're allowed numbers, Ginny. It's good to hear from you. Is everything okay?

Ginny: I've had a glass of wine so guess I've worked up the guts to text you

Me: You need guts to text me?

Ginny: It appears so

The smell of something burning causes me to drop the phone to the side. "Shit!"

"Nate!" Sophia scolds. "That's swearing!"

"Yeah, I know. I'll put some money in the jar," I concede, taking the pan off the heat.

Great! Burnt burgers and another coin lighter. I'll be broke before the month's end at this rate. That swear jar is getting damn heavy. Then I remember Ginny, so I quickly type out a text.

Me: Sorry, in the middle of a burnt dinner crisis, can I text or call you later?

Me: Oh, and Ginny, I'm glad you messaged

Ginny: Me too and yes, I'd like that

Begrudgingly, I leave the phone and try to make a meal out of the mess in front of me. Thankfully Sophia's burger has come out relatively unscathed, unlike my crispy chunks of beef.

"Sophia, can you turn off the television. Dinner's ready," I call from the kitchen and glance down at the plates of food in front of me. "I think today, I have excelled myself," I state admiringly at her meal but then frown at my own.

"Cool," she says running into the room. "So what have you tried to make tonight?"

"Tried?" I ask with a smile. I was alright at cooking before, but it was food such as steak and chicken with rice. Learning to expand my culinary skills to please a child's palate is proving to be a little harder. I think I'm doing okay... well, I thought I was.

Taking our usual seats, I sit down, and Sophia plonks herself opposite me. We both look at our plates and stare.

"So, what is it?"

I burst out laughing. "It's my take on homemade burgers," I say with pride, flicking a pea from my plate at her.

She dodges it before staring back at her meal. "Burgers. Okay, if you say so." Instead of picking up the bread roll, she scoops up her knife and fork, pushes the burger from the bread and starts cutting up the meat. I watch with interest as she hesitates with the food in front of her. Finally, her fork is at her mouth, but she stills, almost as though she thinks the damn cow is going to miraculously revive itself and jump off the fork. Swiftly she puts it into her mouth.

"Actually," she says between chewing, "it tastes like a burger!"

"In that case, I'll eat mine," I add with a wink. I bite into it, and even with the taste of charred meat, it isn't that bad. I silently praise myself for another meal I can *almost* cook.

Mid-chew, I glance over my shoulder to my phone, but immediately stop myself from focusing on why Ginny messaged and instead turn back to Sophia.

"So, Grandma and Grandad rang earlier. They wanted to let us know that next week, they've both been invited out on Saturday night."

Her face drops, demonstrating how much she looks forward to seeing them.

"Sophia, it'll only be for a few hours. It will be the same as every weekend, only I'll be looking after you on Saturday night instead of them."

"So you'll be there?"

"Of course I will. Where else would I be?"

"But you're normally out on Saturday nights."

"That's only to give your grandma and grandad some special time with you." I reach over and cover her small hand with mine. "I know how many sweets they spoil you with, kid. I can't be around to watch them contribute to dental decay. It can't happen on my watch."

She looks happy with my answer and continues to eat the rest of her dinner. There's no need for Sophia to know things are developing slowly for the folks and me. They think they're doing me a favour by giving me a 'night off' from Sophia. But, the first time I dropped her off, she clung to my legs, scared of me leaving just like her parents had done. The difference being, leaving Sophia hadn't been their choice.

If there's one thing me and my parents agree on, it's that Sophia's happiness takes precedence for all of us. So if she needs me to stick around, that's what I will do. Her grandparents take her out for the day, watch DVD's at night or whatever they choose to make sure she feels loved. I ensure I'm always around at breakfast and at various points throughout the day, to remind Sophia I'm still here.

"Nate, I don't want you to marry Grace's mum." I almost choke on my burger, and she sticks out her tongue in disgust at the idea.

"Where the hell's that come from?" Her eyebrows dip at my choice of words. "Sorry, but I don't plan on marrying Grace's mum."

"But why don't you have a girlfriend?"

"I've not met anyone I want to marry, Sophia. It's okay that it's just you and me though, right?"

"Yeah." I watch her deliberate over what's on her mind. "But mummy used to say you had a lot of girlfriends." I can't help but feel slightly embarrassed about that. "Now you don't have any."

Whoa! I put down my knife and fork and lean back in the chair. "Life is a bit different now, for both of us. Before I wasn't too fussy." She looks a little confused. "You know how you don't want to be Jack's girlfriend because you're not going to marry him?" She nods her head. "Well, I met a lot of girls that I didn't want to marry."

"So you're saying, when you have a girlfriend, you're going to marry that one?" she asks excitedly, and I widen my eyes. *How will I ever figure out what the right thing is to say to kids?*

"Not necessarily." I squirm in my seat.

"You're waiting for someone special."

"Maybe."

"Phew. So you definitely won't marry Grace's mum then because I've seen her scratch her bum and that is not special, it's gross!"

"It sure is, kid." I grin.

"I'm done." Sophia puts her knife and fork down. "Can I go back in and watch the television." I take a look at her plate. There's bread left but little else.

"Sure, but when I've cleared up from dinner, it's homework time." She groans before getting down from the table and disappearing into the other room to continue watching her programme. I get up and follow her, wondering what it is she's actually watching. There's too much crap on the television these days, placing importance on stuff that doesn't matter, so a little screening here and there doesn't hurt.

I lean against the doorway and watch as she smiles at some Australian mermaid programme. I've seen her watch it before.

My focus drifts to the photo frame set on the wooden corner unit. The pain hits me at full force, but it's closely followed by the hatred I feel towards the man who caused all of this. Blake Daniels.

The image of Katie and my brother shine back at me. I remember the day Katie turned up at our school. It was a different image from the one staring back at me now. Her glossy blond hair was dull, and her smile barely lifted the edge of her lips. She'd walked into the playground alone. Nobody was there to keep her company—to tell her how exciting her day would be at the new school. Katie had to suck it up. Aaron had been talking to me when he stopped mid-sentence and froze. Other kids kept walking by, staring at her, and when John Tanner opened his mouth and said something as he passed her, it was obvious by the look on her face his words had been callous and unkind. That was all it took. My normally calm, level-headed brother changed. He set off towards them, knocked Tanner clear out of the way, and he never left Katie's side from that day.

My brother soon became the kid that everyone looked up to, but also the one that they watched with caution. From early on, it was apparent how Aaron felt about Katie, subsequently, she became like a sister to me.

Some days, she'd let him walk her home but not every day. We eventually came to understand why. Her mum's boyfriend was a low life that came in and out of town. Katie pretty much acted like the buffer between them. When Aaron first saw a bruise on her, he flipped. It took me and three other friends, including Olly, to hold him back. When in reality all we needed him to do was look into Katie's eyes because the second he did, he stopped fighting us and went to soothe her.

My parents didn't take well to Katie at first. Aaron was the star of the family. The child who would go far, achieve so much. They saw Katie as somebody who would impinge Aaron's success. Their ignorance and refusal to acknowledge the truth behind Katie's withdrawn and nervous manner irritated the hell out of me. I was ashamed of them. Aaron, on the other hand, felt sorry for them and their inability to show compassion.

Aaron always knew what would happen in the end. He told me that he would always choose her and that's what it came to. Katie fought hard. She didn't want us to part from our parents. She didn't want us to choose her over them, but she wasn't the one who was forcing our hand. They were.

When Sophia came along, Katie finally won the battle and Aaron got back in touch with our parents.

After the accident, I was awarded custody of Sophia—it was Katie and Aaron's wishes. Seeing her grandparents—my parents—was part of the agreement. Which means the bridges that were knocked down are now slowly being rebuilt. It's taken a little longer for me to move forward than it did with Aaron, but because of Sophia, we're getting there.

"Mummy said you and daddy were her knights in shining armour. Why did she say that?"

Sophia looks at me and back at the frame where my focus must have been all this time, worry evident in her eyes.

Instantly, I go and sit beside her. She pushes herself close and nestles her way under my arm.

"You don't ride horses, do you? Did daddy?"

I can't help but smile at the image of Aaron and me trying to ride a horse. "No, neither of us did."

"Then why were you knights? I thought you worked at the gym."

"I do, kid."

As I sit here with Sophia in my grasp, I wonder if Katie or Aaron were ever at a loss at how to answer Sophia's questions. I drag my hand through my hair and seriously doubt it. They kind of rocked at parenthood.

"A knight in shining armour means we kind of rescued her. It's not an actual job."

"Rescued her from what? Was she hurt?" Her voice fills with panic, and I realise I've already screwed up.

"No, but you know how your mum was always right about everything? Well, this time she wasn't. We didn't rescue your mum, kid, your mum rescued us."

"From what? Were you and daddy hurt?"

"No. It's hard to explain, but if your mum had never met your daddy and me, life wouldn't have been the same. She made everything fun." Even on the days she didn't feel like it. "She made us get out there and do something with ourselves. She made your daddy smile, every single day and, believe you me, he was a right misery before that!"

"Did she help you too?"

"Too? What do you mean?"

"Her job. Daddy said she helped people every day. He said that some men weren't always kind, so mummy helped the ladies feel better."

I sit, stunned. I had no idea Sophia even had a basic understanding of what Katie did for a living, but I guess we can only protect kids for so long before they realise life isn't always easy and carefree.

I pull her closer, and the emotion stirs once again. "She did." I know Katie had worked with many women over the years, but there's only one woman that I can focus on. Ginny. She helped her, but it came at a colossal cost.

"Do you think she was their knight?"

"I know for a fact that she was." She settles back in my arms acting impressed with my answer.

"Do you think there are still some ladies out there that need help?"

"Unfortunately, Sophia, yes I do."

"Then maybe we should help them. When I'm older of course." The urge to protect her from men like Blake Daniels comes crashing through me. I can almost hear my brother laughing. *You can't stop the Dawson women, bro, and my daughter, she's going to be a force to be reckoned with, mark my words.*

Peering down, Sophia smiles back at me. One of the hardest things will be to say no to this kid.

"You know something?" I draw back slightly so she can see my face and the forced happiness I've put there. "The first time I saw your mum smile was when she was with your daddy.

Whenever you miss her, go to a mirror and smile because it's exactly the same as hers."

Her face lights up. "Really?"

"I promise."

With that, she picks up the remote, directs it at the TV and changes the channel. "You're nice, Nate," she claims, throwing me. I don't watch the TV like she does. I don't clear away the pots or even try and tackle the homework. I just enjoy the closeness of the child I will love like no other.

Each day that followed Katie and Aaron's death, the same name haunted me—the driver of the other car, Blake Daniels. When I spied his name in the funeral section of the newspaper, I had no intention of going, until that day arrived, and I found myself standing outside the church. One person after another walked past me, to say goodbye to the man that was responsible for killing my brother and sister-in-law.

Then I saw Ginny. As she climbed out of the car, her eyes lifted and she looked around at all of the people that were arriving like they were strangers. Only to me, she wasn't a stranger, I'd seen her before.

I was meeting Katie for lunch one day, and there was a woman, so beautiful but with an abundance of pain in her eyes, sitting on the bench opposite Katie's place of work. She had a bruise on her wrist, most likely more marks were there but hidden. I stood Katie up that day so that the petrified woman—Ginny could see her. I always knew I'd never forget her face. And then there I was at the funeral, staring right at her.

She stood on the same spot for some time. Her friend Marci talking quietly in her ear. I didn't see Ginny speak to anyone nor did I see anyone talk to her. It was as though they didn't know who she was.

When they started walking toward the church entrance, a man went to Ginny's other side. But she didn't really pay him any attention. All she did was scan her surroundings, looking through people and past them.

She was looking for one familiar face. For Blake Daniels, her husband.

The fear in her eyes shook me, and I was taken back to years earlier when the same terror could be found in Katie's eyes.

Only this was different because Blake Daniels was dead, yet Ginny was clearly finding it hard to believe.

CHAPTER NINETEEN

GINNY

I quietly close the bathroom door behind me, wanting to escape for a few minutes. We've been at Ryan's less than an hour and already been roped into playing beer pong. Luckily, by some fluke, my aim, mostly, has been right on target, so most of the drinking has fallen on Marci and Ryan's side of the table.

My body shudders at the thought of my game partner, Shawn. He's not breached any of the boundaries I'd put in place until about five minutes ago when he held on to me a little too tight and for a second longer than was necessary. It wasn't a grope or anything, in fact, it was probably nothing but a friendly gesture, but it made me clam up all the same. I tried to brush it aside, but after a few minutes, I needed to make my escape.

Now here I am, feeling like some crazy woman in Ryan's bathroom *not* actually needing the bathroom. Resting my hands on the washbasin, I look at myself in the mirror and try to figure out what my problem is. But deep down, I know. I'm just fighting with the willingness to accept it.

Nate. We've batted light-hearted and amusing texts back and forth throughout the week—we've even spoken a couple of times on the phone, and I'm not finding it difficult to think of anyone but him. When Shawn hugged me after I'd won another shot, it may have purely been down to excitement on his behalf, but for me, they were the wrong arms.

"You're crazy," I whisper to my reflection. "You barely know him."

Yet, there's something different about him. Last weekend he didn't look at me as though I was liable to break any second. Even after I told him I was damaged goods. It seems Nate doesn't scare easy, but there's still time and plenty more for him to learn that will change that. For now, I just have to get through this party.

I reach up and smooth my fringe to the side. My hair's grown a fair amount in the past few months. Although I've kept most of it short, the longer hair at the front manages to soften my face and also serves a purpose, hiding one of the scars Blake left me with. No one would know by looking at me that the mark came from him. Unfortunately, I do, and that's enough.

"Ginny!" Marci's muffled voice sounds through the wood panelling of the door. "Are you okay?"

Quickly, I press the flush, then run the tap. "Yep, coming now." Rubbing my hands on the towel, I unlock the door and open it to find Marci standing there with a concerned look on her face. "I've had two beers, Marci," I say, explaining why I've been a little longer.

She holds me back with her hand extending over my stomach. "Nate's turned up." Instantly, I feel a sense of relief mixed with excitement but try not to show it. When I see the concerned expression still lingering, I question why.

"Is that a bad thing?"

"No, but... well... he came in looking for you then when I told him where you were, he kind of did some weird glare thing at Shawn, stepped towards him and muttered something I couldn't hear."

"Then what happened?"

"I don't know! I ran up here to find you! Quick!" She steers me in front of her, suddenly desperate to get back downstairs.

As we make our way down, I glance outside to the lumbar decking where the beer pong table is. Nate isn't there but Shawn and Ryan are waiting, and Ryan appears a little uneasy. I'm about to swing around and search the rest of the house for Nate when Shawn calls out.

"There you are!" Obligingly I smile, trying not to appear rude.

"He's probably gone to get a drink," Marci's says quietly in my ear. "Finish the game. I'm sure he'll turn up."

But the second my foot hits the decking, I know he's close. There's a shift in the air. The same thing used to happen when Blake was near but in a totally different way. With Blake, the atmosphere turned cold, and my skin would spike with fear. Now, at this exact moment, all senses are heightened as anticipation runs through my body.

I move my feet, rotate around and see him standing a few feet from me. A smile starts to appear on his lips causing a stir in my chest.

"Hey," he says, his voice low. All I can do is smile back. He tilts his head, widening his own smile further and for a second, I can't look anywhere else. A silence falls upon us, not one that's filled with fear or discomfort, but expectation.

"You look good, Ginny... happy."

"Maybe I am," I answer in honesty. "Happy, I mean," I rush out, hoping he didn't think I meant beautiful.

He chuckles. "So, I'm reliably informed you're playing beer pong." Nate peers over my shoulder.

"Oh crap! I um, I was." Looking in the same direction, I see them all waiting for me.

"You're on Shawn's side right? You still have a lot of cups left. It looks like you're winning."

I laugh. "Surprisingly so. I guess I should finish the game. You're staying, aren't you?"

"I'm staying, Ginny. You promised cake, remember?"

"Ah! Cake! Of course!" I reply jokingly. During one of our conversations over the past week, it had been after he told me he'd burnt dinner, we'd got to talking about cooking and baking. Nate asked if I was any good at it. Apparently, he has a sweet tooth. I happened to mention that I'd been roped into baking a few cakes for Ryan's party, as per the demands of my best friend.

"Ginny!" Marci shouts over. "You playing or what?"

"Yeah, of course she is." Shawn's voice carries in our direction. "I need my good luck charm back!"

Very slowly, Nate drags his focus to Shawn. His eyes narrow slightly, and he clenches his jaw before his eyes once again find mine. "Don't trust him, Ginny."

"I think you and I both know I don't trust easily, Nate," I state not telling him anything I'm sure he doesn't already know.

He gently nods his head. "I'm here if you need me, okay? I'll go and catch up with some of the guys. I won't be far away."

"You going to come back for cake?"

"Wouldn't miss it," he says before he heads outside. I see him slow when passing Shawn before he walks down the steps and approaches a group of people at the bottom of the garden.

Begrudgingly, I walk back to the game, and as I do, Shawn throws his arm over my shoulder. Clearly, he's had a few more drinks in my ten-minute absence, unless the alcohol has suddenly entered his bloodstream, but nothing has changed from when I was last standing on this side of the table with him, so I shrug his arm free and take my shot, making it clear I'm not interested in him.

Marci and Ryan have only one cup left on their side of the table, and we have four on our end. Hoping the game will be over soon, I throw the ball, and when it lands in the last of the plastic cups, Marci screams in defeat. I accept Shawn's offering of a high-five then glance down the garden and see Nate looking in our direction. His smile appears strained.

"You know," Shawn leans towards me, the fumes from his alcohol breath tinging the air, "if you want to make him really green with envy, I could think of a thing or two that could get him worked up." He winks. "Play him at his own game, if you know what I mean?"

"No, I don't know what you mean." Is Nate playing a game?

"You see that woman who's standing to his left side." I twist and scan her briefly. Nate watches me with interest and then looks at the woman in question.

"Her and Nate had a thing. She still has a severe case of the hots for him. Maybe you could show him which direction he should be heading."

Whether out of frustration at the lack of clarity between Nate and me or whether it's my intolerance of playing games when it comes to matters of the heart, I turn so Shawn can see me clearly.

"I don't play those kind of games. I never have," not voluntarily at least, "and I never will."

Marci arrives at my side, catching my hand. "You okay?"

"Yes," I answer matter-of-factly, hearing yet another, 'Are you okay?'

"I was explaining to Shawn. I'm done with games." Without appearing even a little abashed, Shawn shrugs and moves away. For once though, I mean it. I've been to hell, and no matter what happens, I won't be going back.

"You going to see him?" Marci nudges her head in Nate's direction.

If that woman is interested in Nate, I'm not going to start a public duel, but then, what if Shawn was only trying to cause trouble. Nate said not to trust him. "I don't know," I state with uncertainty. I want to, but—

"You want cake?" Marci wiggles her eyebrow. "It's good. I know the woman who made them and damn, that girl can bake!"

Cake sounds like the less troublesome option, so we weave our way back into the house and through the group of people hanging around the kitchen table. I hear the word 'pizza' and see a stack of boxes piled high. I glance at Marci, and we shake our heads simultaneously as she hides a giggle. As much as we love pizza, puddings have always been our favourite.

When we make it to the part of the kitchen I'd put the cakes, I stand shocked. There's less than half a chocolate cake left. I brought two. I search for the third plate, the lemon drizzle. There's not even an empty plate to show evidence of its existence.

My hand is yanked unexpectedly by Marci. She tugs me towards a full length wooden slatted door tucked away in the corner of the room.

"Shhh!" Marci whispers holding her fingers against her lips.

She closes the door, and I look around, surprised to see the size of the room. "A pantry!" I say in admiration.

"Not just any pantry, Ginny. A pantry that contains the best lemon drizzle cake this side of the ozone layer!"

"What?"

Marci releases a giggle and pulls my cake off a shelf.

"You actually like the cake. You didn't say it to make me happy?"

"What?" she asks, her face creasing in confusion. "I put it in here because I'm not willing to share it, Ginny!" She dips her finger in the frosting. "Maybe when we're close to nausea I might consider sharing a slice but—"

At the sound of a soft tapping on the door, Marci stops talking and looks at me with wide eyes.

"Ginny?" It's Nate.

"Um, yeah?" I answer, subsequently receiving a dead eye from Marci. I shrug my shoulders and whisper, "I can't not reply!" She purses her lips and points to the cake. She *really* doesn't want to share any. She truly likes my cake. The declaration brings a smile to my lips.

"Is everything okay?"

"It's fine!" Marci states on my behalf but then the door slides open. Almost filling the entrance, stands Nate. I draw in a breath having him in such close proximity.

"Did Shawn just do anything to upset you?" I shake my head wishing for everyone including Nate to stop checking on me and asking me if I'm okay. There's only so much concern I can handle.

"No, he didn't," I reply managing to sound curt and regretting it immediately.

"Oh. I'll um leave you to it."

But I don't want him to go. "We have cake!" I blurt out.

"Cake?"

"Damn it, Gin. I didn't even tell Ryan about this one, and it's his birthday!" Marci tuts.

"Well, we can't eat it all."

"I bet we can now that muscle man's in here!" She moans before stepping aside revealing the cake in its full view. Nate brings himself closer, and I'm suddenly very aware of how small the room is. While I try and maintain a normal breathing pattern, Marci proceeds to cut three large slices. What if he doesn't like the cake? What if he pretends, just to be polite?

As they start to eat the cake, I hold off on mine, suddenly feeling exposed. Blake didn't think I was any good at baking, so for a while, I stopped. I can tell by the embarrassing sounds of pleasure that are coming from Marci that I did a good job. Fighting the desire to run, I peer up at Nate. He catches me watching him and stops chewing.

"Gus is gooooood!" he garbles through his mouth full of food, and I break out in a smile. I am good at baking, goddamn it!

Once Marci's polished off her slice, she rubs her hand over her face and concentrates on Nate and me. There's more than enough room for us all to stand comfortably, but Nate steps to my side, his arm presses against mine making it hard to concentrate.

"I guess I'll leave you to it. I'll be back, so don't go thinking you can eat any more without me!" she orders before leaving.

Nate still doesn't step away from me. "So you came in here for cake, not because of anything Shawn said?" His voice comes over the brief silence.

"I came in here for cake," I say downheartedly. I don't want to start explaining what Shawn said because I sense that's what Shawn wants me to do and like I told him, I'm not into playing games. Yet here I am, standing beside a man that makes me feel safe and nervous all at the same time, and I daren't even open my mouth to tell him.

"Ginny?" I close my eyes at the soft tone he uses when saying my name. "Will you please look at me?"

I swallow then peer up at him. His eyes are searching mine.

"I don't always need rescuing, Nate."

"Who said I was here to rescue you?"

I push up my shoulders. "Call it a gut instinct."

He exhales. "I can't help but look for you, Ginny."

I stare at him questioningly. "What does that even mean?"

He reaches up, slides his fingers along my fringe, trailing his little finger along my cheek. "I'm not asking for an explanation of what or who it is that's hurt you." He takes a breather before continuing. "I don't know if I'm saying the right thing or doing the right thing. I don't know whether I should be leaving you alone or staying by your side."

"Stop it." I look away.

"Stop what? You want me to leave?"

"You *don't know* what you *should* be doing? Are you even listening to what you're saying? Surely you do what you want, Nate! Marci, her brother Liam, they both look at me like I'm going to fall to pieces any second. Now you're doing it. But last week... you didn't." Maybe it all changed when I gave him the briefest of explanations of my life with Blake. "I don't need people to protect me. I need people around me, but only if they like what they see. So what you *should* be doing doesn't even come into it," I say with defeat. Blake never even met Nate, but the aftermath of his actions keep battering the path I'm trying to make for myself. Why can't everyone treat me as though I don't have a past that's crippling my future? Maybe it's because *I* can't.

The flaring of his nostrils tells me I'm getting to him, but truthfully, I have no idea in what way.

"You want honesty?" His voice is thick with emotion that I can't help but look into his eyes.

"I think it's what I need to hear, don't you?" I challenge him, wanting to fight against the past that's forever dragging down my present.

"I know you've been hurt, you said it yourself, and whether you like it or not, it does still affect you, Ginny which is why it affects me. I don't feel sorry for you. I admire you because I sense you're fighting every day. I do want to stand by your side, and I guess in a way, yeah, it's to protect you, to stop anything bad happening again, but it's not just because of that."

He edges even closer, covering what little personal space I had around me, leaving me with no choice but to breathe him in and only him. But I don't feel like I'm suffocating, I feel like I can breathe for the first time.

"I like you, Ginny. I want to get to know you. You said I should do what I want?" His thumb softly brushes against my cheekbone causing my lips to part. "But what is it that *you* want, Ginny? Because I can't be the only one deciding."

I want to tell him that when I stand like this, so close to him, breathing the same air, his face only inches from mine, I feel all of him around me, and I've never felt so alive. He's entering his way into what I believed was a heart without a chance.

"What do you want?" he asks again.

I want him to see me, but only the good, not the ruined version. I want... no, I need, the past to disappear—to be wiped from my memory, giving whatever this is between us, a chance.

So I stand on my tiptoes and press my lips to his. His arms circle round me, drawing me closer than I ever imagined possible. Our lips move together, and I finally get to recognise what pure pleasure tastes like. It's like nothing else around us exists, only the two of us. The past is no longer in my mind, nor is the future, only right now, this very second, and it's the only place I want to be.

His hands grasp at my clothing tightly, not with force, but with a need. My fingers snake into his hair, wanting to get as much of him as I can. When we finally part, our breaths meet heavily in the air between us.

"Tell me what you want, Ginny?" He's forcing an admission from me, and he knows it, but he needs an answer. He's seeking permission.

"I want to wake up," I whisper. I want to be brought back to life rather than exist in a life that remembers the past as though it's still the present. "I want to live."

"Then let me be the one to help you." His fingers thread through mine, and before I can utter another word, he kisses me again, his strength holding me up through my newfound weakness.

In the distance, I hear a persistent knocking sound. When Nate pulls back from me, I realise Marci is calling my name, rapping on the door. I peer up at him and the look I'm rewarded with causes my stomach to flip. A mischievous grin plays on his lips. "Looks like she came back for cake."

"She can have it," I murmur.

He stares at me with desire, and my stomach does another dip as Marci shoves her way into the room. She takes a look from me to Nate and back again.

"What? What just happened here?"

Nate stands back and folds his arms over his chest like he's interested in what my answer will be.

"I promised him more cake," I announce.

"Cake?" She continues staring at us with doubt written all over her face. "Cake?"

I nod my head, and Marci stands impatiently. She's not going to move.

"Is this one of those moments when I need to make myself scarce?" Nate questions.

"Yes, it is." Marci answers at the same time as I say, "No."

"I'll come and find you in a minute, okay? There's something I need to talk to Ryan about anyway." Nate tries to slide past Marci but pushes himself closer to me in the process. My cheeks warm knowing Marci's watching our every move.

She doesn't pass comment until he's left. "You like him, don't you?" she questions once she's sure he's out of earshot.

"I do."

She nods, already knowing the answer. "Okaay."

I frown at the hesitation in her voice. "Okay? What does 'okaay' mean?"

She starts to look around the pantry and then begins to move the various cans and containers of food into a more organised position.

"Marci?"

"I worry, that's all."

Briefly, I close my eyes. "Marci, I keep telling you I'm alright. You're going to have to start believing me."

In the past five minutes, something has shifted between Nate and me. It's like I gave him the permission he needed. "This is a good thing. I'm trying to have some fun."

"You're not falling for him or anything?" she blurts out, and I now know why she's so concerned. If things don't work out between Nate and me, am I going to fall to pieces? Am I going to hide away for months? Will I jump at every unexpected sound I hear like I did when Blake died?

"Marci, don't make this into something big," I say the words to reassure her and hope that they provide some reassurance to myself. "I want to laugh, to enjoy myself, to let myself go. To move on with my life." I grab both of her cheeks in my palms and stare hard into her eyes, offering a smile because right now, that's what I feel like doing. Smiling from ear to ear. "Now let's get back to this party. Otherwise, you'll have people realising why you keep disappearing," I say with an added cheer to my voice.

I find Nate talking to Ryan. When we join them, I'm not sure where I should stand. Marci instantly presses herself close to Ryan's side. Is that what I should do? I mean, Nate and I kissed, but we haven't said *exactly* what this is. With indecisiveness ruling, I stand in the middle, between Ryan and Nate, on neutral ground.

Nate coughs, so I glance his way and catch him frowning at me. A few people come to join us and start to chat away. When I hear my phone alert, I take it from my bag and check the screen.

Nate: I'm not forgetting what just happened

His message brings a smile to my lips, and I type out a reply.

Me: Neither am I

Nate: But I can't kiss you again when there are two people between us blocking my path

I look up at him in shock, and a grin plays on his lips. "Who's got you smiling?" Marci pipes up.

"Erm, no one," I answer. I can hardly tell her the texts are from Nate when he's standing only a few feet from me. But when she peers across at him, he pushes his phone back into his pocket at the same time as I receive a text.

We spend another half hour or so pretty much like this, minus the text messages. Various people come up and chat to Ryan. I'm introduced to them all. Nate appears to know most people here, but it doesn't go unnoticed how his attention diverts to the clock on the wall frequently.

During a lull in the conversation, Nate sidesteps the crowd and comes to stand behind me. "You got a minute?"

"Of course." He waits for me to join him before he leads us both out of the front of the house. When his fingers brush against mine, I'm the one who links my fingers to his. He peers down at me and smiles then continues walking until we get to his car. I recognise it from when he parked outside the coffee shop.

"You going somewhere?" I tease.

Then with a look of regret, he nods his head. He leans back against his car, keeping me close. "Ginny, I had already made plans. I'm sorry. I didn't know that this," he smiles, "was going to happen. Although, I might have secretly hoped!" he states with a grin.

He raises his free hand and brushes his thumb along my bottom lip causing them to part. I feel my heart rate increasing as his blue eyes delve into mine. But it's when I look into his that I see pain and torment and it stuns me.

"What is it?" I question.

He blinks, and the pain disappears. "*You*. You make everything feel better, and it's hard to get my head around why that is," he says, confusion clouding his expression.

"What do you mean better?" I ask. I hadn't even considered

that Nate has his own worries. But he doesn't allow time to answer my question. Instead, he silences me with his lips. Clasping my waist, he pulls me close, and I wrap my arms around his neck and kiss him back, the hunger and desperation flowing from me. My stomach aches as the kiss strengthens, and we become lost in each other.

"Jesus, Ginny," he breathes into me.

When he pulls away, my face feels flushed, and I'm breathless. As I look at him, I still see torment in his eyes. He quickly turns away like he's trying to hide it. Then he glances at his watch.

"I'm sorry, I've got to go." His attention flicks to Ryan's house behind me. "Shit! Why do you have to be so damn appealing?" Finally, he grins at me, and it's like a weight is lifted from my shoulders. "Will you promise me something?"

"That depends on what you're asking."

"Ring me. If anyone's out of order in there." He's trying to smile light-heartedly at me, but I see the tension beneath his words.

"I'll ring you, Nate." And I mean it but not because of what someone may or may not do, I'm going to ring him because I want to.

"Ginny, next weekend… is there any chance that I could take you out. Just you."

I lean forward and kiss him lightly on his cheek. "I thought you'd never ask." Then I set about walking up the path towards Ryan's house, silently giving myself a high-five for moving forward with my life.

∼

"This guy throws one hell of a party, right?" Shawn stalks towards me and leans against the wall of the house next to me. Marci's down on the deck in the hot tub and has been for the past hour. Luckily for her, she's wearing a tank top beneath her clothes although I'm not sure it would have stopped her if she hadn't. I've managed to make small talk with a few people Ryan had introduced me to earlier, and I feel good. But I'd been trying to avoid Shawn.

"So, you and Nate? You an item?"

I shift uncomfortably on my feet not wanting to explain what Nate and I may or may not be.

"Sorry," he says sensing my unease. I notice Ryan watching us from across the room, then he starts to make his way towards us. "Probably none of my business. I get the impression he's been through some shit though."

"Hasn't everyone?" I reply, questioning why I feel like this guy has an ulterior motive for talking to me.

Ryan appears in front of us and looks from Shawn to me.

"Where is Nate anyway?" Shawn enquires.

"He had other plans," Ryan answers vaguely.

"Oh right, the girl!" *The girl? What?*

"Shawn!" Ryan only says his name, but I can tell it's meant as a warning.

"What? Well, that's where he'll be isn't it?"

Ryan steps towards Shawn and ushers him away forcefully while muttering something in his ear.

Nate has a girlfriend? He has a girlfriend? How the hell did I not realise? Why was I so blind? He already had plans with her. I briefly look at Marci who's still busy in the hot tub, before I slink back inside wanting to find an area of quiet where I can try and make sense of it, but people keep stopping and talking to me. So

I escape upstairs to the bathroom again. It takes me all of one minute to decide it's time I left, so I ring for a cab. I feel relief when they say they're around the corner because it means I can get out of here.

Heading back, I walk outside to Marci. "Marci, I'm going to head off."

"No!" She stands up, almost spilling her drink. "Not yet."

"I've already called for a cab. You stay. I told you I wouldn't be staying much longer."

"Ginny, you don't have to go." Ryan comes up from behind. "Don't worry about what Shawn said." I flutter my eyes closed before glancing back at Marci ready for the onslaught.

"What?" Marci steps out of the hot tub and grabs a towel from one of the chairs. "What did Shawn say?" she asks straight to my defence.

"It was nothing," I say trying to play it down. "And I'm not leaving because of Nate," I direct to Ryan.

"Ginny?" Marci tilts her head and raises her eyebrows. "Tell me!"

"Shawn happened to mention that Nate will be with someone tonight." I see Marci's face flash in anger.

Marci swings her focus to Ryan. "Well? Does he have someone? Because how he's been flirting with Ginny and hanging on every single word she's said means he's a total son of a bitch!"

Ryan rubs at the back of his neck and shifts on his feet. "This isn't my business." Ryan sighs.

Marci in her tanked-up state, shouts, "So, it's true!"

"Marci, leave it!" I stare at her, and she calms somewhat. "It's a party. That's what people do at parties. Stop making a scene," I hiss under my breath.

"He wasn't acting the way he was around you because it was a party!" she says quieter now. "It was clear to everyone in this room that he couldn't keep his eyes off you." Marci crosses her focus to Ryan. "Is this seriously the kind of guy you let me introduce my friend to?"

"It's not like that, Marci." Ryan bravely enters the conversation before turning away from Marci and bringing himself towards me. "Ring him. Let him explain."

But I don't want to hear any more. I need to get outside. As I head towards the door. Marci reaches me and spins me around.

"Ginny, please."

"What do you want from me, Marci?"

"I can't just let you leave. Wait for me. Let me get my stuff."

"No." I puff out a breath hating the attention and pity that once again has fallen on my shoulders. "I want to go home. Not because of Nate. You know this," I sweep my hands across the gathering of people around us, who thankfully appear unaware of what's unfolded around them, "this isn't me. Please… sometimes, Marci, you have to let me go."

As though she's heard me for the first time, she releases her hold on me. "I'm sorry. I just—"

"Worry. Yeah I know," I say on a sigh. "Do you know what it feels like to be the one that everyone worries about all the time? The one that's always being watched? I'm not falling to pieces, Marci. I want to go home." She blinks rapidly, and I'm overcome with guilt at being so abrupt. "I'll message you when I get home."

Then I walk out of the door, closing it quietly behind me. The cab should be here any minute, so I venture only as far as the roadside.

The darkness of night always has me on edge, but when I'm

in a neighbourhood I've never been to before, it heightens my unease more.

I hear every sound around me, no matter how small. I scan around me feeling the presence of someone close by, but relief fills me as I see Marci looking out of the window. When I see a set of headlights approaching, I raise my hand, and the car pulls up. I get in and give my address.

Only then do I allow a small tear to escape but that's all it can be. One tear before I close my heart back up.

∼

When I enter my house, I secure all of the locks and hear the sound of my phone beeping like it did in the taxi. Again, I ignore it.

Removing my shoes, I put them on the floor and make my way into the kitchen. Switching on the light, I immediately pull the blinds closed then move to the living room and do the same there. Then I collapse down on the two-seater sofa, removing my bag from my shoulder.

When I expect to hear nothing but silence, the faint sound of music comes from upstairs. My body becomes immobile. *Why can I hear music?*

I lift my focus to the open staircase in front of me, and my lips part as rushed breaths seep in and out.

I had music on before I went out, but I'm sure I turned it off… I couldn't have done. That's the only possible explanation. Slowly, I stand and make my way towards the stairs. When I pass by the small table that has my jar of chocolate mice in I reach out to pick it up. Then realising how stupid I'm being, I put it back down. With my hand on the bannister, I steadily make my way up.

The music grows stronger the closer I get. Once I reach the outside of my room, I stare at the closed door. My hand is now shaking as it hovers over the handle. I swallow then push the door open with force. As it hits the wall, it ricochets back. Quickly, I switch on the light and scan the room. Seeing nobody there, I try to steady my breathing. Making my way to the stereo, I turn it off before backing up and sitting down on my bed.

"Okay," I say out loud. "You left the stereo on. Jesus, Ginny."

The unmistakable sound of my mobile ringing causes me to jolt from the bed. "Shit!" I utter as my heart starts pelting once again in my chest. I dash down the stairs and retrieve the phone from my bag. The relief I feel when I see Marci's name nearly finishes me off.

"Shit, Marci, you scared the shit out of me," I answer

"Why? What's wrong?" she asks sounding panicked.

"Nothing!" I exhale.

"Ginny, you sound out of breath."

"I had to run down the stairs to answer the phone." I walk towards the door to double check I've locked it then start to work round the windows.

"So you're in. You're home. Everything's good?"

"Yeah, sorry. I've only just got in. I was about to message. You still at the party?" Turning off the light downstairs, I head up to bed.

"Yes, I'm still here."

"Okay, well stay safe and Marci? Thanks for letting me go."

"Didn't really have a choice did I?" she says, and I can tell she's smiling. "You know, Ryan's keeping quiet, but I think he's right, I think you should ring Nate."

"I'll see." But I won't be ringing him. There was no label on what we were. We kissed, and he asked me out on a date. A date that I'll no longer be going on.

Slumping down on my bed, we end the call. I notice the text messages that I've yet to open and a missed call, both from Nate. I open the first text.

Nate: Hey. How's the party going? X

That was sent over an hour ago. He then sent another message.

Nate: I'm sorry I couldn't stay. Like really sorry x

I sit and stare at the messages, my finger itching to reply, but instead, I turn off my phone without listening to his voicemail. It doesn't matter what he has to say.

With tiredness wracking my body, I curl up on my bed and beg for sleep to come soon. Sleep without a nightmare.... Now that would be a miracle.

CHAPTER TWENTY

NATE

"Are you sad today, Nate?"

I look down at Sophia walking beside me. Christ, I've got to do better than this.

"Why would I be sad when I'm spending the day with you?"

"I dunno." She shrugs before running to the biggest slide in the park.

I look back at mum and dad. "So much for her being too big for the park, eh?"

When they'd suggested a quick visit to the park before we left for home, Sophia had initially turned her nose up at the idea claiming she was too old for the park. Until I mentioned that even at my ancient age, I still enjoyed the swings.

We stand and watch her repeatedly go up and down the slide.

"She certainly looks to be enjoying it," My dad exclaims. "She's doing well, Nate, don't you think?"

"She is." Sophia surprises me each day. Some days are worse than others, but kids' resilience to events that can crucify us amazes me. It doesn't mean she doesn't care because I know she does, and I'm going to make sure she remembers her mum and dad every single day.

With a brief glance at the sky, I offer a wink. "Let's see if I can still do it," I state under my breath.

Steadily, I walk to the biggest of the swings. I twist my head slightly to see if Sophia's watching and sure enough she is. She's standing intrigued at the foot of the slide. Trying to hide a grin, I swiftly sit on the swing and try and remember how the hell to do this.

Kicking forward with my feet, I pull on the chains like Katie once taught me. Then I see Sophia pick up her feet as she charges towards me.

"Nate! Wait! I want to go on the one next to you." The grin makes its way across my face. Then my heart catches in my throat as I see how happy she is. I briefly glance at my parents. They're standing, watching, arms around each other in support, mum with a glistening to her eyes.

I slow down on the swing as Sophia climbs on hers. Then she gets herself moving and manages to exceed my own swing.

"You're better than me, kid!"

"That's because my mummy taught me." She smiles.

"Guess what?" I say as I start to swing just as high.

"What?" She gleams as we pass each other, her blonde hair trailing behind.

"Your mummy taught me too!"

Her mouth and eyes simultaneously open wide. "Really?" she questions in awe.

"Yup! And she taught your dad. We were pathetic before!" It's not that we never had a chance to go on a swing or anything when we were younger, we chose to do other things, like skateboarding. That was our firm favourite.

With a smile that displays a flash of white teeth, she pulls on the chains and propels herself forward at a greater speed.

When I glance back at my parents, two figures, standing in the background, catch my eye. One of them I'd recognise anywhere. I glance at Sophia and fear starts to encroach as the repercussions of what I've been doing become realisation. I sit up straight and slow the swing down.

"Stay with Grandma," I say to Sophia. "I'll be back in a minute." Getting off the swing, I walk towards the two women, but my focus is only set on Ginny.

As I draw closer, I can tell she's confused as she looks from me to Sophia. *Christ. This is not the way I wanted her to find out.*

When I set out looking for Ginny, I hadn't intended on ever actually meeting her face to face. I only knew from what Katie said that I had to make sure she was okay, that she was free. But seeing her from a distance wasn't enough and now staying away is something I'm unable to do.

Perhaps this was always going to happen. I just wasn't prepared for it today.

"Hi," I say as I reach them, but Ginny seems intent on refusing me eye contact. So I glance to Marci wondering what's going on. Yet she can't take her eyes from her friend. I watch as she steps a little closer like she's trying to reassure Ginny that she's there, right by her side. "What's going on?" I ask, unable to mask the concern in my voice.

I didn't hear back from Ginny last night, and her behaviour now tells me she's upset about something. "Did something happen last night? Did Shawn—"

"No, Shawn didn't do anything," Marci says with a glare, making it sound more like an accusation against me, but I can't figure out why. "Nice little family outing you have going on here."

Although the attitude comes from Marci, it's Ginny that has me worried. Her focus is still and directed at Sophia.

"Ginny?" I want her to look away. I don't want to risk her finding out who Sophia is, not until I've had chance to explain. Not until I'm sure Ginny's ready to hear the truth.

"Who's the kid?" Marci questions as she narrows her eyes in interest at Sophia. At the sound of little footsteps running across the grass, I briefly close my eyes.

"Hello," Her innocent welcoming voice sounds.

I glance down at the girl standing beside me. Feeling the need to protect her, I wrap my arm around her shoulder before looking back at Ginny.

She's looking down at Sophia, smiling. "Hello," Ginny replies. "You were very good on that swing."

"Thank you. My mummy taught me."

"Well, she did a very good job." Ginny's response is delayed but genuine all the same. I can only stand and watch in fascination as the two talk to each other.

"Who are you?" Sophia asks kinking her neck in order to look up at her.

"I'm Ginny, and this is Marci," she says pointing to Marci.

"I'm Sophia."

"You have a pretty name," Ginny comments. I want her to lift her eyes to mine so I can try and read what it is she's thinking, but she's still refusing to look at me.

"Thank you, so do you. I'm nine years old!"

Marci ignores Sophia and glares at me. "So is this your kid?"

Ginny hushes her friend, appearing embarrassed by her intent to interrogate. But as I stand there, my arm protectively resting on Sophia, I want to answer. As Sophia stares back at me, I have no idea if I'm about to say the right thing by her, but it feels right at this moment.

I witness Marci take hold of Ginny's hand. I turn to Sophia, knowing I should have told Ginny about her before now but holding back meant I managed to evade questions that I'm not sure Ginny's ready to hear the answers to.

"Yes, she is." I exhale and wait. Sophia stares at me, and I wonder if I've overstepped the mark. When her face transforms into the biggest grin, I breathe a sigh of relief knowing I've said the right thing.

"Well, it was lovely meeting you, Sophia," It's Ginny that makes the comment and her who's decided our little meeting has come to an end. Then she turns and starts to walk away.

"Ginny, hold up!" I jog a few paces to get to her side, but she continues walking, acting like I'm not there. "I should have told you," I say quietly not wanting Sophia to overhear. The last thing I want her to believe is that I'm keeping her existence secret.

"Yes, you should!" Marci turns on me stopping me in my step.

"Marci!" Ginny calls out stopping her friend from saying anything farther. Then, with a subtle nod in Sophia's direction, Ginny states, "Now isn't the time."

"I rang you last night. Were you okay?" I say, but with an impassive glance, she looks over me to Sophia and smiles.

"Bye, Sophia. It was nice meeting you," she says kindly before steadily moving away.

Sophia levels with me and watches them too.

"Sophia? Are you okay? Is what I said okay?"

"She's pretty. Ginny I mean. The other one seemed a bit angry."

"Yeah," I agree and can't help but look after Ginny for a second. "But I need to know if what I said was okay. I'm not taking their place. You're going to remember your mum and dad forever, but I don't ever plan on leaving you. Got that?"

"Yes, Nate," she says softly. Then she herself looks to Ginny. "But you should kiss her."

"I should kiss her?"

"Yes. You should. Definitely. She made you smile."

"Sophia, you make me smile."

"I know, but sometimes you're sad too. Ginny looked sad." She did, I agree to myself. "You should take her out."

"I should?"

"Of course, stupid! She needs to be happy, and you make everyone happy. I think she'll have a really pretty smile."

My arm reaches back over Sophia's shoulders, and I tug her to my side. "I make everyone happy?"

"Errr yeah! When I felt sad all of the time, you made me happy, didn't you?" I don't know what to say to her. She smiles up at me as though everything is *that* simple, and I wish more than anything that it was.

I know no matter how close Katie got to the women she worked with, she never told them about her personal life, for fear of one day putting the people she cared about in jeopardy. Ginny wouldn't have known about Sophia. Which means the truth, that I'm keeping hidden, continues to hang over me like a heavy weight.

There's a connection between Ginny and me that I can't explain, and with each day that passes, my feelings are becoming stronger. But I'm not ready to tell her yet because when I do, I'll be adding to her grief.

When I get chance later, I'm going to call her, again, and hope that this time she answers. For now, I'll have to settle for providing her with an apology.

I carry the bags out to the car ready for home. We don't need to bring so much now, mum and dad have made sure we have most of what we need here already. My phone vibrates in my pocket, so I lower the bags to the ground and pull the mobile from my jeans. When I see its Ryan, I lean back against the car and answer.

"Nate, we have a problem man. Well, let me rephrase that, you have a problem." Immediately, I'm put on edge by Ryan's tone.

"What problem?"

"Well, for starters, I've hung up on Marci. Fuck!" I hear something thud over the line. "I can't believe I've put the fucking phone down on her."

"I don't mean to sound like I'm not bothered, but why is this my problem?" I pick the bags back up, open the trunk and start to load them in one by one.

"Because, Nate, Marci was giving me the third degree about you! Which, by the way, why the hell didn't you answer my call last night?"

"I didn't get a call from you last night," I state.

"Well, I rang you! Oh, shit!" He sighs. "My cousin's called Nate. Shit man, I'm sorry."

"Ryan, what the hell is going on?"

"Last night someone happened to mention to Ginny that you'd left to be with another girl."

"What?" I went home to Sophia, so yeah technically I was with another girl but my niece.

"Then today they saw you with Sophia right?"

My head feels like it's ready to explode. No wonder Ginny was off with me earlier and didn't return my calls.

"Marci said her and Ginny saw you with Sophia," he

continues when I don't reply. "Marci wants to know if you're single or if you're a total bastard and are still with Sophia's mother."

"Fuck!"

"Yeah, like I said, your problem." I hadn't even thought how Ginny could see the situation for anything other than what it was. Me and Sophia. Of course she'd question where her mum was.

"Right, I need you to rewind a little. What exactly did she say?"

"Really? Fuck man. Right, something like 'So he has a kid. Nate has a kid, and you didn't think it appropriate to share such information with me?'" I told her it wasn't my place to be telling her. She mouthed off a bit about not being able to trust me if I'm withholding stuff from her. She then went on to demand that I tell her if you are in fact single or a total and utter bastard who is leading Ginny on when that's the last thing Ginny needs. Apparently, she's seriously got the hots for you."

"What? I want the actual words." I need to know exactly what it is Ginny believes.

"I'm not a Dictaphone, Nate. Christ!" He sighs. "She's getting attached or reliant on you maybe. That was about it. I put the phone down because I didn't have a clue what to say to her because, for whatever goddamn reason you have, you didn't want her to know about Sophia. Chicks love men with kids you know. Sophia is like your very own chick magnet!"

It's not that I don't want Ginny to know about Sophia. It's because knowing about Sophia brings the truth even closer to Ginny's door, and I'm not sure she's ready to hear it.

I sigh loudly and slam the trunk closed. "Cheers, Ryan. I'll sort it and limit the damage control with Marci. Okay?"

We hang up, and I start to pace the drive. I've not had enough time with Ginny yet, not nearly enough.

I glance back to the house, Sophia's still inside with my parents, so I scroll through my phone until I get to Ginny's number. I was hoping to ring her later when I had more time to talk, but after speaking with Ryan, I'm scared I've screwed this up for good. My finger hovers over the call button. I draw in a deep breath then with one final look at the house, I ring her.

It takes a while for her to answer but when she does, I experience a slight sense of relief that she's at least answering my call.

"Hello?"

"Hi, it's Nate."

"Yeah, I know." Was that a good 'I know'? Christ! Doubt floods my mind, but then I picture how Ginny looked when I first set eyes on her, and I know she deserves the truth. Selfishly, I push the image aside.

"You answered." I kick some gravel with my feet.

"I did."

"Ginny... about the park. I should have told you about Sophia, but well, she's special to me, and until I knew where we were at, I didn't think it right to tell you about her."

"I understand that. If I had a child, I wouldn't be introducing her to every man I kissed." I can't grasp what her tone means. She's hard to read over a phone call. And kissed? Surely she knows there's more to how I feel about her than just a kiss.

"Ginny, that's where I had to be yesterday. I had to get home to her. I'm single. Sophia's mum... I'm not with her."

"Oh." The hint of a smile touches my lips because I know that was a damn good 'oh'!

"I never have been." What? I told her she was my daughter,

that answer makes it even more unbelievable. "Can I still see you at the weekend?" I rush the question out.

I walk around in a circle, trying to kick the gravel back off the lawn and onto the path. Briefly, I glance up at the house and see mum looking back at me. She smiles and walks back inside.

"What would you do if I said no?"

My lips kick up as I sense the tease in her tone. "I'd keep asking. But you want to say yes, so I think for once you should go with what *you* want."

Again, she pauses, this time her wavering setting me on edge. "You're definitely single? Nate, breaking up marriages or relationships isn't anything I would ever do."

"I know that, Ginny, and I'm definitely single."

"Then yes, Nate." I release my pent up breath and turn back round to the house, grinning ludicrously. Sophia appears at the door and skips over to me.

"Great. Saturday? I'll ring you, okay?"

"Okay. Bye, Nate."

"Goodbye."

The call ends, and Sophia starts bouncing on her feet. "Was that her? Was that Ginny?"

"Erm, yes, kid, it was." I ruffle her hair, and she grins back.

"Yes! I knew it." She plonks her hands on her hips. "I told Grandma that it was her because you were smiling."

"Come on, let's go say goodbye."

"Nate and Ginny sitting in a tree. K.I.S.S.I.N.G." Sophia sings, and I stare after her as she runs to the house shouting for her grandad.

My mum watches me as I grab some more bags. "This one's different, isn't she?"

I pause before looking my mum in the eye. "Yeah, she is."

Then I go in for the kill, knowing my comment will hurt. "But what if she isn't who you want her to be?" Without saying her name, she knows I'm referring to Katie.

"We learnt from our mistakes, Nate. We won't be making them again." Mum approaches the doorway, assuming to check Sophia isn't in range. "I was scared, Nate. I knew what you boys were like. Once you got an idea in your head, there'd be no changing your mind. We... I didn't see it as your fight. I know you don't believe me, but I honestly didn't know what was happening to Katie at home."

"You thought we were better than her," I point out the irony. "When ignoring a troubled girl put you as being inferior, don't you think?" I witness the grief on her face and instantly feel remorse. "I'm sorry."

"Don't apologise for pointing out the truth, Nate." Her eyes fill with tears. "I spoke to Katie about this, so don't look at me as though this is all brand new! Nobody was fighting for Katie—until my two sons came along." Her tears spill and a look of pride graces mum's face as her hand reaches out and she touches my cheek. "That girl loved you both endlessly. I'm so proud of you, Nate." She chokes on a sob, and I pull her into my arms as she cries for the son and daughter-in-law she lost.

I also know some of those tears that are soaking through my shirt are for me, for the one son she has left.

"We were wrong for turning our back on you all. All I can do is promise it won't happen again." But as I look at my mum, I wonder if she truly understands what she's saying. Bringing Ginny into our lives will test her theory above all else.

CHAPTER TWENTY-ONE

GINNY

I take another drink from my glass of wine, hoping it will fill me with the miracle of courage. Nate's due any second, and the anticipation is causing a severe case of fluttering in my stomach. The feeling is becoming regular where Nate's concerned, and it seems impossible to shift the smile from my lips.

"I'm saying I think you need to be careful." I continue listening to Marci on the phone. I thought she'd rung to wish me luck, but the conversation has veered into another direction.

"Careful?" I lower my glass to the worktop, my smile fading.

"I'm not sure we know enough about him. I mean, he said he's single, but where's Sophia's mum? Are you sure it's over between them?"

I can hear the concern in her voice, and as much as her apprehension worries me, it's also a source of irritation. "He said it was, Marci, so I have no option but to believe him."

"Because believing a man is always the right thing to do?" It's hard not to miss the sarcasm in her voice, and I can't deny it hurts. "Shit! I'm sorry. I'm worried. You've been through a lot and, I don't know, I'm not sure you've had time to grieve."

Her comment upsets me. I thought she'd understand that whatever this is with Nate, is making me happy. I'm not asking for wedding bells or any form of commitment. I'm not sure I'll want any of those things ever again. What I do want, is to move on from my life with Blake.

I decide to end her way of thinking bluntly. "Marci, I've grieved from the first moment Blake thrust his fist into my stomach. From the second he made me feel guilty for wanting to speak to you. My life with him was one drawn out stage of grief. He changed everything about me. Now, I'm starting to smile again, but more importantly, I want to smile. Surely that's a good thing? I need to do things I haven't yet done—hell, some of them will lead to mistakes, but that's what everyone does, right? I mean Christ, Marci, I've never had a one night stand, never got so drunk that I struggle to remember my own name. I want to experience more than the darkness my memories create. I want to move on." *I have to move on.*

When I can only hear the sound of her breathing, I hope it's because she finally understands.

I see Nate's car pull into a space on the opposite side of the road. "I have to go," I say quietly.

"I'm sorry, Ginny, I didn't think about it... not properly."

"You have to let me try and do this. I'm not going to break if things don't work out between us."

There's a hesitation on the other end of the phone leading me to think she doesn't believe me. "Call Liam or me if you need us, promise?"

"I promise," I say with sadness. We finish the call, and I slip my mobile into my bag.

When I see Nate get out of the car, I push Marci's doubt from my mind.

He said for me to dress casually and although he's in jeans and a t-shirt, I've never seen a man look so good. Reluctantly, I tear my eyes away, suddenly feeling sick with nerves, expecting Nate to be a pro at this and me a mere amateur. I move towards the door, taking in a deep breath before pushing the handle down.

He's there, looking right at me, and I feel like I've forgotten how to breathe. His eyes never sway from mine. The shape of his eyes remind me of Sophia's, but whereas his are blue, hers are a dark brown.

"Hey," he says on an exhale

"Hi," I answer coyly.

His focus continues to hold mine. "You're beautiful, Ginny."

I don't know how to respond. When Blake called me beautiful, it meant he approved of what I was wearing, or how my hair was styled and that approval was usually gained by wearing the clothes of his choosing and my hair styled to his liking.

Being called beautiful by Nate puts an entirely different spin on it.

"Shall we go?" I ask, and he nods but then seems to remember something.

He pulls a bunch of beautiful colourful flowers from behind his back. I stare at them dumbfounded before looking up at him as he holds them out towards me.

"Thank you," I mutter taking them from him. "I'll put them in a glass for now and sort them when I get back."

"Oh and, um, Sophia made you something." He takes a coloured band from his wrist. "She told me I had to put it on so I wouldn't lose it. Sorry, I've probably stretched it a little." He holds out a multi-coloured bracelet made out of tiny elastic bands. "It's a loom band bracelet. All the kids are making them apparently."

I take it from him and stare at it in wonderment. *She made me a bracelet?* Immediately, I put it on and smile. "Can you tell her, thank you?"

"I will. You don't have to wear it," he says with uncertainty.

"No, I want to."

Remembering the flowers, I quickly pop them into a vase, before locking up the house. Nate hangs back and waits for me, again something I'm not used to.

He steps aside for me to lead the way down the short path but ensures he reaches from behind to open the small wrought iron gate for us to pass through. He does the same for the car door.

I can't help but compare him to Blake. But the word 'comparison' shouldn't even exist because Nate does everything differently and just sitting beside him as he gets into the car creates a wealth of new feelings.

He looks across at me and smiles. "Are you okay?"

"Yes, you?"

He keeps his eyes locked on mine. "No I'm fucking nervous as hell," he says, and the tension around us splits apart, and I let out a small chuckle.

"Really? You're nervous?"

"Yeah, trust me, Ginny, this is all new to me." Knowing that he's equally as nervous as I am is enough to make me feel more at ease.

He scrapes his hands down his jeans before turning over the engine. We pull onto the road and make our way deeper into town.

"So," he peers over at me, "How's Marci? She forgiven Ryan yet?"

"Yes." I smile. It didn't take long, with a little coaxing. I understand why Nate didn't tell us about Sophia. She's not a pawn to be used. She's an innocent child.

"Are you actually going to tell me where we're going?"

"You'll realise soon enough. It's not that big a deal. I didn't want to do the usual date in a restaurant thing," he says with a nervous smile.

A few miles further and he pulls into a car park. We get out of the car, and he grabs a bag from the boot. "It's just a few bits to eat. Come on." He smiles. "We'll be late." He reaches out and takes my hand then draws me closer to him as we cross the road. I fit into him with ease and enjoy the closeness. I think he experiences the same feelings when a satisfying sigh escapes from his mouth.

I see a few more people heading in the same direction as us, and we finally come upon a sign that tells me where we're going.

"An outdoor cinema?" I say in delight.

"Yeah, it's some chick flick. Is that okay?"

"Yeah, I've never been to one before but a chick flick? That okay with you?"

He pauses as we reach the path beside the open green. "I was kind of forced to watch chick flicks throughout my teens, so I'm good."

"You watched chick flicks? So either there's something you're not telling me, or you have a sister," I tease, but he goes quiet, leading me to believe I've said something I shouldn't. "Sorry," I mumble.

"Don't be sorry," he answers, but he sounds sad. "You haven't said anything you shouldn't have." But he chooses not to expand further. Instead, he tightens his grip on my hand, and we make our way into the crowd of people already sitting down ready for the film. I wonder what it is that's forcing his silence and wonder if it's something to do with the sorrow I saw in his eyes at Ryan's party. I lean into him further wanting to ease whatever it is he's gone through.

He stops walking and once again holds me with his gaze. I question if I'm pushing boundaries that should still be in place.

"Stop questioning yourself," he says in reassurance. "I stopped because I think we've reached a good spot. Ginny, when you're near, I can barely think straight. When you're far away, hell, I can barely think straight then either. Trust me, the only problem I'm having right now is my self-restraint."

"Oh." I breathe out.

"I like that 'oh'."

He bends down and starts to open up his rucksack. I take the chance and explore his body with my eyes. When he peers up at me, he notices and laughs while he straightens up.

"Damn, Ginny, you can't look at me like that and expect me to be the gentleman I'm trying to be."

"Who said I liked gentleman?" Whoa! What the hell did I just say? He looks as surprised as I am, but in a way it's true. Everyone believed Blake to be a gent, but they couldn't have been further from the truth. "I don't know how to do this." I let out an uncomfortable laugh.

"Only do what *you* want, Ginny. It's that simple, and it should always be. Your terms."

"And if I want more?"

His lips kick up into a slow grin, and I almost stagger at the vision. With only one man in my sights and the same man domineering my mind, I take a step closer so our chests meet. His breaths turn heavy, and I know I'm affecting him in ways I could only dream possible. I stand on my tiptoes, my lips move to his and when they touch it's like he's bringing me back to life. Waking me up, pulling me from the shell of the person I'd become.

My skin tingles as his hands rake over my back. When his fingers caress my head, kneading my hair, I welcome his touch, leaning into him further.

Only when the kiss starts to slow do I remember where we are. I draw back slightly, and he laughs. Looking around, it seems no one took any notice, they are all busy in their own conversations, and I wonder why I drew away so easily.

"Now, that was a kiss." He grins at me, and I can't help but beam back. This man is getting to me, big time.

Suddenly the big screen lights up, the sound of whoops and cheers erupt in perfect timing mirroring my own happiness.

"Ginny?" When I turn round, Nate is sitting on a blanket with some bags of snacks scattered around him, so I sit down and join him. He hands me a plastic glass with white wine. "It's chilled and pinot, that's what you like right?" I look at him astonished. Even Blake didn't know what my preferred drink was, although maybe he did, but he chose to change it.

"It is," I say taking the glass from him. Nate then opens a can of coke and takes a drink. "You not having wine?"

"Driving." Now I get why he rarely drinks. He has to be back for Sophia. This man becomes nobler with each piece of information I learn.

He shuffles back, puts the backpack behind him and lies down, resting his head on it so he can see the screen. I lounge back, expecting to put my head on the part of the backpack that sticks out from behind him but instead he guides my head to his chest. The sound of his heart beating fast fills my ears.

He places his hand on my shoulder tugging me even closer to

him. "You okay?" His breath skims the top of my head. I close my eyes and breathe him in, wondering why I couldn't have found him years ago.

"Perfect," I mumble. My eyes are still closed making it dark, but I'm not scared. I want to anchor myself to him, and his firm hold on me tells me that's what he wants too.

"Ginny?" I hear his voice soft and gentle. "Ginny?" he says it again. I open my eyes with a start, bolt upright and look back down at Nate, remembering where I am. He sits up, propping himself up on his elbows, looking amused.

"I fell asleep?"

"You did."

"Christ, I'm so sorry—"

"It was worth it," he says, and I blush when I think about falling asleep on his chest. Glancing around, I see only a few people scattered around, the park almost deserted.

"How long ago did it finish?"

Appearing dubious he answers, "I'm not certain. I've just woken up myself."

I open my mouth wide before spurting out laughter, feeling free. When his focus freezes on my mouth, I stop laughing and start to squirm uncomfortably underneath his stare.

"You have dimples," he exclaims incredulously.

"What?" I feel my cheeks warm as he sits up.

"I've never seen them before... your dimples." His hand lifts and his finger skims the softest part of my cheek where my dimples are now hiding. I watch his Adam's apple bob up and down as he swallows. The intensity starts to build between us, and I look away.

"Don't turn away from me, Ginny," he pleads.

Slowly, I twist back to face him and find a look of remorse on his face. "I owe you an explanation." I frown at his words. "Sophia's mum, she died. Sophia's a part of my life that I need to protect above anything else and it's her story as well as mine. It's not something I go about telling people."

I hang my head in regret at my actions last weekend and remorse filters its way into my heart.

"I'm so sorry. I shouldn't have questioned you. Somebody said at the party that you'd left to be with a girl, we jumped to conclusions." I raise my chin and look at him apologetically.

"I'm single, Ginny, like I told you."

I close my eyes and think of the little girl with blonde hair and brown eyes we met last week at the park. "She's wonderful, Nate."

"Pardon?"

"Sophia... she seemed so happy with you. You're obviously a great dad." He's taken back by my compliment, but it's well deserved. "I don't know how you'd ever get over something like that, losing a parent at that age."

"She's doing okay."

"What's it like bringing her up by yourself?"

"It's hard, really hard, but amazing too. Since her mum died, people have been great, kind. They offer me parenting advice. I know they mean well, but it's almost like they're saying I don't know what I'm doing. Which, I guess I don't half the time."

I reach my hand out and slowly sweep my fingers down his jaw. "You're an amazing person, Nate. When you said she was your daughter—" I look away briefly remembering her expression. "She looked up at you with a look of disbelief on her face. Then when she smiled at you... she knows how lucky she is to have a father like you."

"I worry that I won't be enough for her. My life was a lot different before I had Sophia."

"Well sure, isn't everybody's? I mean, I know I don't have any children, but before kids, you only have to worry about yourself."

"Do you ever see yourself with children?"

I glance down. "I didn't. I couldn't have done that. Not with him." I shiver as a chill from the night air passes over me. Nate retrieves a blanket from the bag and drapes it over my legs. "You have a spoonful of sugar in there too?" I question with a smile.

"I have a daughter remember? You have to be equipped for rain, sun, cold, hot." He glances at my neck. "In fact, I have one of Sophia's scarves in here." Before I have chance to respond, he's pulled the scarf from the bag.

"No!" I elevate my hand, pushing the scarf away. "No scarf," I state and inwardly cringe at the fear in my voice. Nate clearly recognises it and slowly lowers the scarf to his knee.

"Okay. No scarf."

An awkward silence settles between us. I keep my focus down for fear of what I will see if I look at Nate. He knows I have a past that I've been keeping hidden, but he's never pushed for answers. It's like he's giving me the time I need. Or maybe he's worried about what he'd hear.

"You've never asked me about him," I state bringing up the one subject we both are managing to avoid.

"Because I know it still causes you pain. I don't like seeing you in pain, Ginny."

"He's dead," I blurt out. "And I'm not sorry," I whisper under my breath. "Bet you never thought I was crazy, huh?"

"You're not crazy, Ginny," he says with a sad tone.

"I can't remember it being like this before," I say on an undertone, and I feel him tense beside me.

"What was it like before?"

I inhale deeply before my eyes lift to the stars above. There isn't a cloud in the sky, and it's beautiful. "I can't remember ever talking to him like this. Y-You…" I stutter on my words wondering how much I should be telling him. "You make me feel safe."

"He didn't?"

"No." Lifting the blanket from me, I twist around and sit forward on my knees. "You can't fix me, Nate, nor will I blame you if you get up and walk away because that's what you should do. You should leave."

"I'm going to stay as long as you let me, Ginny."

"Well, I'm not willing to ruin today."

He looks at me, pain oozing from him. Without him actually knowing, I feel he understands. He once told me I reminded him of someone who experienced pain. I want to ask him who it was, but if I'm not willing to ruin today with details of my own past, I can't expect it from him.

"We all lose at some point and have to learn how to get back up again. One day, the pain will no longer drench you and what comes after the fall… it can be everything." His words remind me of what Katie once told me, and for a second I wonder what she'd think of Nate. I wish she'd returned my call and then maybe I'd be in a position to introduce them.

His fingers knot into mine.

"You want to get out of here?"

"What did you have in mind?"

"Whatever you want. What have you always wanted to do but never have?"

It only takes me a second to answer. "I don't want to think about the past, nor the future." I want to let this damn guard down that I permanently have erected around me. "I want to drink, Nate, laugh, and fall over because I'm that drunk I can't stand."

"I was expecting a skydive or something, although something like that would be a little harder to organise last minute and in the dark. Getting drunk, I can do that." He grins a smile of mischief. "You trust me?"

"Like I've never trusted anyone before." His whole body stiffens, and it can only be because he understands how hard trust comes to someone like me.

CHAPTER TWENTY-TWO

NATE

I watch her as she stands at the end of the bar sipping on her drink. I've moved to the door so I can make a call to my parents to let them know I'll be out a few more hours yet, as long as everything is okay with Sophia—which it is.

She's already on her third drink since entering the bar, equalled by as many shots. Yet she still appears closed off to everyone else but me, which makes me feel on top of the world, but I also know it's not normal. Not healthy. I worry that our time is limited, selfishly needing to have as much of her as I can before she finds out. I told her I'd stay as long as she lets me and that's the truth.

Pushing my phone back in my pocket, I make my way over to her. The glow from the dimmed lighting in the bar emphasises her beauty, and all I see is Ginny. The haunted look in her eyes that usually taunts me is slowly easing. She doesn't want to ruin this evening, and as much as I feel she needs to talk about her past, about him, right now, selfishly, I don't want it to be ruined either.

When she turns and smiles, I have no choice but to follow

her wishes because she's so damn happy. "So how drunk are we talking?" I meet her grin head on.

"Well," she closes one eye and skims over the choice of alcohol behind the bar, "I'm talking like really drunk. Puking in the morning kind of drunk."

I call out to the barman in front of me. "Can I have two more lagers please?" The male bartender acknowledges my order with a nod, but his gaze settles a second longer than necessary on Ginny. She doesn't notice of course. Ginny's beauty is rare because her looks should dictate a confidence that she doesn't possess.

The barman hands over the drinks, and I thrust a note towards him, adding a scowl in for good measure.

"Sorry, man." He nods and takes the money.

"No chaser?"

I widen my eyes, amused by the already tipsy version of Ginny standing in front of me. "I have a feeling we should be pacing it a little," I respond, finding it damn difficult to take my eyes from her.

"Quit staring at me like that." She giggles, the alcohol apparently lifting some of Ginny's defences.

"How am I staring at you?" I tease, enjoying this side of her.

"Like you want to kiss me," she adds.

It's as easy as that, one glance, one sentence, and I'm rendered speechless. I do want to kiss her, desperately. I want to hold her, forever. Every minute I spend with her increases the feelings I have towards her. I want to make everything better. I'm falling for her. But how can I fall for someone who keeps half of them hidden? How can I expect her to fall in love with me, when I'm withholding secrets?

I stand back, and she frowns. "You don't have to kiss me. It's okay."

I don't know what to say, how to react. The only way this will ever work is if she knows the truth. Yet, learning the truth could elevate a permanent barrier between us, and I'm not sure if I can risk it, not yet.

So I take back the step I put between us. "I'll always want to kiss you," I breathe the words so only she can hear. She has to believe that she's worthy of so much happiness. She has to believe in herself. She widens her eyes, and I reach out and take her with my mouth. She gives back as much as I give to her. It's a kiss of desperation, a plea for something good to come from a nightmare she has no idea we share.

When the kiss ends, she buries her head in my chest, and I wrap my arms around her, wishing... hoping that I never have to let her go.

"Do you ever wish you could forget?" she mutters.

Gently, I take her face in my hands, spread my fingers over her temples, guiding her head back so I can see her. The pain emanates from her like it has no way of stopping. A groan of agony escapes from deep within my throat at the anticipated answer to my question. "What do you want to forget, Ginny?"

"Everything." She drops her head so I can no longer see her face. Muscles twitch in my jaw, and I find it hard to catch a breath. Then she looks back up. "If I'd have met you first, I'd want to remember every single second."

Heavy breaths break free from my lips, landing on her head of soft dark hair as she continues clutching me. *If I'd have met her first?* I blink rapidly, wanting to take away the anger, the injustice that's dredging its way through me.

Before I know it, someone crashes into our side. I turn, ready to attack, but its Marci.

"Hey!"

I glance at Ginny, wondering if she asked her friend to join us but judging by the look on her face, she didn't, and surprise reverts to annoyance.

"Why are you here, Marci?" Ginny asks sounding curt.

"I honestly didn't know you were here, not until I saw you a minute ago. I'm sorry, I'll leave you to it," Marci says, appearing full of regret.

"I'm fine, Marci." She stands up straight. "In fact, I'm better than fine. So quit your worrying. I'll be back in a minute," Ginny directs at me. "I need the ladies room."

Marci hangs back, and we watch Ginny head towards the toilet.

"What was that about?" I direct at Marci. "What have you done?"

"Excuse me?" she replies, glaring at me. "What have *you* done? What the hell was going on between you two because she looked as upset as she was the day I got her back?"

"The day you got her back?"

She shakes her head, trying to cast my comment aside. "Look, Nate, there's more to Ginny than you'll ever know. You've been around five minutes, so don't start preaching about her welfare as though you know what's best. My concern is exactly what's caused this mess."

"What mess?" I tackle.

"It doesn't matter." Again she tries to shrug off her comment.

"You talking about her ex?"

"You know? She told you?"

"I know enough."

It takes a moment for my comments to sink in. "Then you'll understand where my concern comes from. Ginny isn't happy with me because I've questioned her over what this is between you two—"

"Now hang on—" I begin.

"Hear me out," she interrupts. "I want her to be happy, Nate, Christ, if anyone deserves it, she does. I think you should maybe ease off a little."

"Ease off?"

"She's becoming reliant on you. I've been watching her the past few weeks, and the moment you appear, it's like she can breathe again, without pain."

"So why the hell would I walk away from her?"

"I didn't say walk away, just slow down. She needs to grieve. What if you hanging on tight to her allows her to continually bypass the grief stage? What will happen then?"

"I've no idea. You seem to have all of the answers." I'm coming across as angry, but I shouldn't be aiming it at Marci. I know what I'm doing is wrong, not because of the past, but because I'm withholding information from Ginny that she should know. Marci adding another concern makes it two too many.

"I worry that it won't be great for Ginny. Part of me wants to keep my mouth shut because she's happy, Nate, she barely knows you, but when she looks at you, it's so different to how she ever looked at Blake. You remember that night in the restaurant, our kind of double date?" At least she has the decency to appear embarrassed.

"Of course I remember."

Sheepishly she glances in the direction Ginny just went. "I missed her when she was gone. She rarely came home. I'm pretty certain it's because that's how Blake wanted it. When she came back, I knew everything was going to be alright. Then I saw her with you, and I heard her laugh. I hadn't heard that beautiful sound for so long that I'd forgotten what it was like. I stared at her, but she heard herself laugh too, and I knew she felt guilty for it. I went home and cried that night because I felt like I was getting some of the old Ginny back but, I don't know... she doesn't talk about him." Her voice fades, and it's hard to hear with the chatter that's going on around. "She hasn't told me what he did. With this kind of thing, I don't know, shouldn't she be talking about it with someone? What if she's covering up something that shouldn't yet be buried?"

I feel like someone's punched me in the gut. I thought I'd been helping but what Marci's saying makes sense. I knew from the moment I first saw her that she was hiding, submerging her pain beneath a blanket of false smiles. Yet I've chosen to stop seeing it because even a false smile from Ginny is better than a normal smile from any other woman.

"She came to me once for help. She was beaten, still bleeding." She shakes her head in disbelief. "But then he showed up, and it was like he'd pressed some kind of automatic behaviour button. She willingly went to his side and left. I still can't get my head around it. Even now. Why she chose to go back."

My shoulders slump because this bit I do know. Aaron and I, we learnt it all from Katie—her mum had been the same. Ginny had no choice. She would have done it to protect others, to stop the beatings from getting even worse. She did it because she was goddamn petrified.

"When she's with you, it's like it never happened." Surely that's a good thing? I don't quite understand what her problem is.

"What are you trying to say?"

"You've somehow become her crutch, her lifeline. It's you she seeks out, but what if one day you're not there. I'm not sure she can take more pain, not when she can't bring herself to talk about what she's been through." Marci nudges me in my side, and I lift my lids to see Ginny making her way back towards us. "I better go. I'm trying to help you both here, Nate," she states as she slides away into the crowded part of the bar, disappearing from view.

She can't take any more pain. Which means the secret I'm keeping hidden has the capability of not only ruining us but destroying her.

Lifting my focus, I watch as Ginny gets closer. She looks around. I'm guessing to see where Marci is. When she reaches me, she takes the beer from my hand and raises it to her lips.

"Bottom's up," she announces, and I drink my own beer like it's going to give me all of the answers I need.

"Oh my God!" she calls out. "You normally drive because you have Sophia at home and I'm making you drink." She glares at my beer. "You're not having any more. Shit! I'm sorry!"

Gently, I offer my reassurance. "Ginny, my parents are with her. She's safe." I usually drive because I want to be there if she wakes in the night but these past few weeks her nightmares seem to be easing somewhat. So I didn't see the harm in drinking earlier. Now, I think I'd have been better with a sober mind to assist with the bombshell Marci's added to the one I've been burying my head under.

"Are you sure? I can't be the reason you're not there when she needs you."

I stare at her, wishing I'd met her years ago, before he managed to get his bastard hands on her. Before our future held a link to a broken past.

I have to tell her, or I have to walk away. But I want a third option. Something that doesn't involve causing her pain. I'm riddled with desperation, unable to see a way through this without hurting her. Although it was her husband that caused this, I can be the only one to let her know the true extent of damage he created.

When she grabs my hand, I let her lead me outside as the words I wish never to be spoken, hang in the air.

The second we hit outside her lips land on mine. At first, I don't respond, but she only tugs me closer towards her, wrapping her arms around my neck. She appears to acknowledge my hesitance but refuses its existence, instead, deepening the kiss. When my hands instinctively grasp her waist, she lets out a gentle moan. I want to please her, to touch her skin, feel her near me, with me. To allow this connection that's been smouldering away to ignite.

She stretches herself higher. The action causes her top to lift slightly and my fingers land on her naked skin. It's soft, smooth, and so damn inviting. My fingers can't help but travel further up her back, exploring as much of her as I can. When my touch lands on a roughened part of skin, I trace over it, recognising it as scar tissue.

She flinches and pulls from me. Her breaths come short and fast as a look of shame crosses over her expression.

"No!" I say aloud. That one act of disgrace proves Marci's point, and I can't bear for it to be true. My hatred for Blake grows beyond what I ever thought possible. She turns away, but I step around her and lift her chin so she's looking at me. "Don't turn from me like you're ashamed." She won't look at me. "Ginny, you didn't create this. You have to believe me." As she stands in front of me, her focus on her feet, a single glistening tear falls from beneath her lashes and slowly makes its way down her cheeks. "You can't take any blame." The words fall helplessly from my tongue as what Marci said haunts me further. I turn my back on Ginny needing a minute.

"He hurt me. Repeatedly. How can I not take any of the blame?"

"What?" I swing around and look hard in her eyes. "You didn't do anything wrong! You have to talk to somebody, Ginny." Men like him, they control, making women like Ginny believe they're partly responsible. Marci was right. "You need to talk to someone," I utter again.

"Why? So I can relive it?" She looks at me with a wounded stare. "So I feel all of that pain again?" I pull her to me, never wanting to let go. But I know that's not the answer. Finally, she holds me too and slowly our breaths calm and leave our chests in synchrony. "I can't, Nate." I want to give in. To let her forget the memories that cause her agony but then I'll never be able to talk to her about my brother or Katie, and I can't act like they never existed.

"You have to, Ginny."

Her body steadily tenses within my hold, but her arms ease their grip. She shuffles back and straightens her shoulders before raising her eyes to mine.

"My husband was an abuser. But he wasn't always like that. At first, he was kind, attentive, caring. When we met, I was caring for my mother. She only had a matter of weeks left when Blake came into my life. He would sit with me and let me be sad. Blake entered my life when all I could see was the darkness."

Ginny backs up, her hands clasp together in front of her, and she swallows. She's talking, but I'm not sure I'm the right person.

"When she died, Blake took care of things, helped with the

funeral arrangements, the house, everything. He made me feel as though I was the only person in the world. At first, he started worrying about me, about my safety, I'd never really had that before. Then he started to get jealous. That was bearable to start off with—it kind of made me feel wanted. But then it started to get out of hand. To the point, I thought it best not to go out because it made life easier. Then we moved away and... everything changed. Everything."

I step towards her, needing to be by her side but she shakes her head. "No! The truth isn't something people always want to hear, but *you* seem keen on hearing mine."

I retreat from her and can only stand and watch as the girl I'm falling for withdraws further into herself, immersing into a life she wants to move on from but hasn't yet come to terms with.

"I didn't have a job. I gave it up to move with him. I started making mistakes with dinner... with his ironing... I made a lot of mistakes. At first, it was a smack across my cheek—" She stares at me to check my reaction. I shove my fists in my pockets to avoid giving anything away, but I can already feel the muscles tensing in my jaw hearing about that sick son-of-a-bitch.

"I should have tried harder to protect myself—"

"You shouldn't have to protect yourself from your husband, Ginny. He was supposed to love you, protect *you*!"

"Somebody doesn't suddenly start hitting out for no reason."

Holy shit! She can't see that this is not of her doing. "Whatever made him do it, Ginny, was nothing to do with you." I want to reach out to her, but she won't let me.

"We'll have to agree to disagree on that one, Nate!"

Anger starts to bubble away at what Blake has made her believe. Blake! If I could get my hands on him... Without warning, the image of him lifting a finger to Ginny flickers into sight. Then suddenly I need to hear it all. I need to know everything. To know his death was the only thing right in this horrid situation. I turn back around. "You said *at first* it was a smack across the cheek? What else did he do?"

She scans our surroundings like she doesn't want anybody hearing what he did. When the entire world should know exactly what he was.

"Why do you need to know? It doesn't matter anymore," she pleads.

"*I* need to know." I'm pushing her, but I have to know.

"Remember you're the one who asked, Nate," she says by way of warning. I nod my head. "He would punch me." Ginny drops her focus, shame once again unjustifiably becoming hers. "Kick me. Pinning me up against the wall became his favourite for a while. He used a scarf around my…" her hand flicks to her neck before she drops it helplessly. "Towards the end, he'd knock me about so much that I'd drift in and out of consciousness, then he…" It's only then, the tears start falling from her eyes. She looks at my fists. They're clenched tight, and my jaw is set in a tight line. She shakes her head. "You've heard enough. I don't need to go on."

"Enough? There's more?"

Oh God… no… no… The truth registers. "He…" I close my eyes as reality sinks in, and I can't bring myself to finish my own sentence, but as I look at her now, I know she's confirming my fears. He raped her.

"Why the hell did you not leave him?" I hate myself the minute the words leave my mouth. I can't put any blame on her, not even to cause a single doubt in her mind. "Don't answer that," I sneer. "You shouldn't have had to leave him. This was all on him." This is why Katie worked with women like Ginny because she knew what it was like first-hand and wouldn't have made a callous remark like I just did.

"I tried twice. But somehow he knew within hours where I was."

"He tracked you," I say matter of fact.

"That's what I was told by a friend." She laughs, but it's cynical. "Isn't it pathetic? I moved miles away and only made one friend, well she wasn't even a friend, not in the true sense of the word but she was the only person who knew *everything,* and she understood."

I still at the mention of a friend. "A friend?"

"Yeah, she helped me get out, but somehow it was more than just a job to her." *She... Katie.* "She worked with me for a while. If it weren't for her, I'm not sure I would ever have left. People like Katie, the work they do... no amount of thanks would ever be enough. She was my saviour."

Katie. She said her name. Tears sting my eyes. Each muscle in my body tenses, waiting to hear more about the relationship they had, no matter how brief.

"I rang her mobile and left a message. I wanted her to know that one of the women she'd helped had made it. It wasn't due to our plan, but all the same, I wanted her to know. I never got a reply. I shouldn't be surprised really, you see, the original plan was to never look back, Katie taught me that. I was not to make contact with anyone from my previous life. It would put them in danger, as well as myself. But circumstances changed." She looks at me now. "I was going to leave. I had somewhere to go. My bag was packed, I was following through every single part of the plan I'd made with Katie. I wasn't going to put up with it anymore Nate. But then I saw the police car drive up the lane."

"The police?"

"Blake had been in an accident." She hangs her head as though in disgrace. "There was another car involved. I know there were more fatalities than him. The police said it was an accident, but I still buried my head, Nate. I should have found out who they were. If they left people behind. Who does that? Who doesn't even have the decency to face disaster in the eye?"

Even now, without knowing the entire truth, she's managing to place blame on herself. If she finds out *everything,* Ginny will hold herself unrightfully responsible.

I could stay here. Act like nothing happened. Try and live as though it didn't matter, protecting Ginny from the truth of what her husband did. But, I know what he did would matter to her. More than anything.

My eyes seal closed as I beg to remember how she has been tonight. Ready for something new. Possibly with me.

If she found out who was in the other car, she'd put the pieces together, possibly believe that Blake was at fault in the end. She'd know who me and Sophia are, wonder why I reached out to her. I've been keeping too many secrets.

I know somehow Ginny would end up blaming herself because that's who she is. Whether he made her this way or she's always been like it, I'll never know. She'll take the blame. She won't pass it where it rightfully belongs, to Blake Daniels.

"Now tell me what you see when you look at me?" She asks the question with disgust, and I recognise what she's waiting for. She's expecting me to stand back, but I can't handle the space we've already created, so I walk towards her. She's holding my stare but not in fear of coming to harm, in fear of what I think of her.

I stand so close that I feel her breath. "I see a beautiful woman who has been hurt badly, and I know all you deserve from this point onwards is happiness and safety. You need to trust." My words die off as reality sinks in. I can't give her that. When she finds out who I am, and what I've kept from her.

I take a step back, and she looks at my movement in panic.

Fuck! I don't know what to do. I'm standing facing the one woman I want to protect but being with her will mean I will be the cause of her ruin. *What have I done?*

I shake my head, not wanting to believe how selfish I've been. I feel like I was falling for her before we even met but how can that be? How can you love someone you've never even spoken to? It's like Ginny was always meant to be with me and a bitter fucked up twist of fate led to this moment. Her broken heart, her aching body, was brought into my life. I have no doubt I was born to love this woman, but I'm not sure she'll allow it.

"You need to see someone," I utter helplessly.

"You said I needed to talk. I'm talking to you."

"I'm not the right person."

"What?"

I take a step back and witness the panic on her face, but I can't see any other way out of this. "I despise him. I see you—it's only a tainted version of you, and I know there's still a part of you missing. But I'm still falling in love with the part of you that's here."

"You're what?" A smile tinges on the edge of her lip, and she makes a move towards me.

"No! I'm falling in love with the part you allow me to see, but I want to see all of it, and because of him, I'm not sure I ever will. I'm glad he's dead because if he weren't, I'd go there and finish the job myself. You need to talk to someone, Ginny. You need to grieve."

"Why would you want me to grieve for a man like him if you despise him so much?"

"I want you to grieve for you. Not for him. I want you to grieve for the years you spent with him. The times he took your smile, for how he removed your freedom." I clench my jaw excessively. "For when he hurt you." I clamp my eyes closed as images of him laying his hands on her crowd my mind.

I know I'm acting like the biggest cock in the history of fucking cocks! But I have to leave. She's starting to heal, but all it is, is a cover, a scab holding together wounds that are still very much alive and flourishing beneath. If I remain with her, I can't continue to withhold the truth, but maybe she can get better without knowing the extent of what happened that day when they all died.

Hearing her talk of Katie has made me aware of what she meant to her. She doesn't know she died. She doesn't know it was her husband that was driving the car that hit her.

When I link my eyes to hers, she sees straight through me.

"No," she utters. "Nate, please—"

"I can't do it," I whisper.

"Can't do what?"

"I can't do this. Y-You have to believe what I'm about to say. You have to trust me. Staying with me will only cause you more pain. You think you suffered before? I have the potential to scar you for a lifetime, and I can't be that person."

Tears fall down her cheeks, and I want more than anything to be the one to wipe them away, but I can't.

"Ginny." Her name comes out like I'm choking, the emotion hitting me hard. "You are worthy of so much, but I can't be the one to break you. I'm sorry. So sorry."

"I'm already broken, Nate, can't you see that? You can't hurt me any more than I'm hurting now."

Behind Ginny, I see the outline of someone as they walk towards us. When I recognise Marci, I don't know whether I'm grateful she showed up or want to push her away for making me see everything in bright shitty neon lights.

I swallow hard and gulp on a breath. "I have the capability to finish you off, Ginny." I take steps backwards and make myself watch as she falls to the ground. Pain rips through my body, slashing through my chest. I take it because it's what I deserve.

I may despise Blake Daniels for everything that he did, but that disgust, the hatred is now self-owned as I see the woman I love fall to pieces in front of me.

Marci rushes to Ginny and cradles her in her arms as I turn away.

"I said slow down!" Marci shouts. "Not leave, you bastard."

Blake Daniels was the cause of Katie and Aaron's death, Ginny's abuse, Sophia becoming an orphan. His life came at a disastrous cost to all I love. Now one more thing has come of it. The price of us. Ginny and me.

CHAPTER TWENTY-THREE

GINNY

$\mathcal{A}$bsentmindedly, I wipe Marci's table free of crumbs from the bread selection that she has partly devoured her way through.

"Ginny, will you please eat some?" Marci holds up a slice of olive loaf as though that's what I need right now, that the bread will somehow make everything better.

"I told you, I'm not that hungry." I'm not hungry at all. In fact, the half-slice I forced myself to eat still feels like it's lodged in my throat, ready to make a reappearance.

"Do you want to talk about it?"

"No." Marci brought me back to her place last night. She's been watching me like a hawk since. The only reprieve I had was the four hours I was left alone in the spare room. I wish I could say I slept soundly for those few hours but it would be a lie.

"You haven't heard from him?" she enquires, her tone soft.

"I'm not expecting to, Marci. It was clear what he wanted."

Standing up, I take the plates over to her sink and turn on the tap. Marci warned me not to get too close, but I refused to listen, thought I knew best. I still don't understand though... he was right there one minute, acting as though I meant something. He even said he was falling in love with me—the brief second that followed I was floating on air—and my heart had a reason to keep on beating. But then I told him about Blake, and he froze, no longer able to look at me.

"I'm heading back home soon," I comment as I submerge the plates in the warm water.

"Ginny?" I lift my focus wondering how long Marci has been saying my name, a look of worry is in her eyes, so I smile, but she only looks away. "There's something I should tell you."

I turn around sensing what she has to say isn't something I want to hear.

"I told him you needed to grieve. That you were becoming reliant on him, and I didn't think it was healthy. You haven't seen anyone... like a counsellor and I think maybe it would help."

"Maybe. You told him I was becoming reliant on him? Was I?" I question staring at her. "Or was he helping me, Marci?"

"I'm sorry," she repeats. Perhaps I should be angry with her for interfering, but Nate didn't walk away because of what Marci said. I just wish I knew what the real reason was. None of it makes sense, and while Marci's watching me with a keen eye, it's hard for me to try and get to grips with the situation. "Ginny, you know you can stay as long as you like."

"I know." But I'll be going home.

The sound of someone knocking on the door breaks through the momentary silence, making me jump. Marci's quick to stand. "It's okay." Her brow creases. "I should have said. Ryan's due over."

For that split second, I was taken back to the time Blake turned up at Marci's house. All of the progress I thought I'd made disappeared with that one knock. I force a smile and nod.

"He made me jump, that's all." I lick my lips and close my mouth, forcing rapid breaths through my nose.

When Ryan walks in, he takes Marci's face in his hands and kisses her hard. Appearing uncomfortable, I'm assuming in my presence, she pulls from him, and then he sees me.

"Oh, hey, Ginny." His welcoming smile turns to a look of sympathy. "How are you doing?"

"I'm fine." My answer sounded genuine, but I can't tell myself if I'm actually fine or not. "I'm going to go and grab my stuff," I say heading out of the room.

"Stay for another drink, Ginny. Please?" Marci doesn't want me to feel like I have to go because Ryan is here. To ease her conscience, I agree. She moves towards the kettle, setting about making us all a drink while I nip upstairs.

When I make it into the bedroom, I lean back against the door taking in the neutrally decorated room. It reminds me of the rooms I used to see Katie in. I shake my head, wanting to stop the reminders that keep coming at me. I've tried hard to forget, but for some reason, recently, they keep reappearing more frequently. Hastily, I pack up my few belongings and go back downstairs.

Ryan's sitting at the table alone. "She's gone to the toilet. She won't be long," he adds as though I may be worried about being alone with him in the room. I sit down in a chair opposite him, and he pushes a steaming cup towards me. "That one's yours, I think."

"Thanks." I hold the cup in my palms and keep my eyes low. I know he's looking at me. No doubt noticing my puffy swollen eyes due to lack of sleep and my tears. But I've had enough of being the one everyone talks about behind my back. The one who's had so many awful things happen that all everyone wants to do is protect me from anything bad happening further. Like Nate last night. He told me he could finish me off. *Why would he say that?*

"Ginny," his fingers twiddle together like he's nervous. "For what it's worth, I'm sorry about you and Nate." *Another apology. It's all anyone has for me.*

"Thank you," I say the words but don't really mean them.

"I don't get it though. I don't understand," he mumbles. "Sorry, I'm probably speaking out of turn but Nate, he could never take his eyes off you. It doesn't make sense how he'd walk away from you like that. I'm not trying to get you to fight for him or anything. I just... it doesn't make sense."

"I think," *I know,* "I've got some baggage, and he was right to walk away."

"I can't imagine Nate would let any kind of baggage stop him from doing what he wanted." He glances over his shoulder to the doorway to check if Marci's in earshot. "What if it's something else?"

"What do you mean?"

"I don't know. He's a great guy. I've only known him eight months or so, but since I met him, there's been something I can't put my finger on. I've always felt like Nate is holding back on me. Like there's something on the tip of his tongue, but he stops himself from saying it. Maybe he is ill." His eyes open wider as thoughts run through his mind. "He wouldn't want you to see that," he adds after contemplation.

Eight months? That's roughly the time I came back here. "Eight months? You met him eight months ago?" I query trying to figure out if the span of time has any relevance to anything at all, but I can't think of a reason it would.

"You met who eight months ago?" Marci questions as she enters the room.

"Nate," Ryan answers indifferently, but Marci focuses on me with questions of her own.

"That's when you came back," she points out. "That doesn't mean anything. Does it?" She frowns.

"How would I know?" But an unnerving feeling is settling itself in the pit of my stomach. I sense dots scattered all around me, fighting to be joined up in order to give me a bigger picture, but I'm not sure if I want to know it. Nate said he could break me. What does he mean?

I look at Ryan. "You know where he lives right?"

"I do, but I'm not sure if it's the right thing—"

"What are you talking about?" Marci barks.

Ignoring her, I continue looking at Ryan. "Please... next weekend?"

He sighs, and I know it's a sigh of resignation. "Okay."

"What the hell, Ginny?" Marci shrieks.

"I need to talk to him."

"You're doing no such thing!" Marci calls out her order. She wants me to grieve. Nate wants me to grieve. Yet they're both expecting me to walk away from Nate without a single question.

I stand up from the table and look my friend right in the eye. "I *am* going to see him next week. You will not be coming. You've been worrying about me hiding from my past. Well, how can I go back there without getting some kind of explanation about the present? I have to close this door first—then I'll step back into my past, Marci."

CHAPTER TWENTY-FOUR

NATE

She continues reading next to me, and I stare at the page following the words. It's a book about a group of girls at a school. I've already lost what's happening, but Sophia looks to be enjoying it. Until that is, she makes up an entirely new sentence about a monkey riding a bike with a tattoo on its forehead. I frown and lift the page.

"Where does it say that?"

She lets out a little laugh. "I didn't think you were listening, so I was tricking you."

"Ha-ha, well there you go, I was listening." I smile at her, and she looks at my lips.

"That's not a proper smile."

"Excuse me?"

"When Dylan smiles in class, he smiles like that. Miss Spencer always notices and talks to him a lot. Do you need to talk?"

Fuck! I have to stop letting my feelings show to Sophia. She needs me to be her safe, her happy.

"Of course I don't need to talk, kid, everything's as it should be. Except..." I twist my wrist around and glance at my watch. "My watch tells me you should be in bed."

"Yeah yeah. I'll go upstairs and brush my teeth."

I ruffle her hair, and she groans before running out of the room.

Picking up Sophia's half-drunk cup of hot chocolate, I take it into the kitchen at the same time as Olly taps on the door, proceeding to walk through. Max follows behind. The sound of little footsteps resounds on the landing before cascading down the stairs. I mockingly display a disapproving glance at the doorway, knowing Sophia will rush through the living room and bound through into the kitchen any second to join us.

"Olly!" She cries as she enters the room before dashing towards him. In style of their normal greeting, Olly scoops her up, then tickles and fusses over her, causing spouts of laughter to leave her lips.

"Oh my God, Sophia, you've grown! I'm sure of it. And..." Olly sniffs around her face and neck. "You smell of –"

"No!" Sophia wriggles happily in his arms knowing what's coming.

"Mint! I can smell mint and the sweet scent of strawberries!" Olly sniffs all around Sophia's neck and hair while she squirms in his grasp, giggling her way through his tormenting. Finally, he sets her back down to the floor and ruffles her hair before she lifts up a hand finally acknowledging Max.

"Hi, Max," she remarks before they greet each other with a high-five. I smile at the different versions of greetings that pass between Sophia and my friends. The difference is that Olly was also a friend of Katie's, so he's been in Sophia's life from the day she took her first breath. He's seen her almost as much as I have.

Max, on the other hand, I've only known for a couple of years. He doesn't have experience with kids, but he's still good enough around her.

She wanders back towards me and wraps her arms around my waist.

"I definitely have to go to bed on time now, don't I? Because they brought beer round?"

"That you do." I turn and squat making it easier for her to jump on my back. As always, she climbs on, and I give her a piggyback up the stairs to bed.

Once I've tucked her in, I come down the stairs, the top of Olly and Max's heads are visible on the sofa, showing they've already made themselves at home. I walk past them to the spare chair and take the beer that Max holds up as I do.

I sit down with a sigh and stare at the television, not caring what's on.

Looking across at the guys, I watch as a knowing look passes between the two of them. Olly raises his eyebrows at Max, clearly wanting to silence the more outspoken of the two. Max shakes his head in frustration and pushes himself back on the couch, his eyes purposefully pointing at the television, avoiding me. I squeeze the bottle in my palm, feeling the tension radiating from me.

Olly turns his attention my way, exhales, then hoists himself up, resting his elbows on his knees. "So what's going on?"

"Why should something be going on?" I retort.

"Um because today is Monday and you didn't make it to work? Because you look like a seal slapped its flippers back and forth over your cheeks, oh, and if you squeeze any harder you're going to break that bottle in your hands."

"Basically, you're uptight, twisted, and fucking in love with her. Is that right?" Max adds but continues to glare at the television.

I scowl back wondering what his problem is. Everything is too raw at the moment. Only they don't have a clue as to why.

"Nate, does she know who you are yet?" Olly broaches more tentatively.

I slump back. "No, and she doesn't know about Katie. For definite. She has no idea she died," I exclaim.

"How does she not know it was Katie in the car? It was in the papers, the same article that reported on her husband's death!"

"I dunno," I utter with sarcasm but immediately jump to Ginny's defence. "Why would she? Katie's birth name is Kathryn, and they used that in the newspaper. They only ever used first names at work. She wouldn't have had any need to connect the two names and maybe she was too torn at the time to take notice or even think about it. She definitely wouldn't have known who Aaron was," I say quietly.

Jolting up from my seat, I tug on the patio door and step outside, dragging my fingers through my hair. It's all getting too much. I've overcomplicated everything. I should have been upfront with Ginny in the first place.

I pace back and forth then stop dead in my tracks. Max has yet to say a word, so I turn round and look through the open doorway in his direction. He's avoiding me. With his lips tight, it's like he's holding his thoughts in. Then I see the tick in his jaw. I'm ready for him and decide a fight might be what I goddamn need right now.

"You're keeping quiet, Max?"

His eyes briefly swerve my way.

"Max," Olly says his name in warning.

"No, I want to know what he has to say."

"I don't think you do, man," Max taunts with a tight grimace flashing over his expression.

"I said I wanted to know," I state impatiently.

Max leans forward, his posture tense. "Fine—" he starts, but Olly interrupts.

"Outside," Olly orders as he glances towards the staircase. Sophia is upstairs. Her bedroom window overlooks the front garden, so Olly knows whatever is about to be said, will be done without her ears listening in.

Narrowing my eyes, I watch Max as he comes outside, Olly slightly in front of him like a visible shield between the two of us. Max is going through a tough time with his girlfriend, so Olly thought it'd be good for him to get out. I'm guessing the issue here is that he and Katie had some strange kind of respect for each other. Max looked at her like she was on some pinnacle. Which she was, I just have no idea why *he* put her up there.

"Out with it, Max," I demand.

"You seem certain that this Blake purposefully killed Aaron and Katie, yet you've stood by and not sought any kind of justice, why?"

Olly widens his stance sensing I'm ready to react, but if anything, I envy Max's naivety. "He's already dead. Katie and Aaron, they're dead. It would have served no purpose."

"I imagine your brother and Katie would see it differently," he chunters in response.

"Well, that's where you're wrong." I flex my fingers, my patience wearing desperately thin. "Blake was an abuser. He killed the one woman that tried to set his wife free. What sort of message would that give to people who suffer abuse and for people that choose to help? It destroys... wipes out all that Katie was trying to achieve. What happened was the worst case scenario possible, and I hope to God it doesn't happen again. Katie saved many women before Ginny, Max and if she were still around, she'd continue helping them, no matter what!"

I stand straighter, facing him head-on, almost daring him to continue with his current line of questioning because I won't falter. Not on this. "Anything else?" I jab.

"Well, if you ask me, this chick is and will continue being totally screwed!"

"What?" I say narrowing my eyes.

"She's been beaten. Battered, right? I have no idea how people get over something like that. I don't think they ever can. Surely it's like a self-destruct button, and at some point, she's gonna—"

"Self-destruct? Max she didn't *choose* for this to happen to her."

"How the fuck do you know? Maybe she's some psychotic woman and deserved the beatings. Women can be—"

He doesn't have chance to finish his sentence. I charge towards him, too quick that even Olly can't prevent the inevitable contact. Knocking Max clean to the ground, I straddle over him and draw back my fist.

"Nate!" Olly grabs hold of my hand, and I twist round in anger. "Enough!" he hisses. "Sophia's upstairs for fuck sake." That's all it takes, I sink back to my heels, heavy breaths firing from my chest. Max shuffles his way back, before sitting up, his arms come to rest on his knees.

"Max, I told you to keep your mouth shut. You don't have a clue what you're talking about," Olly states as he tries to calm his own breaths.

"I don't get why you'd voluntarily choose a woman like that? Aaron, Katie, they died and for what? For her?"

"What the hell?" I snap. "I didn't voluntarily choose Ginny like some kind of arranged relationship. It just happened, and none of this was Ginny's fault, Max."

"Wasn't it?"

I stare at him hard, wondering how I can make him see sense. Then it clicks into place. "You liked Katie," I state.

"Everyone liked Katie," Max retorts, but he liked her more than your average friend. Not that he would have acted on it. Max knew how my brother and Katie felt about each other.

"So, what if I was to tell you she came from the same kind of background Ginny did? Would it make you think any less of her?"

"What?" Max glances confusingly between Olly and me, looking for confirmation. "Your brother—" He clamps his jaw shut in anger.

"NO!" I yell. "Not my fucking brother! Are you insane? No, it was years ago. It was her mum's boyfriend and the boyfriend after that one. But no matter what *they* did, what *they* caused, Katie was never to blame."

Max inhales and exhales heavily. "Man, I didn't know. F*uck!* I'm sorry."

I don't say anything else in response. I've said enough. He stumbles his way up to standing then approaches me, extending his hand out. I slap my palm to his, and he hoists me upright.

"And no woman deserves a beating. You got that?"

"I'm sorry." His eyebrows draw in as a pained expression crosses his face. His hands fall to his side before he turns and walks away. He stops and looks over his shoulder at me. "Katie? That shit happened to *her*?" His voice loses power.

"It did."

"Fuck!"

His pained expression is too much to bear. "Max, you don't have to go," I state regretfully.

"Yeah, I do."

I bow my head as Olly's hand rests on my shoulder and Max makes his way out of the house.

"I totally screwed that one up, huh?"

"He's having a tough time with Nadine. He shouldn't have come tonight. I thought he could use the company but, in hindsight, I should have left him with the bottle of Jack he was already cradling. Talk to him tomorrow."

I pull out one of the chairs from the patio table and collapse down on it. Olly nips back into the living room to collect the beers before coming back out and joining me.

We sit like that in silence for a few minutes, thoughts swamping my mind. Max didn't get it because I never gave him the opportunity to learn the truth. I miss Aaron and Katie, more than anything, but it wasn't Ginny's fault. We have both suffered pain at the hands of her husband.

"They'd be proud of you," I look at Olly as he speaks again. "Proud that you're putting everyone else before you. But Aaron..." He goes quiet. "I think he'd understand the most. He got to save Katie. You both did. That little speech you gave Max? I hadn't seen it like that. I know he'd be rooting for you, Nate and he'd be on Ginny's side. I'm sorry it took me so long to see it."

What a mess. This entire situation is all kinds of fucked up. But at the root of it all is a woman that I can't get out of my mind. I want her safe like Katie did and the only place I can see that happening is with me. But I can't do it.

"She has this power," I begin, "this ability to turn me into a goddamn caveman. I want to be there, by her side all of the time, to protect her, but I'm also the one person that can knock her down to her knees if the truth comes out."

"I don't know what to say to you, man. I wish I had the answers."

"There's more."

"More? Like this isn't enough."

"Her best friend. She thinks Ginny's bypassed the grieving phase or something. That I've become the distraction, so she doesn't have to face up to her past. What happened to her, it can affect people in so many different ways. Katie had help, Aaron and I made sure of it. She spoke to people. Ginny's only briefly touched on it with her friend and me." I stop talking and shake my head. "How can I tell her about something like this, when she hasn't even handled what happened to her? If she finds out about Katie and Aaron, she'll take the blame."

"You've already said it's not her fault."

"It isn't, but she'll not see it that way until she gets help for herself."

Which means walking away was the right thing to do, not for me, but for Ginny. It was always about everyone else with Katie. Always. *It looks like I'm getting to honour your memory in the same way, sis.*

"Nate. I've never seen you this crazy about a girl before. Is it her or because of where she came from? That she was married to him?"

"At first, I would have said where she came from. That was why I found her in the first place. But it's her, Olly. It always has been, I just didn't know it until I met her. The outcome still has to be the same though."

"So you're going to walk away." I peer sideways on at him. "You've already left haven't you?"

"Yes," I reply stoically before I take a swig from my beer, permitting myself to wallow in pity for a few hours. Because tomorrow I need to get up, give Sophia breakfast and do the school run with a smile on my face that she believes is genuine.

CHAPTER TWENTY-FIVE

GINNY

"Thanks for this, Ryan."

He glances nervously from the driver's side at me. Ryan picked me up ten minutes ago, and we're on our way out of town towards the house that Nate stays in at the weekend with Sophia. I'm reliably told by Ryan that it's his parents' house.

"Make sure to tell him this was your idea and not mine."

"What time did you tell him you'd be there?"

"Quarter past. So we'll be five minutes early." I twitch about in the seat, the confidence I felt earlier waning dramatically.

"For what it's worth, Ginny, I think what you're doing is cool."

"Cool?"

"Yeah, it's like the reverse of Romeo and Juliet, an updated version. This time it's the chick that's going to save the man."

"Did you read that book, Ryan?" I enquire, his take on the story not quite how it was portrayed. "Besides, I'm not saving him, Ryan. I'm after an explanation, an answer."

"Sorry, Shakespeare wasn't my forte in school."

"Well, they both died in the end," I explain. He pulls the car to a stop and turns off the engine.

"Oh! Then you're nothing like them." He winces then nods

his head towards a detached brick built house set far back from the road. "That's it. Listen, Ginny, I know he's been on radio silence ever since last weekend, but it's killing him being apart from you. I don't know what went on, but I sure as hell recognise a heartbroken man even if I've only spoken to him on the phone."

I recognise Nate's car in the driveway. "And Sophia, she's definitely out?"

"Yeah, with his parents. Look, he thinks I'm here to take him out to kill a couple of hours before Sophia gets back. You'll have the house to yourselves if you know what I mean."

"Not the intention," I say rolling my eyes.

"Whatever."

After my talk last Sunday with Ryan, self-pity altered its path. Something's happened, I sense it, and I have a feeling that the answer lies with Nate.

I take a deep breath and undo my seatbelt. It's strange that when the fight turns and it becomes about somebody else, I feel like the bravest warrior I could be when all I felt before was the weakest link.

Ryan twists in his seat and faces me. "You've got this, Ginny. If he tells you to leave, tell him to go fuck himself and that he's made the biggest mistake of his life," he shrugs, "that ought to do it."

"Thanks, Ryan," I say even though he hasn't quite grasped why I'm here. Ryan thinks that we'll be having some kind of reunion. But something inside of me is preparing for something else. I can already sense my defences starting to rise. I just don't know why.

We both notice the door to the house open at the same time. Nate stares in our direction. It's him, yet there's something different... like the energy has been drained from him.

"Come on. He's waiting." Ryan gets out of the car. Nate smiles, but I can tell it's not genuine.

As I climb out, Nate notices movement and shifts his attention in my direction. The second he recognises me, his shoulders drop and grief washes over him. He doesn't want me here, that much is obvious. Part of me wants to turn away and run, but if everyone wants me to move on with my life—if I want to move forward—then I have to face whatever it is that Nate is keeping from me.

Ryan walks to my side. "You deserve an answer." I nod my head before finally walking forward.

Nate steps out of the house and meets us halfway. He takes his hands from his pockets, letting them hang loosely at his side. He appears uncomfortable and out of place. But he doesn't stop looking at me. Whatever it is that's weighing on his mind is ruling him with sadness.

"I'll um wait in the car?" I hear Ryan state. "Unless you want me to... you know... make myself scarce?"

"Can you wait in the car?" Nate says, sounding defeated. A sound I don't want to hear.

"Yeah, I guess." He starts to walk away, his strides slow and unsure.

Then Nate turns, with his head bowed, he walks inside. I follow anxiously. He closes the door quietly behind me. We're standing in a grand-looking hall. There are a couple of framed photographs set neatly on the wall farther in, but I don't look. I only concentrate on him.

"Do you want a drink?"

"No."

He moves through a doorway, so I continue in the same direction and find myself in a small lounge. Judging by the size of the house on the outside, I'm sure this isn't the main room everyone congregates in.

He stands there, in the middle of the room, appearing lost. His refusal to look at me causes me to bridge the gap he seems intent on making.

"You shouldn't have come." His breaths sound crushed as he retreats a step. Pain rushes through me.

"What is it?" I question helplessly. "Am I that repulsive to you now? Knowing that he—"

"No!" He's quick to answer. "What he did to you has no bearing on how I feel about you, Ginny. You have to know that."

"But I don't know that. I told you, and then you left."

He stays mute. Unmoving. Looking only to the floor at his feet.

How can he do this? I opened my heart to him. I told him everything. Then he turned his back. The never-ending unanswered questions that have been playing on my mind all week, continue to drive me insane. As I stand and take in this strong, caring man before me who appears as lost as I once was, I'm riddled with confusion. Why would he want me to tell him about Blake and then walk away from the truth?

"Do you know what it took for me to open up to you?" I exclaim.

He becomes still. Deathly still. His attention still diverted from me.

"There's something else going on here. I understand that I have to get some help, but I don't think that's it. Is it?"

"I want you to get help. Then maybe..." He struggles "No...

you have to come to terms with everything that's happened to you, Ginny."

"Come to terms?" I screech. "Why the hell would I keep reliving what I've been through? You sound like Marci!"

"You have to leave." Finally, he looks at me. So much pain and anguish gleams in his eyes that I know I can't walk away from him. Not when he's like this. "I'm begging you, Ginny."

"I'm not leaving." I move closer and witness the restraint he's showing at our close proximity. I lift my hand and touch his cheek. He exhales and steps away shaking his head.

"Please... this is hard enough." His voice cracks.

"Nate?" I say. "Please, what's going on?" I'm even more confused at what's transpiring.

He wants to be touched but feels he has to walk away. He knows I've been hurt before but believes he can scar me for a lifetime. He told me he was falling in love with me, but he's trying to let me go. My focus darts around chaotically as I desperately try and figure this out.

He's protecting me. But why? "What are you protecting me from? That's it isn't it? You're protecting me! No matter what you think you're doing right now, it's wrong! I deserve the truth. I need for people to stop shielding me!"

With his focus on the floor, he leaves the room without saying a word.

I stare at the doorway, wondering where he's gone.

The sound of heavy footsteps fills the air, which is strange because I didn't hear the sound when he walked out, only now as he makes his way back into the room. His head remains dipped, his focus on something he has in his hand.

When he pauses a few steps from me and lifts his lids, I already see the apology on his face.

"I wanted to wait until you were ready. Because I don't think you are ready, Ginny. But you're refusing to leave." He holds out the object in his hand. It's a photo frame. Confused, I take it. "I'm sorry," he murmurs.

"What are you sorry for?"

"For breaking you."

I look down at the photo I'm holding. My eyes first find Sophia. I briefly smile before I look at the people sat either side of her. My smile disappears as I face Katie?

"I-I don't understand?" I glance at Nate, but he refuses to look back at me. His hands reach out to the sides of his head as though blocking out the reality. He slides down the wall, his body curling over his chest "Look at me," I whisper but he avoids me. "I said look at me," I say in desperation and anger. "Why am I holding a picture of Sophia... with Katie?"

"The accident... Your husband..." Nate's eyes close, and he exhales a long breath. "He was driving."

"I know my husband was driving. I buried him," I accuse.

"There were two cars involved."

"I know. I told you that. What the hell are you saying to me?" My words come out desperate, frantic, wanting an answer that's different to the conclusion I'm already making.

"Katie was in the car that Blake hit. She was with my brother. Aaron. He was killed instantly."

"No." I shake my head refusing to believe his words. "No. You're lying." It's all a lie. They couldn't have been in the same accident as Blake. It doesn't make sense.

"I wish I was."

The nightmare... it's back, but with the sickest twist I could have ever have thought possible. I can't stop shaking my head.

My chest starts to hurt, and dizziness comes over me as I try and gasp for breath.

"Blake... he hit their car? You said *he* hit their car!" I accuse. "He..." I harden my jaw, "Blake hit them?" I turn away staring into the air around me as it begins to suffocate me. "Katie? I-I don't understand. How did that happen?" I mutter to myself then turn on him once again, but he's still averting his eyes. "Your brother? Your brother was in the other car?" He drops his head to his knees in pain and desperation. "You lost your brother?" I cry.

My mind swings back to the day I was leaving. He never finished his breakfast. He may have picked up the newspaper, but he didn't read a single page. Instead, he talked about us going away. If there was one thing I was certain of, in all our time together, it was that Blake was a stickler for routine, except that one morning.

I swallow the knot of emotion that's risen in my throat and look to Nate. "Were you there? When he hit them? Were you in the car?"

"No, Katie rang me just after."

"I was leaving him..." I grow silent and close my eyes before pain, so intense, bounds through me. I had thought it was an accident. There was a married couple in the car. "He couldn't have done it. The people who died..." Aaron and Kathryn... oh my God, what was their surname? I look around in panic, the room spinning in a haze. Why can't I remember their surname? "Katie is it short for Kathryn? I never knew her surname."

"She used to go by her maiden name at work anyway. You couldn't have known."

I stare at him, shaking from head to toe. Then I move towards the hallway. I hear Nate calling after me, as I open a door and walk into the kitchen. Mail... where's the mail? When I spy a letter on the side, I retrieve it. Mr & Mrs Dawson... Nate's parents... Dawson... Aaron and Kathryn Dawson.

I turn swiftly, my focus wide. "Nate," I sob, "Nate Dawson. That's your name?" I knew his name. He told me. How did I not connect it to them? "He didn't know who she was?" I look at him, pleading for it not to be the case. "He couldn't have." Unless he followed me.

"I can't be certain."

"But you think he knew? She didn't ring me back."

It's as though time stands still. He knew I was leaving him. He must have known when I met with Katie. Katie... He hit her car on purpose. Katie? Katie died because of Blake? My eyes lift to Nate's. Blake killed his brother. A sob rips from my chest. Sophia? The tears tumble from my eyes.

I hear a painful howl come from deep within, and I fall to the floor. Strong arms surround me. His grip tightens and his body trembles against mine. I clutch onto him distraught at all that this beautiful man has lost.

CHAPTER TWENTY-SIX

NATE

She's sobbing uncontrollably, and I don't know what else I can do. I have her in my arms. I never wanted it to be like this... never. I slam my eyes closed, not wanting to see her pain, pain that I have caused. My arms encase her entirely. Her cries tearing me apart, one by one.

The memory of that day comes flooding back, too vividly...

I'm about to set off for work when my phone rings. I turn over the engine, switch the phone to hands-free and answer the call from Katie.

"Hey, you on your way to work—"

"Nate..." Fear engulfs me instantly at something in her voice. "Please come... help."

Panic takes over, hearing my sister in law's plea. "Katie, where are you? What's happened?"

"We're on Briar's Lane... we've been in an accident." Fuck! I ram the car into reverse. "I'm coming, Katie." With the squealing of my tyres, I thrust the car into gear and pull away from the house. "I'm only a few minutes from you."

I can make out her breathing over the phone, but it doesn't sound right. It's noisy and strained.

"Katie, who's with you? Have you called for help? Is anyone hurt?"

"I've rung for help, but Aaron... he's quiet... He won't talk to me. Nate... I don't know—"

Not Aaron, please God, not my brother. I hear her soft sobs that hitch like she's in pain. "Where's Sophia?" *I swipe a tear from my cheek.*

"She's at school." *A temporary relief washes over me.*

"Stay good, sis, okay? Keep talking to me."

I press the horn on my car as the car in front sticks to the speed limit. Their brake light shines back at me, so I pull around, swerving to overtake them, almost colliding with an oncoming van. I curse under my breath but get straight back to Katie.

"Katie, how are you doing?"

"I'm cold, Nate."

My blood turns to ice. No! This is not happening.

I jab at the horn, warning everyone out of my way as I charge through the traffic.

"I'm almost there." *I drive like a maniac but finally pull onto Briar's Lane looking for them. It's a quiet road they must use as a shortcut to get to work. When I'm met with the sight of two cars splayed out in different directions, varying degrees of mangled metal, I ease my foot on the pedal and draw to a stop. Shit!*

Rubbing at my eyes, I blink fast to regain my vision and jump out of the car.

"Aaron? Katie?" *I shout as I see the extent of damage to their car. I run to Aaron's side, but when I crouch down, nothing could have prepared me for what I see. His head is twisted, blood seeps from his nose, and I know before I even feel for a pulse that he's gone. A strangled moan resonates from my throat. My brother...*

"Nate?" I lift my focus and see Katie's seat has her crushed, pinned against the dash.

"I'm here."

"I can't see him, I'm stuck. Is he okay?" She's struggling for breath. I stand up, scrub my hands over my face before kneeling back down to Aaron. I lean toward him, smashed glass from the window clawing at my arms, but the pain is nothing, minute to what I'm really feeling.

"I got her, bro." I fight with the strain in my voice, keeping it low to avoid alarming Katie. "I love you, man." The words come out broken.

"What are you saying?" Katie shouts in panic.

I get back up and rush round to her side.

"I'm here, Katie." I breathe out and wipe down from my mouth.

Her eyes flicker open before widening in fear. "Nate!" she manages to croak. "What about Aaron?"

"He'll be fine. Just fine," I force the words out.

The sound of mumbled shouts distracts me. A man stumbles towards us. He must have come from the other car. I can't believe someone managed to get out of it.

"Where is she? Where is the fucking bitch?" he calls out while appearing agitated and confused.

Katie starts crying with the pain.

"You can't take her from me!" Again the man shouts. "And I'm not leaving her!" He follows with something I can't make out. But as I look back at Katie, it's clear she heard what he said.

"Who is he?" I question, but Katie's eyes remain fixed on the man staggering around in the road.

Blood pools over his face and eyes. He glances at his hands as though he's seeing his blood for the first time before he starts shaking, shock clearly beginning to take effect. "No... God no! Ginny! I won't leave her!" he shouts before gripping at the side of his head.

"Shit!" He falls to his knees still clutching his head. I should go to him, but I don't want to leave Katie.

"Leave him," Katie manages to speak out, and the hatred in her tone shocks me.

"What? Who is he?" I ask again.

Slowly, like she's fighting to control her focus, her eyes find mine. I see the hesitation on her face and know that she's telling me only what *she* wants me to know, not what *I* want to know—like she did when we were younger. "He's nobody, Nate. Nobody."

I know she's lying, but right now my priority is her. "Katie, keep your eyes on me. Focus on me." I glance over Katie's shoulder at Aaron. There's no movement. Nothing. The sound of sirens explodes in the air. "They're here, you see. It's going to be okay."

"She'll be gone now," she mumbles.

"She's at school." I look confusingly to the back of the car assuming she's talking about Sophia.

"No, Ginny." Even though chaos surrounds me, it's Katie's words that matter. "Ginny." She smiles through her pain. "She never had... the knights... not like I did." She lifts her hand to my cheek. "Don't cry, Nate. You saved me. Both of you did." Then as though realisation sinks in she turns, but then shouts out in pain. "Aaron! Oh God."

"Katie, look at me." I can't cope with seeing her in such pain.

"You have to pick Sophia up from school. Nobody else!" she says with a fight I didn't know she had. "Only you, Nate!"

"I'll get her. Don't worry, and I'll bring her to see you straight away."

She smiles weakly and appears to struggle as she swallows. "Tell her how much I love her." Her eyes fill with tears, and I can't remember a time I've seen her cry. She was always so strong, but then she always had Aaron to lean on. I take a peek over at my brother, and *my shoulders suddenly start shaking with the emotion I'm battling to keep hidden from Katie.*

"You remember the climb, Nate? Tell Sophia don't ever be afraid to fall."

"I remember... because the climb is the best, right?"

She smiles through her pain, and I watch as she reaches out blindly for my brother's hand. I guide her to it, and she grabs onto him.

"Remember, Aaron, you helped me climb," she says to him.

I shake my head. "You're not doing this, Katie, you're not saying goodbye," I warn. Her face grimaces in pain.

"I don't want to leave you," she gasps, and a wheezing sound comes from her throat. "I don't want you to be alone," she adds, her eyes heavy with tears as she looks at me. As her mouth opens to gain another breath, I see the stain of blood inside her mouth. She must have noticed my focus lower to her lips, and she swallows. "I'm sorry," she gasps. "He's so proud of you, I'm so... proud of... you, Nate."

Her eyes start to lose focus as the paramedic arrives asking me to step aside.

She shouts at the paramedic. "Wait!" She orders the paramedic. "Sophia... You. Only you!"

"I wouldn't ever let her go there, Katie." I allow the words to hover briefly before I utter what she needs to hear. The words I don't want to say because a world without my brother and sister in law in it doesn't bear thinking about. "I remember, and Sophia will stay with me. I promise."

Powerlessly, I stand back, grip onto the sides of my head and watch the scene in front of me. I can't lose them both. I can't.

I hear the hitch in Ginny's breath, and the sobs start to ease. I want to hold onto her for as long as possible, but when she draws from me, I don't stop her.

"You think he knew who Katie was. I can see it in your eyes."

"I'm not sure, Ginny." The name he called that day had been Ginny. I'll never forget Katie's face when she saw him and heard Ginny's name. She knew who he was. I knew the moment I saw the obituaries in the newspaper. At the time, I wondered who Katie was protecting by not telling me. Now I know it was Sophia and me. If Blake had survived, I would have sought revenge. Katie wouldn't have wanted that for me, or for Sophia.

"Blake died... Katie died... Your brother died..." She confirms with a frozen, wide-eyed stare. "My life wasn't... isn't worth that amount of loss."

"No!" I state adamantly. "That's not what happened. Their lives weren't taken so you could live. They died in an accident. This wasn't some kind of trade of one life for another."

She turns away and mumbles, "It's three lives. Three lives for mine."

I strengthen my hold on her, refusing to let her be alone in this. But then she twists steadily, returning her focus to me.

"You came to find me. I kept seeing you... you were watching me. You wanted to find me." She's not asking me. She's trying to figure it out for herself. "Why would you want to find someone like me? A battered, weak woman?"

My jaw hardens at her own label.

"That's what I am, Nate."

"No, Ginny. That's not who you are."

She rises to her feet and looks down at me. "Did you want to make sure I paid for your loss? Is that it?"

"No!" I assert and quickly join her in standing. "Ginny, I wanted to make sure you were okay. I had to know."

"Well, clearly, I'm far from okay. You can't be either. I'll never be alright. All of this... it's all because of me."

She wanders aimlessly around the room moving further from my reach. I need to bring her back, but I don't know how.

"If there is fault to be placed anywhere, it's with me, Ginny."

"How could any of this possibly be your fault?" she continues in a dazed state but there's something else she needs to know.

"Do you know where you were the first time I saw you?"

"At the bar," she states absentmindedly.

"No, it wasn't. I'd gone into the city to meet Katie for lunch, but I was early, so I sat down on a bench. There was already a woman sitting on one side, so I sat the opposite. She was fidgety and nervous." I watch Ginny intently as I try to explain. "I remember briefly looking up and taking in her side view—she was beautiful." Ginny stops walking. "She is beautiful. For a second I was like, 'What the hell is she sitting alone for? A woman like that.' Then you looked at your watch, and I saw your bruise."

She turns around and stares at me in disbelief.

"You looked at me briefly, but you didn't really see me. I knew you needed help the second you looked my way." Her brows furrow. "You looked straight at me, but the fear and panic that stared right back at me made it impossible for you to actually see me."

She stands motionless, tears in her eyes, shaking her head as she tries to remember.

"I knew then you were trying to find the courage to go into the refuge. Katie," I exhale at the sound of her name, "was the best at her job. It was her you needed. So I rang and stood her up. Told her you were on your way over, that you needed help, that you needed *her*. I made her stay that day, so if you want to place the blame anywhere, it should be with me. When I saw his name in the obituaries, I had to try and find you." I swallow hard, choking back the emotion. "Katie... the day of the accident... in the car, she said she hoped you'd got away. When I saw you again, I couldn't turn away because you still weren't happy, and I know that's what Katie would have wanted."

The tears roll down her cheek, but she stares at me blankly. "So you hung around because of Katie."

"You know that's not true. I've fallen for you, Ginny."

"I need to leave," she mutters. "Sophia will be back. Sophia," she says her name so quietly that it hurts.

"Even though I only saw the tiniest part of you, I never forgot what you looked like."

"Don't, Nate!" She holds up her hand, stopping me from approaching. I know her boundaries, and I know why she has them. She places the photo on the table before raising her eyes to me. "She was a mother. I never knew that." Her eyes overfill with tears. "I'm so sorry, Nate. I would never have tried to escape if I had known my freedom came at such a high price. I would have stayed and taken it all."

I watch as she turns towards the door.

"Ginny, where are you going? You can't leave."

"Why? In case I do something stupid? I've spent years being stupid... naïve... weak. For years, I've done what someone else wanted me to do. Things with me, they won't end well, it appears they never do."

"You can't go."

She ignores me and keeps walking. A vacant look sweeps over her expression, and I frown.

"You should never have tried to find me, Nate. Sometimes, when a person is lost, they don't deserve to be found."

I race towards her, reaching out. My hand slides down her arm as she tries to pull it away, but I manage to grip onto her hand. "I can't let you go."

She looks over her shoulder at me. "You have no choice, Nate. You'd never try to stop me because I know you're different to the man that gave me my scars. I'm so sorry for what he did, Nate. Do you know, part of me actually felt sorry for him, even when he inflicted pain on me? I didn't think he could help it, but I will no longer pity that man." She curls her lip. "I'll despise him for as long as I live."

She slides her hand free from mine and walks out of the door.

What was I thinking? What have I done?

That same haunted look I saw in her eyes all those months ago has returned. Only this time, I'm the one who put it there, which means I'm no better than that scumbag, Blake Daniels.

CHAPTER TWENTY-SEVEN

GINNY

I haven't said a word the entire journey home. I've felt Ryan looking at me repeatedly but, I can't talk because I wouldn't know where to start. As the car draws to a stop, I climb out, find my voice to mutter my thanks before taking the short path, which leads to my house, in a state of confusion and disbelief.

Katie... Katie and Aaron... Nate and Sophia...

When I find myself standing at my front door, staring at the handle, it dawns on me that Ryan hasn't yet left, that he's watching me, but I don't have the energy to turn round, to even offer a wave in thanks because right now, nothing else really matters. Nothing, but what happened at the hands of my husband.

Marci! Ryan will tell her how strange I'm acting. So, I turn and force a watery smile in place, knowing that I'm most likely too late. He's probably already calling her. I watch him drive away until he's out of sight.

I'm about to turn back to the house when something causes me to halt my feet. A state of unease starts to spread through my body. Nervously, I glance around me. I search the expanse of road, paths, cars, and trees. Anywhere my eyes land, I look for something to account for my worry. The sound of my breaths becoming more rushed alert me to a danger that I can't see.

A car travels over a dip in the road causing me to jump and shriek out.

Quickly, I retreat into the house, closing the door and fastening the locks behind me. There wasn't anybody there, yet I can't shrug this dreaded feeling. Every time I experience the same sensation, the fear I suffer reminds me of when Blake was alive. It feels like he's taunting me, which is stupid because it's impossible.

The house feels cold, so I tug my hoodie over my hands as a chill emanates through me. Dropping my bag to the floor, I head for the stairs. When I get to my room, I go to the wardrobe and slide the door open. With a stretch, I reach to the shelving at the top, and my fingers skim the edge of the box that hasn't been touched since the day I moved in here.

Retrieving it, I push my heels back to the floor and collapse down on the bed. My fingers continue to shake as they skim along the plain brown cardboard. I could have chosen a prettier box—one with butterflies on maybe, but I didn't deem it appropriate at the time. I still don't.

Taking a deep breath, I lift the lid, opening up the past I thought I'd left behind. I turn my head away for a moment when a familiar scent wafts beneath my nose, reminding me of a home and life I left behind. My lips curl up in revulsion.

When I look back, our wedding picture stares back at me. Out of all of the photos I saved, I chose this one? I glare at it before pushing the photograph aside and searching underneath. There are another few photos I kept, all of Blake and me in the early days. Then I see the cards we'd both written our wedding vows on. Scanning over the words I stop and a shudder racks through my body as though someone has walked over my grave.

I will never leave you, Ginny, I promise. It will forever be you, forever be us. You are my everything. You are my perfect.

I start ripping at the card, tearing until it's in the smallest of pieces. Then I resume my search. Immediately, I see part of what I'm looking for. A cut-out from the newspaper providing the details of Blake's funeral. *In memory of Blake Daniels...* I remind myself of every word... *Husband to Ginny... To be held at St. Lawrence Church...* I ensured terms such as 'beloved', 'celebration of his life' were omitted. It was informative, but without a doubt, lacking the sentiment of a heartbroken widow.

When I glance back inside the box, I know the article that reported on the accident isn't in here. I'd chosen ignorance. I didn't want to deliberate over what Blake may or may not have done. I'd remembered their names but chose not to continue remembering. Not for one minute did I believe it to be a deliberate act of malice... of murder.

I slide off the bed until I'm in a tired cowed heap on the floor. The weight of guilt has never been so heavy, forcing all strength to leave me.

"I'm so sorry." My voice breaks through the silence. "We did this to you." I want to drown in my tears, but they now refuse to come. *What's wrong with me? Everything that's happened... that happened because of me, and I can't even cry for them?*

I let out a squeal at the sound of loud knocking on the door.

"Ginny! Open this door!" Marci shouts through the letterbox. Quickly I jump up, throw the box to the back of the wardrobe and rush downstairs.

When I come to a stop in front of the door, something tells

me I need to play this calmly, or she's not going to leave, and being with people... talking... it's not what I want to do right now.

On an inhale, I pull open the door.

"Hey." She looks at me with a sad smile, and it throws me. "Can I come in?"

"Um, yeah." She walks past me. I take a glance outside before quickly closing the door behind her.

"Are you going to tell me what happened?" She pulls out a chair at the breakfast bar and sits down. I sigh, resigning myself to the fact it isn't going to be a short visit and fill the kettle.

"Marci, I didn't want to start explaining myself to Ryan. I was probably rude wasn't I?" I twist to face her. "I'll apologise."

Turning away from her, I click the kettle on to boil and start grabbing cups out of the cupboard. "Ginny, I'm not talking about Ryan. Nate rang me."

My hand hovers over the cups momentarily as a sense of fear starts to enter my stomach. *Has he told her?*

"Why would he do that?" I question simulating indifference.

"I guess because he's worried about you. Gin, will you look at me?" I can tell by her voice that she's now standing behind me, so I turn round and face her.

A thought suddenly comes to me. What if she's known all along? What if Nate told her and Ryan before?

"What happened? He wanted me to check you were okay. Ryan said you didn't say a word in the car." She scours the room, and I'm not sure what she's looking for. "Yet, you're here, making tea, acting normal. I thought—"

"You thought what?"

Appearing embarrassed, she drops her focus. "I th-thought maybe you were going to do something to yourself." She looks back up at me. "Nate, he sounded distraught."

A laugh bursts from my mouth, a strange sense of hysteria taking over before a determined seriousness takes over me. "If I were ever going to do something to myself, it would have been before, when Blake was here. Trust me, that's not my plan." No, I prefer to live with this newfound torture and own it because rightfully it is mine to possess. "What exactly did Nate say?"

"He told me to come. Said I needed to make sure you were okay. He sounded... I don't know, Gin, kind of distraught. He wanted me here now." It's still hard to tell if she knows. I'm trying to decipher meanings and actions between her words

"That's all he said?" I ignore her description of Nate and concentrate only on what Marci knows. I have to know what I'm facing here. I'm on tenterhooks waiting for the bombshell to drop and for her to tell me she knows what sickening act Blake did in his final hour.

"Yes. Why? What is it Ginny, please for God sake tell me what's going on!"

I indicate for her to sit down while I finish making the drinks. I remain standing, leaning against the worktop.

"Nothing, Marci. We talked a little about our past." I pause, struggling with the truth, "I'm going to get help."

"What?"

"I'm going to take some time off work, and I'm going to see somebody. You were right Marci, as is Nate."

"But you and Nate? You're together? Over?"

"Over." Definitely over. I can't bring myself to try and understand why he would even want to look at me. "I'm okay with it, Marci." Blake has left me with no alternative. I turn on my feet and stare out of the window at the open fields over the road. I will get help. But first, there's something else I have to do.

I remember the funeral, the burial, but I need the vision of his headstone permanently marked in my memory. I've had enough of him haunting me. It's time I said my goodbye. I don't think I was ready all of those months ago, but I certainly am now.

"I need you to stop worrying about me. I'm going to stay with an old friend for a few days. Then when I get back, I'll talk to someone. I promise."

"Whoa! What? Who's the old friend? You never said you had a friend. Where?" Once again she's beside me, her eyes open wide. "There?" She looks at me incredulously.

"Jesus, Marci. I had other friends, not many, but I had some. I wasn't a total recluse." I sound hurt, and she recognises she's upset me. But it's not what Marci said that caused me upset—it's the truth behind her statement. I didn't have a friend, not a true one. How pathetic is that? This is all too much to process, and the lies roll off from my tongue with ease. It's as though I can't stop them spilling from my mouth, but I have to keep going so I can try and work this through in my mind.

"I'm sorry," she says full of remorse.

"It's going to be okay, Marci." I smile, but it's false. Because I've allowed yet another untruth to leave my lips. "I need some time. I'll be back by the weekend. I'll call you then." Where I'm going, I have no intention of staying longer than a day, but Marci doesn't need to know that. "Let me do this," I plead.

As she stands and looks at me, I'm not sure she believes me. I will get help, but first, I need to pay a visit to my husband. I haven't been to his grave in over eight months. In fact, it must be nine by now.

I'm not going because I feel like I owe him a visit, which most definitely is not the case. I'm going because although I identified his body, I need to make certain the bastard is still well and truly rotting away.

I've been parked for over an hour now, with a strange sense of déjà vu, a knot of fear churning away in my gut. The cemetery, the final resting place of Blake remains in my vision. Even now he has me terrified.

I change the position of the visor as the sun starts to peer through a gap in the clouds, grateful for the disruption of my focus. Glancing up at the sky, I see a flicker of blue. I'd normally be looking forward to summer, but my thoughts are elsewhere. Besides, a storm's been forecast for the end of the week so the blue skies and sun won't last for long.

Averting my eyes, I force myself to step out of the car. Feeling the need to look around me, I see a couple glancing my way. Their stares linger a little longer than needed, so I dip my head and shuffle my feet forward, making my way to the path.

I recall the route I made months earlier, tracing over the steps I made then. I haven't allowed myself to remember this day, to remember what he did, yet as I continue walking, the memories come flooding back.

Before I even look up, I know I'm now standing before him. I can feel his presence surround me, like a huge black cloud manifesting itself until it clings to me.

Closing my eyes, I sink to the damp earth below. It must have rained here in the last twenty-four hours. Or maybe it's what the ground feels like in spring, and I'd never taken notice before.

Avoidance, Ginny! Look up. Silently I instruct myself. Finally, I raise my focus and see his name in front of me.

There are no flowers on the grave. No evidence of personal belongings or treasures left by family and friends as a reminder of a life that is missed. There is nothing. Only a headstone and grass.

"It's strange how I knew where you were without even looking. I could taste the putrid air that surrounds you," I snarl. I can almost hear him laughing and taunting me, knowing I only have the courage to say such a thing because he can no longer lay his hands on me. "I imagine this is hard for you, not being able to reach out and hurt me."

Then, as though I need convincing, I reach forward and splay my hands over the grassy area that now covers his decaying body. I sink my fingers into the soil making sure it's tightly compact, the grass well and truly seeded.

"You're gone, Blake." I dig in my fingers and scrape at the soil like it's his skin. "You can laugh at me all you like. Continue to haunt me. But I'm still here, and you're not. What you did appals me. To think I married a man as vile as you makes me feel sick to my stomach." I pull my hands from the dirt and stare at them. "Scum of the earth," I whisper. "It's not what you've become, it's what you always were." A short, brittle laugh bursts from my mouth. "Everything you did to me was hard to forgive, but I did forgive you. Many times. But, Blake, I will never forgive you for what you've done to that beautiful little girl. Nor will I forgive you for taking away Nate's family. Nate." I allow his name to hover in the air, hoping that on this one occasion, above all others that Blake can hear me. "Can you hear his name? Can you hear what it means to me? He's come into my life and taken hold of my heart in a way that you never could. I want to give it to him fully, Blake, but I can't because you made sure I'd be ruined for any other man."

I sit back and blow a heavy breath from my mouth. I meant everything I said, everything. Yet my hands are shaking, and all I want to do is run from here, but my legs are trembling so much, I'm unsure if they'll carry me.

"Even now you control me. I hate you."

Then, as though the devil himself heard my words of loathing, an eerie silence engulfs the air. I draw in a deep breath as unpredictability—uncertainty disables me. It's how I was before... when he was here.

The sound of movement behind me causes me to stiffen. I twist slightly and glance over my shoulder, but there's nobody there. The atmosphere thickens, and small breaths seep from my lips. I turn back to Blake's headstone, but as I do, the ground groans beneath a footstep.

Get ready to run, Ginny. I hear Blake's voice. But I can't have.

I should never have come back. Never.

CHAPTER TWENTY-EIGHT

NATE
PRESENT DAY

I relax back on the worktop in the kitchen. No, that's incorrect. I lean back. I'm so far from relaxed right now.

With a beer cradled in my hand, I look around at the group of people at Ryan's. Most of them I know, but there are a few I've never spoken to. Not that I have any intention today. The only reason I came was to see Ginny. If there is even a chance she is going to be here, I have to be too. It's been almost a week, and I haven't heard from her. She told me I had to let her go and because I'm different to the man she married, she believed I'd follow her wishes, but it's been damn hard. If I don't see her today, then I'm not sure I can do what she wants. I have to at least catch sight of her.

"Nate, will you *try* to look like you're enjoying the party?" Ryan hollers across the room.

Out of the corner of my eye, I notice a brunette shift her focus in my direction. I keep facing forward, but she approaches anyway.

"Hi."

I give her a brief glance trying not to be too rude. "Hey," I respond casually.

"So, I'm guessing you're Ryan's hot friend with the broken heart?"

I swing round to look at her properly. "What?"

She eases back. "Sorry, it's just... you're Nate, right? Ryan told me about you."

"Did he now?" I exhale. "What exactly did he say?"

"He-he..." she stutters on her words, but my attention has already moved on as I notice a commotion at the front door when it slams against the wall. A gust of wind takes whoever it is by surprise. I straighten up, checking who's arrived. Marci. Alone. She takes down her hood and removes her jacket before shaking the rain from her. I briefly glance through the window. The wind's picked up, the storm that's been forecast looks like it's making its mark.

Immediately, Marci looks over at me with a look of apology on her face before she notices the girl at my side. Then her expression changes.

Shit! I rub at the back of my neck in frustration before flanking the brunette and turning away from her.

"Well, charming!" she mutters before flouncing off.

I watch Marci as she walks towards the refrigerator and takes two beers out before heading in my direction. She doesn't even search out Ryan, she just comes to stand directly in front of me and hands me the beer.

"Thanks," I mutter.

She rotates, positioning herself at my side, facing the room. "You doing okay?" she asks. "You know, I'm still not sure if I should be angry at you or if you parted ways amicably. Ginny gave me the impression it was amicable?"

Amicable? How can what I told her have been amicable? Hearing Ginny's take on what occurred sets me even more on edge. She hasn't told Marci. Which means what? I try to absorb the information.

"So was it amicable? Because you look all worked up about something, Nate."

I look back at her and wonder how much she knows. "What did she tell you?"

"Other than it's over between you, nothing! Absolutely nothing. At least she's accepted she needs help though right? That's got to be a good thing. I wish she'd get her arse back here." She shakes her head, and I freeze at her words.

"Get back? From where?" I ask, as slowly the unease continues to build.

"There! Hereford!" she exclaims in disbelief. "I mean, I didn't even know she had friends there, which is stupid because she must have. I can't remember her mentioning anyone though. But she's staying with a friend now."

Yet, Ginny told me only last week, the only friend she had was Katie. I reach out behind me and put the untouched bottle of beer down. The perpetual feeling that something isn't right continuing to gnaw away at my mind.

She looks to my beer on the side. "What are you doing?"

"When did she go?"

"Sunday." The day after I told her about Blake.

"When did you last talk?"

"Tuesday." Her voice fades, and she looks up at me. I come to stand in front of her, so the only thing she can see is me.

"What are you not telling me, Marci?" I know there's something. Although I'm standing in front of her, she's shifting on her feet, appearing ill at ease.

"She was rushing me on the phone, told me everything was fine. But she seemed distracted. That's when she said she was staying longer. She couldn't give me a date when she planned on returning."

"And that worried you?"

She nods her head in confirmation. "I went to her house on Wednesday with Liam, my brother. I thought... I don't know what I thought. I guess I thought maybe she was lying to keep me away, but all the curtains and blinds were shut. There was no sign of life in there, so she must have been telling me the truth," she says on a sigh. "She's asked me repeatedly to let her live her life. There comes a time when I have to trust her and stop interfering. I probably shouldn't have gone round but..."

I stand rigid, my gaze unfocused, and I grow quiet. Although she's trying to sound convincing, Marci's holding back on something.

"But what? Marci, Goddamn it, what are you not telling me?"

"It's nothing. I've been watching too many horror movies recently. Liam's already told me I'm being stupid—"

"What are you not telling me?" I demand. If Ginny's in trouble, I can't walk away. I've tried that before and failed.

"When I spoke to her, she sounded like she did before when she was with him. Back then I didn't realise what was going on. She always sounded so busy, rushed our phone calls, only ever provided the very basic of information. That's what she did this week. It was like going back in time." She casts her eyes down, and I know there's more.

"And?"

"For Christ sake, you don't give up easily do you?" she huffs. "I said to Liam. It was as though Blake was alive. Like he'd never actually died in the first place. You can go ahead and laugh at me now," she adds rolling her eyes.

But I don't laugh. Nor do I pass comment. I push my fists in my pocket, my fingers brushing against my car keys. Then I glance at Marci. Blake Daniels is dead. I saw him collapse to the ground with my own eyes. Besides, a man like Blake couldn't have lived on the sidelines for months watching his wife move on with her life.

"Nate?" I sense the fear in her voice and see it echoed in her expression. "He is dead? Isn't he? Because if he's not..."

"I need to tell you something, but we're going to have to do it on the way." I stalk towards the door.

"On the way where?" Her heels click on the floor as she follows closely behind.

"We have to find her. We'll start at her house."

"But she's not there," she practically screams at me.

I stop, and she almost crashes into me. I lower my voice in response. "She told me she didn't have any friends, Marci. There's something wrong. If she isn't at the house, then we'll drive to where she used to live. We're going to find her."

Ryan calls out from the doorway, but I keep moving. I can explain to him later. But he jogs after us. "Where the hell are you two going?" he questions with mistrust in his tone. "Is this a party for two?"

Marci opens her mouth. "It's Gin—"

"This isn't what you think," I fire back. "We'll be back soon." I get in the car. Sensing the urgency, Marci does the same. Then as I turn the engine over, I feel her staring my way.

"Nate? What's going through your head? Because you're scaring me."

I push my foot to the pedal. "There's something you need to know about the day Blake died," I begin.

CHAPTER TWENTY-NINE

NATE

The tyres skid on the wet ground as we pull to a stop outside Ginny's. I know Marci's still reeling from what I've told her, but there isn't time for further explanation.

The first thing I notice is the curtains are drawn and blinds shut on all of the visible windows like Marci said they had been days earlier. I glance at Marci with unease before we both jump out of the car.

I push through the gate, ready to bash on the door, but a broken shopping bag stops me in my tracks. Reels of brown parcel tape poke out of the plastic. We both look at it in confusion. Is it Ginny's? Why wouldn't she pick it up if she dropped it? Why does she need all of that tape?

"That wasn't here the other day." Marci peers from around her hood apprehensively to me.

Immediately, I step forward and bang on the door. "Ginny?" I shout. "She normally parks her car in the garage, not on the road?" I question Marci looking at the white painted garage door.

"Yes." She rushes in that direction and tries to open the garage door, but it's locked, so I bang again.

"There's no answer, Nate. She's not here." She splays her arms out in helplessness. "Maybe she's still there, Nate. In Hereford."

"She told me the only friend she had was Katie. Why would she be there?"

The fear in her own eyes brings about a panic in mine. Something isn't right. I can feel it. I've felt it for days but put it down to me not hearing from her.

"Ginny?" she calls joining me at the door.

I step to the kitchen window, trying to peer inside. Rain runs down the window and drips from my brow, distorting my vision. I can't see a thing inside. The blinds are completely closed.

"Damn it! Move!" I exclaim, jutting my head to Marci instructing her to step aside.

"Nate!" I hear Marci shout, but I ignore her, take a few steps back, then charging at the door.

Christ! The impact hits my shoulder hard, stinging like a bitch. The door doesn't budge. Why the hell would it? Couldn't she have had a wooden door that was rotting? No. I scowl at my own dumb thoughts. That wouldn't have been safe. Even though I know I'm not going to be able to get through the door, I run back and charge towards it again.

"Nate. NATE!" Marci shouts.

"What?" I spin round, rubbing my shoulder.

"You're never gonna get in like that. There's a window at the side. It's small, but if you break it, I think I can climb through."

I search for something to throw at the window, but there's only a small patch of grass. Marci disappears into the garden next door then comes back with a large, heavy stone that must have been used on some garden feature. I grab it then thump it on the window. We hear a crack, but I can't see any damage. I slam it to the window again, and this time the pane splinters. One more time and it shatters enough for me to clear the glass to create an area for Marci to climb through.

Bending down, I help lift her, and she scales through the gap in the frame. The second the door's unlocked, I push past.

It's dark, and there's a strange smell. My eyes quickly take in the room. A few cups, only half-filled with remnants of tea or coffee are scattered around the room. The sink contains dishes with curled up dried food on that looks days old. Then I look at the window sill. The flowers I gave her are now wilted, the colours faded... lifeless.

"Ginny?" I say her name, don't shout it. Marci moves from the room.

I feel Ginny here... somewhere, but everything is wrong. I can't look away from the mess before me. Then the sound I'll never forget, surges through the house.

"Nate!" I move, fast at the sound of Marci screaming my name.

When I turn the corner, nothing could have prepared me for what I see. Ginny. She's wearing a black, thick-knitted jumper that's too big, making her look small and frail. Her face is pale. She's sitting on the floor, leaning against the wall, her sleeves almost covering her hands, her wrists pressed firmly to her temples like she's fighting to block out sound.

Marci's talking to her, trying to get her to listen but Ginny sways back and forth squeezing her head.

I'm there in a second, dropping to her feet, calling her name. Her sleeves are pulled tight over her palms, but her hands are dirty, mud embedded under her nails. It's dry and looks like it's been there for days.

Her eyelids dart open. "No!" she cries in desperation. "Go! Leave! Now! He'll find you! You can't be here, Nate. He'll already know about you!"

"Who, Ginny? Who will know?" Marci quizzes.

"Blake," she whispers his name and a heavy sensation rolls through my chest, crippling me.

"Blake's dead, Ginny," I say.

But as she looks at me, her normally soulful brown eyes are lacking warmth. They're bright yet at the same time dark, carrying with them an intense sentiment of dread. "No... he's not." She shakes her head, and I witness the panic spread through her. "He's been watching. He's back!"

A chill spreads through my spine extending to my neck and shoulders. My body becomes rigid. *He can't be.*

"He's dead," Marci repeats looking at me for confirmation, but I don't know what to say. They said he died. The police... the newspaper... he had a funeral.

When Ginny's focus bolts above my head, I shoot around, the urge to fight and protect kicking in. He won't hurt her again. I'm up on my feet, but there's nobody there. Nobody. I look back at them both on the floor. The same look of fear on Ginny's face, an expression of confusion on Marci's.

"Noooo!" Ginny wails, continuing to clutch at the side of her head. I'm spinning around frantically searching for... for him? "He was at the graveyard." Her eyes widen. Her fear creating my own. "He was watching... been following me... he's here." Her words appear jumbled and confused.

"Where, Ginny? Where the hell is he?" Marci's crying now, her focus darting nervously around the room. "Nate, what's happening?"

I shake my head, the movement spreading to my body. "I don't know. I don't..." When I look back at Ginny, something shiny on the floor, half tucked under her leg reflects back at me. A knife? My skin turns cold.

I fall to my knees and take the knife. There's blood on the blade. I grab Ginny by the shoulders, as she continues to cry out, shouting for us to escape.

"Ginny? Where are you bleeding? GINNY!" I holler over her voice.

Marci hits me, telling me to leave her alone when the action causes one of Ginny's hands to fall. Blood starts to appear from under her sleeve—the deep red colour descending to her palm.

"Get a towel or cloth Marci, NOW!" I bellow.

"Oh God!" Marci's cries break out around us. "Ginny, no! Oh God no!"

"Marci, towels now!" I grab her wrist and feel the warm damp material of her jumper. Blood spreads onto my own skin. The darkness of her jumper had been hiding her injury.

I seize her other hand, that wrist feeling exactly the same.

"We need more!" I shout as I hold both her wrists upright. I desperately scan over the rest of her body for any other signs of bleeding. "Ginny," I gasp, "my God, what have I done?"

"There's nothing left of me now," she utters, her screaming now calmed. Her eyes start to glaze over. I'm not sure what's worse, her panicked screams or the picture of Ginny losing a fight she shouldn't have been forced to make.

Marci's back with us and starts to wrap a towel around Ginny's wrist. "Pull it tight," I instruct. "Tighter!" While she keeps hold of one arm, I encase the other.

"Did he do this?" Marci's questions continue, but all I can do is concentrate on Ginny and her wounds. I pin Ginny's arm against the wall with my elbow and pull the mobile from my pocket, dialling the emergency services.

"Nate. The hospital's five minutes away."

I let go of the phone. "You drive," I instruct. "Ginny, I'm going to carry you." My arms scoop underneath her, and she falls into my hold, the fight leaving her. "No. Ginny!" I hold her close, gripping on, wanting to pass life from me to her.

"Please leave, Nate. Please!" Her despair hangs in the air, but mine meets it head-on.

What have I done? Why the hell did I let her go?

She starts to mutter about Blake again. Her focus flitting in every direction, causing me to continually look around me for any sign of him. Her fear is so raw, it's difficult not to believe her.

Marci rushes out in front of me, holds open the back door of the car so I can sit down with Ginny cradled in my lap.

"Nate, what—"

"Get us there quick, Marci," I interrupt unable to answer whatever she's asking. I raise Ginny's arms above heart height, and the car jerks into action as Marci hauls the car into motion.

Wiper blades swipe back and forth over the window. It's the only thing I hear. The only thing I can focus on. I can't look at her. I can't see what I've done.

"Talk to her, Nate," Marci instructs from the front. "We're nearly there, Gin," she calls over her shoulder, then glares at me through the rear view mirror. "What's wrong with you? Talk to her!"

As I gaze down at her. I know why I'm scared to. Her face is paling. The empty look is taking over more of her eyes. I'm losing her.

"You're going to be alright. You hear me?" My voice is unrecognisable. I had a chance to save her. Instead, all that has happened has led to this moment, and it's now no longer in my control. "We're here, Ginny. Always will be."

My eyes fill with tears, but I fight desperately to blink them away, the need to keep seeing her paramount. My fingers are pressing hard onto the towels that cover her wounds and time seems to pass in a daze.

"He can't hurt me now," she breathes. "It's... all on... me." Her eyes close, and I clench her wrists tighter, not wanting to hurt her but needing her to survive.

Marci slams her feet on the brakes. I look up and see the bright lights of the accident and emergency department.

"Ginny, we're here. It's okay." Marci races round and yanks the door open. Tucking my head on top of hers, protecting her from the doorframe, I get us out, then charge to the emergency room.

"HELP!" We both shriek as we run through the doors. A nurse turns and spies the broken girl in my arms and runs over, shouting for a gurney.

I lay her down gently. Marci's talking fast, telling them what's happened. The nurse takes Ginny's arms from me. At first, I resist.

"We've got her," she tries to offer reassurance, but it falls on deaf ears. I once thought I had her too.

We watch on helplessly as they wheel her away.

"Nate," Marci whispers my name. "He's dead. He's definitely dead?" She peers up at me. I don't know which answer is the worst? That somehow that bastard is alive, trying to get back to Ginny like she says or that he's dead like we all believed him to be. I want him dead, but if he is, then it means Ginny is more broken than we ever believed possible.

"I'm going to talk to them... to tell them what she said. Maybe the police should be here or something."

"He's dead, Marci." I know he is. What reason would he have to fake it? He'd have known he was letting Ginny go and that's not something a man like Blake Daniels would ever have tolerated.

She stares at me hard. "How can you be sure? You saw what she was like!"

"I saw a woman so scared by what she believed to be true. I saw what Ginny must have looked like all of those times he lifted his hand to her. I saw the broken version of Ginny she's been trying to keep hidden."

"Then what? It was a flashback? So she tried to kill herself?" I don't know what any of the answers are. But I know the man who was so desperate to punish Katie for trying to help Ginny escape, would not have allowed his wife to experience months of freedom. There isn't a chance.

Yet, Ginny believed Blake was there. That he'd found her. So I voice the only possible explanation. "Ginny's ill." I turn and walk away.

∽

I sit, my back stooped, elbows resting on my knees, hands clasped in front of me. I can feel my body seizing up under the tension and worry, but I don't move to try and ease it. All I do is glance at the clock for the thirtieth time in as many minutes. Why are they taking so long? Marci's already been to the nurse's station, and all they could tell her was somebody would be out to speak to us shortly. She told them what Ginny said relating to

Blake, and I watched as they nodded their heads taking it all in. They promised they'd tell the doctor.

"Hey!" A man, a few years younger than Marci walks up to her and grabs her tightly. He looks familiar. He was at the funeral, standing next to Ginny.

"Liam!" Marci cries, the sounds of her sobs fill the waiting room

"What the hell happened?" I see Marci look down at me out of the corner of my eye. Then they both shuffle away to talk. Their voices hushed beneath the even quieter atmosphere of the waiting room. He keeps directing his gaze my way. No doubt she's telling him exactly where the blame lies for this. With me. The person sitting in this shitty plastic hospital chair. The selfish motherfucker who decided screwing up Ginny's life further was the best idea.

I've failed her. She's been hurt, in mind and body. She suffered loss and yet through it all, she fought to get her life back. But I had to make contact, couldn't settle for visual confirmation that she was alive. No, I had to talk, to push my way into her life so she had no option but to learn the truth. I've done this.

I stand up, twist around and kick out at the seat I'd been sitting on. People in the waiting room stop talking and stare at me. I glare back. When I feel someone touching my hand, I swing back, ready to knock whoever the hell it is, out. But it's Marci.

"Hey!" Liam bellows, thrusting himself in between his sister and me.

"Sorry, I didn't know it was you."

She smiles, offering her understanding. "It's okay. Nate, this is my brother, Liam."

I dip my head in acknowledgement, but he remains in

position in front of me, trying to stare me down. I won't be moved. So, levelling my shoulders, I stare right back.

"What are you going to do?" If he's asking for a confrontation, then he's got one.

"Excuse me?"

"Are you hanging around? Leaving? Expecting her to pick up the pieces?"

Although the question comes from Liam, it's Aaron that I see. He's shaking his head, wondering what the hell it is I'm playing at. *You know the answer to this, Nate. You're not going to move on from her. So don't lose her. It's your turn to fight. You should never have left it all up to her.*

"I'm staying."

He tilts his chin up. "Right answer," he replies, steadily dropping the attitude and relaxing his fighting stance. "You got to kind of give me a minute. This whole situation is one big mind fuck. I mean, Ginny's in there?" He twists, briefly looking to the door they took Ginny through. "Fighting for her life... believing that fucker is still alive. You're here." His eyes level with me. "Looking like your world has come to an end. You gotta be in love with her then?"

"What?" Marci says in shock.

"Jesus, sis! You don't hang around for someone in this situation if it's only lust. I thought you girls knew about this kind of thing." His smirk quickly drops, and he holds his hand out to me. "I'm sorry... about your brother and his wife. It's got to have been tough." I accept his condolences. "But the girl... I'm sorry. Marci's only just told me. What's her name again? Sophia?"

"Yeah, it's Sophia."

"She's doing okay?"

I'm surprised at the matter-of-fact way he's speaking. There appears to be no judgement—no questions about how I came to be in Ginny's life. Maybe they'll come later. "She's doing alright," I acknowledge.

"Good." He grabs his sister by the shoulders and starts to walk towards the chairs, appearing to be accepting of my responses. "Ginny's stronger than everyone believes, you know. We'll get her through this."

The three of us go to sit within the same cluster of chairs, hoping above everything else that Liam is right.

∼

When two doctors come into the waiting room, simultaneously, we get out of our seats and meet their approach.

"Are you here for Ginny Daniels?" All three of us nod. "And you are?" He starts with me.

"I'm Nate, um, her friend." I stumble on what I now am to Ginny.

"I'm Marci, her best friend, and this is my brother, Liam. We've known each other all our lives."

"So are there no family members here?" He glances to his female colleague standing at his side.

"We're not related by blood, but I'm all the family she has. Her mum passed away, and she's never even met her father. And don't go thinking you can get in touch with him because she doesn't even know who he is. So when you ask who her family is, it's me!"

"Then follow me." He walks on ahead, Marci and Liam follow closely behind. I hang back slightly trying to push back the reminders of the last time I had to go into the 'relative's room'. I dig my hands deeper into my pockets and claw away at the material like I need to hold on to something to stop me from falling completely.

"We've stopped the bleeding." A breath abandons my chest. He's stopped the bleeding, which means she's alive. He wouldn't have said that if she wasn't.

"So she's okay! Can we see her?" Marci asks.

The doctor looks to his colleague at his side as a grave expression is passed between the two.

"What is it? You said she was alive!" I question.

The doctor who has yet to speak, finally talks. "Does she have any health history that you think we need to know about?" I look at Marci, and she moves her head from side to side. "What about a history of psychological illness with Ginny or within her family?"

Again Marci shakes her head no but this time appears more unsettled by it.

"At the moment, Ginny is an extremely scared young woman. She is convinced her husband is following her and that he is trying to cause her harm. She truly believes this, which is why she was looking for an escape—"

"So she *did* do that to her wrists?"

The female doctor looks to Marci. "I'm afraid so. I believe you told the nurse that Ginny's husband died not so long ago?"

"I did, but..." Marci looks between Liam and me.

"He's dead," I state in confirmation.

"We're trying to get a picture of Ginny's life so we can help her in the best way possible. If you could give us as much information as possible about Ginny, her life now and what it was like before her husband died?"

Marci nods her head. "He was abusive towards her," she says in a quiet tone.

"Excuse me?"

I clench my jaw and listen to Marci unload Ginny's history with Blake. They discuss it between them while I remain quiet. They talk about Ginny's marriage and how everything seemed perfect until they learnt it wasn't. They try and determine how long the abuse had been going on for, but nobody really knows. They question whether Ginny received any counselling or went to therapy. Again Marci answers, but then when there's a pause in speech, I look up to see all eyes now resting on me.

"Nate? You need to tell them about Katie." I glance helplessly between them all, but after a long-suffering silence, Marci continues. "Ginny had someone. She worked for women's aid. Her name was Katie. Ginny went to her for help. I'm not sure how long she saw her for or how often, but I know she was helping her escape from Blake."

"Is there any chance I can speak with this person? Do you know where I can contact her?"

"Katie died. Along with her husband. They all died in the same accident as Ginny's husband." The short explanation is unreal, but sadly it's the truth.

"Oh," he replies, taken aback. "So Ginny's husband died in a car accident that also killed Katie, the woman who was helping Ginny?"

"Yes, and Katie's husband died in the accident," Marci repeats.

I see both doctors working it through in their heads.

"It was never proven as an intentional act," I finally speak. "It was ruled an accident. Ginny only found out a week ago that it was Katie and her husband in the other car. She didn't know."

"Right," she says slowly, putting all of the jagged, ugly pieces together. "You've all helped enormously. Thank you. Ginny is currently awaiting an assessment by a mental health professional. It would be beneficial for us to share this information with them. After that, we'll know more."

"A mental health professional? Can you not even tell us what you *think* is wrong with her? You're a doctor!" Marci cries out.

"By what you've told us and by the observations we've taken so far from Ginny, it appears she may be suffering from psychosis. Psychosis has a strong link with trauma including abuse, loss, and bereavement—all of which you have identified that Ginny has suffered. Learning what happened to Katie... it could have been a trigger. Until we know more, it's very difficult to pass further comment."

I provided the trigger. My gaze darts from each person in the room, guilt crushing my chest. I did this.

"Will she get better?" The question tumbles desperately from my lips.

"It's too early to say anything at the moment, I'm afraid. Like I said, we'll know more once she's been seen by a specialist in this field. Our priority at this time is to keep Ginny safe."

"You mean from herself?" Desperation clings to each word Marci speaks. "Can we see her? Even if only for two minutes?"

"I'm sorry. It would be best for us to concentrate on helping Ginny. We'll let you know more when we do."

They dip their heads and leave the room, stating we can sit in here for a while longer. But I know it's time for me to leave. I don't need Liam and Marci to confirm what I already know. I said I was going to stay, but how can I now?

I move towards the door, and Marci calls out to me.

"Nate?"

"I'm going home to Sophia."

"Nate." My name is the only thing she says. But I understand why. She can't provide any words of reassurance because there aren't any that can be said.

One week ago, I provided Ginny with the trauma that caused her to finally fall to pieces. Like I told her I would. Blake may have created the damage, but I was the one who broke her in the end.

CHAPTER THIRTY

NATE

Four weeks and I've heard nothing other than little snippets of information relayed from Marci. Marci promises me that Ginny is getting better—becoming more like her old self, but she still has a long road ahead of her. The main one being therapy.

I'm desperate to catch sight of her, but I worry that if I do, I'll send her spinning back into the past, and I can't be responsible for that again. Being unable to help or see her hurts in a way that's indescribable.

Now I'm here, at Ryan's, waiting for news of her.

"She'll be here soon."

"What?" He must have recognised the look of hope flash across my face.

"Marci! I meant Marci." Of course he meant Marci. He clamps his hand to my shoulder like Aaron used to on many an occasion. "Maybe she'll bring good news."

Maybe.

"Shots?" Ryan nods in the direction of the table in the middle of his back garden. A group of the guys are already crowding round with glasses in their hands at the ready. It can't hurt, in fact, it may help alleviate some of what I'm feeling.

We make our way over, and Ryan slides a glass to me.

"Right, this bottle of Jack has to go by the end of the night!"

They all holler out calls of excited approval. Ryan dips his head in my direction. "Well?"

"I'm in!" Sophia hasn't had a nightmare in a month or more now, so I've started to have a few drinks on a Saturday with the promise that my parents will ring if Sophia needs me.

We bang the glasses on the table, three, two, one, then it's on my lips, the liquid hits my tongue before seeping down my throat giving me a false and temporary feeling of warmth.

The glasses are refilled until the bottle is two thirds empty. I know I'm nearing that wall when it's time to call a cab and get home, but as I lift my eyes, Marci appears.

She smiles at Ryan first. He grabs her by the waist, lifting her and making her squeal before setting her back down. She then sets her sights on me and calls my name. I follow her to the end of Ryan's long strip of garden.

It's the same routine every week. The venue may be different, but it's always at the same time, once she's finished visiting Ginny. I take whatever scrap of information she's willing to provide. I'm not sure if Ginny wants me to know anything, but as always, I can't stay away.

"You might want to sit down," she says pointing to the rattan furniture. Silently, I do as she suggests, wondering why this feels different to last week and the weeks before. "I know this has been hard on you, Nate and so does Ginny."

"What? She told you that?"

"Yes." She smiles. "She's doing really well." She puffs out a laugh. "You still don't believe me, do you?"

If I could see her... maybe, but I won't make that move. I refuse.

Then, I watch as she pulls something out of her bag. It's a small envelope with my name on it.

"She wanted me to give this to you." She holds out the paper, and I take it from her, resting it gently between my two hands. A letter. Why is she writing me a letter? "She planned on writing it last week, but she has some doubts that this is the right thing to do, even now." Marci fixes her eyes on me. "She wants you to be happy, but she doesn't want you to wait for something that may or may not happen between you." Marci's lips spread into a straight line. "She wants you to move forward with your life, for you and Sophia." She bows her head and leaves me with a letter and heaviness weighing in my chest

My finger tugs at the envelope, revealing paper with Ginny's handwriting on.

Nate,

I'm sorry it's taken me so long to write, but it took me a while to believe that you might actually be waiting to hear from me. No matter how many times Marci told me you were waiting, I didn't quite believe her.
I'm not sure where to begin, Nate.
In the beginning, I tried to move through each day like I was getting better, as though I was dealing with what had happened. But there were still moments when I felt like I was falling. I'd try my hardest to escape these moments by doing anything to distract me.
Then I met you.
You became the good in days that previously were merely bearable. I

wanted to cling to those times with you. In fact, part of me still does because it gives me hope.

When I found out about Katie and your brother, something happened, I can't explain it. The doctors say it could have been the trigger which finally caused me to slide into the craziness that you saw. Everything felt real... the delusions, the paranoia... I was so scared, and all I wanted was you, but at the time, I thought making contact would put you in danger. I genuinely thought he was there, back with me. I know it's difficult to comprehend.

That day, I wanted peace, for everything to end, to escape him in the only way I could see possible. I am so sorry, Nate for letting you see me fall as low as I could go. I can't really remember what I said, but if I hurt you even more than I believe I have, then I'm truly sorry.

I drag myself away and look at the sky above, not wanting to believe what I had thought all along... I gave her the trigger telling her about Aaron and Katie. It was me.

"She said to keep reading." Marci's somehow standing in front of me. I didn't even see her draw near.

"What?"

"She told me if I saw you look away from the letter, looking like you kind of hate yourself, then I was to tell you to keep reading." She shrugs her shoulders. "So keep reading."

Taking a deep breath, I dip my head and continue.

You saved me, Nate. Like you helped save Katie. The doctors also say that this could have happened months, possibly years from now and anything could have triggered it, so don't feel guilty. At least this way, it only affected a handful of people. In years to come, I hope to have many more friends, maybe even family around me. So, thank you for saving me when I needed it the most.

"She's thanking me?" I gape over at Marci. *Why the hell would she be thanking me?*

I once had a friend. She helped me break away from a nightmare, from a monster. I still wish I hadn't involved Katie, tried to leave him without her help and that wish will never leave me. But Katie also told me something that I'll never forget. She told me that we all fall. It's an inevitability of life, but when you've fallen, the climb becomes the making of you. If you're lucky, you get to climb with somebody special holding your hand.
Because of how I fell, I have to start the journey by myself. Please understand that. Maybe one day I'll see you again, when I've made more progress, but I don't want you to wait for me. It would be unfair to ask, and if I'm being honest, I still don't believe I deserve you. We have no idea what the future holds, we both know that. But know that you set me free, and I'm now ready to start my journey.
All my love, Ginny

I can't look up, not forward to the future, nor behind to the past? "I have to sit and wait? Do nothing?"

This time Marci approaches before sitting on a chair beside me. She scoots it closer.

"All through our childhood, Ginny was so strong." She smiles at the memory. "It was always her and her mum. They did everything together. Her mum made sure Ginny never missed out by not having a dad around. When her mum became ill, she fought for as long as she could. Blake turned up at the same time as Ginny was falling to pieces. He took over. At that moment, I think it's what she needed. But then it continued. She doesn't want to fall again, Nate, nobody does, but she wants to know that if it happens, she'll be okay. That she won't… that she won't try to hurt herself like she did this time."

"Fuck!" I breathe. "I want to be there." I collapse back. "Do you think… does she care about me, Marci?" I have every intention of waiting, but I don't want to add any pressure to Ginny. If she doesn't feel the same, then it changes everything.

"You're serious?" She shakes her head and lets out a gentle laugh. "You're under her skin, Nate. I think it's always been you, but she couldn't find you."

"But you said I should move forward—"

"No, Ginny said it, and she said it so you won't feel obliged to wait. You're one step closer, Nate. Just hold on."

Hold the fuck on? This is immense. She's doing okay, and she wants me. *She* wants *me!* I jump up, make my way up the garden, charging past Ryan. "I need some paper."

"What?" He curls his head following my steps.

"Paper. Where is it?" I push through the door, entering the house and walk into the kitchen. I pull at the drawers to find the 'junk drawer'. Everyone has one. It contains everything you don't think you need, but one day will find a use for. But each time I pull one open, it's neat and organised. "What is this?" I tackle. "Where's your goddamn junk?"

He tosses an envelope towards me, but it's not even been opened. "Seriously, this is all you have?"

"I'm not a chick, Nate. I don't have pretty, embossed writing paper in my cupboards."

"Pen?" I hold out my hand, but he stares at it blankly. Then Marci comes to the rescue and hands me one.

While they both edge to the corner of the room, I set about sending a message to Ginny. If she's not ready to see me, the least I can do is let her have some hope.

So I write the only thing I can.

Don't complete your journey without me, Ginny. Keep climbing, but meet me halfway. x

EPILOGUE

FIVE MONTHS LATER

We walk side by side along the path together. As the sun shines, warming my face, I stop and close my eyes. I know Marci has slowed down because I can no longer hear her feet on the pavement. No doubt she thinks I'm crazy for standing in the middle of the path with my eyes closed, but I can't help it. My cheeks bunch as a smile spreads across my face.

I hear the birds, nestled within the branches. A gentle breeze flows past me, and I don't only feel it, I hear it. Somewhere in the distance, there's an engine, possibly a ride-on grass cutter. It's rare I hear nothing these days. If you try hard enough, there's always a sound you can pinpoint. Which means life is being lived. I hadn't realised how low I'd been until days like today when my senses allow me to experience things that were present all along. I was blinded before.

"You alright, Gin?"

"I'm good, Marci," I reply opening my eyes to look at her. She sees the peace that I no longer have to force into my expression. It's present of its own free will. "I thought I had to do it all on my own, you know." We set off walking again. Neither of us have mentioned where we're going, but we both know.

"No one ever wanted you to do that, Ginny."

"I know, but I was the one who fell, so I had to get myself back up again. It's a certainty of life that we all fall. It will happen again, but I have to believe that I can handle it. No matter what."

"And do you?"

"I do." I have people around me who care. Therapy has helped me immensely and although I will always have doubts and fears. "I'm stronger now," I say aloud.

"Don't let him hear you say that!" And she chuckles.

"Excuse me?"

It's her turn to stop. Her hands reach for mine. "Everything you've been through, Ginny. You've always been strong. You couldn't see it. Neither could I, and I'm so sorry." Her lids close in regret. "But Nate did see. So whether you believe you're stronger now or not, he thinks you've always been strong. He wanted to be by your side, to hold your hand, to help you when you fell, not to catch you. Although he'd have tried his hardest to rescue you if you'd let him."

"But I had to rescue myself. He understands that, right?"

"Where you're concerned, Gin, he understands everything. This man—I think he was always waiting for you. Through the terrible things that have happened, maybe something good could come of it."

"He might not want that."

"But you're ready to find out?"

"I'm ready to see him. The rest... who knows." Marci no longer questions my judgement or my decisions. I know she's found it difficult to keep her opinions to herself, but she's done it for me. "Today, I want to make sure they're both okay."

"And what happens if it doesn't go well?"

"Then I'll handle it. I'm not asking for a marriage proposal,

Marci. I'm not asking for a thing." If Nate comes at me with blame, if Sophia does, then I'll take it. If I fall, I will try and get back up, and that's all I can ask of myself.

"So we're off to the park again?"

We both look to the fenced-off field in front of us. The park where we first saw Nate with Sophia. We've been back here four weeks in a row. I'm aware I could ring him or even turn up on his door, but for now, all I need is to catch sight of him. I have to see that they're both happy, and they're working through their loss.

"I'm so proud of you, but, FYI, if shit turns bad, I'm gonna punch him, and he can fall to the floor."

I laugh, but reach out to her, tucking her hand under my arm.

"He has a right to feel exactly what he wants. I'm not asking for his forgiveness, but it doesn't stop me from being able to apologise. An apology that he deserves." If I have the guts... if he's here. If if if!

"He's not going to want an apology, Ginny. Trust me." I'm aware that Marci and Nate have been seeing each other on a weekly basis. She's been brief about their encounters for fear of adding any more pressure on me.

When we reach the row of trees, I know before looking up that he's here. "They're here, aren't they?" I breathe.

"Yes, they are."

Quickly, I retreat a few steps before taking in the view. My vision briefly skims over the people near the slide and swings, but I know they're not there. When my sight lands on the skateboarding ramp, a whole well of emotion hits me hard.

Unmistakably, he's the man who flew down the ramp with ease. His hair's grown a little, and instead of being covered by a wealth of clothing, he's wearing a t-shirt and board shorts. His skin has a touch of tan from the summer weather. He looks even better than before, which, until two seconds ago, I thought was impossible.

He moves to the side of the ramp and looks up to the ledge, watching Sophia. She's tackling the smallest ramp and giggles at something he says. My eyes fill with tears, and my shoulders start to shake with the relief I'm feeling. They're okay. It's not to say they aren't sad, I imagine they always will be, but they are together, and they're smiling.

"Ginny?"

I exhale heavily. "I'm good. I promise."

Then Sophia rides her board. Her posture stiffer than Nate's, not as fluid, but very impressive all the same. They're oblivious to us watching them, and I want it to stay like this for a few more hours to come yet. But then something changes.

Nate stands up straighter, the skateboard hangs from his hand at his side. Sophia seems to notice the change in him too. Even from this distance, I can see the worry enter her expression.

His feet start to move, turning him around until he stills and looks directly at me. A warm glow rises to my cheeks.

Sophia steps to his side and says something to Nate. Whatever he says in response isn't what she wants to hear because she sets off in front of him, heading right towards me.

"Do you want me to block her?"

I look at Marci incredulously. "Block her? She's nine, Marci." With the sight of Katie's daughter storming towards me, I wonder what I'm in for, but there certainly won't be any blocking.

"Fair enough. I'll stay back here, but you know where I am, Ginny."

I make myself move toward her slowly, so as not to scare her.

She can scare me all she likes. I'll take whatever Sophia wants to offer and without argument. My attention is drawn to Nate as he now follows Sophia, jogging to catch up with her.

When we're a foot from each other, I stare only at the blonde haired young girl in front of me.

"Hi," I say.

"Hi." She smiles, and I'm taken aback. "Nate said you might not want me to come and say hello, but it's okay that I did, isn't it?"

"It is."

"See!" She turns glowering slightly at Nate who I know is standing right beside her, but I can't bring myself to look at him. I always thought he had the power to read me. But I'm not sure I'm ready for him to see the version that I'd always kept hidden. I'm not the person he met all those months ago, and it's like I'm meeting him for the first time. Although I feel better in myself, he may not see it that way.

"Ginny?" he says my name. I swallow then lift my eyes to his.

I bite my lip at the sight of him so close, then have to blink rapidly so I can see him clearly.

"You look... great, Ginny."

A relieved laugh escapes from my mouth and more moisture wells in my eyes. From my periphery, I see Sophia looking repeatedly from Nate to me and back again.

"I saw the dimples, Nate!" Sophia exclaims excitedly before turning to me. "You look pretty when you smile with dimples."

I look at him aghast, and he shrugs. "I had to tell someone about them." He smiles.

"You're really good on the skateboard," I praise.

"Thanks, Nate taught me." Again she watches Nate before her

delicate lids lower, and I wonder if me coming here has disturbed her fun with Nate, but when I look a little harder, she's not looking down in sadness, she's staring at my wrist. "You still have the bracelet?"

"Oh!" I glance at the colourful set of bands that I've cherished since the day I received them. "I do."

"It looks pretty on you."

"It's a pretty bracelet," I respond. "Although, I'm not sure how much longer it's going to last. I think I've worn it too much," I admit with a shy smile. I want to take a look at Nate, but nerves seem to be getting the better of me. I've spent some time dreaming about this moment... wondering what it would be like to see him... to see them again.

"I can make you another one," she offers. "My mum helped people." I swallow at the change in topic. "Sometimes she saved them." My head does a little quiver in confirmation. "She helped you." I choke up. "Nate told me."

"She did, Sophia. She helped me a lot."

"I think my mummy liked you." I can't talk through the sadness I'm experiencing. I'm learning to understand that Katie and Aaron's death is not of my doing, but it doesn't take away what Sophia and Nate have lost. "We can tell you more about her if you want? And my dad."

"I'd like that."

When Nate asks Sophia to give us a moment, she skips away happily, back towards the skateboard ramp.

"Don't you need to go? I mean she could fall or something," I query worrying.

Instead of looking her way, he takes a step, bringing himself closer. "No, she has this. Trust me. She's been learning for a while now. I used to take her to a skate park closer to home to give Katie and Aaron a couple of hours to themselves." I'm glad he feels like he can talk about them with me. I hope that one day I get to learn more.

I keep my eyes on Sophia and inwardly smile seeing Marci approach her. "I can't guarantee everything Marci says will be appropriate. You might want to screen her conversations."

He doesn't respond. I only feel his eyes on me.

"Ginny... Will you look at me?" I do as he asks. Not because he requested it but because I want to, and he's so damn close I can't think straight. "Fuck!" he exclaims as he takes in my face. "I- I can't believe—" He frowns. "I'm not sure what I'm supposed to say. Whether I can say what I want or damp it down and keep everything on a safe level."

I smile. "Say what you want, Nate." And I mean it.

"Seriously?"

"Yeah. Seriously."

"What if I scare you?"

"I'll handle it." And it's true. More than anything, I want to have Nate in my life, but if it's not what he wants, I'll understand.

"Then fuck, Gin! You look so damn good. Better than good." He fixes his eyes on mine. "Your dimple. I've seen it like four goddam times in the past five minutes."

I lower my head, feeling a little embarrassed, but he soon hooks his finger under my chin, bringing me to look back up at him. "Don't hide from me." His thumb gently rubs at the spot where my dimple sometimes appears. "I've been waiting for you. I see you, Ginny, and I see what worries you the most. Sophia knows."

"What?" I pull from him, but he reaches for my hand, already anticipating my move.

"She knows the man who was driving the other car was your husband. Sophia was the one who asked me if he'd hurt you too."

"How could you have told her that? She's a child," I whisper shout at him.

"Yes, she's a child, but she's had to face things that no one should have to face, even adults. She already had an understanding of what her mum did for a living. I may have been wrong to tell her but kids, they see things differently, usually for the better." He glances back at Sophia and she waves. "Hell, I'm going to make mistakes, Ginny, plenty of them, but she's kind of good at pulling me up on them," he adds with a free laugh.

"It's good to hear you laugh, Nate."

"I didn't do much of that before, huh?"

I shrug. "I guess you were too busy worrying about everyone else." We stand and gaze at each other and without a single analysing thought passing through my mind, I lean forward and kiss him softly on the cheek. "Thank you."

He's surprised. "Why are you thanking me?"

"For waking me up, Nate."

"How's your journey going?" he asks referring to the last piece of communication we shared when he asked me to meet him halfway. I treasure that note each day. Nate has no idea what those few words meant to me.

My hand grazes his. "I reckon I'm about halfway." Our fingers intertwine, the touch bringing a sense that I've made it home.

"Halfway, huh?" His lips spread into a smile at the same time mine do. He can't help but look at my mouth. I see his hesitation but refuse to allow it. I reach up and stroke his cheek, and his dark lashes flutter closed before his eyes open, bearing a heat and intensity I've never seen before. It takes my breath away. His hand glides to my cheek then tangles its way into my hair. "Don't ask me to let you go again."

I expect tenderness, but his lips crash into mine, knocking me off balance. His arms close around me, protecting me, and I hold onto him just as tight. He mumbles something that I can't make out because I'm lost in him. His muscles tense beneath my grasp as somehow he draws us closer together.

When the kiss slows, our touch becomes more tender and gentle.

He tilts his head so he can see me clearly. "What are your plans tonight?"

I lift my shoulders. "No plans."

"Can I take you out?"

"You don't have to ask, Nate."

"I'll always ask, Ginny."

I don't know what the future holds, none of us do. But as I stand with Nate by my side, my body pressing against his, I dream it involves him and Sophia.

Today's a good day. You can't expect them to be like this all of the time, I know that, but now I believe I'm worthy of them.

Sometimes we have to face a fight we can't ever imagine encountering. It can be forced upon you. Life can treat you with unkindness. If you're lucky, some gentle hands will be present to help ease the pain.

I am a stronger person now. Perhaps I have Blake to thank for that. But I won't be thanking him. Blake is a part of my past that I won't ever forget yet a part I have every intention of moving on from because now, I am free.

Try not to let the fight consume you. It can be a sick twisted part of a journey you have to travel but keep going, keep climbing. You never know who or what might be waiting for you when it's all over.

The End

ACKNOWLEDGMENTS

Ginny's story has consumed me for well over a year and has been the most difficult book I've written to date due to the subject it covers. For this book to be what it is, there are many people to thank.

Darren, thank you for believing in me and for being one of the first to read this book. Oh and for forsaking lengthy facetime calls because I was busy immersing myself in the book world!

To the amazing ladies that beta read for me – Zoë, Trenda, Becky, Tara, Kat and Rebecca—I kind of went all out this time and although there were so many of you, each one had qualities that strengthened Ginny and Nate's story. Thank you all for your expertise and your honesty.

Thanks to Jo for providing your specialist advice and to Sofie, for giving me huge cover love!

Claire, not only are you are a damn fine editor but you rock at brainstorming! I do believe you got to name the book! Thank yoooouuuuu!

Bloggers. To say thank you doesn't seem enough. I am

gradually meeting more of you, and it's a total pleasure. You work tirelessly and with passion all due to your love of reading.

To the ladies in my reader group that bravely came forward (who shall remain nameless as per your request), thank you so much for your input. I am humbled that you agreed to read and put forward your views, and I am so sorry for all that you went through. Thank you seems too small a word!

Finally, to you, the reader for adding another reason to the list of things that make all of this worthwhile.

ABOUT THE AUTHOR

R.G. Corr is a mum of three, who loves to read almost as much as she does to write. When she's not working or writing, you'll find her nose deep in her kindle swooning over her latest book boyfriend.

Having had an overactive imagination for many years, a discussion in a soft play area, amidst the noise and mayhem of toddlers, finally convinced her to put pen to paper and write her first novel.

You can keep in touch with her via:

Goodreads
https://www.goodreads.com/author/show/14898944.R_G_Corr

Facebook
https://www.facebook.com/RGCorr1

Twitter
https://twitter.com/RGCorr1

Instagram
https://instagram.com/rgcorr

Printed in Great Britain
by Amazon